OCTOBER 2, 9:30 A.M.

WENT TO THE DANCE AND HAD A LOUSY TIME. Mag was wearing some hideous outfit she called her "Butterfly Ensemble." All kinds of bright colors that didn't seem to go together. During the fast songs, Mag would step away from me, raise her arms above her head, and shake her hips. Trying to turn me on? I just laughed at her. During the slow dances, she put her arms around my shoulders and tried to nibble my ear. I kept moving my head out of reach and kept my arms loose around her waist. I didn't even try to get excited about holding her body. It felt like a soft sack of flour to me. I kept one eye on the door and the other on the clock. Didn't see a single good-looking guy all night. . . .

Entries from a Hot Pink Notebook

Todd D. Brown

WSP

WASHINGTON SQUARE PRESS
PUBLISHED BY POCKET BOOKS

New York   London   Toronto   Sydney   Tokyo   Singapore

This book is a work of fiction. Names, characters, places and incidents are products of the author's imagination or are used fictitiously. Any resemblance to actual events or locales or persons, living or dead, is entirely coincidental.

A WASHINGTON SQUARE PRESS *Original* Publication

A Washington Square Press Publication of
POCKET BOOKS, a division of Simon & Schuster Inc.
1230 Avenue of the Americas, New York, NY 10020

Library of Congress Cataloging-in-Publication Data

Brown, Todd D.
    Entries from a hot pink notebook / Todd D. Brown.
      p.   cm.
    ISBN 0-671-89084-0
    1. Gay youth—United States—Fiction. I. Title.
  PS3553.R733E58 1995
813'.54—dc20   94-48440
                                                CIP

First Washington Square Press trade paperback printing June 1995

10 9 8 7 6 5 4 3 2 1

WASHINGTON SQUARE PRESS and colophon are
registered trademarks of Simon & Schuster Inc.

Interior design by Irva Mandelbaum

Cover design by Patrice Kaplan
Front cover illustration by David Kahl

Printed in the U.S.A.

For all those
about to make the journey

Acknowledgments

Thank you to the multitude of friends whose paths I've had the good fortune to cross during what has been an amazing quarter century. Though you are now scattered across the country and around the world, I think of you often. Far too many to name individually, if you're reading this, you know who you are.

Thank you to everyone at the Tisch School of the Arts, for teaching me about my own fortitude and the best way to express my voice.

Thank you to John J. McNeill, whose book *The Church and the Homosexual* proved invaluable.

Thank you to Arthur Woodstone, who read the first hundred and fifty pages of this and told me to keep going.

Thank you to Debra Ely, who was the first person to read the whole thing and tell me it was good.

Thank you to my agent, Jane Dystel, for not giving up, and for being herself.

Thank you to my editors, Julie Rubenstein and Liate Stahlik, for their insight, and for helping me find the right ending.

Thank you to Elizabeth Blake and Geneva Brown, the "Grams," for making me laugh without even trying.

Thank you to Tracy Allen and Tammy Brown, my two beautiful sisters, for years of love, grace, and support.

Thank you to my parents, David and Beverly Brown, for letting me know I can always come home, for understanding the difference between fact and fiction, and for personifying the true meaning of "family values."

Entries from a Hot Pink Notebook

August 30

I just got this notebook for school, but I'm gonna use it as a journal instead. I looked at my class schedule and figured I'd need two notebooks, one for taking notes and one for paper bombs. High school starts tomorrow and I wanted to be prepared. Somebody told me that in Basic Ed. everybody throws paper bombs, so I figured I'd better buy a notebook for that. But then I thought, I've got better things to do than throw paper bombs. Paperclips work better, anyway. They make a neat sound when they hit a guy's head. So I've got this hot pink notebook that I don't need. I didn't have any other choice but to get hot pink. By the time I got the money from Mom, the General Store was down to their last two notebooks, and I'd rather pick up a piece of manure in my teeth than ask Jeff for a ride to Kmart, which is 12 miles away, in Lipton.

Mrs. Kendrick, my English teacher last year, told me that a blank page is a crime. I was goofing off when I was supposed to be writing and she walked up to me and said, "You know, Benjamin, a blank page is a crime. Make use of it. Fill it with words. Give it value." She had her heart set on teaching me good grammar. "I hate to see such a powerful mind muted by ignorant speech," she'd say to me when I said

1

"ain't" or "don't got." "Speak English," I'd tell her, even though I understood her perfectly.

"Your power lies in the written work, Benjamin," she'd say to me. "Your experiences, Benjamin? Write them down! Your memories? WRITE THEM DOWN!!!" She was always telling me to keep a journal. "To record your feelings, Benjamin. To provide an outlet for your brain. I don't want to see you ending up a juvenile delinquent." I liked the old broad, even though she was a pain in the ass.

I'm so nervous about tomorrow. It's like my stomach's doing back flips. Whoops! The light from the Texaco sign out my window just went off. Midnight. Bedtime. Way past bedtime.

Here's to you, Mrs. Kendrick . . .

▶ August 31

First day of high school. It's gonna be a breeze. Got stuck in Basic Ed. with all the other idiots. Mom told me they're the classes I should sign up for, so I did. It's the same crowd I went to junior high with, except Mag isn't there. She's in the College Prep. courses. I ask her what college she's going to and she tells me to leave her alone. She doesn't have any idea.

I don't give a flying fuck about college. Basic Ed. is like a vacation for me. Eighth Grade: The Sequel. The teachers are all Nazis. My math teacher, an old bitch, made me spit my gum into the trash right in the middle of class. I cracked it by mistake when she was passing by. She scrunched her lips together and bellowed, "In the trash!" at me. Before class was over I chewed up another piece and stuck it on her chair when she wasn't looking. I hope she sat right on it.

Lunch is a joke. Mr. Duff marches around looking constipated. He kept passing by our table with a frown. He knows we're from Tranten Township, so we're bad news. It's true. We *are* bad news. It's the same gang I hung out with in junior high. Les tossed some butter pats up on the ceiling, where they got stuck. The crowd all thought that was pretty funny.

All the Lipton freshmen snobs sit at a table on the other side of the room making faces at us. Mag's in all of the College classes with them and she wants to get out of them. She says they treat her like a freak. I tell her to act stupid and then she'll be put into Basic Ed. She doesn't think much of that idea.

▶ September 1

We had standardized testing today instead of classes. What a pain. While we were taking the test, I looked around at all the other Basic Ed. guys and almost cracked up. Les wasn't looking at the test book. He was just filling in the dots so they made a straight line. Sid didn't even fill the dots in. He wrote "This sucks my dick" on the answer sheet and started reading *Guns & Ammo* magazine. Kuprekski sat there looking into space.

I finished early, so I started reading *Planet of the Apes*. It's what we're reading in Basic English. It's pretty good. After I read it for a while, I looked around the room and knew how the astronauts must have felt landing on that planet.

▶ September 2

Turned fourteen today. Dad didn't call, but Grandma made a cake and Jeff got me a new T-shirt that's got "GOING PLACES" written across the front of it. He bought it for five bucks at the General Store. I know because I saw it in there. It was in a bargain rack of stuff they couldn't sell. At least he remembered. Grandma and Mom both chipped in and got me a new parka, because my old one ripped out last winter. Mag came over tonight and gave me a card with a naked woman holding a box of chocolates in front of her boobs. On the inside it says, "Saving the best piece for you." I laughed because Jeff thought it was real funny and then I tacked it up on my bulletin board.

3:36 A.M.

Two guys out my window are fighting. Even though they're both ugly as sin and probably got dirty fingernails, I pretend they're fighting over me. Maybe it'll give me good dreams tonight.

September 3

7:15 A.M.

No good dreams. Try again tonight.

5:20 P.M.

It's probably good that I don't carry this notebook around school. You start carrying a hot pink notebook around Chappaqua High School and you're asking the student body to call you a faggot. That word is such a pisser. Even Mag uses it, and that ticks me off. It's so weird that people who wouldn't dream of saying "nigger," "chink," or "wop," scream "Faggot!" like it's going out of style. They just don't get it. Not Mag. Not Jeff. Not the kids at school. And not my parents. I've had these feelings for about a year now. It's like a part of me now.

What turns me off about women is their softness. You can't touch a single part of their bodies without squishing something. When I think about a time last year when Mag put my hand on her boob, I get physically ill. I like hardness.

I'm not about to tell anybody about it, either. Rural Maine isn't the place to announce that you're queer. Last fall at school there were rumors going around that a guy in the junior class was a homo. The guy—his name was Dion Hatch—moved here from some place in Massachusetts, and he was sort of a fem. He had a very girlish face and a way of fluttering his hands when he talked. I know because we rode the same bus as far as Tranten Junior High, where I got off. I'd see Dion every day, sitting in the front seat, talking to Ray, the bus driver. As a rule, all of us kids from the junior high school would steer clear of Dion and try to find a seat as far away from him as possible. We heard he made a pass at some guy in the school library. The rumor was all over town and the school.

Dion survived at Chappaqua High School for two months, then the school royalty, which includes my shit-for-brains older brother who's the crowned prince, struck. Jeff came home one night bragging about it to his girlfriend. He and his band cornered Dion in the locker room, tied him up with gauze bandages, and plastered his face with makeup. Jeff was laughing hysterically as he told his flavor of the month how Dion got a mouthful of lipstick. The Cro-Magnons carried him out to the football field, where the cheerleaders were practicing, and strung him up from the goalposts, where he hung for ten minutes. While Jeff told the story, I was laughing like crazy on the outside, screaming my head off on the inside.

After a while, Mr. Duff came out and cut Dion down. He made a good show of screaming at the guys, but realized the prank was just a joke and decided to let it pass. After all, the boys had state championships to win and scholarships to qualify for. They were entitled to let off a little steam, weren't they?

The following Saturday, the Chappaqua Lions beat the Poolon Red Devils for the class-D football championship. The following Sunday, Dion Hatch shot himself with his father's gun.

Dion's mistake was that he advertised himself. There's a big difference between being gay and having people think you're a fag. This notebook's gonna stay carefully hidden.

▶ ## September 4

Saw Dad today. He was in the coffee shop with Carol, the whore he left Mom for. He saw me through the window and sort of gave me a little wave. Carol pretended not to see me at all. I hate her. She works as a teller at the bank. Dad started seeing her on the sly last April. By July he was off the sly and spending whole nights with her. He started showing up at different places with her. They'd turn up together at potluck suppers and town meetings. Mom would see them walk in and hightail it out the exit, dragging us behind her. She'd say, "Damn them both to hell," when we got outside. Then she'd tell us not to say anything about Dad and Carol to anybody. She didn't want to give the Tranten Township grapevine any gossip to spread. Didn't matter. Everybody in town knew what was going on. And everybody talked about it.

The night it all came to a head, Dad took Jeff and me out to dinner. We should have known something was up when he showed up sober. It was supposed to be this father-son evening, but Dad spoiled all of the fun by announcing his plans to leave us and live with Carol for good. She made him "happy," he said. I remember Jeff running out of the coffee shop and throwing a rock through Dad's windshield, Dad cursing down the street after him, and me saying "No," over and over to myself. I went home and Mom was shut up in her bedroom. She didn't come out for two days.

Now everything's back to normal, except that Dad has a new mailing address. And Grandma moved in to give Mom a hand. Mom's back in school to get her high school diploma. Dad married her when she was sixteen and she dropped out her junior year to have Jeff.

She's trying to move on with her life, but the past won't leave her alone. Every month, Mom has to walk into that bank and face Carol as she cashes her Aid check. I wish she had the balls to punch Carol, or better yet, plant a bullet between her eyes. But Mom barely has the guts to stand up against the breeze, much less challenge Carol in head-to-head combat. So Carol sits on her fat ass behind the bank counter, hands Mom her money, and then goes home to make Dad "happy." I hate her.

▶ September 5

Friday night and nothing to do. The Palace closed, so can't go to the movies. The Rusty Nail won't allow anybody under 21 inside, not that I'd wanna go there anyway.

Lived through my first week of high school. I don't think I'm gonna like it that much. It's too much like a concentration camp. Bells ringing and teachers patrolling the halls, watching out for any slackers. I was walking in the hall today and saw Mr. Duff and a cop searching through some kid's locker.

I was gonna ask what they were looking for, but Duff barked "Move along!" at me, so I didn't.

My classes are all real easy. My Basic English teacher tries to make it good, but nobody gives a fuck and she ends up talking to herself half the time. Scott Pushard, one of the guys in Phys. Ed., was talking about dropping out today. He says he can earn more working a skidder than he can sitting in class all day. I'd drop out, but Grandma would throw a fit. She says, "Your High School is your last chance to have fun before the real world." I just want to find something I'm good at.

I passed Jeff today in the hall and he acted like he didn't know me. He looked in the other direction, like I was from outer space or something. I don't care. I don't claim to know *him* half the time. I've still got Mag.

Mag and me have been best friends ever since grade school. She moved to town when we were both in the second grade. She was this sort of pretty girl who sat behind me and smart-assed the teacher. Mrs. Donahue hated her. I think she figured that Mag was sent by the devil himself to torment her.

One day, a car backfired outside our classroom window and Mag's eyes went wide and she screamed, "Jumping jackasses!" The whole class laughed and Mrs. Donahue grabbed Mag by the ear and hauled her to the principal's office. Mag came back to the class the hailed hero. "Jumping jackasses" became the buzzwords on every Tranten Township second-grader's lips. Later, while Mrs. Donahue was lecturing us abut something or other, I turned around and looked at Mag with a questioning look, as if to say, "Where did you learn to say *that*?" Mag shot me a grin that screamed, "I know a lot more." I went to her house that night to find out how many bad words she knew. We've been best friends ever since.

We started with the basic swear words: *bitch, damn, suck, ass,* and then she advanced me to the "big guns": *fuck, cunt,* etc. Mag told me to never use the "big guns" unless I was really mad. The basics were pretty much accepted in most groups, but the "big guns" could get people pretty ticked.

I found out how ticked one night when I said "Fuck" at the dinner table. Dad picked me up by the hair, carried me to the next room, and thrashed me with his bamboo cane. He asked me who I learned the word from and I said, "From . . . Jeff." So then Dad hauled Jeff into the room and thrashed him. This was way back when he towered over both of us. Poor Jeff didn't have a clue why he was getting the bamboo until Dad told him. Jeff denied that he ever spoke the word, and Dad whacked him again for lying.

Even with the beating, I kept being Mag's friend. She was so glamorous to me. She knew the latest words before the high school kids did. It turned out, she learned them from her father, who was an even worse boozer than mine. He could turn your hair gray with his curses. Her mother is built like a truck driver and's got a face to match. She could make a charging bull turn on his ass and run away crying. She scares me sometimes. I've seen her beat up a man twice her size. Mag isn't afraid of her, though. She smart-asses her mother to beat the band.

Mag and me can count on each other. I was the first person she told when her father drove his car off Lucifer's Chasm. After that, when her mother went crazy for a few days, Mag even came and stayed at my house until the storm passed. Now her father's a vegetable hooked up to a machine in the Veteran's Hospital in Portland.

Mag was the person I told first when Dad left. I can't remember what she said to me, but I know we were laughing before long . . . And then crying. I can count on Mag. I tell her everything.

Well, almost everything.

▶ September 6

Grandma's planning on staying for good now. She had most of her furniture auctioned off and the rest she's moving into her room here. It used to be my room, but now I'm bunking with Jeff, which is a different story. I'm kind of glad to have her around. She got Mom rolling again.

After Dad left us, Mom locked herself in her bedroom for hours on end. Jeff and me didn't know what she was doing. We called Grandma, who came over and pounded on the door. Mom wouldn't answer, so Grandma took a hammer to the doorknob and smashed it off. We walked in and Mom was lying face down on her bed crying. Grandma told us to leave and we did.

Everything was quiet for the longest time, then we heard glass smashing. We ran into the bedroom and saw Mom flinging Dad's beer-bottle collection into the alleyway under her window. Grandma was standing beside her screaming, "That's it! Pretend they're his head!" We just stood there in the doorway watching her. Our mouths dropped open a mile. Grandma saw us and waved us out of the room. As we walked out, I remember Jeff saying, "They've gone berserk." For once I agreed with him.

A couple hours later, Grandma came out and told us Mom was sleeping and we should keep quiet. She made spaghetti for supper and told Jeff and me that it would be our job to do the dishes from now on. Jeff didn't like that, but he doesn't dare talk back to Grandma.

Now Mom is going to night school. Grandma says she always wanted Mom to go back, and now Mom's got the chance. We've got Grandma's pension, plus the Aid to live on. Jeff works three nights a week at the feed store, but all that money goes in his fund.

So every day at three in the afternoon, Grandma drives Mom to her classes at Lipton, then she comes back and makes our dinner, and then she has her nightly poker game with three of her friends in the kitchen. They drink apple juice and have wicked gas. I don't dare walk into the room when the four of them start tooting. At ten, Grandma drives to Lipton again to bring Mom home.

Grandma's always got some hobby going. One day it's crochet and the next it's collecting bottle caps. It's hard to believe she's my mother's mother. It seems like Mom doesn't

9

do anything except cook and clean. And she hardly ever smiles.

Now she studies all morning and goes to school all night. In between she looks for stuff that Dad left behind that she can toss out the window and break. Grandma says Mom's gotta find something to get excited about again.

September 8

There are no good-looking guys in the freshman class. Out of sixty-seven guys, there are five passable-looking ones in the lot. Of course, all of the girls flock around them like ants on a piece of cake. One of them is Les Numer. We've been going to school together since the first grade. Even then he was popular with the ladies. He had a way of moving which he practiced all through grammar school and junior high so that he could use it in high school. He sticks his chin out and clenches his fists when he walks. I think Mrs. Feely, our first-grade teacher, had a crush on him. She swallowed a bottle of aspirin after Les went on to second grade.

Today, Les's got an endless parade of bimbos (Lipton sluts mostly) coming up and asking him all kinds of stupid questions, like "How's your tuna casserole?" or "Would you like my chocolate pudding?" Stupid questions. Stupid people. Any idiot can see what they're up to. They want to be *seen* talking to Les Numer. Whenever Mag sees one of them walking away, she'll whisper to me, "If he got her pregnant, she wouldn't know whether to brag or complain."

There aren't any decent guys to dream about around here. I was sort of worried about locker-room behavior. I mean, what if I went all hard while I was taking a shower after Phys. Ed.? I shouldn't have worried. I learn to turn it off. I pretend I'm taking a shower with a bunch of ugly statues. The guys in my PE are all pretty gross, anyway. They've all got dirty fingernails, or they're fat, or they're in Special Ed., or something.

All last year I had a crush on Les. He was, to me, the perfect guy. Unfortunately, there were about fifteen girls in the class who felt the same way I did. They had the advantage too. They could bat their eyelashes at him, giggle, touch him—in general, act like simpleton asses—while I had to just look at him from my desk. But that was enough. Just watching Les run across the gym floor, wondering what he had under that shirt of his, was enough for me.

It was just a crush. After school one night, I was with Les when he beat up this kid with a baseball bat. They were fighting over a pack of cigarettes or something. He was a turn-off from that day on. The bat episode made him more of a hunk to the girls in class. "Les had his reasons," they would say, defending him to their parents. "The other kid started it. Les was just defending himself."

Les didn't need a baseball bat. He had an army of thirteen-year-old girls (and one thirteen-year-old boy) who were willing to kill for him.

September 9

Man named Burt came from the factory and spoke to the school today—the seniors mostly, but everybody had to go. He spouted on about employee benefits and pensions and this, that, and the other. All this for a lifetime of making plumbing supplies. Dad worked in the factory for five years and he hated every second of it. He said his foreman was a son of a bitch and the work was a pain in the ass.

Every morning when I wait for the bus, I see the people coming off from the nighttime shift. They look like walking dead people, like they've been run through the spin cycle or something. When I was in sixth grade, the class took a tour of the factory. All I remember about it is the smell of the disinfectant chemicals used to sterilize the equipment. It smelled horrible to me and I wondered how anybody could work all day with that stink attacking their noses all the time.

Mom's never worked at Plumbco—you need a high school diploma—but Grandma Maisie did, for thirty-six years. The morning after she graduated from high school she showed up for work. That's the way it goes. She never even bothered to look anywhere else. She still talks about her time there. "They knew how to treat their employees," she'll tell you to this day. "Then those union people came in and started shitting up the system." Grandma quit two years after the Plumbco workers unionized.

While Bert drawled on about the wonderful world of plumbing parts, I looked at the seniors sitting in a group on the highest bleachers. Jeff and his jock crowd looked at each other with smirks on their faces. They'll never end up working in that hellhole. After graduation, they'll charge out of town clutching footballs or dribbling basketballs. The class brains weren't even listening to Bert. They were smirking at each other like they knew some secret nobody else knew. Then I scanned down to the front rows of the senior section where the rest of the class sat. They all looked the same. Doomed.

I looked around the freshman section and discovered I was in the "doomed" section. Got scared.

September 10

Tonight after school I went with a bunch of my old Tranten Township crowd to the foot bridge over the river and smoked cigarettes. Had a shitty time. Les told a joke about Nancy Reagan and Barbara Bush. Can't remember what it was. Wasn't funny. Sid started talking about Ellen Carriker's boobs. He said they're like two oranges. I said grapefruit would be a better word. Everybody laughed and started talking about her ass. I tuned them out after a while. I just sat smoking my butt and tried to figure out why I was there. I don't even like those guys. They're not going anywhere. They don't want to budge. I started getting real afraid when I looked at our reflections down on the river. I couldn't see any difference between me and the rest of the gang. We were all a big blur in the water.

They talked about school and what a crock it is. School is a crock, I thought, but so is this.

I mashed my butt on a rock and got up and left. One of them asked me where I was going and I said, "Away from here." They all cracked up like it was a joke. But I was serious.

September 11

Jeff's latest girlfriend is Cindy Jones, a redhead who streaks her hair with bleach. She meets Jeff's two criteria: she looks good and she puts out. Mag asked me how long they've been going together and I told her, "The length of your average fart."

That's about how long Jeff's relationships last. It all seems so footloose the way he picks up and drops girls. It's almost like, they're in the same room at the same time, so why not go together?

Mag and me had a great time watching Cindy act like queen for a day in the cafeteria. She sat there looking at Jeff stuff his face on chop suey and smiled like a fool. She tried acting interested in what he was saying when you could tell she just wanted to jump him. I give them two weeks.

September 12

Bad news. They got my standardized test scores back and I scored in the top five percent on everything but General Science, which I got ten percent. I got this note in homeroom today that said I had a new schedule. Now I'm in all the top College courses. Double shit. I went from reading *Planet of the Apes* to some piece of crap called *Lost Horizon*. Just got done reading the first two chapters and it's boring as hell.

We had to write a short story in college English class today as part of a writing exercise. Mrs. King, the stony old bag who teaches it, said it could be about anything. I rewrote something I read in *Reader's Digest* while I was on the hopper this morning. It was one of those "drama in real life" things about a little girl who got bit by a snake. I changed it to a little boy who got bit by a rat and almost died of rabies.

The only good thing about this is that Mag's in all my classes now. She's supposed to have a genius IQ. Mr. Duff sent a note home with me tonight. It's to my parents telling them about my "great achievement" and how proud they should be of me. Mom hasn't got back from her class yet, but Grandma read it and told me she was proud. She stuck it up on the refrigerator and said I should show it to Mom.

When Grandma wasn't looking I took it down. It's in the garbage can now.

September 15

I *hate* the College courses. Mrs. King said my story about the rat and the boy was the best in the class and made me read it to everybody. I felt like such an ass. Mag kept making faces at me and trying to get me to laugh but I didn't. I wanted to sink into the earth. Mrs. King sat at her desk filing her nails the whole time I was reading. Don't think she was even listening. All of the snobs from Lipton were looking pretty constipated by the end of my paper. I wanted to crumple it up and cram it up their noses.

French class is a nightmare. The teacher, an old crow named Mademoiselle Chanson (I call her Old Lady Song behind her back), stands up in front of the class and has each kid give the French name for an object. I sat there like a moron while she pointed at different people and said things like *"le stylo"* and *"le crayon."* She told me since I'm new to the class she'll leave me alone this week, but next week I'd better be on my toes. I didn't tell her I wasn't staying in her class that long. I'm getting out.

September 16

Today Jeff broke up with Cindy after four days. A new record! They had a big fight in the cafeteria. I saw it all. Jeff went out with Lucy Boress (college student) last night and got lucky. He told his friends about it and one of them told Cindy. Cindy bombed over to Jeff's table and asked him if what she heard was true. Jeff said, "Wouldn't you like to know?" Cindy got mad and dumped a bowl of chocolate pudding in his lap. Mr. Duff dragged her to his office and sent her home to cool off. Everybody at my table was looking at me. I shrugged my shoulders and said, "What a tangled web we weave." Mag laughed but nobody else did.

Tonight I heard Jeff talking on the phone to one of his friends. He said Cindy was frigid and a lousy fuck. When he got off the phone he said to me, "Watch out for women who bleach their hair with Clorox. It seeps into their brains and wipes out their hormones." Then he laughed and took off for the river to get blitzed.

Somebody should slug Jeff. He can be such an ass sometimes.

September 17

Weeeeeha!!! Somebody slugged Jeff. Cindy's father came around tonight and told him nobody treats his daughter that way. He's the same size as Jeff, but he's got more muscles on his arms (!) and legs. Jeff looked like a stick figure next to him. Jeff started to apologize but Cindy's father punched him before he got the words out. Jeff went down for the count and Cindy's father took off. Grandma got wicked mad and said she was calling the police on him. Jeff told her not to and took off for the river. Still not back yet.

1:07 A.M.

Jeff's back and down in the bottom bunk. I think he's jerking off because he's breathing real heavy and making sighing sounds.

September 18

School still sucks eggs. The Lipton snobs are all jerks and the teachers are pains. Today in Earth Science, Mr. Henderson called me to the board and asked me if I could label a diagram of layers of the earth. I pretended not to know because I don't want him calling on me. I don't belong in the College courses and I don't see why everybody's pretending I do. This one guy named Ralph doesn't even pretend. He looks at me with this tight-lipped expression on his face and passes his pen back and forth from hand to hand. He's Old Lady Song's little pet with his preppy shirts. I hate him. All the Lipton snobs are like him. Tomorrow I'm gonna talk to Mr. Duff and ask him to put me back in Basic Ed.

September 19

No dice on putting me back. Mr. Duff told me I'd be wasting my potential if I was in Basic Ed. When I got into the locker room before Phys. Ed. I wrote "Duff is a prick" on the stall door. Then I watched as a group of guys dumped Kuprekski headfirst in a garbage can.

Kuprekski is what I call a dreg. He doesn't have a damn thing going for him. He's ugly, fat, dumb as an unlit bulb, and poor as dirt. He lives in a shack with his father who spends all his welfare money on lottery tickets. One day I saw Bill Kuprekski buy fifty tickets and a box of Twinkies. I had a feeling that was his grocery money. He kept saying he was gonna win "the big one."

Later that day I saw Kuprekski asking at the coffee shop for a handout. "My dad got laid off and we don't got no money for food," he told the waitress.

She knew the truth. Hell, everybody in the coffee shop knew the truth. She fixed him a sandwich and told him to scram. Kuprekski wolfed down that sandwich in three bites and walked out. When he walked by me, I saw a big piece of lettuce on the front of his shirt that survived the attack. I figured he was saving it for later.

I feel kind of bad for Kuprekski. We used to sort of be friends. But some people you can't help. Some people you don't want to help. With Kuprekski, it's a little of both.

September 20

I was walking down Main Street today and I saw Jeff toting Marsha Depuis on his arm. She's his latest flame. I don't know much about Marsha except that she lives in Nome and she works in the library sometimes as an aide. She's sort of pretty from what I've seen of her, though she's nothing to write home about. She definitely isn't Jeff's type. I don't think she's been to the Free Clinic once her whole life.

I think she might be a Brain, but I don't know. Mag told me today that Marsha's family makes "big bucks." I guess it's good that Jeff's planning for the future. They sure make a weird pair. I wonder what they talk about. What could either one of them say to the other that could be interesting?

▶ ## September 21

Went to the movies last night with Mag. A bunch of the school elite walked in and sat behind us before the show. Jeff was with them, and they acted like jerks all through the movie. Throwing popcorn and talking back to the screen. Mag and me just looked at each other and rolled our eyes. When we were riding back, Mag's mother had a man in the front seat with her. She met him in a bar. He kept snapping her bra strap and trying to undo her pants. Mag's mother slapped his hands and said, "There are kids in the car." I don't think she minded, though. She was smiling. Mag was getting pretty antsy herself. She'd look at me and then we'd both start laughing like someone just cracked a joke.

I got a ton of homework this weekend. I wanna just blow it off but I haven't got anything better to do. Anyway, I've got a feeling that my brains are what's gonna get me out of Tranten. Jeff hardly ever cracks a book. He's sure he's getting a sports scholarship. When basketball season comes, he says the college scouts will be here in droves and he'll be able to write his own ticket to any college he wants. I asked him what he's going to study and he said he didn't know yet. Basketball probably. I don't think any school offers a degree in Sexual Prowess.

11:15 P.M.

Jeff's making the moves on Marsha in the living room now. It doesn't sound like things are going good for him. They'd better cut it out. Grandma's coming home soon. She doesn't believe in sex before marriage. I know this because she's announced it to Jeff and me about a thousand times.

Jeff says she must not have believed in sex after marriage, either. How else could you explain the pained look on Grandpa Gerald's face? I asked him what he meant and he showed me a picture of them taken on their honeymoon in Boston. Grandpa Gerald looked like somebody just kicked him in the balls. I never looked close at his face before. Leave it to Jeff to notice something like that.

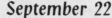

September 22

Mr. Duff is starting a new contest series. Every Friday during announcements he's gonna ask a trivia question and stick all the right answers in a hat. The name drawn wins a pizza. Hooray . . . It's something he's doing to show he cares.

Mag and me worked together on a written conversation today in English. It was supposed to be between two fictional characters so we picked Paul Bunyan and Wonder Woman. We made Paul Bunyan madly in love with Wonder Woman, but she's more interested in tying him up with her golden lasso and making him submit. We got laughing so hard I almost wet my pants. Anything to get kicked out of these classes.

September 23

Kuprekski won the first trivia contest. The question was: "Write the chemical formula for table sugar." I answered it and put Kuprekski's name on the paper and it got drawn. Kuprekski heard his name and didn't have a clue. He didn't even know he entered. Hope he likes the pizza.

Mag and me got an A– on our dialogue. Mrs. King called it "very original." Shit . . .

September 24

I hate to admit it, but I kind of like Marsha. She's funny and seems to have brains. Tonight when she was making dinner (Mom was out practicing her driving with Jeff), Grandma cornered her and asked if she was gonna marry Jeff. Marsha said, "Not anytime soon. I like to try out a man before I buy him." Grandma frowned at this and wanted to know what she meant, and Marsha said, "I want to make sure the shoe fits." Then she made a circle with two of her fingers and stuck her index finger through it a few times to illustrate. Grandma's mouth dropped open and she stamped out of the kitchen.

I can't blame Marsha. Grandma was asking for it all night. She walked in and wrinkled her nose up at Marsha's cooking, in front of Marsha. And then she asked what nationality Marsha was. When Marsha told her French-Canadian, Grandma muttered, "Figures," under her breath. Of course, Marsha heard this. Things didn't get any better when Grandma told Marsha she was burning the stew and turned the stove down without asking. If you ask me, Grandma had the dirty finger moves coming to her.

Later, I heard Grandma tell Mom that Marsha's a "hussy." I don't think Marsha's a hussy. To hear Jeff complain about her to his friends, you'd think she was a nun. Grandma was getting on her nerves and she wanted to stir Grandma up. That's all. If I could get away with half of what Marsha does, I wouldn't need this notebook.

► September 25

Got my first French test back today, a 62. It was a pretty easy test about common nouns: *pencil, paper,* simple shit like that. Old Lady Song gave me a list of the words we had to know and I threw it away. Mag got a 91 and she was acting pretty cocky for the whole class. She sat there with a smug expression on her face and crossed her arms in front of her. Old Lady Song came up to me and said I should have tried harder. I pretended like I couldn't understand her and crumpled up the test after class. I've gotta read five frigging chapters in *Lost Horizon* tonight. Damn . . .

► September 26

Had to work with Ralph today in French class. Old Lady Song broke us up into pairs and gave us a list of verbs to conjugate. Ralph just kept looking at me with that sour look on his face. I asked him what was wrong and he said he had allergies. I thought he was gonna be mean and say he was allergic to me because I'm from Tranten, but he's really allergic to *everything*. Dogs, cats, dandelions, you name it. Chalk dust really sets him off, so he's gotta wrinkle up his face all the time to keep from sneezing. He showed me all the pills he has to take. They're in five different bottles. He also has to go have shots once a week or else he breaks out in hives and can't breathe.

I felt a little bad for him. He's not a bad person at all. He's really kind of nice. He offered to help me get caught up in French if I'd show him how to make a paper bomb. I didn't answer him one way or the other. I'm still trying to worm my way out of the College program.

I've gotta be careful about pegging people before I get to know them. I mean, just because Ralph's from Lipton that doesn't make him an instant ass.

▶ ## September 27

Had to work in groups of four today in French class. Old Lady Song grouped me with Ralph and two girls named Lesly and Theresa. Theresa's a snotty bitch but Lesly's pretty cool. She whispered to me that she thinks Ralph's a geek. Glad I'm not the only one.

We played "go fish" speaking only French. It was to get us practicing saying the numbers. Theresa was acting pretty bored. She started yawning and sucking on a lollipop. Lesly told me Theresa likes only senior boys. Don't we all. I looked at Theresa a long time and tried to see what there was about her that a senior would like. I figured Theresa must fantasize about older men, because with a face like hers, she should have been licking a salt lick, not a lollipop.

The game got really boring so I tried picturing Ralph out of his clothes. I only drew a blank. When Ralph took all of Theresa's fours, she said the game was stupid and tossed her cards down. She started painting her nails while Lesly and me lied to Ralph about what we had in our hands. The poor guy had to go fish every time.

▶ ## September 28

Had a long talk with Mag this morning on the phone. I told her I hated the College courses and I was gonna flunk out of them on purpose. Mag wasn't sympathetic at all. She called me a lazy bastard. She said if I was any kind of friend to her I'd stay in the classes. She doesn't want to face the

Lipton Snob Patrol by herself. Mag never spoke to me like that before. I decided if you can't beat 'em, join 'em. The guys from Lipton aren't any better-looking than the guys from Tranten, but they're cleaner. I guess it's better this way.

Mom's going for her driver's test tomorrow. She's awful nervous about it. Jeff's been going over all the rules of the road with her. After supper tonight, Jeff went to shoot hoops and Marsha took Mom out for a drive. I went with them. We drove all the way to Lipton. I could tell that Mom was nervous about driving with Marsha, but Marsha was cool about it. She cracked jokes and tried to make Mom laugh. Mom passed a herd of cows in a field and Marsha said, "Cows at nine o'clock!" and then made a sound like a machine gun. Mom told Marsha she didn't think that was very funny. Marsha apologized and kept quiet, even when Mom almost ran into a telephone pole.

▶ ## September 29

Mom flunked her driver's test. The guy who gave it to her was in a hurry to get it over with and he made her nervous. She flubbed both tries at parallel parking and when she was pulling into the DMV parking lot, a hornet flew in her window and landed on the steering wheel. She screamed and drove into a row of garbage cans. The guy got out of the car shaking and white-faced. Mom waited for Jeff and me to get in and gave Jeff the evaluation with "flunked" on it. She was ready to cry.

During the ride home, Jeff asked her all kinds of questions, "How was parking on a hill?" and "Did you signal when you turned?" All Mom said was, "I don't remember. I don't remember." Jeff got pretty mad at her and said he couldn't take her out driving anymore with basketball season coming up. Mom got mad then and said, "That's OK, because I'm not driving anymore. How much humiliation do I have to take?"

Nobody said a word the rest of the way home. Marsha had dinner ready when we got back. She knew by the look on Mom's face that she flunked. Marsha was full of funny stories when we ate. She had to take the test three times. The first time, someone behind her honked his horn and she was so startled she ran a stoplight. The second time, she hit the car she was parking in front of during parallel parking. The third time, the guy who gave the road test was so sick of her, he gave her the license without even getting into the car. "He was scared for his life," she said.

I thought this was pretty funny, so I started to laugh. Mom just looked down at her food and coughed. Jeff didn't think it was so funny, either. Grandma clucked her tongue and started clearing the dishes away. Marsha kept quiet the rest of the time.

September 30

Mag and me have moved tables in lunch. It seemed kind of dumb for us to keep eating with the Tranten Troublemakers. Now we're sitting at the way end of the senior table with Ralph, Lesly, and some other misfits. People don't mind because I'm a blood relative of Jeff. Besides, there's always at least two empty chairs between us and the closest senior, so it's OK.

Mag's been bugging me all week to go to the Autumn Dance with her. She brings it up every day on the bus, at lunch, in French class, you name it. I'd rather be strung up by my fingernails, actually. I've told Mag a million times I don't like dancing, and she says we won't have to dance, we can just go and "mingle." I know I'll give in to her. Who knows? We might have fun.

October 1

Today when we were waiting for the bus in front of Plumbco, this guy came running out of the building holding on to his hand and screaming. Blood was running out of his fingers and he passed out on the sidewalk. These other two guys in suits charged out holding a stretcher and carried him back in. It all happened so fast that Jeff and me weren't sure what we just saw. It'll probably be in the paper tomorrow.

Lesly asked me to go to the dance with her tonight. Told her I already had a date but thanked her anyway. She's not bad. She hates school so much. She's really rude to the teachers and gets away with it. She told Mr. Henderson today that she had a headache so she couldn't go to the board and label an earthworm diagram. When Mr. Henderson asked her if she wanted to go see the school nurse, Lesly said, "Just stop talking and it'll go away." Everybody laughed and Mr. Henderson's mouth dropped open. He didn't do anything to her though. That took balls. Mag told me that Lesly's father is on the school board and he's got power over teachers' salaries, so they don't dare do anything to her. That must be nice.

Jeff's out driving with Mom tonight. She was real angry when we came home from school this afternoon. She must've seen Dad and Carol when she went to the store or someplace. When we walked in the door she told Jeff not to take his coat off. She wanted to drive. Jeff couldn't even eat a snack. They were out the door in five seconds. After they left, I went out in the alleyway to see if there was anything new. Found Dad's framed picture of Dolly Parton. The glass was broken and the picture was all covered with mud.

▶ October 2

9:30 A.M.

Went to the dance and had a lousy time. Mag was wearing some hideous outfit she called her "butterfly ensemble." All kinds of bright colors that didn't seem to go together. During the fast songs, Mag would step away from me, raise her arms above her head, and shake her hips. Trying to turn me on? I just laughed at her. During the slow dances, she put her arms around my shoulders and tried to nibble my ear. I kept moving my head out of reach and kept my arms loose around her waist. I didn't even try to get excited about holding her body. It felt like a soft sack of flour to me. I kept one eye on the door and the other on the clock. Didn't see a single good-looking guy all night.

Mag's mother drove us home. During the ride, Mag kept edging closer to me like she was expecting something, I don't know what. I kept edging away from her and looking out the window. She said, "What are you looking at?" and I said, "The moon." I was really looking at her reflection in the window, trying to figure out what I was seeing. I didn't have a clue.

Nothing in the paper about what Jeff and me saw in front of Plumbco yesterday. I guess it never happened.

5:57 P.M.

Saw Dad today in the General Store. He was all clean-shaven and slim-looking, like he's taken up exercise or something. He saw me and walked over. "How are you doing?" he asked me. I said, "Fine" and turned to the cake mixes like I was trying to pick out a flavor. He told me he's got a new job. Carol's father arranged it for him. I just said congratulations and pulled down a box of Duncan Hines German chocolate. The next thing I know, Dad's cramming a twenty-dollar bill in my hand and walking away fast. When I turned to say something to him, he was out the door.

I told Mag what happened tonight when she came over. I showed her the bill and asked what I should do with it. "Spend it," she said. I asked Jeff the same thing and he says I should throw it away.

► October 3

Decided to take Mag's advice. Seemed a lot more practical. Mom's birthday is next week so Marsha took me shopping in Lipton. We had a great time joking around about Jeff. Marsha says she's "training" Jeff for life. He's got to know he can't just have any woman when he snaps his fingers. With men, you've gotta make them realize you're something special before you let them invade you. I'll have to remember that.

Marsha also thinks Jeff has got to shape up when he talks. When he says a double negative now she punches him in the arm—real hard, so he says, "Ow!" Like last night, Marsha was making popcorn and she asked Jeff where the margarine was. Jeff said, "We don't have no margarine." Marsha asked him to repeat that, so he did. Then she turned around and punched him. She was laughing, but Jeff looked like he wanted to kill somebody. I smiled and he started walking toward me. I hightailed it out of the room. The next thing I knew, Jeff and Marsha are laughing like crazy.

Marsha bought Mom a sterling silver engraved key chain as a sort of incentive for when she goes for her license again. I bought Mom a bottle of perfume that Marsha says is the "downfall to all males" (maybe I should try it). It's called "Seduction." Marsha put some on her wrist and then held it up for me to smell. It smells sort of like wildflowers and bug spray. If that's what turns men on, fine. I hope Mom likes it.

Saw Theresa from school in the store. She pretended not to see me. I was gonna play along with her game but I accidentally knocked over a rack of scarves when I was backing away from her. It made a CRASH sound so she *had* to look at me. I almost died. She sniffed "Hi" at me. I snorted "Hi" back and watched her for a while. She bought two sweaters and a pair of Calvin Kleins. She had her own charge card, the rich bitch.

7:35 P.M.

Grandma just had a long talk with Mom. Or had a long fight with Mom, is more like it. "You've gotta decide for yourself," Grandma spouted. "Either you sit around on your butt all day, waiting for him to walk through the door, or you can start playing the field." Mom mumbled something about not knowing anybody she'd want to start over with, and Grandma snapped, "I know plenty of good men!" "What am I supposed to do? Call them?" Mom screamed back.

Grandma told Mom to get out of the house and let people know she's available. Mom acted irritated and said, "That would make people think I'm lonely." "You *are* lonely!" Grandma bellowed at her.

Mom was quiet for a long time, then she started sniffling like she does right before she's about to go on one of her crying jags. She looked at herself in the mirror and said, "I can't," real soft, like it was almost a whisper. Grandma said, "No more tears. Maybe if you'd been strong in the first place, he never would have left." Then Mom started crying for real.

Jeff came home from shooting hoops and asked what was going on. Mom ran out of the room and Grandma just shrugged her shoulders and shook her head. Jeff looked at me and I told him, "They were just talking about Dad."

I hated Grandma for making Mom cry, but I had to agree with her. Mom never fought it when Dad took off. I don't know what she could have done, but anything would have been better than what she did. She just sat back and let it happen to her, like she was helpless or something. That must really bug her when she thinks about it. I know it bugs me.

▶ October 4

I ran into Carol today. Mag had to go to the bank and cash her mother's paycheck for her, and I went too, forgetting that Carol might be there.

She was standing by the watercooler, smoking a cigarette. She looked at me and started to turn away. She stopped though, and forced a smile. "Hello," she said.

I didn't say a word.

Carol puffed on her cigarette for a minute and then said, "Your Dad misses you."

I looked away and mumbled something about I missed him too. Mag walked over from the cashier's desk and nudged me out the door.

Standing there with her cigarette cocked and ready to fire, I wanted to slug her. She was so trampy, like such a slutty whore. After we left the bank, Mag said to me, "She probably stuffs her bra."

▶ October 5

Mr. Taylor (guidance counselor) cornered me today and asked me to be on the decorating committee for the Halloween Dance. He started giving me this talk about how important extracurricular activities will be when I apply to colleges. Why should I give a shit about that? I've got about as much chance of going to college as farting myself to the moon. I wanted to tell Mr. Taylor that but he started going on about my joining Student Council and I couldn't get a word in. Before I knew it, he was shoving a Student Council application in my hand. He told me to give it some "serious thought," then he took off down the hall.

Why don't these people leave me alone?

Crumpled up the application.

It's in the garbage can now.

▶ ## October 6

School is getting really boring really fast. I don't think anyone wants to be there. Not the students, who have to be, not the teachers, who don't know anything else, and not the janitors, who clean up after the rest of us go home for the night. The only person who seems happy to come to Chappaqua High School is Duff. He's always got a bug up his ass about something.

Today he called an assembly to tell all of us the new school policy on drugs and alcohol. It's an automatic suspension if any illegal substances are found in our possession. Duff did a lot of huffing and puffing when he walked across the stage giving his speech. He tried to look scary when he wrinkled up his eyebrows at the mention of "marijuana and liquor." Instead, he looked like the guy from the hemorrhoid ads who complains about having an itchy crack. I said this to Mag and she snorted at me like a pig. We both got laughing and Old Lady Song came over and gave us detentions.

After the assembly, a few kids ran out to their lockers to get rid of the "illegal substances" they had stashed away. I saw beer, joints, and different colored pills fly into pockets. It's common knowledge where all that stuff comes from. There's a house on Crooked Lane where everybody goes to get it. People keep their eyes on the front door. If it's got a handkerchief hanging from the doorknob, that means the drugstore's open. I'd say drugs are a problem around Tranten Township. Getting high or loaded or wasted seems a lot more appealing to some people than a lifetime of inspecting

27

faucet ratchets and then going home to their trailer to watch Vanna turn letters on *Wheel of Fortune*.

▶ ## October 7

Had detention with Old Lady Song tonight. When Mag and me walked in, she made us sit on opposite sides of the room. I pulled out *Lost Horizon* and started reading it. Starting to enjoy it. I was thinking about Shangri-La when Scott Pushard got up and started to leave the room without asking. Old Lady Song asked him where he thought he was going and Scott told her, "To the bathroom. I'm sick of this shit." Old Lady Song told him to sit down and Scott walked right by her. Old Lady Song grabbed his arm and tried to pull him back in the room. This was a mistake. Scott shoved her away and sent her sprawling on the ground. She sat there stunned as Scott took off.

I got up and helped her to her feet. Her glasses were hanging down on her chin but she didn't seem to care—just stood there shaking and moving her mouth with no sound coming out. I reached out to push her glasses back up when she screamed and told me to get Duff. Before I had a chance to leave the room, Duff was there. He told us all to scram and we did.

▶ ## October 8

Old Lady Song didn't come to school today. Her substitute said she's sick. Scott Pushard dropped out of school. I saw him out in front of the gas station tonight whistling and throwing rocks at the road. I've got a feeling that's where he'll be ten, twenty, thirty years from now.

▶ ## October 9

Dad called tonight asking to talk with Jeff. Mom begged him to come to the phone but he wouldn't. So then Dad said he wanted to talk to me, I got on and he was all concerned about me, which sort of surprised me. I didn't think he cared anymore. He asked me if I wanted to drive to Boston with him and "a friend" next weekend. I said, "No . . . not really."

He asked why not, and I said, "Because I can't stand your friend, Carol the Cunt."

Dead silence on the other end.

Then, "What did you call her, you little bastard?"

"Carol the Cunt. Didn't you know that was her nickname?"

Dad cursed me and slammed the receiver down. I looked over at Jeff, whose eyes were as wide as silver dollars. I was happy to see him IN SHOCK. Then I looked over at Mom.

It was the first time I've seen her smile in about three months.

October 10

Mom's birthday today. Marsha made a cake and brought it over. She sang an "R-rated" version of the birthday song that she said her father taught her. We all laughed except for Grandma. Marsha didn't seem to mind. Jeff was acting pretty funny all night. He put a party hat on Mom and snapped her picture. I couldn't tell if Mom was enjoying herself or not. A few times you could tell she was trying to smile, but couldn't quite make it.

Grandma gave her a new sweater, Jeff gave her a gold-plated bracelet, Marsha gave her the key chain, and I gave her the perfume. Mag showed up and gave Mom a T-shirt that said "33 AND STILL SEXY" on it. This got a laugh out of everybody except Grandma, who sniffed at it. Mom seemed to like everything. She even blushed at Mag's T-shirt. She kept looking over at the phone, like she was waiting for it to ring. It stayed quiet all night.

October 11

Jeff and Marsha are in the other room arguing. She came over tonight to help him study for a physics exam, but all Jeff wanted to do was shoot hoops or suck face. Marsha got pretty angry and asked him what he was gonna do with his life, work at Plumbco? Jeff laughed at her and said his ticket out was basketball. Marsha snapped back at him, "That'll get you a basket-weaving degree at some second-rate school, that's all." Jeff just grinned at her and made a kissy face and reached for her boob. Marsha whacked him over the head with his physics book. Jeff saw stars for a few seconds.

I left them alone after that. It was the start of the fifth fight they've had this week. Marsha wants Jeff to start taking things seriously, and Jeff just wants to play games (basketball and sex, in that order). If he isn't careful, he's gonna lose her and then there'll be no hope. She's the best thing to happen to him since the invention of the condom. Their fights always start out funny and lighthearted, then the name-calling starts (where fight number five is right now). Marsha calls Jeff a "brainless jock" or something like that, and Jeff calls Marsha a "preppy snot." After that, they start wrestling, fighting viciously one minute and then laughing and necking the next. It's a kick to watch these fights. They scrap on the floor like pro wrestlers, trying to get each other in headlocks, screaming bloody murder at each other. Marsha may be small, but she's more than a match for Jeff. The fights never last long. Soon, they're kissing like they never hated each other.

I was right. Just went in the room and they're necking like crazy.

▶ October 12

Today in lunch I thought I was gonna die laughing. Some juniors brought in a female mannequin with a picture of Duff's face taped at the head. She was wearing a bra and panties and had an empty beer bottle glued in her hand. They stuck it up on the radiator in back before the lunch bell rang.

When people came in they started laughing. Duff came in and got wicked pissed. He screamed at George the janitor to take it down, then he looked at all of us. We were all laughing hysterically. He bellowed, "Be quiet!" at us and we did. He started pacing back and forth between the tables, saying how the people who did it had better confess or he was gonna give everybody in the cafeteria a detention.

Everything was real quiet as he looked at us, then Ralph started sneezing like crazy. I think he must have drunk some milk by mistake because he was sneezing up a storm. Duff just scowled at him and asked him to control himself but Ralph kept right on sneezing. Duff screamed, "Detention for everybody!" and then he stamped out of the cafeteria.

October 13

I think Ralph has a crush on Mag. He goes out of his way to sit by her in lunch now, and today he gave her an apple. It was sort of comical. He polished it up and set it down on her tray while she was up going to the bathroom. She came back and saw the apple. She looked at me and said, "Where the hell did this come from?" I kind of looked at Ralph, who was grinning at Mag. Mag made a face at me and then said, "Thank you," to Ralph. Lesly was laughing like crazy.

Mag and Ralph were pretty quiet the rest of lunchtime. When we were riding home on the bus I kidded Mag about it. She told me to "Shut up" and just looked out her window.

October 14

Mom goes for her second road test the day after tomorrow. Grandma just came back from driving with her. She seems a lot more confident this time around. Less ready to cry, anyway.

Grandma's sure she's gonna pass. Last night, she went with a church group to see Timmy Will preach, and now she believes that God will be watching Mom from up in heaven. He'll put His hands on her wrists and guide her as she turns the steering wheel. He'll place His feet gently on top of hers and direct them as to how much pressure to apply on the brakes and gas pedal. To hear Grandma tell it, God's like a fast-food joint for wish granting. You just drive up to His window and tell Him what you want. If you don't have a license, like Mom, I guess you have to walk. But the wishes do get granted, if you pray hard, and believe.

Grandma must've really taken Timmy Will's words to heart, because she didn't say a swear word all night.

October 15

At dinner tonight, Grandma made us all join hands and pray that Mom will get her license tomorrow. Mag thought it was pretty funny and giggled all through the prayer. When the prayer was done, Grandma glared at her and asked me and Jeff why we both had such disrespectful girlfriends.

Is Mag my girlfriend? I never bothered to think about it before. We do everything together, and we talk on the phone every night. I can't picture life without her. In a lot of ways we're closer than Jeff and Marsha, or Dad and Mom were, or even Dad and Carol are. We can read each other like books, spending a lot of time on the good pages and skimming the bad ones.

I guess I love Mag.

But not in the biblical sense. I'll save the Bible for a good-looking blond hunk with brown eyes and a bare chest.

Beg your pardon, Grandma.

October 16

Mom got her license!!! She dropped Jeff off at basketball practice and then she drove home alone, waving her license out the driver's seat window. Grandma screamed, "Wonderful!" and grabbed the license from Mom's hands. She raised it up to the heavens for Him to see and then gave it back to Mom.

Mom was so excited when she told us about the test. The examiner was a kindly old man who had a nice smile. He complimented her turns and said the way she parked on a hill was "first rate." To top it off, Mom did parallel parking right the first time! No second tries for her. Mom smiled when she told us that part. It was great seeing her excited about something. Grandma had her eyes closed as Mom told us all about the test. When Mom was finished, Grandma smiled and said she knew she could do it.

Now Mom says she's gonna drive Grandma around, instead of the other way around. She won't have to bum rides off her night school classmates now, either.

▶ ## October 17

Today in English something strange happened to Ralph. It was the weirdest thing. He was sitting there fine, listening to Mrs. King read out loud from *Lost Horizon*. The next thing we knew, he was falling out of his desk and lying down flat on the floor. He let out this long moan, "Oooooooooooooooh," and his body went all stiff. Everybody just looked at him for a second, then Mrs. King snapped into action. She barked at Theresa to go to the office and call for an ambulance. Then she knelt down beside Ralph and unbuttoned his collar. Ralph's mouth started to foam and his body shook like crazy. We all sat there like dummies. It was scary. Pretty soon, Ralph went limp. He breathed deep and looked like he was asleep. Duff came in all serious like and told us to go to the study hall room, so we did.

When we were walking in the hall, Mag looked real shook up. I asked her if she was all right and she said, "I was passing a note to him and BANG! What the hell happened?" Said I was damned if I knew.

In lunch, everybody was talking about it. Everybody thinks it's drugs. Lesly said she didn't think Ralph ever touched them, but she couldn't think of anything else that could cause that kind of reaction. I feel bad for Ralph, the way people are talking about him.

8:20 P.M.

Mag just called. Ralph had an epileptic fit. She said he's fine now and he'll be back to school tomorrow. He called her and asked her what our math homework was. Mag said he sounds good. I'm glad.

▶ ## October 19

Ralph came to school today. Everybody in the College classes was happy to see him. Mrs. King treated him like an invalid all through English class. When we were taking a quiz, she asked him (in front of everybody) if he wanted her to come pick up his paper so he wouldn't have to walk up to her desk and exert himself. He didn't say a word. He just walked up to her desk and put the paper down like it was crown jewels.

Mr. Nolier (PE teacher) asked him if he wanted to sit out the flag football game. He said no and charged onto the field. It was pretty amazing watching Ralph play football today. Usually he doesn't give a damn about the game and just goes through the motions, but today it was like he was gonna prove something. The other team threw a long pass. Kuprekski wasn't looking and the ball bounced off the back of his head and landed in Ralph's hands. Ralph looked real surprised for a second and then he took off like a bat out of hell. The guy *ran*. He was bobbing and weaving down the field like one of the *Solid Gold* dancers. The other team was so shocked that they didn't even try to steal his flag. Ralph tripped once on his way to the end line, but he covered it up like a pro and crossed the line in midair, barely landing on his feet. He slammed that ball down and ran back to the huddle for the next play.

Mr. Nolier, who was in shock, blew his whistle and said, "Six points." Ralph was acting like that sort of thing happened every day. He high-fived me and said, "Not bad, huh?"

"Good run," I told him. Good day, too . . .

October 20

Mr. Mariner, my World History teacher, is a god. I don't understand how I could have missed it before. Maybe because I was too busy looking at the guys in class, trying to find someone passable, I never bothered to pay attention to the man in front droning about Germanic tribes. He is a man.

He is *such a man*. How could I have missed it?

Maybe it's because I thought his class was dull. Maybe it's because I never looked past his sort of plain face. Or . . . Maybe it's because I'd never seen him wearing a T-shirt before today. In class he always wears bulky sweaters or three-piece suits. But after school when he's getting ready to do laps around the track, his clothes improve.

He was in the guys' locker room posting a sign-up sheet for indoor track, which he coaches. And he was wearing one of those netted T-shirts that show a lot, but not enough to give you the whole picture. I looked at the outline of his chest and his iron stomach and it was really tough for me to keep from going hard. Hell, I would've paid him to take off his shirt and show me what was underneath if I had any money. I did see his belly button when he raised his arms and that was enough to make me wanna drool all over the locker room. Then I looked down his washboard stomach to his dick. It was hard to tell how big it was through the material of his sweat shorts, but I could tell there was potential in that area. Then I moved on to his muscled-up legs and I was Jell-O.

I was afraid I was gonna start panting so I looked away from him real fast and came face-to-face with a poster of Brooke Shields puckering her lips up. That cooled me down.

I figure Mr. Mariner was in front of me for about ten seconds—the time it must have taken him to tack up the sign-up sheet. After he was done, he turned around, said "Hi, Ben," and left the locker room. I sat there watching his ass and tried to remember I was in public.

Signed up for indoor track today. Mine was the first name on the list.

▶ ## October 21

Somehow, Mr. Taylor (guidance counselor) found out that I'm going out for indoor track. He cornered me in the hallway and gave me the thumbs-up sign, saying, "Track will look great on your college applications." "What college applications?" I wanted to ask. Instead, I acted like I was in a big hurry and started backing away from him fast. He mouthed, "Way to go," to me and grinned a stupid grin. I pretended not to see him and turned around.

Old Lady Song came back to school today with her arm in a sling. She says her arm was fractured but it doesn't hurt anymore. She called me up after class to thank me for helping her up from the floor. I feel kind of bad for Old Lady Song. She's a recent widow. She quit her job teaching a few years ago so she could spend more time with her husband. And

then he got killed in a hunting accident last fall and Old
Lady Song went back to work. Mag told me all of this on
the bus ride home tonight.

It must have been a real slap in the face. She was planning
on traveling in France with her husband and seeing all the
places she'd been talking about all those years, and now look
at her, back in the classroom, teaching a bunch of kids who
don't care how to conjugate verbs.

I'm gonna be nice to Old Lady Song from now on. She
needs a break.

October 22

Today in History, Mr. Mariner said my name and smiled.
It was after the bell rang and everybody was just leaving. I
walked by his desk and he stopped erasing the board and
looked at me. I stopped and looked at him. His eyes looked
like two pieces of chocolate.

"I heard you're going out for track."

"Yes. I decided I could use the exercise." (He laughed like
I'd just cracked a joke and patted my butt.)

"I thought you were looking a little . . . robust." (I laughed
like he'd just cracked a joke.)

"It looks like it's contagious." (And I patted his stomach.
Then I left.)

This could be the beginning of a beautiful relationship.

Ralph told me that Mr. Mariner lives on the old Potter
farm in Nome. That's way out in the middle of the woods.
Maybe I'll go visit him sometime.

This afternoon I told Mag I was going out for track and
she laughed like it was some joke. She asked what events I
was gonna compete in, and I said I didn't know. "I'm just
doing it for fun," I told her. She's not convinced. I'm not
sure I'm convinced, either.

October 23

11:30 P.M.

Went to the fair in Lipton tonight with Mag and her

mother. It was kind of a last-minute decision to go. Mag called up at five o'clock and said they were going, so I decided to tag along. I usually hate the fair. I never have any money to spend, so it's no fun. But tonight we went with Mag's mother and her latest boyfriend who's in the American Legion. He had a ton of tickets he got for free. He gave Mag half of them and told her to "Live it up."

Mag and me went on every ride in the place. When we were on the Ferris wheel, Mag started talking about how great it would be if we could just stay on it and never get off. That didn't make any sense to me and I told her so. "Who wants to spend their whole life going up and down in circles all the time?" Mag said, "It beats being stuck on the ground and going in circles all the time, which is what living in Tranten is like." I understood her. Mag put her head on my shoulder and started whistling "Zip-a-dee-doo-dah." That cracked us both up, so then we started to sing the song. We couldn't remember the words, so we made them up as we went along. My voice started cracking bad and Mag laughed. I stopped singing after a while.

We went on all the other rides. The Whip, the Merry Mixer, the Paratrooper. You name it, we went on it. My favorite was the Skydiver because of the way Mag screamed "Holy Jesus!" every time we went upside down. We were both real dizzy after all the rides and we couldn't walk straight.

We went into the Freak Show where we watched some guy swallow swords. Later on, this Fat Lady named Dolly came out in a red fringe miniskirt and started dancing to an old big-band song. Her thighs were as big as watermelons and her boobs looked like a pair of bowling balls bouncing around under a blanket. Her whole body shook like Jell-O when she danced. Everybody was laughing at the poor broad. I felt bad for her. The funny thing was, she didn't seem to care. She was smiling away and waving her arms up in the air like a professional. It was like she didn't know everybody was making fun of her. It sort of scared me she could be so blind.

Mag's mother snagged us when we came out of the Freak

Show and told us it was time to go home. She must have had a fight with the American Legion guy because he didn't ride back with us.

3:47 A.M.

Just had the worst nightmare. I was up on a stage in this red fringe miniskirt in front of a crowd of Fat Ladies. Music began and I started to dance. The Fat Ladies all laughed and cheered me. After a while I started to sing, "I like men, I like men," and the Fat Ladies cheered even louder.

Suddenly the lights all went out and I couldn't see anything. Pretty soon I discovered I couldn't breathe. I got so scared. I woke up and my face was buried in my pillow and I was suffocating. I was real relieved when I found out all I had to do was pick my head up to breathe again.

What does it mean?

October 24

I'm getting real nervous about indoor track. I saw a couple of Lipton snobs running around the track tonight and they meant business. I don't wanna make a fool of myself. I keep telling myself that I'm gonna do it just for fun. But I keep thinking that I'm gonna come in last in every race I'm in. That would be a nightmare. But then I tell myself not to worry.

I'm a pretty fast runner—in fifth grade I even won a race. It was a fifty-yard dash at the fair and all the kids were invited to run in it. It was sponsored by some dairy and this guy in a cow costume was calling, telling all the kids we'd get free milk if we ran. I hated milk, but I decided to enter when I saw the trophy. A solid-gold runner frozen in mid-stride on a wooden podium.

The cow got us lined up at the starting line ("Mooooo-ve along, kids! Mooooooo-ve along!") and then raised a starting pistol in the air. I don't remember anything about the race—it's just a blur of cows, cheering faces, and visions of that trophy. Jeff told me later that I left all the other kids in the dust. I cruised over the finish line and then the cow ran at me waving the trophy and a gallon bottle of milk. I was the new town hero.

The milk might have been a decent prize if its expiration date hadn't been the next day. The trophy turned out to be solid plastic, painted gold. It broke a week later. I've got the pieces somewhere in my bureau.

Who knows what might have been if someone had encouraged me? Maybe indoor track is the start of a whole new career for me.

October 25

Grandma is driving us all crazy with her preaching. She damns Jeff and me to hell if we swear now. God hears and see *everything*, she tells us as she shakes a finger. He's standing up there with a big book, making big black checks in it every time one of us says "damn," "shit," or "fuck." Once the book is full, we've reached our limit on swear words, and then there's no use apologizing. We might as well get on the "Down Escalator" and prepare for a hot ride.

Grandma figures since Jeff and me are so young, we've probably still got time to keep our quotas down, but only if we stop swearing now. It kind of puts a crimp in suppertime talk. We have to say the cleaned-up versions of swear words. Now, instead of saying "Holy shit!" we say "Holy crap!" For "fuck" we say "caca." I feel so dumb saying "caca"—like I'm in first grade—but Grandma likes it.

Someday when I'm feeling brave, I'm gonna ask Grandma if she's reached her quota yet. Her lifetime of "damns" and "shits" must have left a line of check marks a mile long in God's book.

October 26

Kuprekski got revenge today. Les Numer was shooting elastics at the back of his head on the bus. Kuprekski just sat there like a bump on a log. After a while, Les got bored with the elastics and started calling Kuprekski names like "Spazman" and "shit-for-brains." He'd call out to Kuprekski,

"Hey you, Shit-for-brains! When's the last time you took a shower?" When Kuprekski wouldn't turn around, Les shot a paperclip at the back of his head. Kuprekski just sat there. Nobody could see his face.

When the bus got to Les's stop, Les got up to leave. When he was walking by Kuprekski's seat, Kuprekski stuck out his foot and tripped him. Les went flying down the aisle and fell down, ripping the crotch of his pants open. He had on leopard-skin underwear. He got up and Ray, the bus driver, told him to be careful going down the steps. Les shot Kuprekski a look that could only mean murder.

I wouldn't want to be Kuprekski tomorrow. Hell, I wouldn't want to be Kuprekski ever.

▶ October 27

Kuprekski disappeared today. Nobody knows what happened to him. He was on the bus this morning. Sometime between first and second period he vanished. Duff called the police in and they searched the school grounds but they couldn't find him. Mag says it's no great loss. "Let him stay lost," she says.

Ralph says that he saw Kuprekski in Lipton last night. He was in the trash bin behind McDonald's, picking around for food. I just shook my head and shrugged my shoulders. Some people don't have any pride at all.

▶ October 28

They found Kuprekski today. He was shut up in an unused locker, bound and gagged with dirty sweat socks. He spent the night in there. He probably thought it was nice, compared to his house.

Been invited to a Halloween party. Kimby Quinn asked me. As a rule, I don't like Kimby. She stabbed Mag in the back last year. They both made it to the finals of the school spelling bee, representing our class. Mrs. Kendrick only had one list of the bee words and she gave it to Kimby, telling her to make a copy of it and give it to Mag. Kimby conveniently "lost" the list, and so Mag didn't have anything to study. She got knocked out in the third round. Kimby went on to win the school bee and made it as far as the states, where she lost to a guy from Rumford. Mag never forgave her.

Mag was sick today, so I paired off with Kimby in French class. We had to conjugate a bunch of verbs. Kimby says the party's gonna be "awesome." She says I can bring Mag "if I want." Everybody's gotta wear a costume.

I've known Kimby since the first grade and I'm still not sure if I like her. She's one of those people who act like your best friend for a few days and then when you really need them they disappear. She's also an obnoxious flirt. She's got the movement of picking lint off a guy's sweater down to a science, and she can laugh at any witty thing a guy says. She pisses me off sometimes.

Lately Kimby's set her sights on Mr. Mariner. She grins at him during class and laughs at all his jokes. Today she couldn't find Yugoslavia on the map in front of the class. She put on quite a show of scrunching up her eyes and moving her finger helplessly across the map of Europe. Finally, she turned pitifully to Mr. Mariner. Mr. Mariner sighed dramatically, put his hand on hers, and put her finger on the right spot. Kimby loved every second of it. I felt like screaming at her when she was doing it.

Today in lunch, Lesly said that Kimby reminds her of Erica Cane on *All My Children,* the way she hems and haws around men. Ralph said he really likes her. He thinks she's nice, the way she puts her arm around his shoulder and acts so familiar all the time. Ralph doesn't know that she does that to every person with a penis. It's Kimby's Way.

October 29

Told Mag about Kimby's party and she wants to go. It's either that, she says, or staying home and watching her mother molest trick-or-treaters. It should be an interesting evening.

Since Grandma found God, she doesn't approve of Halloween. She calls it "the devil's holiday." Instead of candy, she's gonna hand out slips of paper with Bible verses on them. I'm not sure how this is gonna go over with a bunch of greedy trick-or-treaters, but Grandma's sure she can handle them.

Jeff and Marsha are going to a kids' party at the Town Hall. Marsha promised her mother she and Jeff would help with the games. She's here now fitting him for his costume. They're gonna go as Superman and Lois Lane. I think that's real funny.

Last night, Marsha asked him what he wanted to go as and he said Adam and Eve. They fought for a while, and finally decided on the man of steel and his faithful female reporter. Jeff's not gonna wear the tights, just blue jeans, the shirt, and a red cape. Marsha also told me she's gonna try to get him to slick his hair back like Christopher Reeve. We'll see. He's not very happy about it. He got invited by some of his jock friends to a keg party by the river. I think he's planning on cutting out of Town Hall early.

Mag and me are going as married zombies. We're both gonna make up our faces. Over her face, Mag's gonna wear a wedding veil and hold a bouquet of flowers. I'm wearing a bow tie and cummerbund over mine. Whoops! Grandma's in the next room condemning Marsha. Better go see if I can bring peace.

October 30

Mom's got a date for Halloween. Her night school class is giving a party and this guy asked her to go with him. She says it's not a date, just two people riding together to a party. Grandma asked her what his name was and she wouldn't say. Jeff seems happy about it all.

Mom tried to call Dad at Carol's tonight after dinner, to see what his Halloween plans were, and no one answered. She tried the number four more times and there was still no answer. Finally, she slammed the receiver down and went to the kitchen where she started making candied apples. She's got about fifty of them done.

Just went in and asked her what she was going to go as

for Halloween this year—to try to cheer her up. "A ghost," she said.

▶ October 31

6:46 P.M.

Happy Halloween. A bunch of kids wore costumes to school today. Ralph came as a mad scientist and Lesly came as an Indian squaw. Mag and me wore our zombie costumes. It was fun. Old Lady Song came dancing into class in a ballerina outfit. She had on a crown and this big tutu with long underwear and tennis sneakers under it. That got a laugh out of everybody. I like Old Lady Song. She's all right.

Mr. Mariner came as the Lone Ranger and he was looking good. He told us that the Lone Ranger was his hero when he was growing up and that he loved those old movies. I never got into the Lone Ranger, because I felt bad for Tonto. I always thought he was an idiot for doing everything the Lone Ranger said. The poor bastard always got the crap beat out of him so the Lone Ranger could come save the day. After seeing Mr. Mariner, though, I could relate to how old Tonto felt. He must have been crazy about the guy. The next time one of those old movies is on the tube, I'm gonna watch it.

Mrs. King didn't wear a costume. She just wore her regular clothes. Mag whispered to me that Mrs. King should get the "Scariest Costume" award. I just grinned at her and rolled my eyes. Mr. Duff dressed as Santa Claus. He came into the cafeteria today with a sack full of pamphlets on how to enjoy an alcohol-free Halloween. He passed them out to all of us, saying, "Ho-ho-ho!"

"No no no!" Mag whispered in my ear as she crumpled up her pamphlet.

Mr. Duff announced that the PTA is throwing an alcohol-free Halloween party tonight in the Lipton Town Hall. Hooray . . . Lesly and Ralph asked Mag and me if we were going to it. We said, "Nope." I kind of wish we were going. I'm not looking forward to tonight at all. Kimby came to our table in lunch today grinning from ear to ear. Mag told Kimby that her costume was great, and she wasn't wearing one. Kimby asked Mag, who was wearing her zombie costume, why she forgot to put her costume on. I could tell they were on the verge of a cat fight, so I asked Kimby what time we should be at her house tonight, to sort of change the subject. Kimby said, "Eight o'clock, and it goes until dawn." Right ... If Kimby's parents are around we'll be lucky to go to ten. They're religious.

Old Lady Song won the teachers' costume award, and Ralph won the students'. The prizes were big Hershey bars. Ralph gave his to Mag. She tried to look happy about it but—Whoops! Mag's at the door. Gotta run.

November 1

Halloween was a disaster. Went to Kimby's party with Mag. What a mess. I knew we were in trouble when Kimby answered the door. She was dressed in this harem girl's outfit with veils and sequins. Mag took one look at her and asked, "Where's the camel you just laid, Kimby?" Kimby glared at Mag and asked how she thought she could get away with wearing a white wedding gown. It went downhill from there. It was tough work trying to keep the two of them separated for the night.

Kimby's brother Frank brought in three cases of beer and everybody started drinking. Mag went at the beer like she'd been on the wagon for a year. She downed one in five gulps and then reached for another one. I don't like to drink. When we were twelve, Mag and me stole a bottle of tequila from her mother's cabinet, took a jug of orange juice from my refrigerator, mixed the two of them together, and drank it straight from the Tupperware jug. We'd heard about someone getting "plastered" that way and we wanted to know what it felt like. We were both out cold when my parents came back. Mag's mother had to carry her home. I woke up the next morning feeling like someone was pounding my head with a hammer. I puked up buckets and got grounded for a month. Mag's mother grounded her for three days.

I learned my lesson, but Mag obviously didn't. She was

working on her third beer when Kimby broke into her dance of the seven veils. Kimby was working on her fourth at the time. Everybody cheered like crazy when she started taking off her veils while trying to dance to "Heart of Glass." She was having trouble with one of her veils, so Frankenstein (Les Numer, I think) yanked it off from her. She was down to her last veil when her parents came in and started screaming at us to get out of their house. I can imagine how shocked they were to come home and find their daughter, the honor-roll student, stripping for a room full of monsters, super-heroes, and hoboes.

The next thing I knew, Mag and me were on the front lawn with the rest of them, wondering what to do next. Someone mentioned the keg party down by the river and everybody started to leave. Mag was pretty wasted, so we decided to skip the party. As I watched people leave, it amazed me how much better everybody looked with masks on.

Tried to walk Mag home but she wouldn't go. "Can't go home. Mom's got a date in the house." She cried as we walked in the direction of her house. "I wanna sit down."

We sat down on the town fountain where Mag started to throw up. When she was done, I wiped off her face with a rag I found and we just sat there for about an hour. Mag was so drunk she talked mumbo jumbo. "My mom hates me. She's ruining my life. She hates me!!!"

I just sat beside her and said, "No, she doesn't."

We were both getting cold, so Mag decided it was time to go home. When she stood up and tried to walk by herself, she fell face first on the grass and got a mouthful of leaves. "Tastes like shit, Ben." I got Mag to her house and nobody was home. What a relief. I helped her up to her bedroom and settled her on the bed. I didn't know if I should take off her clothes or not and decided against it.

Got home and Jeff and Marsha were sitting on the couch making out in their costumes. I left them alone and went up to my room. Mom and Grandma were in bed. I looked at myself in the mirror and decided I liked myself better as a zombie.

This morning the lawn's covered with Grandma's Bible

verses. "The kids in this neighborhood are all demons," she says.

4:45 P.M.

I walked the five miles to Mr. Mariner's house in Nome this afternoon. I started thinking about him this morning and decided I really had to see him. It was either that or listen to Grandma quiz Mom on the Table of the Elements for a chemistry test.

A couple of cars slowed down when they saw me walking but nobody stopped. I didn't care. It was sunny and pretty warm for November 1. When I got to where Mr. Mariner's house is, I slowed down and started feeling dumb. I was sort of wishing I hadn't come when his front door opened and he came out holding an ax. I ducked behind a tree and watched him walk to the big wood pile beside his house. It felt real good seeing him like that.

He picked up a piece of wood from the pile and put it on the chopping block. He looked at it for a few seconds, like he was meditating, then he raised the ax over his shoulder and brought it down on the piece of wood. His first blow was way off and he just cut a little piece of bark off. He said, "Damn," and tried again. The next time he took off some more bark but still didn't come close to chopping the wood down the middle. After a while, he had a pile of wood chips from that one piece of wood that was still up on the chopping block. It was hard not to laugh. He looked so helpless and funny. Finally, he threw the ax down and ran into the house. The next thing I knew, he was driving out of the driveway in an old green car.

I waited a few minutes for him to come back but it looked like he was gonna be gone for a while. I don't know why I did it, but I walked over and chopped all the wood in the wood pile and stacked it while he was gone. When I got to the last piece, I heard a car coming up the road. I threw down the ax and ran for my hiding place. It turned out to be a red pickup truck, not Mr. Mariner's green lemon. I breathed a sigh of relief and took off.

Ran like a bat out of hell the whole way home, feeling stupid and achey. I don't know why I chopped the wood for him. It was such a crazy thing to do. Mag says love makes you do crazy things. Maybe it's love.

How would I know?

6:39 P.M.

Just saw Mag at the store. Her eyes were all bloodshot and she looked green. I told her she looked like shit and she told me I could kiss her ass. She was picking up some soda and cigarettes for her mother. I walked home with her and tried to make her laugh, but she just glared the whole walk home. I tried asking her what was wrong and she said her mother was bugging the hell out of her.

When we got to her house, her mother was sitting at the table smoking and filing her nails. She told Mag to put the soda away and go to her room. Then she asked me to leave.

I tried calling Mag tonight but her mother said she couldn't come to the phone.

November 2

Grandma came home from church today and started going on about how Mom, Jeff, and me ought to start going with her. She says it helps her a lot when she has to face "daily challenges." Listening to the choir when they get singing, and hearing Reverend Silk preach about God and the world, "recharges" her, she says. Reverend Silk's sermon must've been a powerhouse today, because Grandma talked a blue streak. Things about how God has a plan for each one of us but we've gotta give our lives to him if we want to know what it is.

When she was done with her speech, she gave us all the eye. Jeff and me looked down at our Pop-Tarts. It was easier than saying, "No thanks." Grandma cleared her throat and made a face like she was waiting for one of us to talk. Finally Mom said to her, "You've got religion, and I've got *As the World Turns*. When my soap opera starts getting boring, I'll go to church with you."

Grandma nodded and left the kitchen without saying a word. I thought she was mad, so I went to her bedroom to talk to her. She was folding her clothes and stuffing them in her bureau. I asked her if she was OK and she said, "I try to help. I'm not always right, but I do try to help. In my own way."

I sat on her bed and watched her fold clothes. It took me a minute to figure out her mood. She wasn't mad. She was discouraged. All of a sudden I couldn't blame her. When she had her back to me, I said, "Thank you, Grandma," and left the room fast.

▶ November 3

Jeff got in a fight in school today. Some guy named Kirk made a remark about Dad. He wanted to know if Dad sleeps between Carol and Mom when he comes home, or if he hops from bed to bed. Jeff beat the shit out of him and made hamburger out of his face. Mom had to go bring Jeff home.

"You can't be doing stuff like that," she told him.

Jeff didn't say anything. He's suspended for three days, and he's got to write a formal apology to Kirk. Marsha's with him now. She came over tonight after she heard about the fight. She's in the living room with him rubbing his hair. I walked in to say hi and she put her finger to her mouth like Jeff was asleep. Jeff kept his eyes glued to the TV set.

▶ November 4

I've started noticing little things about Mr. Mariner that I never saw before. He's left-handed, and his nose is slightly crooked. He told us today that he played hockey in college. He probably broke his nose doing that. Maybe I'll ask him sometime. I know he's not married, and I don't think he has a girlfriend. God, it doesn't hurt to hope.

We were labeling maps of Europe today and he was going around the room looking at our papers. He stopped at my desk and patted my shoulder (!) and then said, "Good job, Smithie." He used his finger to point out the Red River and I thought about how good it would feel to hold that hand.

I've never held a man's hand before. Jeff stopped holding my hand once we hit grade school. Dad never started.

▶ November 5

Mr. Mariner has the nicest smile I've ever seen. His laugh is kind of goofy, but his smile is something else. I see him smile and I think about touching his lips with my finger. Just running my fingertip across them. Then I imagine what his crooked nose feels like. I touch my own nose to get an idea. Then I think about running my fingers through his hair. It's real dark. When I walked up to his desk to hand in my paper I got close enough to smell it. It smelled clean. Like a man.

He's got Kimby Quinn all hot and bothered. I can tell by the way she laughs at all his jokes and looks at his ass when he walks by. She tries her old picking the lint off the sweater routine with him every other day. I don't think he appreciates it. He kind of nudges her hand away and looks sick of her.

I like to give him a hard time. In class he'll ask me some question like, "Where did the Turks resettle after the Celtic invasion?" and I'll say, "Jamaican Club Med." That always gets a laugh out of him. None of the other kids in the class think I'm very funny, but I can always make Miles laugh.

I like his name. Miles. Rhymes with smiles.

▶ November 6

I daydreamed about Miles Mariner today. Almost got into deep shit, too.

He was going on about the Yalta Conference when I droned out his voice and started concentrating on his body. He was wearing his green sweater and I got thinking about what he looked like under that sweater. Before I knew it, I had a boner. Miles called on me to go to the board and point out Yalta on the map. I wanted to die. I can just imagine what would have happened if I'd gone to the board with my dick sticking out like a flag. I told him I didn't know where Yalta was and Kimby, thank God, raised her hand and pranced up to the board. I think she stuffed her bra today because she was sticking out a little more than usual. I fixed my eyes on the toilet paper jutting out from Kimby's chest and started going soft again. Just in time too, because the bell rang and I had to get up anyway.

When I was walking out, Miles stopped me at his desk and asked me if I knew where Yalta was *now*. I said, "Yah," and ran out of the room. That was too close for comfort. In the hall Mag asked me if I was OK. She said I looked pale. I smiled and said, "Never been better."

▶ November 7

Mom brought her friend home tonight. Grandma told her she wanted to meet him, so she asked him over for dinner. His name is Chuck and he's shorter than Mom. I could tell that Grandma was sort of disappointed, but she seemed happy to meet him. Chuck drives a truck for Beck Lumber and is almost bald. His big dream is to work as a parts inspector for Plumbco.

Mag came over for dinner and I could tell she was sizing up Chuck. She's always on the lookout for "stable" men for her mother. She asked him what he did in his spare time and Chuck said, "Ceramics." Grandma asked him all about his religion and seemed happy with the answers.

The funny thing is, Mom doesn't seem to like him all that well. She smiled when Chuck complimented her cooking, but I could tell her brain was somewhere else. They had to go to a class after dinner and Mag stayed and helped me with the dishes. She told me that Chuck reminds her of a little mole. He makes me think of Dopey, the seventh dwarf. I told her she should introduce him to her mother. He seemed pretty stable. She said, "There's a big difference between being stable and being comatose."

Grandma must've been eavesdropping in the living room, because she charged right in and gave Mag hell. She said Chuck is a good man. He's got a steady job and he goes to church every Sunday, and if Mag couldn't say anything nice, she should go home until she learned some manners. Grandma stamped out of the room and Mag and me just looked at each other. The next thing I know, we were laughing hysterically.

▶ November 8

Indoor track started today. Miles had us all sit down on the gym floor and write which events we thought we wanted to do. I put down 50-yard dash and 200-yard dash. He read my paper and then grinned down at me. "You're a sprinter, heh Smithie?" I wanted to tell him that my name is Ben, but then I figured that I liked him calling me Smithie. Nobody else does. It's kind of like a pet name.

He showed us the stretching exercises we have to do before every practice. The elastic on his shorts was kind of coming loose, so he had to pull them up every time he bent over. Then he had us run laps around the gym. He called me over when I was running by and told me to relax my arms. I was flapping them up and down and wasting too much energy. Then he grabbed my hands and shook my arms until they were loose. This turned me on like a light. I turned around to get back on the track and he slapped my butt. I was running on air after that. I felt like I was passing everybody on the track.

He stopped us and said we would all work on sprints after that. We each got a turn to do it. He screamed, "Go!" and I streaked across the gym floor like I had a herd of cows after me. When I got to the finish line, I stopped and looked over at him. I waited for him to say something to me, but he just wrote my time down on his clipboard and got ready to start the next runner.

▶ November 9

I'm in heaven.

After practice tonight everybody else went into the locker room to take showers. I stayed behind to watch what Miles was going to do next. He started running laps around the track, just jogging around and around. I hid behind the bleachers and watched him the whole time. After a while, he started breathing hard and wiping the sweat out of his eyes. He looked so good.

Some of the guys were coming out of the locker room and getting ready to go home. I decided I'd better go shower too. When I got in there, the showers were empty and everybody was clearing out. I got into the shower and started soaping up. I heard the shower next to me turn on and a familiar voice said, "You still here, Smithie?" I opened my eyes and there was Miles standing next to me, naked as the Fourth of July. The next thing I knew my eyes were burning because I got soap in them. I made a noise and Miles said, "Soap in your eyes? Here." And he handed me his towel and I rubbed my eyes. It smelled like Old Spice. I didn't dare look at him at first. I was afraid if I did, I'd go all hard. I would *die* if that happened. Miles isn't the kind of man you can pretend is an ugly statue.

He asked me how I liked track and I said, "It's great." Then he said it looked like it was going to be a pretty good team this year and I mumbled something. I don't remember what. He started shampooing his hair and I decided to sneak a quick look at him. His back is a wonder. So many places to touch on it. And his butt is two perfect bowls of flesh. I wanted to grab them. He closed his eyes and started soaping up his face and I looked at his dick. It looked kind of small to me, but then I looked at my own and saw that mine looked small too. He cleared his throat like he was about to talk, so I jerked my eyes away from him and turned up the cold water on my shower.

He said he'd help me with a weight training program if I wanted, to build up the muscles in my legs. Runners need strong legs. I said I'd like that. And then he said that he liked my form when I ran. I had a lot of potential. I was gonna say something back but I started getting all wrinkled so I had to leave the shower. I turned it off and said goodbye to him. When I walked by him, I sort of accidentally on purpose rubbed up against his back. He didn't seem to notice, but I did. It felt like I was touching love. It was so hard and so nice-feeling.

I dried off and got dressed as quick as I could. I couldn't

face him again. I think I was afraid of getting too much of a good thing. All I know is, my ass was out of that bathroom in five minutes flat.

When I got outside, Jeff and Marsha were waiting for me in her car. Marsha had a Student Council meeting, so she had to stay after. Jeff was pissed at me because I kept them waiting. "Where the hell have you been?" he growled. I told him the locker room was crowded and I couldn't get into a shower until ten minutes ago. He said try harder next time and then Marsha told him to cool it. She looked back at me and said it was all right.

I'm dying to tell somebody about what I feel for Miles. During the ride home, I thought about telling Marsha. I've got a feeling she'd understand. When we stopped at the store on the way, I stayed in the car with her while Jeff ran in to pick up some chips. She looked back at me and wanted to know if something was bothering me. She said I looked kind of dazed. I just shook my head. For one split second I almost blurted out, "I'M HOPELESSLY IN LOVE WITH MILES MARINER!!! I CRAVE HIS BODY LIKE WATER!" Instead, I said, "Thanks for the ride."

▶ November 10

Lifted weights with Miles today. He got me going on this program and he's gonna work with me every night after track practice. He shows me an exercise to do and I'll pretend like I don't get it and ask him to do it again. He does it and then I'll try to get away with getting him to do it again. He usually refuses and makes me do it then. It's kind of fun. I tried to get out of the session without breaking a sweat, but Miles wouldn't let me. He said, "No pain, no gain," and nudged me toward the weight bench every time.

He asked me if I had any problems at home that I wanted to talk about. I said no and he said, "Because I'm here for you if you ever need to talk." I just shook my head and got down on the bench. He's the last person I want to talk about my home life with. It would ruin everything. I just wanna hit the sack with him.

November 11

Miles gave me a ride home tonight. I missed the late bus home and Jeff forgot to wait. Miles's car is an old rusty clunker with a bad green paint job. It looks even worse close up than it did from my hiding place behind the tree. The inside of it smells like fast-food grease and is a mess. He cleared off a bunch of papers and books from the passenger seat to make room for me. It took him three times before he could get the motor to start. When it finally turned over, he looked at me and smiled, saying, "You got a rubber band for the engine?"

I love his smiles.

I guess he figured one of us should start talking, because he said he was gonna fly home to Florida for Christmas this year. I told him I've never been to Florida and he said, "You're welcome to my plane ticket." Then he made a face. I didn't know what to say to that, so there was another long quiet spell. Then he started talking about why he went into teaching. He said that his mother wanted him to be a doctor and his father wanted him to be a pilot, so he thought teaching would be a happy medium. His parents aren't so sure, though.

He groaned and said something strange. Something very strange. He looked at me with a serious face and said, "Don't fall into the traps your parents set for you." I was real confused by that and couldn't figure out what he meant, so there was another long quiet spell.

He asked me what I wanted to do with my life and I said, "Be an astronaut." He asked if I was serious and I said, "No. I really wanna be a reporter for a newspaper." He thought that was great.

Nobody ever asked me what I wanted to be before. People around here just assume you're gonna go work at Plumbco, or else they don't care. Miles is different. He started getting interested in the idea of me becoming a reporter. He said I ought to ask Duff about starting a school newspaper. I said I'd have to see about it.

Another long quiet spell. Miles stuck in a Dire Straits tape

54

and started singing with it. This was strange to me. I never knew a grown-up could like rock. Grandma doesn't let it in the house.

There were all kinds of questions I wanted to ask him. What does he look for in a person? What are his favorite TV shows? I never get to be alone with him. There's always some dippy girl hanging around his desk during class, or there's a bunch of brainless jocks sweating up a storm in the weight room. Here I was, finally alone with him, and I couldn't find out all of these things.

Before I knew it, we were in front of the Texaco station. I said, "Here," and he stopped. He said, "See you tomorrow, Smithie," and punched me right on the arm. I got out of the car and said, "Goodbye, Mi——." I almost called him Miles but I stopped myself in the nick of time and finished off with "Mr. Mariner."

He smiled at me and drove away. I am hopelessly in love with the man.

1:56 A.M.

Can't sleep. Can't stop thinking about Miles. When I do, I feel lost. I keep thinking about the stuff I've seen him do the last few days. Running around the track, taking a shower, driving his car, walking by my desk in those tight pants of his. He's all I think about these days.

It feels so great to think about him. I rub myself all over and pretend it's him I'm touching. My face becomes his face. My arms become his arms. My legs become his legs. My body starts tingling and my dick starts dancing and—Whoops! Jeff's talking in his sleep. He keeps saying, "Come on, Marsh." His dream must be a funny one. He's laughing.

Mag says you can program your dreams. You've gotta decide who or what you want to dream about and concentrate on it right before you fall asleep. I've tried it a couple of times before and it didn't work. Maybe I wasn't concentrating hard enough. I'm gonna try again now.

Come on, Miles . . .

November 12

Kuprekski's going out for indoor track. I couldn't believe it when I saw him in the locker room. He's gonna throw the shot put. Miles was staying with him the whole time, showing him how to hold the shot, placing his arm in the right position, touching his feet so they moved the right way.

Kuprekski walked up and tossed it forty-seven feet. He must have been imagining the shot was Les Numer's head. Everybody's mouth dropped open, mine included. I thought Miles was gonna bust. He ran up to Kuprekski and started slapping his rear end and putting his arm around him. It was gross. I hope he remembered to wash his hands after he did it.

For one split second—the only second in my life—I wished I was Kuprekski.

3:29 A.M.

Just had a dream about Miles. He was running toward me naked with a smile on his face. When I tried to touch him he'd jump back out of my reach and laugh. It was scary.

November 13

10:07 P.M.

Went to a square dance tonight with Chuck and Mom. It was the last thing I wanted to do. I was gonna go over to Mag's but her grandparents are in town and they took her out to dinner.

Chuck came over at around seven wearing a cowboy hat and a plaid shirt. He looked so stupid. Mom, Grandma, and me were watching the opening round of *Star Search* when he do-si-do'd in. He said they were having a square dance at his church and Mom and Grandma were invited to come "cut the rug" with him. Grandma said she was too tired to dance but that I would love to go in her place. I wanted to kick her. Chuck looked at me and I said, "No thanks." Then Grandma starts carrying on about how it'd be good for me to meet some "nice Christian girls." I made a face at her and quietly told her to butt out. She got all mad at me and said

I was going. It would be a good chance for me to get to know Chuck. Grandma was using her "don't you dare argue with me" tone of voice, so I knew I'd better do it. Mom was in the doorway, getting her coat on. I heard her mumble, "He can go to hell." I didn't know if she meant Chuck or Dad.

When we were driving over, Chuck got talking about the truck his brother-in-law was going to sell him. "It's got everything but the kitchen sink," he said. I didn't even try to get excited about the truck. I just looked out the window. Mom turned on the radio and Charlie Rich came blaring out. Chuck started talking about meeting Charlie Rich once when he gave a concert in Augusta. "It was the most exciting day of my life," he said. To me this was even more boring than the truck story. I just nodded and counted the little dots up on the ceiling of his truck.

We got to the church hall and I found out there wasn't a "nice Christian girl" there under fifty years old. All the women were *old*, and all the men had beer bellies and chain-smoked. For the first dance, I got paired off with a four-foot-tall crow who came up to my waist. We did the "Virginia reel" and she kept screaming over the caller that I ought to meet her daughter. After about the third time we went around the circle, she found out I couldn't square dance. She didn't like the way I do-si-do'd, so she stamped on my feet and told me to forget about her daughter.

The next dance was "Duck for the Oyster" and I got paired with this old bag named Josie. Josie danced with a limp and liked to click her false teeth in time with the music. She grabbed my fingers with her sandpaper hands and almost pulled my arm out of the socket when we ducked for the oyster. By the end of the second dance, I got the hell out of there. When I was out in the fresh air I thanked God that Mag wasn't around to see me. I looked out at the open field across from the church and wondered what Miles was doing.

Mom came out after a while and said we were going home in a minute. Chuck just left to get the truck. She looked out at the field with me for a second and said, "There must be something better than this."

Chuck drove up in his truck and honked the horn at us. I think he was angry at Mom, because he didn't say a word. Neither did Mom. I sat between them and wished I was someplace else. Chuck turned on the radio and a Crystal Gayle song came on. After a while, he started singing along with Crystal. Mom just kept staring straight ahead. It was hell. It's a good thing Grandma was in bed when I got home. I think if I'd seen her I would've strangled her.

November 14

Grandma joined a church group called Christian Helping Hands. Every week now after church she drives to the house of an old person who lives alone and helps out with cleaning and cooking. Grandma says it makes her feel "valuable in the eyes of our God." She says it'll make the admission price into heaven a little easier to pay when the time comes.

I was still mad at her about the square dance, so I asked her if God gives heaven discounts to people who give money to Timmy Will. She scowled and sent me to my room.

November 15

Ralph had an asthma attack today in Phys. Ed. They were playing volleyball in the gym, which I hate. Mr. Nolier asked for a couple of volunteers to go outside and take the soccer nets down. I raised my hand and Ralph said he'd help. It was freezing outside and we weren't wearing jackets. Mag came out and told us we were both crazy. She was skipping girls' PE. She offered to breathe on Ralph to keep him warm. He thought that was pretty funny and asked her if he could breathe back on her. I called them both sex fiends and climbed up on the net frame.

I was unhooking the net for Ralph to catch when he started heaving and fell to the ground. I screamed at Mag to get Mr. Nolier and she took off for the gym. I just sat beside Ralph and looked at him. He looked scared. I don't blame him. He was trying to breathe and no air would go in. Suddenly he grabbed hold of my arm and looked at me like he expected me to save his life. "Tell me what to do!" I screamed at him.

That was so stupid of me. Of course poor Ralph couldn't speak. His eyelids fluttered and he passed out.

The paramedics came and slapped an oxygen mask on him. One of them said "Asthmatic" as he gave Ralph a shot. I was gonna ride with him in the ambulance but Duff barked at me to go to my next class. I wanted to strangle the bastard.

I walked into History ten minutes late and Miles ribbed me. He called me the "freshman tardy animal," then he asked me where Ralph was. I blurted out everything that happened in one long sentence, my voice getting louder so that I almost started crying. Miles took me out of the classroom so I wouldn't embarrass myself. We got to the hallway and he put his arm around my shoulder and walked with me up and down the hallway, saying, "It's all right." I was so upset I didn't give a fuck about how good it must've felt. The next thing I knew, we were in the office and Miles was calling Grandma to come take me home. He sat with his arm around me while I waited for my ride. His face was so close a couple of times I could've kissed him, but I didn't want to.

Grandma showed up and took me home. She was confused about what happened, so I had to explain it all over again to her. Just tried to call Mag and nobody was home.

Shit . . . I never said "Thank you" to Miles.

9:30 P.M.

Mag just called. She said Ralph's condition is stable. I asked her where she was and she said, "The hospital." She snuck onto the ambulance when Duff wasn't looking and rode up with Ralph. She told the attendant that she was Ralph's sister and he didn't ask any questions. She said Ralph's Mom was with him now and she's a snobby bitch. She breezed in at a quarter to five, told Mag to go home, and didn't even thank her. I wish I was with Mag now.

 ## November 16

During homeroom I saw Miles. I told him "Thanks." He smiled and said, "I'm here if you need me."

If he only knew how much I needed him.

Mag was quiet all day. I would've tried to make her laugh but she looked too shook up to laugh. I was shook up too. During lunch we called the hospital and asked about Ralph. His Mom came on the line and said, "Ralph is resting comfortably," and hung up.

Mag was right. She is a bitch.

▶ November 17

Dad and Carol broke up. The news is all over town now. Carol told everybody in town that she was just plain sick of Dad. Last week, she got loaded at the Rusty Nail and started wailing about how she couldn't stand him another minute. Mag's mother told me all about it. She said lately Carol's started showing up at truck stops with this guy named Rudy. It got pretty serious between them, because yesterday while Dad was at work Rudy moved his stuff into Carol's house. Carol tossed all of Dad's stuff on her front lawn.

Dad went home and saw his clothes getting rained on and got wicked pissed. He ran into Carol's house to slap her around. He met up with Rudy and got punched in the face. The next thing Dad knew, he was flat on his back on the wet grass. Mag gave me a play-by-play of the whole thing. She heard it from her mother, who heard it from Carol's sister. Now Dad's walking around town with a shiner on his left eye. He's moved into the Wagon Wheel Motel on Main Street.

"The heathen had it coming to him," Grandma said.

I still hate Carol, but I think it's great that she gave Dad a shot of his own medicine. To let him know how Mom felt when he took off, and to cause him a little physical pain to boot, was just what he deserved.

Mom didn't say anything about Dad all night. She must know about it. *Everybody* knows about it. I just wonder if she's gonna let him move back in. I wouldn't . . .

▶ November 18

Dad's the laughingstock of the town now. And so are we. He's out of work and he just wanders Main Street picking up returnable cans and trying to hitch rides to Lipton. I walked by him today and he started to sing. Mag told me to just keep on walking and not pay any attention to him. "That's my son," he screamed. Everybody on the street looked at me. I wanted to sink into the earth.

Came home and was gonna tell Mom about my seeing Dad. It turned out, Grandma and her were talking about him already. Grandma told her that everybody in town was taking bets on whether Mom was gonna take Dad back. Mom made a face and mumbled something about how it was nobody's business. Grandma looked at her real serious and asked, "Well, are you gonna take him back if he asks?" Mom said she hadn't decided.

Grandma got wicked mad and screamed at her, "What does he have to do to you before you give him the boot?"

Mom shook her head and said, "When he left, I didn't put up any kind of a fight. You can blame me just as much as him."

When she said that, I felt the bottom drop out of my stomach. It sounded awful to me, and I felt bad for thinking the same thing. Grandma looked like she was gonna scream bloody murder. I took off for my bedroom. Before I could slam the door behind me, I heard Grandma scream at Mom, "You think you're dog poop, don't you?"

They're still going at it.

7:38 P.M.

Mom just came in. She said she needed to talk to somebody else besides Grandma for a while. She said Grandma's too stuck in her ways to reason with. I wanted to say, "Grandma's not the only one," but I didn't.

Mom started going on about how much she hated Dad when he left, and that she thought about asking him for a divorce but she didn't think she'd better. She knew Dad and Carol wouldn't last out the year. It was just a matter of time. She didn't want to blow it again when Dad came back for a second chance.

"How do you know he'll come back?" I asked her.

"He'll be back," she said. "I know it like I know the sun's gonna come up tomorrow."

For some reason, I knew it too. Mom seemed so sure that I couldn't think anything different. "Are you gonna let him come back?" I asked her. It's what I was dying to know.

Mom was real quiet for the longest time. She was just tapping her fingers against the windowpane. I didn't think she heard me, so I was gonna ask again when she said, "If I do let him come back, I'm gonna call the shots."

Then she walked out of the room. I was afraid she'd say something like that. She'll call the shots for a few days and then it'll go back to the way it was. She loves him, and I can't figure out why.

► November 19

"You're not a sprinter, Smithie." That's what Miles said to me when he pulled me into his office tonight. I was disappointed. I was hoping maybe he was taking me aside to tell me how much he loves me, but instead he said that. "You don't look like you're trying very hard," he said. I told him I was doing my best, but I'm really not. I love lifting the weights with him and seeing him smile at me when I cross the finish line, but the actual running is a pain in the neck. All the other guys are faster than me, so I don't even try to beat them now. I just go through the motions and run the hundred yards trying not to break a sweat.

Miles looked at me like he was going to say something real serious. I just looked at him and smiled. "Do you want to talk about anything, Smithie?" I told him no, and just looked at him, trying to keep a straight face. He took a deep breath and said, "I know about your Dad."

I didn't know what to say to this. It took me totally by surprise. Finally I said, "You and everybody else in town." He nodded his head and started to stand up. I took the hint and got out of my chair. Miles told me he wants me to start working out with the distance runners. He said I might be more suited for the mile or two-mile run. I said, "OK," and started to leave his office. He touched my arm before I was out and said, "I'm here for you."

It might have been my imagination, but I think I heard goddamn pity in his voice.

▶ ## November 20

Bad scene today in front of the barber shop. Jeff sort of got into a fight with Mr. McPheran, the barber. We were gonna go into McPheran's and get our haircuts when Dad showed up, swinging a broken bottle in the air, trying to hit his shadow. He slammed the bottle on the outside of the building and McPheran came running out screaming and calling Dad names.

He said Dad was a bum who couldn't keep a job. Dad tried to shake his hand, but Mr. McPheran knocked him to the ground and said, "I wouldn't shake your hand if it had a million dollars in it." Dad started bawling then. When he hit the ground he cut his hand on the bottle. He was holding it and looking up at Jeff and me like he was expecting us to hand him a Band-Aid or something.

Jeff turned on McPheran and called him a stupid old bastard. McPheran begged his pardon and asked him to repeat what he just said. Jeff looked at McPheran and said he was a constipated old shit who didn't know his ass from his dick. McPheran scowled at Jeff and said that he knew which one of us took after our father.

The next thing I remember is McPheran walking back into his shop. I guess this means he's not gonna cut our hair anymore. Jeff took off down the street and I just stood there and looked at Dad for a minute. He looked like such a bum. Just lying there holding on to that bottle like he was trying to squeeze some more booze out of it. I probably should have helped him, but where has he been when I've needed him. Out humping Carol or getting drunk. He's gonna have to work at it before I help him with a bleeding hand.

Tonight Marsha cut our hair. She did a pretty good job on everything except my bangs. They're pretty crooked. I told Marsha my bangs look like a lightning streak and she said,

"If you want straight bangs, go to a professional." Then she said that it'd be five bucks for the haircut. We laughed until Jeff told me to get lost.

8:47 P.M.

Ralph just called. He's home from the hospital. He asked me to come over to his house tomorrow to help him get caught up on his homework. I said, "Sure." His mother is coming to pick me up. Hooray . . . He said he tried calling Mag and she wasn't home. I could tell he'd rather have her come than me. I'd better call her.

► November 21

Ralph's mother came and got me a couple hours later than the time she said she'd be here. She didn't apologize or anything. She was driving a Lincoln Continental. It's a real nice car with a fancy interior. She was pretty quiet riding over, like she didn't want to be seen in Tranten Township. The only thing she said was, "Ralph is a very sick young man." I wasn't gonna argue with her. I know that. I was just wondering what else Ralph has besides epilepsy and asthma. Then I thought, That's enough to make a person crazy.

We got to Ralph's house and he was sitting up in his bedroom with a humidifier going. The first thing he asked me was, "How's Mag?" I told him, "Fine," and that she wanted to come but she had to baby-sit. That was a lie. When I asked her this morning, Mag said she didn't want to come at all. Ralph's been giving her the creeps lately and he makes her nervous. She never knows when he's gonna pass out or go into spasms or just stop breathing. She says she could be talking on the phone with him making him laugh, and Ralph could just keel over dead and she'd feel responsible. She can't handle it. I couldn't tell Ralph that, so I lied.

Ralph looked pretty pale and weak. He didn't seem that interested in doing homework. I just got out my French book and we started conjugating verbs. We got laughing a couple of times when I told him about things Old Lady Song did in class last week, but I could tell Ralph wasn't up to it. He kept pulling out his inhaler and taking a swig. I asked him if there was anything I could get him. He was quiet for a second, then he said, "A new body."

I thought he said it to be funny, so I laughed. I realized after a minute that Ralph wasn't laughing along, so I shut up. We'd conjugated about ten verbs when his mother came in and asked me if I'd like a ride home. Ralph told her he felt fine but she waved him off. I said, "Sure," and got up to leave. Ralph looked up at me and said, "Thanks, Ben." I said, "No problem," and hightailed it out of there. I hate to say it, but I was real happy to get out of that room.

Ralph's mother and me didn't say a word to each other the whole ride home. I wish we had, because I kept thinking about what Ralph said: "A new body." It made me so depressed.

November 22

I *hate* the two-mile run. It's a nightmare. Twenty laps around the track. I did it for the first time tonight. I was fine the first four laps, but then I started getting tired. By the tenth lap I was breathing real hard and thinking about stopping, but I didn't want to let Miles down. By the fifteenth lap I started seeing double and felt like I was dying. I must've been delirious for the last lap. I don't remember anything about it except floating over the finish line and trying to breathe again. The only fun part of the whole thing was seeing Miles at the end of it. He walked up to me and said, "Good job." I couldn't ask him what my time was, because I felt like if I talked, I'd puke all over his feet.

Mag keeps trying to get me to quit track, but I'm gonna stick with it. I tell her it keeps me well rounded. Mag says if I wanna be well rounded I should get a dog and read Shakespeare. Ha . . .

November 23

Mom's gone bonkers. Tonight when I got home from track practice she was shut up in her room. She didn't come out for supper. Grandma pounded on her door and Mom said she was fine. She came out of her room at eight o'clock with her hair permed, her face with an inch-thick layer of makeup on, and she was wearing her best dress. We all looked at her for a minute. She looked kind of pretty. Grandma asked her if she was going out with Chuck and she said, "No," and walked to the front window humming. She sat on the chair by the window, looking out of it, like she was waiting for something. Grandma, Jeff, and me all looked at each other and then back at the TV. It was so strange.

At ten, Grandma shut off the TV and told Jeff and me to go to bed. She walked to Mom and asked her if she could get her anything. Mom shook her head and kept her eyes glued to the Texaco sign out front. It was like she was trying to see through it to something else. Grandma came in and told Jeff and me to say a prayer for Mom tonight.

Just went out to the living room. Mom's still sitting by the window, looking out. Except now the Texaco sign is out and Mom's just looking at the dark. She's made her decision.

November 24

Today in English Mrs. King gave us a pop quiz. It had one question on it: "What are you most thankful for and why?" I was feeling creative, so I wrote, "I'm thankful that the geese remembered to fly south this winter, because it's too far to walk, and it's cheaper than the bus." I thought she'd get a kick out of that.

What do I have to be thankful for? I've got a drunk for a father, a basket case for a mother, a dimwit for a brother, and a religious fanatic for a grandmother. We live in an apartment above a gas station. Not exactly your all-American family.

There must be something better than this.

I see myself ten years from now and I'm still in this same place and I get scared to death. Some people stay in Tranten Township their whole lives. They never leave the state. Hell, some of them never leave the county. I've gotta find a way out.

Basically all I've got to be thankful for is Mag and Miles. M&M. Melts in your mouth, not in your hand.

 ## November 25

Another Thanksgiving at home. Grandma invited Chuck over without asking Mom. He showed up carrying a casserole dish full of stuffing. Grandma let him in and gave him a seat. Mom came home from the store and saw Chuck there. She dragged Grandma into the kitchen. "Can't you mind your own business?" she asked Grandma, quiet, so Chuck couldn't hear. Grandma just looked up at the ceiling.

When dinner was ready, Grandma made us shut up while she said a ten-minute prayer. While she was thanking God for the paper napkins on the table, I snuck a look at everybody. Jeff was chewing, like he'd snuck a piece of turkey during Grandma's prayer. Chuck had his eyes closed and was moving his lips. Mom looked like she wished she was someplace else. I knew how she felt. Grandma kept filling up Chuck's plate, telling him that Mom cooked this and that. The table got pretty quiet, so Chuck told a joke about a Frenchman and a hound dog. I can't remember what it was. Wasn't funny.

I wonder what Miles is doing tonight.

November 26

Jeff and Marsha are cooking in the kitchen. I never saw Jeff near the stove before tonight. It's the funniest thing I've ever seen. Jeff should have known he was in trouble when Marsha came over this afternoon and said her mother was sick and she needed to bake five loaves of bread for a church sale. Jeff told her to get her sister to help her, but Marsha told him to shut up and get the mixing bowl. When I went in there, Jeff was measuring out flour and saying how stupid he felt. I was gonna ask him if he wanted to borrow Grandma's apron, but I knew if I did he'd slug me.

Mom's sitting by the window again tonight. She's got on the perfume I gave her.

November 27

Mag came over today. Her mother had a pair of men over and Mag wanted to get out. We started talking about Christmas and what we wanted. Mag wants a new stereo and her own MasterCard. I just want peace at home. It seems like so long since I've had a happy day.

I want a happy day *and* Miles Mariner.

Miles *is* a happy day.

November 28

Got back my quiz from Mrs. King today. She said she wanted to see me after class, so I walked up to her desk. She said, "Ben, I'm worried about you. Do you want to talk?" I said, "No. I want to pass your class." She said she wasn't trying to be funny and I said, "I know."

She wants to help me but there's nothing she can do. Short of hitting my father with a Mack truck. She's not the hired-killer type, though. She put on her concerned face and tried telling me everything would turn out fine, but how the hell does she know that?

I let her touch my shoulder and sigh. It made her feel better. Her breath smelled like peanut butter and celery sticks.

November 29

Tonight at track practice, Miles gave us each a progress report. Everybody improved on their performance except me. He told me not to worry about it. I'm not gonna set the track world on fire—so who cares? He said to go out and have fun. Meet people. Kuprekski's showed the most improvement. Balls.

I feel like I'm letting Miles down. I want him to be proud of me. To be happy with me. To let me kiss him and feel his tongue inside my mouth.

10:46 P.M.
Dad's back . . .

He just showed up at the front door crying and saying, "I've gotta take a leak. I've gotta take a leak." Grandma slammed the door in his face so he ran under Mom's window and screamed, "LET ME IN! PLEASE, LET ME IN!!!" The next thing I heard were doors opening and closing.

Mom went outside and helped him in.

I can't believe it.

She took him by the hand and led him inside. They're in the bedroom now and everything's quiet. She didn't even have time to put her makeup on or slip into her good dress. Dad didn't care. He was ready to come in the first door that would open for him. I can hear him crying now. "Help me. Help me," he keeps saying. Mom's making hushing noises and humming "Rockabye Baby."

I don't wanna wake up tomorrow . . .

▶ ## November 30

What a day. Dad's back and life is strange. This morning he came to the table for breakfast and tried acting like everything was back to normal. Grandma came in and said, "It's nice of you to drop by," really sarcastic like. I didn't know what to say. Jeff came in, saw Dad, and ran out of the room, slamming the door behind him. It's all a big mess. The only person who seemed comfortable about it was Mom. She fried up eggs like a crazed woman and shoved them in front of us.

After breakfast, Dad took Mom to Lipton to go shopping. I felt like screaming at her. "Did you forget what he did to you!" I don't think she cares.

Saw Mag first thing on the bus.

"Dad's back," I told her.

"For how long?" she asked.

"Good question," I said.

Ralph came back to school for a half-day today. It was good to see him. He has a tan and looks healthy for a change. In lunch, Lesly told us that Ralph's parents bought him a sun lamp that he sits under while he watches TV. Must be nice.

I had a chance to talk with him during lunch. He said he was feeling a lot better and it was good to be back. I rolled my eyes and said, "Are you sure?" Ralph looked right at Mag who was standing in the chow line and said, "Yah."

Miles was in a grumpy mood today. He barked at Kimby for cracking her gum while he was speaking, and he didn't smile once at me the whole class. In fact, he didn't smile at all. I got thinking he must be lonely living so far from his family. When class was over I waited until everybody left and then I walked up to his desk. I was gonna try to cheer him up. He looked up at me like I was lost and said, "Is something wrong?" I felt dumb all of a sudden, so I just said no and took off out the door.

Got home from school today and Mom and Dad were shut up in their room. I went to the door and I heard Mom laughing. It's been so long, I forgot what it sounded like. I'd give anything to know what's going on in her head.

I just asked Grandma if she thought Dad was gonna stick around and she said, "Does the devil have a conscience?"

▶ December 1

This morning Dad made a little speech for us all. He said he was never gonna touch booze again. Mom smiled, Jeff got up and left the room, and Grandma said God forgives everybody once. I looked at Dad, who's still got a trace of a shiner on his face. He was trying to look sincere but he just looked desperate.

I don't know what to make of his speech. Mom seems to think he's got his shit together. I'm not so sure. I'll believe it when I see it. Hear it. Smell it. Feel it.

▶ December 2

Mag is determined to lose ten pounds in two weeks. Her mother won a trip to the Bahamas and she's gonna take Mag. Today Mag came to school toting a carton of yogurt and a plastic bag filled with celery sticks. I told her the best way to lose weight is to exercise and she stuck out her tongue and crammed it in my ear. Really gross.

I've got other things to worry about. My first track meet is tomorrow and I'm scared to death. What if I trip while

I'm running the two-mile and everybody laughs at me? What if I come in last? I tried talking to Miles about it but he was too busy with paperwork in the locker room to give me any time.

I keep thinking about calling him tonight. I know it would feel better just to hear his voice. But what would I say? "Miles, I'm nervous. Could you come over so I can look at you?" Out of the question.

Jeff just told me not to worry. I'm just a freshman. Nobody'll expect me to do good.

Thanks. I feel much better.

December 3

The track meet was a semi-success. I came in ninth out of twelve runners. Eleven, technically. One guy dropped out after the tenth lap because of heat exhaustion. I didn't embarrass myself once, though, and I finished without tripping. Met some awful cute guys too.

After the race, Miles came up and started congratulating me. Any other day I would have welcomed Miles, but he was looking so old to me all of the sudden. The lights in the gym were real bright and I could see every nook and cranny on him. His hairline is starting to recede and he's got wrinkles on his cheeks that I never saw before.

Kuprekski won the shot put. I couldn't believe it. He couldn't either. Miles was all over him when it was announced over the PA system. He slapped him on the back and kept shaking his hand. I was gonna go congratulate him but I decided I better not. I wouldn't have meant it.

On the bus ride home, a pair of sprinters named Cole and Ted sang dirty ditties. A guy and girl who came to watch the meet started making out behind me. Miles told them to break it up and separate. He didn't want any of that stuff going on while he was in charge. When did he get so old?

December 4

Today Old Lady Song taught us a French song to sing for Christmas. *"Il Est Né."* Old Lady Song has got a pretty nice singing voice. She was singing around the room with a smile on her face. I was singing too, but I wasn't really sure what the words meant. When we were halfway through the song, Old Lady Song stopped in front of me and asked real quiet, "Why are you frowning, Ben?"

The funny thing was, I didn't even know I was frowning. I got confused and didn't know what to say. Mag looked at me and then at Old Lady Song and said, "He's got a lot on his mind these days."

I don't have a clue what I had on my mind. I guess a frown comes naturally to my face these days.

► December 5

Got back a paper today in English. A-plus. Mag was pissed because she got a B. The paper was a story I dashed off about an Indian named Joe who takes over an innocent family's farm. He does it because years ago the white settlers took over the land by force from Joe's ancestors, and so he's taking it back in the same way. He figures it's only right. The people of the town get mad at Joe and they all invade his farm. There's a shoot-out and Joe is killed defending his land. His final words are, "It's my land."

Mrs. King wrote on the paper, "A story filled with emotion and suppressed rage."

Suppressed rage? Where did that come from?

► December 6

Mag's father died last night. Mag said she wasn't surprised. They finally got permission to unhook the machine and he just checked out. Mag got the call and told her mother, who used the news as an excuse to get drunk. Mag came over here and stayed for the night. She and me watched *Friday Night Videos* and ate popcorn all night. I tried getting her to talk about her father but she just shook her head and told me, "No way." Jeff was staying over at Marsha's so Mag slept on the bottom bunk.

When I turned out the light, Mag started talking a blue streak. She went on about how once her dad took her on a long drive to Boston, just her and him. He bought her candy and took her up to the top of the Prudential Building so she could see the city. The city was all lit up like the Fourth of July. She can still remember those lights. They reminded her of Christmas, only it was in the middle of summer.

The next thing I knew, Mag was crying. I climbed down and sat on the bed beside her and held her hand. She kept saying, "Hold me. Hold me," over and over again. I put my arms around her and rocked her back and forth until she was asleep. It felt so strange to be holding her like that. It was almost like holding Mom or Grandma.

When I woke up this morning, Mag acted like nothing happened. I was relieved. I thought she might take it as a sign that I want to get it on with her, but she didn't. When she left this afternoon, she kissed me on the cheek and said, "Thanks."

 ## December 7

10:15 P.M.

Went to second track meet this morning. Disaster. Came in last out of ten people. Kuprekski won again. Hate him. Too tired to write. Going to bed.

December 8

I almost died today in homeroom. Duff was doing morning announcements. When he announced the results of the track meet last night, he gave all the names of the people who placed. Then he read the names of "others who participated" (losers). My name was the only one he said. I wanted to sink into the floor. When I was in the hall on my way to first period, Mr. Taylor (guidance counselor) grinned real stupid at me, lip-synched "Way to go," and gave me the thumbs up. I pretended not to see him.

Got to French class and Old Lady Song announced that we're having a party before vacation and everybody's got to draw names. I drew Kimby. We have to make something homemade for a present. I don't know what in hell I can make for Kimby. I tried trading her name with Ralph, who drew Lesly, but he was only interested in trading if he could get Mag.

Came home and Dad was in a coma in front of *The Guiding Light*. Grandma told me that's where he's been all day today. At least he's not drinking.

December 9

Dad sat around the house again all day today. He says he's just taking some time off to "figure it all out." I wanted to know what he has to figure out, but I didn't say anything. Tonight he tried helping me out with my homework but I didn't want him to. I didn't know how to tell him to leave me alone, so I let him look at the pictures and give me his opinion. His ways of dividing fractions are strange. He kept saying I ought to use a calculator to do it. I didn't tell him that calculators don't have fractions on them.

After a while Mom came in and smiled at us like this was a normal evening in our house. She asked how we were doing and Dad said, "Great. Great." I looked down at my homework paper that was covered with wrong answers and said, "Great." When Dad was leaning across me to sharpen his pencil I caught a whiff of his breath. It smelled like Listerine.

December 10

Ralph has got a plan on how he's gonna give Mag a present. He wouldn't tell me how he was gonna do it, but he says Mag will be surprised. I don't doubt it. I was gonna tell Ralph maybe he ought to back off from Mag a little bit, but he's awful excited about it. He's making her a stained-glass ornament. I don't know how Mag feels about stained glass.

Tonight Grandma and me made my present for Kimby. It's a bread-dough wreath. You make the bread and then braid three strips of it into a circle. You bake the circle, let it cool, and then shellac it to preserve it. You tack a red bow on it and you've got a "classy present," Grandma says. The bread's baking now.

Grandma warned Jeff not to touch the bread when he walked in. He glared at me and said he wasn't hungry. Then he hightailed it to Marsha's house. I don't know why he's taken off so soon. Dad won't be home for hours. I saw him behind the factory with a couple of other beer bellies using some tin cans for target practice.

9:30 P.M.

Gotta bake my bread wreath over again. Dad came in when we were watching TV and ate it before I had a chance to shellac it. He said he was hungry after looking for work all day. Grandma just nodded and said we'd bake another one tomorrow. Great. I didn't even wanna bake the first one.

Dad seems kind of lost at home now. It's like we've all got parts to play and he doesn't know what his is. Maybe he never had one.

December 11

Dad applied for unemployment today. I heard Grandma talking on the phone and she said it was a disgrace for an able-bodied man to be collecting welfare. Dad wasn't anywhere around. Mom came in and Grandma cornered her. Grandma told her, "It's time for you to take control of your life." Mom made a face at her and said, "Mind your own business."

Mom's got a black and blue mark on her cheek that wasn't there yesterday. I asked her where she got it and she said she had to stop quick in the car and her face hit the dashboard. I asked her why she had to stop quick and she said a dairy truck cut in front of her. I tried to get a closer look at it but she wouldn't let me. Grandma just shook her head. "Those truck drivers are all crazy," she says.

7:30 P.M.

Just tried to go into Mom's room to get some ribbon for the wreath. Dad was in there with her. I could her him talking softly. "You know I didn't mean it," he said. I cracked the door and saw him holding her, kissing her gentle on the top of her head. She kissed him back.

Shut the door quick.

▶ December 12

Marsha came over for dinner tonight. We were all waiting at the table for Dad to show. He came in and laughed at us. His laugh sent a shiver down my back. I'd heard it before. We'd all heard it before. Many times. It's what Jeff and me used to call "Dad's whiskey laugh." A high-pitched giggle. Grandma closed her eyes and looked down at her plate (a silent prayer?).

Mom started filling Dad's plate. It took a while for Dad to get into the rhythm of eating. He missed his mouth a few times but he got the hang of it. Nobody said a word. I felt bad for Jeff. And Marsha. I just felt sick of Dad.

Mom was cheery all through dinner. She was humming as she served everybody their food. She had on a lot of makeup. Her bruise was almost invisible. Grandma asked Marsha how her school was going. Marsha said, "Fine." That was all anybody said. I wanted to scream at Dad and Mom. It was so embarrassing. Dad ate about three helpings of everything and then told us he was so stuffed he couldn't even suck a tit. He pulled a bottle of beer from his pocket and grinned at all of us. He had a piece of lettuce stuck between his teeth. He popped the cap off and took a long swig. Mom closed her eyes while the beer went down. She looked like she was trying to wake herself up from a nightmare.

Everything got real quiet and Dad burped. Grandma scowled and left the room. Mom blushed and tried to laugh. Marsha looked down at her plate. Jeff and me just looked at each other. After a second, Dad called Grandma's name ("Maiseeeeee!") and went looking for her. Mom got up and started clearing the table. Jeff looked at Marsha and said real angry like, "You wanted to meet my father."

They both left the room and I heard the door slam. Mom came back in for another load of dishes. Her eyes were all red. She looked at me and said, "Could you clear away the rest? I'm real tired."

Sure, Mom . . .

December 13

Bad fight tonight. Jeff missed a foul shot and cost Chappaqua the game by one point. On the ride back, Dad was real pissed and asked Jeff, "Where did you learn to shoot? From your mother?" Jeff called him a horny bastard. Dad stopped the car and told him to get out. We left Jeff standing in the middle of the road. When I turned around, he was giving our car the finger.

As soon as we got home, Dad dropped us off and drove away. Mom's called all of Jeff's friends but nobody's seen him. She started crying and went to bed. I was gonna go in and ask her when she was gonna start calling the shots again, but decided I'd better not.

1:36 A.M.

Dad's in the living room with a six-pack and a bottle of gin. God help us all.

December 14

BIG Christmas party today in French class. Old Lady Song made eggnog and cookies for all of us. The presents were a disaster. First, I opened mine from Theresa. It turned out to be a pound of fudge. I hate fudge, but I pretended to be happy about it. Theresa didn't seem to care.

Kimby opened my present to her and let out a shriek. I couldn't tell if she was happy or scared, until she tossed the box on the floor. My bread-dough wreath fell out, along with a dead mouse. Kimby glared at me and screamed, "That's not funny, Ben!"

I said I had no idea how the mouse got in the box, which was the honest truth. Old Lady Song investigated and found a little hole that had been chewed away in the bottom of it. The mouse broke in sometime at night and tried to eat the shellacked wreath and keeled over dead. The wreath had some little bite marks in it. Old Lady Song clucked her tongue and said, "What a shame, Ben. All that work." Then she swept up the mouse and left the room for a second.

I was gonna apologize to Kimby, but I knew if I did I'd start laughing, so I kept quiet. I didn't give a damn about the wreath being ruined. It was worth it just seeing Kimby scream like that.

All the presents were opened and everybody was trying to act happy when Old Lady Song found one last one under the tree. It just had "TO MAG" written on it in big capital letters. Mag took the present from Old Lady Song and looked at me real puzzled. She opened it and inside was a pretty white stained-glass ornament shaped like a dove. On the bottom it said, "LOVE." Mag was totally confused. She'd already got a present from Dana. She looked at me and whispered, "Where the fuck did this come from?" I shrugged my shoulders and said I didn't know.

Kimby, who was holding the half-eaten wreath in front of her like it was a guitar, smirked and said, "It looks like Mag has a secret fan." Everybody laughed at that. I looked at Ralph and he was laughing along, like he didn't know who the secret fan was.

I felt bad for Mag. She looked kind of pathetic holding that dove ornament. She got her revenge on Kimby, though. In English, during free reading, Mag took a red satin Christmas ball and hooked it to the back of Kimby's pants from a belt loop. When Kimby got up and walked out, the ball was dangling over her rear end and bouncing from cheek to cheek. Kimby must have been wearing hiney padding because she didn't feel it. Everybody who saw it laughed. Tonight on the bus, she still had it on, and she still didn't have a clue.

Came home from school today and Dad was sleeping on the couch. Turned on the TV and he growled at me to shut it off. He needed to sleep. "What for? So you can rest up for dinner tonight?" I wanted to ask but didn't.

▶ December 16

What an awful day. It started out perfect but ended up a disaster. Missed the bus, so I had to hitch a ride to school with Miles. He was streaking by in his lemon, so I held my thumb out and screamed, "I missed the bus!" He screeched to a stop and motioned for me to get in. When I did I saw he was dressed in these tight jeans and a leather jacket and he looked good, but still kind of old. My dick didn't jump when I saw him like it usually does. I wonder why? We talked about the track meet and Miles said he was real pleased with how I did. I should just try to have a good time and not worry about placing.

He pressed the gas and all of a sudden started talking about being alone and single in a small town. He said it's "the pits." He looked sort of sad. I was gonna offer to come keep him company during Christmas vacation, but we were just pulling up to the school. He parked and smiled a killer smile at me and my dick started doing the cha-cha.

When I got into homeroom, Duff came at me scowling and accused me of writing graffiti on the bathroom walls. He found the "Duff is a prick" artwork I put on there in September. He said he had the handwriting analyzed (right) and he traced it to me. I had to spend all first period scrubbing it off with blue soap, and I got three detentions to boot. Shit . . .

In lunch, Lesly was balancing a bowl of chop suey on two fingers when she dropped it on my lap. It was hot and soggy. Thank God I didn't have a hard-on when it happened. I had to walk around the rest of the day looking like my crotch was bleeding. In Earth Science, Theresa asked me if it was that time of the month. Everybody laughed. I wanted to die.

When I got home, Dad was sitting at the table, pretending to read *Time* magazine. He asked me to take out the garbage and I told him I had to change my pants first. He said, "Now," and I said "No." He got mad and slammed his magazine down. I told him if he was in such a hurry he could do it himself, and he snapped back, "I told you to do it." I was pretty pissed by this time and said, "Ask Carol to take out your trash for you."

The rest is all a blur. He got up and slugged me across the mouth. Now my front tooth is loose and I've got the mark of his hand on my right cheek.

I wasn't surprised. His breath smelled like a brewery. So much for his little speech. So much for Mom calling the shots. She's not around, so he grabbed something else for a punching bag.

My mouth feels like hell.

December 17

Last day of school before Xmas vacation. We had a dopey assembly where the band got up and played carols. Mr. Duff dressed as Santa Claus and handed out candy canes at the door. Somebody stuck a piece of paper that said "I AM A BIG ASSHOLE" to his back and he didn't know it.

Ran into Miles going out and he told me he wanted me to keep running during the break so I didn't get out of shape. I wanted to kiss him but he reached out and touched my cheek. He wanted to know where the bruise came from. I told him my dog bit me and then I ran out the door. He didn't follow me.

December 18

Went shopping at the General Store with Mag today. She had to pick some things up for her trip. She bought some suntan lotion and said she was gonna come back as dark as Tina Turner. I told her that too much sun is dangerous and she told me to shut up.

I saw her fondling a bottle of Seduction and then putting it back. When she wasn't looking I bought it for her. Had it gift wrapped. Bought Mom a box of chocolates and Grandma a gold cross necklace. They had all kinds of crosses, big and small, for the same price. I got the biggest one I could find because I figured Grandma could use it to scare off a vampire someday. Got Jeff a T-shirt from the bargain rack. Same one he got me for my birthday. He probably doesn't remember it, anyway. Didn't get Dad anything. I'm not sure if he'll even be around for Christmas this year.

7:56 P.M.

Dad and me just went to get our Christmas tree tonight. I didn't want to go but Mom laid a guilt trip on me, so I decided I'd better. It was odd. I could tell he felt kind of guilty for smacking me, but I wasn't ready to forgive him. Drove to Lucher's Hardware to pick it out. Dad didn't say a word to me the whole ride over. Then, when we parked, he looked at me and said, "You gotta understand, I'm doing the best I can." I said, "Right," and he nodded his head like everything was fine and dandy.

We got outside and Dad started scanning the trees. He says there's a science to picking them. I watched him look and remembered a time when I was real young. We didn't have money for a tree, so we sneaked onto private land and cut one. It was just Dad and Jeff and me walking through the woods. Before I got big. Before Jeff turned into a jerk. Before Dad discovered booze.

Dad started singing "Row Row Row Your Boat" and Jeff and me joined in so we were singing in a round. We got messed up with the words and started laughing. We looked for a long time until Dad found a tree he liked. He started chopping away and screamed, "Timber!"

Just as the tree fell, a game warden came by and asked us what we were doing. Dad said, "Getting a Christmas tree for my boys." The game warden said it was private property and Dad acted real shocked, like he didn't know that. The game warden told us to take the tree and scram, which we did, but only after Dad talked him into helping us haul the tree out of the woods.

Dad had his moments.

When we were riding back today, I started to hum "Row Row Row Your Boat," quiet, to see if Dad remembered. He looked at me like I was crazy.

We came back and set the tree up without saying a word. Grandma came in and told me I did a good job picking out the tree. I told her Dad was the one who did it. She snorted and left the room.

December 19

Decorated the tree today. Marsha and Mag came over and Grandma made eggnog. Had a good time, considering that

Mag was in a foul mood all day. She's pissed because her mother isn't taking her to the Bahamas after all. She met some banker in a bar and asked him to go with her. Mag's gonna go stay with her grandparents in Waterton while she's gone. I felt bad for her. She seemed to cheer up after a while. She said it was "par for the course" for her mother.

Marsha and Grandma got into a fight about the Christmas lights. Marsha told Grandma she was overloading the socket but Grandma said she knew what she was doing. Grandma plugged in the lights and sparks flew everywhere. All the lights went out and Marsha made a face at me. Grandma started sputtering about defective lights and said Marsha was too smart for her own good. Marsha said, "And that's a bad thing?" and Grandma said, "If you're a woman, yes." It was hard not to laugh.

Mom and Marsha started singing "Twelve Days of Christmas" and acted out the parts. When they got to "eleven ladies dancing," Mag jumped up, shook her hips, and waved her scarf in the air. Grandma said that was sinful and shook her finger at Mag. I thought it was funny and got up and danced with her. Jeff told us we were all stupid and went to the gym to shoot hoops.

Grandma got out a card she was sending to Timmy Will's TV ministry. She told us all we ought to show God we loved him by sending Timmy Will some money so he could do His work. Grandma folded up a twenty and stuck it in the card. She asked us if we had any money we wanted to give. We all shook our heads. Grandma hissed, "Sinners," and left for the Post Office to mail the card.

All afternoon, Dad sat in the corner and looked out the window. He was turning a piece of paper that looked like a check over and over in his hands, like he was thinking about tearing it up. He left after dinner and hasn't been back since.

December 21

Jeff played in a Christmas B-ball tournament in Freemont today. Mom wanted to go, so I went with her. We stopped and picked up Mag on the way over. Mag told a joke about

Christopher Columbus and Queen Isabella and made Mom laugh. We were gonna pick up Marsha, but she called this morning and said she had to work with her mother.

The tournament was a lot of fun. Miles was there. I saw him standing by the bleachers, talking to Mr. Nolier. I waved at him and he came over and asked how I was doing. I said I couldn't complain and then I introduced him to Mom. I almost blew it and called him "Miles" when I did it. I caught myself just in time though and said "Mr. Mariner." Mom seemed nervous to meet him, but he was cool about it. He shook her hand and smiled one of his knock-out smiles for her. I could tell she was impressed. She looked down at her lap for a second and fluffed her hair up for him. Miles told her that I was a very smart young man. She told him that I got my brains from her. Miles laughed like crazy at that. I wanted to die.

Mag asked him if he was sticking around in Maine for Christmas. He told us he was leaving to go home to Florida the day after Christmas. He winked at me and said, "Economy flight." I almost winked back, but then I thought it would look too retarded, so I didn't.

Mom and him talked for a while about her getting her diploma. Miles seemed real interested in that, and Mom seemed glad he was. When he left, he jumped down over the bleachers in two leaps. It was hard for me to keep my tongue in my mouth. Mag watched him walking toward the door and whispered to me, "Great ass." I almost said, "You can say that again," but I caught myself and called Mag a "sex fiend." She snorted at me like a pig and pinched my cheek.

I looked over at Mom and she was looking dumbstruck at the door. I figured she was probably watching Miles's ass like I wanted to, so I looked too.

There was Dad standing in the doorway.

Mom waved to him and he came over, walking in a straight line, grinning from ear to ear. He looked different to me all of the sudden.

He was sober.

While I was saying silent thank-you's, he sat down beside

83

Mom and kissed her on the cheek. Then he said hi to Mag and me and sat back and watched the game. Jeff came out with the team and started practice shooting. He saw Dad up in the stands and went all white. I knew what he was thinking. He looked at me like a lost puppy. I lip-synched "It's OK," to him and he turned and started shooting.

Dad was happy as a pig in shit. He cheered like crazy for Jeff and told everybody who was sitting by us that Jeff was his son. During halftime of one of the games they had a raffle and Dad's number was drawn for one of the prizes. He won dinner for two at the Rusty Nail. Mag whispered to me that they put cow shit in the food there. I told her to shut up and pinched *her* cheek, so she snorted at me again.

Jeff had a great day. He was high scorer for all three games he played in and won the MVP trophy for the day. He had his picture taken for the newspaper and there's gonna be a write-up about him tomorrow. He acted real humble and nice all day. For once I was proud to know him.

When we were riding back in the car, I told him, "Good job, Jeff," real quiet like. It was so strange. I couldn't look at him. And he couldn't look at me. He kept looking out the window. I didn't think he heard me until a couple minutes later when he said "Thanks" to a passing Exxon sign.

▶ ## December 22

Big write-up today in the paper about Jeff. His picture was on the front page of the sports section. It was a big picture of him shooting a foul shot and looking serious. The article called him the "Hope of Chappaqua." Mom was real excited about it and showed it to Dad. Dad got up and shook Jeff's hand. Jeff smiled a little bit but didn't say anything. Dad said he was going out to do some shopping and asked Mom to go with him. Mom looked a little shocked but grabbed her pocketbook and followed him out the door.

Marsha came over waving the sports section and hugged Jeff. She said she was sorry she missed the tournament. Jeff told her, "No sweat." Grandma made a cake and decorated it so it looked like the front page of a newspaper. She was gonna write "Congratulations Jeff" on it, but she ran out of space, so she ended up putting "Congratula J" on it. It was comical. I kind of laughed when I saw it and that made Grandma mad. Marsha said the cake was "very nice." Grandma thought she was saying it to be mean, but Marsha really meant it. Grandma told her there was no need to be smart about it. Marsha just looked at me and shrugged her shoulders. It's getting so she can't win with Grandma no matter what she says.

There was a thump on the door and Dad came in carrying a new basketball. He gave it to Jeff and said, "Have a ball, Jeff." Mom thought that was so funny she started to laugh. Jeff looked like he didn't know what to do next. He mumbled, "Thank you," to Dad and dribbled the ball once.

I thought Marsha would be uncomfortable around Dad. The last time Dad spoke to her was during his great dinner performance. She acted like it never happened and shook Dad's hand like she was meeting him for the first time. Which she was, really. Dad forgot all about the dinner, and nobody seemed ready to remind him. Jeff least of all. He and Dad started talking about the games and the trophy like it was an everyday thing.

I played along with the show. It's easier not to rock the boat when it's like this.

7:34 P.M.

Mag just left for her grandparents' house. She stopped by on her way and gave me my present, a sweater she knit herself. It's dark green with blue stripes. One of the sleeves is longer than the other but I still love it. I gave Mag her perfume and she said it was great. She said she'd have to wait until she got home to try it on because her grandfather gets confused sometimes and thinks that Mag is one of his girlfriends from the old days. Mag told me that once he tried to French kiss her. Mag said the little part of his tongue that he managed to get into her mouth tasted like Pepto-Bismol. I almost threw up when she told me.

Mag sprayed me with the perfume and kissed me long

and hard so that our teeth crashed. It hurt a little. Then she grabbed the band on my underwear and gave me a wedgie. I squeaked and told her to have a good time. I'm gonna miss her.

▶ December 23

Went shopping with Marsha today. She wanted to buy a camera for Jeff and asked me to come along to help pick it out. I was gonna tell her that what Jeff really wants is a box of condoms, but I didn't think she'd appreciate it. Marsha started asking me all about Mag, things like did I want to get serious and this and that. I told her Mag was just a friend, more like a sister to me than anything else. Marsha smiled and said sometimes they made the best girlfriends. I just shook my head at her and said I don't think so.

I asked Marsha if she was serious about Jeff and she said he pissed her off sometimes, but it was hopeless love. I know how she feels.

We got the camera, a One-Step, and Marsha started talking with the salesperson who was a friend of her mother. I heard Marsha saying that she's already been accepted at Harvard with a free ride. I was shocked when I heard that, but I don't know why. Her SAT's were perfect 800's. I admire her so much. She doesn't show off her brains like some people.

When we got outside the store she told me not to tell Jeff about Harvard. She's saving the news for later. I asked her if she was scared about leaving Tranten. She nodded and said, "A little." I bet I will be too when the time comes. If it ever does ...

They had all of these men's aftershaves on sale in the store. I know that Miles uses Old Spice, so I picked him up a bottle of it with my last five bucks. I don't know why I did it. Probably as a thank-you for what he's done for me. Or probably because since I saw him at the basketball games I can't stop thinking about him. It just seemed like the right thing to do. It made me feel better, anyway.

Got home and Mom was sticking a few presents under the tree. I know what they are. A new hunting jacket for Dad, new high-tops for Jeff, and a Monopoly game for me. I saw her picking it out in the General Store (bargain bin: $7.99). I think Monopoly's boring but Mom always gets me something. She asked me what I wanted this year and I told her nothing. If I told her what I really wanted she'd probably start crying. I'll act happy about Monopoly.

I don't know how I'm gonna give the Old Spice to Miles. Mail it probably. Nope. Can't. Don't have any money for stamps. Have to take it to him.

▶ ## December 24

Wrapped up the Old Spice for Miles this morning. Before I wrapped it I put some on my cheeks. I liked the way it made me think of him. Started really missing him then. I decided to walk to his house and pretend to stop by like I was just in the neighborhood. Then, on my way out, I was gonna leave the Old Spice in his mailbox where he'd find it tomorrow and not know who it was from.

I stuck a tag on the box and wrote "TO MILES" on it in all capitals so he wouldn't recognize my writing, then I walked over to his house. I nearly froze my ass off during the walk over because nobody stopped to pick me up when I held my thumb out. Les Numer bombed by with his folks and didn't even look in my direction (prick).

When I got to his house, it was all dark and nobody was home. I stood outside for about an hour and waited for lights to go on, but none did, so I left the package in his mailbox and turned to leave.

Looking back, it's better that I did it that way. If I visited Miles and then a package showed up in his mailbox right after, he'd know the Old Spice was from me. I would *die* if he figured that out.

Walked all the way home and just got in. My face was all frostbit by the time I got inside, but I'm happy. The apartment is warm and Grandma's baking Christmas cookies. Dad and Mom are in the other room talking low. Everything is calm. Life is good. Even though I didn't see Miles.

9:30 P.M.

Grandma dragged me to Christmas Eve services at her church. I knew we were in trouble when they started out the show by having everybody sing "Happy Birthday" to Jesus. It was the first time I ever sang it for a Holy Ghost. It felt kind of silly.

After the birthday song, the little kids got up and did a living nativity scene. Don't ask me why, but one of the kids playing a shepherd was leading a real sheep down the aisle to the manger. When the sheep got to the front of the church, he took one look at the girl playing Mary and wet on her foot. Mary got mad and tossed Baby Jesus down and ran to the back of the church, screaming. I guess that's show biz. Everybody clapped at the end, even though Mary was gone and Jesus was upside down on the cradle.

Got back and Jeff and Marsha were making out on the couch. I thought Grandma was gonna throw a fit, but all she did was say, "God sees everything," and went to bed.

Mom and Dad came in and sat down. It was all quiet until Mom started singing "Away in a Manger" in front of the tree. Her voice is very soft, but pretty. I looked over at Jeff and he was smiling at her. When she got done, he got up and kissed her. He said she sang every other note on key. Mom laughed and punched him in the arm. Dad told her her singing sounded great to him. She kissed him long and hard and then winked at me. It's the first time I've seen her happy in a long time.

Dad mentioned a party the Elks are having tonight. Mom said she didn't want to go. Dad said, "OK." Case closed. Thank God.

Marsha kissed Jeff and said she had to go. Her family was expecting her. Jeff said, "Okeydokey," and walked her to the door. Then everybody but me went to bed. I'm staying up and looking at the tree. It's been a happy day. Here it is Christmas Eve and I've already got one of the two things on my list.

I wonder if Miles will be waiting under the tree when I wake up tomorrow morning?

Nah ... Don't even think it. It's time for bed.

▶ **December 25**

12:35 A.M.
Dad's car just pulled out of the driveway. What's up?

2:51 A.M.
Dad fell way off the wagon. We should have seen it coming when he left. He still wasn't back by 2 o'clock so Grandma locked the door.

He woke everybody up at 2:30 when he started slamming his fist on the door. Grandma peeked into our bedroom and told us not to come out, then she screamed at Mom not to let him in. I guess Mom ignored her because the next thing I heard was the door opening.

The one time Mom has the balls to stand up to Grandma and look what happened. Dad stormed in and started calling Mom names like "slut" and "whore" and wanted to know who she slept with while he was shacking up with Carol. Mom said, "No one," and he got mad. I heard glass breaking and Mom screaming.

"Where are my sons?" he wanted to know. "Jesus Christ," I heard Jeff say. Suddenly our bedroom door swung open and Dad came in telling us both to get up. He made us stand at attention out in the hallway like we were in boot camp while he screamed gibberish at us about not taking any crap from nobody. We're Smiths and proud of it. I watched Dad walk back and forth in front of us and wondered if he wanted us to salute him. Hell would have to freeze over before I'd do that.

After a few minutes of Dad's carrying on, Jeff called him an ass and started walking toward Mom, whose forehead was bleeding. The window in back of her was broken and she had pieces of broken glass in her hair. Dad wanted to know where Jeff thought he was going and Jeff ignored him. This pissed Dad off, so he charged after Jeff, grabbed him by the shoulder, jerked him around, and shoved him against the wall. Jeff seemed to just bounce off the wall, and then he fell. Mom screamed at Dad and ran to help Jeff, but Jeff wasn't seeing anybody but Dad.

The rest was a nightmare. Jeff jumped to his feet and

89

punched Dad in the nose. Dad let out a yelp as his nose started to bleed. It bled slow at first, and then it started to gush. He started bawling. Jeff cursed him and slammed out of the house. Grandma grabbed my hand and led me into the bedroom, where she's sleeping in the bottom bunk and asking God to put Dad out of his and our misery.

Merry Christmas . . .

6:30 P.M.

We spent all day looking for Dad. We finally found him barefoot and face down in the snow outside of the A&P. Grandma told Mom to leave him there but Mom got Jeff, and me and him brought Dad home. He was all wet and sneezing like crazy. Mom put him to bed and rubbed his feet until he fell asleep.

Grandma just got done having it out with Mom. She says Dad needs the kind of help she can't give—God has to step in. I felt like asking Grandma to pray for Dad and maybe God will touch him with His middle finger and lift the curse of alcohol. I didn't because I knew I'd get whacked.

9:30 P.M.

Just went in to see Dad. He looks like he's dying. His face is as white as a sheet and his breathing sounds raspy, like a bulldozer going up a hill. His eyes look like two little red balls when he opens them. He throws up every hour in a pot Mom stuck by his bed, so the whole bedroom smells like puke. Mom's in there with him now, rubbing his forehead with a wet cloth. She told me to get out when I went in.

I keep hearing him trying to talk. He mumbles gibberish about welding two pipes together and talking with Captain Kangaroo. Not once have I heard him say "I'm sorry."

What do I do?

December 26

Dad's in the hospital with "complications brought on by the flu." He got up this morning and passed out at the table. His face just fell on the table like a ton of bricks. Mom got hysterical and started slapping his face. Grandma told Jeff to call the ambulance and started saying prayers. It got bad. Dad opened his eyes and started to puke on the table. Mom got some of it on her lap, but she hung on to his head.

Finally the ambulance came. When the guys came in I kept thinking what a mess the apartment must seem to them. It's a mess to me, and I live here. The guys loaded Dad onto a stretcher and carried him off. Mom and Grandma rode with them, and Jeff and me have been waiting.

Marsha and Jeff are in the bedroom fighting. Jeff keeps saying Dad can rot in hell for all he cares, and Marsha keeps saying, "Your mother needs you." I think she hit him a couple of times because Jeff said, "Cut that out!" like he's real angry.

Whoops! She just screamed, "You're going and that's that!" and stormed out the door. Where's Jeff going?

▶ ## December 27

Marsha drove Jeff and me to the hospital today to see Dad. He was hooked up to a plastic bag and didn't recognize us. I tried saying hi to him but he kept his eyes shut and flapped his lips around. He started talking about when he was a boy and how his father wouldn't get him a bicycle. He had to go out and earn the money himself and buy one secondhand. He sawed and stacked five cords of wood in three days all by himself. After a few minutes of listening to Dad ramble on, Jeff got up and left the room and I followed him.

Jeff didn't say a word to Marsha or me until we were off and driving. When we got out of town he started crying. He pressed his face against the window and said, "Dad never told me nothing."

Marsha stopped the car and put her arms around him and whispered into his ear. She didn't bother to correct his double negative.

I wish Mag was here.

8:09 P.M.

Grandma got all excited tonight because Rev. Timmy Will said Dad's name on TV today during the special sign-off prayer. In the card she sent him, she asked him to pray real hard for Dad and he did. He said, "God bless Jason, Joe, Jonathon," etc. Grandma got real excited because she said Rev. Timmy *never* said "Jonathon" in the sign-off prayer before. She's convinced that her card got into his hand somehow. As soon as the Timmy show was over, Grandma called the hospital to see how Dad's doing. No improvement.

▶ December 28

Grandma spoke with her minister at church today about Dad. He says there's a place upstate called Riverbrook that cures people of alcoholism. He said they take emergency cases right away if they have to. Grandma made him call and tell them we've got a real emergency. They said they'd send somebody down to interview Dad the day after tomorrow. Dad's gonna have to show this person that he wants help. I don't know how they're gonna get him to agree to that.

Marsha brought Mom back from the hospital and Grandma told her what's happening. Mom said, "No way," and told Grandma to butt out. She said Dad's regained consciousness and knows what's happening. He's ready to come home. They can work it out themselves without anybody's help.

Mom started to leave the room when Grandma took her by the arm and told her there was no other way. Marsha said, "I agree," real quiet like. Grandma looked just as surprised as Mom that Marsha said something. They're still talking in the kitchen now.

Grandma and Marsha on the same team? I never thought I'd see that in my lifetime.

7:37 P.M.

Mom just got off the phone with a man from Riverbrook. He gave her all kinds of advice on dealing with Dad. We're all supposed to tell him that we love him but we want him to get help before he comes home again. The man said Dad's gotta realize for himself that he needs Riverbrook. We can't make him go. I hope it works.

December 29

We all drove over to see Dad this morning when visiting hours started. He looked weak and pale. When we walked in, he tried to smile and asked us what was new. Mom said, "Nothing." Grandma made a face at her and shoved a brochure for Riverbrook into her hands. Dad asked what was going on and Mom showed him the brochure.

He got all mad and threw the brochure on the floor. "I can lick it myself," he said. We were all real quiet for the longest time, and then Mom said, "Don't bother coming home until you do."

Dad looked confused. It was like he didn't hear her right. Mom went on to say that we didn't want him around if he couldn't control his drinking. Dad looked at me and Jeff like he didn't believe her. Like he wanted us to tell him it was OK for him to come home. Jeff and me just shook our heads. That wasn't what Dad wanted to see. He got pissed. Said he didn't need us and we could all go to hell. Screamed at us to get out of his room.

Mom told him she wanted to show him something first. Some things he did to us when he was drunk. She took the bandage off from her forehead and showed him the cut. Jeff lifted up his shirt and showed him the huge bruise on his back from when he got slammed against the wall. I was gonna wiggle my loose tooth for Dad but I didn't need to.

Dad buried his face in his hands and started sobbing. Jeff and me didn't know what to do next. Mom looked like she wanted to run up and hold him. Instead she stood still and said, "We all want you to get better. But not at home."

We stood there watching Dad, waiting for him to say something. Finally he said, "I'm sorry. I'm sooooooo sorry."

December 30

Woman came from Riverbrook today to interview Dad. Mom said he was agreeable for most of it. He only got mad when the woman told him the Riverbrook rules. I guess they're real strict. He asked the woman—angry—why did he need a goddamn baby-sitter? Then he told her to get lost, but Mom calmed him down and said it was the only way. After a while, Dad signed the woman's paper. He told the woman that, yes, he wanted help, and he'd do his best to receive it. He checks in tomorrow.

Thank you, God.

8:55 P.M.

Mag just called!!! She's coming home in three days. Her grandparents are both really cool, but they're driving her "batty." I told her what's going on with Dad. She said she didn't know what was worse, having a dead father, or one who's going through what mine is.

I said I'd take mine dead.

▶ December 31

Dad left for Riverbrook today. Mom drove him.

Mom said he was quiet all through the drive up. He just looked out his window in a daze and didn't say a word. She told him over and over again that it was the best place for him now, but he looked real scared. When they got to Riverbrook a nice woman came out and showed Dad to his room. Mom said he's in a ward with nine other people. They've all gotta share one TV. I hope the nine other guys like westerns. If not, how's Dad gonna live without his *Bonanza* reruns?

Mom's in her bedroom now. I went in to see her earlier and Jeff was sitting beside her on the bed. She was stroking his hair and talking real quiet. I got on the other side of her and she started stroking my hair too. It felt good. I got close to her mouth so I could hear what she was saying.

It was, "I don't think I can make it."

▶ January 1

Happy New Year ... Wild party was going on next door until late this morning. Lots of screaming and laughing. I didn't feel like sleeping anyway. I laid awake and thought about Dad. How did he get to where he is? First I blamed myself, then I blamed Mom. Then I blamed Carol. Then I figured out that Dad was doomed from the start. He never wanted anything more than what he could find in Tranten Township (booze and boredom) and that's what did him in. I got real sad thinking about it. I've got to want more than what I've got or else I'll go the same way. I. WANT. MORE.

▶ January 2

Mag's back!!! She came over tonight and I told her everything that happened. She kept saying, "Holy shit." She brought me back a piece of bourbon cake that her grandmother made. It smelled good. We were gonna eat it, but Grandma got a sniff of it and dumped it in the trash. She said the family's got enough problems without me getting drunk from a cake.

Jeff and Marsha came home and we played Monopoly. They got into a wrestling match when Marsha bought Reading Railroad. Jeff had the other three railroads and needed the fourth to have a monopoly, but Marsha bought it. She waved it in front of his face and stuck out her tongue. Jeff wrestled her to the floor and had her pinned when Marsha flipped him over her. Jeff went flying. Mag and me watched them and laughed. Mom came in and we asked her if she wanted to play. She said, "No thanks," and smiled a little at Marsha. Marsha smiled back.

School starts again tomorrow. Can't wait to see Miles.

▶ January 3

2:30 A.M.

Just had a pair of dreams. In the first one, Mag was in bed with me naked. We started making love—what I think is love, anyway. Mag had to explain everything to me. She was in complete control. I went through that dream real confused, like a blind man. I woke up squeezing my dick and holding on to the side of the bed for control, scared out of my tree.

I fell back asleep and dreamed I was in bed with Miles. It was the most incredible dream. Caressing his chest. Squeezing his buns. Kissing his cheeks. I knew exactly what I was after and I went for it. Before I knew it, there was a flood of great feelings coming from my dick, like a super present I was giving myself. It felt so good. I woke up and my underwear was all wet.

Now I know what Jeff's so excited about.

8:39 P.M.

My life is over. Miles got married over vacation. He came walking into the classroom the same as always, but this time he had a wedding ring on his finger. I saw the ring and felt my stomach drop. Kimby Quinn saw the ring too and asked Miles who the lucky woman was. Miles smiled and said his girlfriend from high school. I felt like someone (Miles) punched me in the stomach. I sat in my chair like a slug and didn't say a word all class. Miles asked me some stupid question about Patrick Henry and I pretended like I didn't know.

He's not mine.

He never will be.

It hurts soooooooooo bad.

January 4

Met Miles's wife. She came to track practice tonight. She's this perky little blond woman who's so small and soft Miles must squish her when they make love. She was running around after Miles holding a clipboard and writing down everything he said. I got sick watching her. She got happy watching Miles. She had this cocky grin on her face like she was thinking, Look at this man who I've got. Isn't he a god? I watched them both as they talked and talked and talked. Miles didn't laugh once. He barely smiled. He can't be happy with her. She looks too much like Smurfette.

3:48 A.M.

Just had another dream about Miles. Same great feelings. But this time I woke up and felt empty.

January 5

Miles introduced his wife to the team today, saying she was going to be his new assistant. Her name is Kelsey. She's got a deep husky voice that sounds like a man. She had that same cocky grin on her face. Miles was smiling today too.

After a while I couldn't look Kelsey in the face. It hurt too bad. I kept my eyes on the ring on Miles's finger, trying to pull it off with my eyes. That hurt too after a while, so I closed them. That was a lot better.

Miles calls her "Kell." What a dopey nickname. When I walked up to Miles to look at the practice schedule, I took a deep sniff. He smelled like Old Spice. That just about killed me.

I'm quitting track tomorrow.

► January 7

Told Miles I was quitting track today. He got all upset and wanted to know why. I told him I was falling behind in my homework and he got a sour expression on his face, like I was letting him down. Bullshit . . . He let me down.

"I'm gonna miss you, Smithie," he said to me. Right. Let him cheer for Kuprekski and kiss his wife. I don't give a fuck. I don't know what I ever saw in him.

Mr. Taylor (guidance counselor) saw me in the hall and lip-synched the word "Why?" to me across the hallway.

"Broken heart," I lip-synched back. He didn't know what I meant, though. He looked at me like I was crazy.

I *am* crazy.

► January 8

There's nothing to live for anymore. Now I know how Mom feels. I feel like I'm going through life in slow motion. Who do I dream about now? What do I do? School sucks eggs. The only thing that made it good was Miles, and now he's what makes it bad. At least when I thought about him, it kept my mind off Dad. Now when I think about Miles I get the same sick feeling I get when I think about Dad, so I'm back where I started.

In English today Mrs. King wanted us to write an essay about what we'd like to do for a career. I passed in a blank piece of paper. How the hell do I know? All I know I can do is run the two-mile run in twelve minutes.

Had a fight with Mag on the bus coming home. She wanted to know what was bugging me and I told her I didn't feel good. She tried blowing in my ear and I screamed at her to "Fuck off." Everybody on the bus went, "Ooooooooooh." I wanted to shoot all of them. Mag got wicked pissed and switched seats while the bus was still moving. Came home and cried.

11:49 P.M.

Just called Mag to apologize. She was real nice. I told her I was just having a bad day and that I was sorry. She told me to forget it and come to school in a better mood tomorrow. Then she said to me, "Ben, life sucks and then you die." The way she said it was real funny and I started laughing.

Feel better. Feel much better.

▶ January 9

Mrs. King cornered me today about the blank piece of paper. I told her I'm not good at anything, so how could I know what I want to do for my career? She put on her concerned face and said my grades were the best in the class. I have a unique mind. I've just never realized my potential. Yeah, yeah . . .

Got watching *Timmy Will's Bible Hour* today. Grandma tunes in every afternoon. He had lots of dumb advice. He says you've gotta have a plan for your life. God can only help you so much. You've gotta go out and find your happiness.

I had my happiness. He was taken away from me by a flat-chested blond midget woman. Hate her. Hate him too.

Jeff came into the room and asked me what the fuck was wrong lately. He says that I've been like a corpse all week and Mom is beginning to worry. I didn't know Mom even noticed me. I've seen her maybe ten minutes all week. She's been studying hard for her midterms. I told Jeff I just feel sick. He said, "I hear you panting at night. I know what you're doing."

I was trying to be quiet about it too.

I just can't help thinking about Miles, and when I do, this urge takes over my hands and the next thing I know, they're down there fiddling around. It feels good at first. Great up until the end, when all of the happiness spurts out of me and I feel empty again. Empty and angry.

Jeff told me if I had any questions I should ask him. The school nurse will just screw me over about it and make me feel dumb.

I told him I knew it was normal and he said, "If you can control it, it's normal. But too much of it is sick." Then he made a face and left the room.

I don't feel any better.

▶ January 10

Kuprekski beat up Les Numer today! I still don't believe it. It started out so typical. Les was pelting snowballs off the back of Kuprekski's head. He made a mistake and stuck a rock in one of them. When Kuprekski got hit, it made a CRACK sound. Before Les could say a word, Kuprekski thundered back toward him and started punching him hard. Throwing the shot must have jerked his confidence into high gear, because he went after Les like he was a punching bag.

Les fell down and Kuprekski jumped on top of him and started pushing his face in the snow. He'd scream, "Eat snow, asshole," and then he'd drive Les's face into the snow again. Les's face turned blue after a while and he started to cry. Kuprekski drove his face down hard one last time and got up. He didn't smile or anything. He just walked away.

He must feel like a million bucks tonight. I know I feel better.

▶ January 11

There's a new guy who sits beside me in my World Geography class and is he interesting-looking. He's got olive-colored skin and dark brown hair. He's also got a pretty nice body from what I've seen—he was wearing a big bulky sweater. His name is Aaron, I think. Whatever it is, he's different, for sure. While Mr. Nichols was droning on about the Aswan Dam, I watched his profile out of the corner of my eye. His nose is kind of big. But nice.

I only looked straight at him once, when I dropped my pencil and he picked it up for me. When he looked at me he sort of smiled like he wants to be friends. He's got a dimple on his chin. He's not what I'd call good-looking, but he's interesting to see. When class ended, I walked with him to the door and got close enough to know that he smelled like Brut.

Today when Kuprekski got on the bus, Les stayed in his seat and let him pass. Les looked like a kicked puppy when Kuprekski walked by. It's the beginning of something new.

January 12

Mr. Taylor called me into his office today and asked me if I wanted to join Student Council. Brett DuShane, the freshman representative, moved away over vacation and they need someone to take his place. I don't wanna do it. Kimby Quinn's the other freshman on it and I couldn't stand to work with her. Mr. Taylor started going on about college applications and how I had to start planning now. I told him I'd think about it and left. I wish he'd leave me alone. Who asked him?

That new kid, Aaron Silver, is in all the College classes. He's in my homeroom too. It was kind of a nice way to start the day, seeing him first thing. He was quiet in every class except French. Old Lady Song asked him how much French he'd had. He got up and recited a poem ("Le Roi du" something) from memory. Old Lady Song's eyes popped open. He grinned at me and sat down.

In lunch, Ralph said that Aaron's a show-off and a conceited jerk. Lesly said he's confident, and what's wrong with that? Mag said, "Who cares? His eyes are dynamite." I didn't really join in the conversation. I was too busy watching Aaron out of the corner of my eye. He was eating by himself at the far end of the cafeteria, making faces at Duff.

9:35 P.M.

Just spoke with Marsha. She says Student Council is a blast and I ought to join. I think I will. Maybe it'll help me forget about Miles.

Speaking of Miles, I might as well give myself a present. Jeff's gone out for the evening.

▶ January 13

Went with Grandma to visit the elderly today as part of her Christian Helping Hands thing. It turned out to be this old gal named Patsy. When we got to her house in Nome, Patsy was out shoveling snow off from her dead husband's tombstone, which is in her front yard. I asked Grandma why the tombstone was there and she said, "That's where her husband is buried. Now shut up." I was trying to figure that out when Grandma called me over to help her bring Patsy inside. She was only wearing a bathrobe and slippers. Her feet were soaking wet from the snow and her teeth were chattering.

Grandma gave Patsy hell when we were leading her inside, but Patsy didn't care. She laughed and asked Grandma if she wanted coffee. It didn't take me long to figure out Patsy was off her rocker. She filled the coffeemaker with jelly beans and set it to brewing. I started to say something but Grandma shushed me and said real quiet, "Take the coffee when she offers it to you and say thank you." I just nodded and looked at Patsy to see what was gonna happen next.

The coffeemaker started burping and spitting out this gross-looking water. Patsy got out dirty coffee cups and gave us some. She sat down and started talking about her grand-daughter who never came to visit. I was gonna ask Grandma if the granddaughter was real or just something that Patsy was making up, but Grandma was too busy nodding and saying, "God help this woman," under her breath.

The next thing I knew, Patsy dashed into the other room to get pictures of her granddaughter. Grandma walked over to the cupboards and opened them up. All that was inside was cans of dog food. I asked Grandma where the dog was

and she said, "No dog. Patsy eats it. All she can afford."
That made me want to puke. Grandma looked at me and
said, "The next time you start feeling sorry for yourself, mis-
ter, you think about Patsy." I didn't know what to say to that.

Patsy came back without the pictures. She lost them.
Grandma said that was OK. Patsy went into the other room
and started watching *$25,000 Pyramid,* and we went into her
room and changed her sheets. I wanted to ask Grandma all
kinds of questions, but I could tell she wasn't in the mood
to talk. We got done with the bed and Grandma went and
told Patsy we were leaving. Patsy didn't care. She was too
busy shouting clues at the TV.

Grandma was quiet during the drive back until we crossed
the Tranten Township line, then she announced that she
wants me to go to church with her next week. She says I
ought to talk to Reverend Silk. She says it's a confusing time
for me and I need a male role model to help me out. I was
gonna tell her Reverend Silk is about a hundred years old.
What would he know about it? But I decided I better not.

▶ *January 14*

We're doing new projects in Geography. It's kind of like a
United Nations thing where we get together with partners
and research a Third World nation, then at the end of the
week, we're gonna be delegates from that nation and present
the nation's plight. When Mr. Nichols said to get together
with partners, Mag and me looked at each other. But then I
turned and saw Aaron looking at me too. He smiled at me
and I felt like I had a buzz. "You wanna be my partner?"
he asked. YES! YES! YES! YES! YES!

"Sure," I said. We're gonna be delegates from Ethiopia.

Mag made a face at me when the bell rang and didn't
speak to me until the bus ride home when she asked, "Why
didn't you wanna be my partner?" I said something about
Aaron being a new kid and not knowing anybody yet. She
seemed to accept that. She showed me her new imitation of
the Pillsbury Doughboy. She makes her voice go really high
and talks about ready-to-bake biscuits and cinnamon rolls.

Then she told me to touch her belly button which I did, and she giggled like she was on helium. We were both laughing like crazy by the time the bus reached my place. I love Mag.

January 15

Worked on the Ethiopian project in study hall today with Aaron. It's very interesting. Just when I think my life couldn't get any worse, I hear about the starving people in Ethiopia and it makes me feel real lucky. It's a bonus that I get to work with Aaron. He's real sad about the whole Ethiopian thing. He says when he graduates he wants to join the Peace Corps and go over there and help them.

Aaron's kind of a rebel. When we were saying the Pledge of Allegiance today in homeroom, Aaron held his hands in back of himself and hummed "Come Together." I never saw anything like that before. I asked him about it and he said the Pledge is a farce. Looked up *farce* in the dictionary and I'm not sure if I agree with him or not.

January 16

We worked over at Aaron's house in Nome this afternoon. He's got a set of encyclopedias. His mother works part-time as a social worker. His father's a lawyer. I read from the books and Aaron took notes. He looks kind of weird when he writes. His eyes go all squinty and he bites his tongue.

While we were working, Aaron got talking about his parents. They were both at Woodstock. Aaron said that they belonged to a nudist colony in Oregon until Aaron was five, and then they traveled around the world. Aaron showed me pictures of him swimming in the Red Sea and stuff like that. His grandmother made them move back east (Boston) so they'd be close by when she croaked. She was "old money," whatever that means. She bit the dust and Aaron's parents took the money and ran. They decided to settle in Maine so he could grow pine trees and she could have a flower garden in the summertime. I listened to Aaron talk and I couldn't believe it. He's seen the whole world.

Aaron's father came out of his office and asked us how

the report was coming. He looks a lot like Aaron but is a little taller. He's got that same dimple on his chin and a kind of big nose. He kissed Aaron's mother for a *long* time and then winked at her on his way up the stairs. Aaron rolled his eyes at me and watched his mother climb the stairs after him. They didn't come down again while I was there.

January 17

I flunked a history test today. I couldn't study for it. Every time I opened my notebook I got thinking about Miles, and that made me sick. When he handed the test back to me with an F on it, he asked me, "What happened?" I told him my dog buried my notebook in the backyard and I didn't dig it up until it was too late to study. Miles shook his head and kept on passing out papers. That was fine with me. When I'm in his class now I don't even try to hear what he's saying. I tune him out and look out the window. It's easier that way.

Came home tonight and Grandma told me Mom got a job at the McDonald's in Lipton. Didn't believe her until Mom walked in wearing the uniform. Asked her, "Why?" hoping it was just a bad dream. She said it was too embarrassing cashing her Aid checks at the bank. Now we've got to live on less money a month. Ronald McDonald doesn't pay as much as Ronald Reagan.

If Mom was embarrassed before, how could she like going to McDonald's every day wearing that dumb uniform? I asked Jeff this and he told me to shut up and stop being so fucking snobby.

January 18

Aaron and me gave our report today. It was a success. Everybody but Mag voted to give us economic assistance. She was grumpy all day because she called me last night and I was on my way out the door to Aaron's house. We had some last-minute things to get done before the presentation today. His mother came in with tofu sandwiches, which we ate while we watched television on Aaron's set. Aaron groaned when he opened the sandwich and saw it was tofu inside. His mother said, "Stop complaining. I'm adding ten years to your life."

While I was eating, I got thinking how lucky Aaron is to live like that all the time. To have parents who like each other and don't drink. I'd give anything for a day like that.

Later, while I was sketching a map of Africa for the cover of our report, Aaron asked me about Mag. Was I serious about her? I said, "No, we're just good friends." And Aaron nodded his head and pulled out a framed picture of the girlfriend he left behind in his old home. Her name is Connie and he went with her all through junior high, then when he moved, he decided to break it off clean. He said they both wanted different things. I wondered the rest of the night what "different things" Aaron wanted.

It was getting to be pretty late, so Aaron asked me if I wanted to stay over. I thought about it for a minute. It would've been nice. But for some reason I heard myself saying, "No. I better get home."

Aaron hasn't been to my place yet. I don't know if I want to invite him. What if Mom walks in wearing her McDonald's uniform, or Dad shows up from Riverbrook out of the blue? I think I'd die.

 ## January 19

2:57 A.M.

Just had a strange dream about Aaron. He was sleeping in pajamas on my bed, out like a light bulb. I was sitting up next to him. I looked at his face and I wanted to kiss it, to touch that dimple. I looked at his shirt and I wanted to take it off, but I didn't know why. I mean, Aaron is pretty good-looking, but he doesn't make my dick dance when I look at him or anything like that. His nose is kinda big, and his arms are awful hairy. He's just a friend. I don't think about touching him when I'm awake. I wanted to touch him in my dream, though.

It was strange. My dick stayed soft and my underwear stayed dry through the whole dream. Tried to go back to sleep, but I can't stop thinking about Aaron. I'm dying to see him.

4:45 P.M.

A woman came into Phys. Ed. today and gave us a sex talk. She told us a little about AIDS and how you can get it. All the guys wanted to play volleyball until she pulled out a condom and a banana. "This is how you put it on," she said. And then she stretched the condom over the banana until it was on all the way. Everybody thought that was pretty funny.

When she left the room for a second, Les stole a handful of condoms from her bag. He handed them out saying, "Use it like a good boy." When the nurse came back she didn't have a clue. I stuck mine in my wallet because I saw a couple of the guys doing that. Les blew his up like a balloon and made farting noises with it all the way home on the bus tonight. After his condom popped, Les took his pen and wrote on his bus seat, "STOP AIDS—KILL A FAGGOT." I cheered with everybody else. Les spelled all the words correctly, after all. That's a first for him.

Aaron smelled real nice in class today—rugged, like Aqua Velva.

▶ January 20

Woke up today and I was all stuffed up with a cold. Grandma took my temperature and it was 102 degrees. She told me to stay in bed, which is what I did all day. Grandma had to go out and see Patsy today but Mom was home. She kept coming into my room and asking if I wanted anything. I'd say, "No," and she'd disappear again.

When the mail came, she got real excited because a letter came from Dad. She ran into my room and started reading it for me, like I was too sick to read it for myself. The letter was short. Dad wrote that he misses us all, but he knows that Riverbrook is the best place for him. He can't wait to come home and eat Grandma's cooking because "the Riverbrook food sucks." He doesn't know when he'll be good enough to come home, but hopefully it'll be soon. Mom folded up the letter and looked up at the calendar, singing, "Happy Days Are Here Again," slow and pretty. I don't know why she chose that song to sing.

Something strange happened to Mom while she was reading the letter. I watched her face the whole time. It started to glow after the "Dear Everybody" part. She undid her hair and let it fall down to her shoulders during the middle part. Then, right before the "Love, Jonathon" part, she smiled. I watched the years disappear from her face and wrinkled up my nose to keep from sneezing. It was itching like crazy but I didn't have the heart to stop Mom while she was on a roll. She's in the kitchen now singing "Happy Days" again. Still don't know why.

▶ **January 21**

I was still honking like crazy, so I didn't have to go to church with Grandma today. Thank you, God. Marsha came over today and asked Mom if she wanted to buy tickets to a lasagna supper the National Honor Society's having in a few weeks. Mom bought two. "For me and Jonathon," she said. Marsha kind of raised her eyebrows but didn't say anything.

Grandma came home all mad with crazy Patsy. She said Patsy was running around on all fours like a dog today, barking and eating her dog food from a bowl on the floor. Patsy wouldn't stand up and play human until Grandma patted her head and said, "Good doggie." Grandma says Patsy needs to have someone go live with her full time. I asked her why nobody does and Grandma said, "Nobody cares."

▶ **January 22**

I'm on Student Council. Mr. Taylor said my application was OK'd by everybody on it. I'm not sure if I'm happy about it or not. Kimby came running up to me between classes today and told me we'd have a great time. She managed to pick a couple pieces of lint off my shirt while she was telling me how much fun we're gonna have. I nodded my head and said, "I hope so." If she touches me during a meeting I'm gonna scream.

In lunch I told the guys at my table. Lesly and Ralph were both happy about it. Mag was pissed that Mr. Taylor didn't ask her to join. I said it was gonna be boring as hell and she was lucky. She didn't believe me. I went over and told Aaron, who was eating alone. He congratulated me and said, "Self-government gives birth to change." Had to write it down so I wouldn't forget it. Aaron's always saying stuff like that. I asked him to come sit at our table for lunch and he said, "Maybe tomorrow."

Miles spared me a second in class and said track wasn't the same without me. Suuuuuuure it isn't, Miles. It's so strange. I still feel like kissing the bastard even though he broke my heart. It hurts. Wonder when that's gonna go away? He assigned us thirty pages to read tonight. I'm gonna blow it off.

Came home and Mom was at class and Jeff was at an away game. Told Grandma about me making Student Council. She said she was proud of me. I could tell from her face that she'd never heard of Student Council before in her life.

▶ January 23

First Student Council meeting today. It was Marsha, Kimby, me, and five Lipton snobs. They got talking about the Valentine's Day Dance and how we had to think of a theme for it. The Lipton Hags are all a bunch of airheads. Marsha's the only person on it who's got half a brain. This one dame named Dorian started going on about crepe paper decorations and shit like that. Kimby started talking like that was the most interesting thing she ever heard and acted like a brown-nosing asshole. I didn't even try to pretend. I made a face at Marsha and rolled my eyes. After the meeting she told me, "It gets better." I wanna quit already.

Aaron ate at our table during lunch today. He was nice to everybody, which was kind of a relief. Ralph seemed determined to hate him but he changed his mind after Aaron gave him his hot dog. He calls hot dogs "cancer in a casing." Mag got kind of mad when she walked in and saw him sitting beside me in her chair. I pointed at some empty seats on the other side. She made a face at me and stamped out of the cafeteria. I don't get her lately.

Saw Miles in the hall after lunch. He was joking with Ku-prekski and laughing that stupid laugh of his. He saw me and said, "How's it going, Smithie?" and then he kept on walking right by me. Didn't even wait for me to answer. Why did he ask? He didn't care. I wanted to kick him. Punch him. Make him hurt like he hurt me.

It's no use. Nothing I could do to him would cause that much pain.

January 24

Jeff came home real excited tonight. He's only fifty-five points away from making a thousand points in his high school basketball career. Jeff says it's a BIG DEAL. There are seven more games left in the season, so Jeff's sure to make at least sixty points before the season ends. It's kind of exciting. But also kind of sad. There are only three other guys from Chappaqua High School who've made a thousand points. Their names are up on this banner in the gym in bright green and blue letters. One of them, Gary Gould, graduated in '80 and he works behind the checkout counter at the General Store. The plaque he got for making a thousand points is on the counter between the Atomic Ball jar and the cash register. Once in a while some customer'll ask Gary about the plaque and he'll go into this hour-long story about the last game of the '79–'80 basketball season. By the time he gets to the part about scoring the winning basket, Gary's as excited as a virgin at a prison rodeo. The customer's usually near a coma. I don't think anybody ever mentions the plaque to Gary a second time.

Marsha was with Jeff when he bombed in with the Big News. She seemed real happy, but I could tell something was bugging her. I asked her and she said things were fine. Didn't believe her. She and Jeff drove to Lipton tonight to go shopping. Wonder what's up.

Grandma got watching Reverend Timmy Will tonight. He's got specials on every day this week—each night he preaches about some deadly sin. Tonight it was taking the Lord's name in vain. He's got this high-pitched voice that gets on my nerves after a while. He sang "How Great Thou Art" and then started gabbing about his "Timmy Fund" to help all the poor people in the world. Grandma called in a pledge ($20) to the fund. I was gonna ask her why she didn't use the money to buy crazy Patsy some food, but I got up and left the room instead.

11:30 P.M.

Jeff just came in pissed out of his mind. Asked him what's wrong and he said, "Marsha's going to Harvard next year." Tried to act surprised but I've known for about a month now. I told Jeff that was good news and he said, "Shut the hell up!"

I know what's bugging him. Marsha's got next year all planned out. Next year for Jeff is a big question mark. He said college scouts would beg him to play for them, but none of them ever come to the games. Chappaqua High School isn't on anybody's map. Not anybody who's anybody, that is. I think he was hoping Marsha would stay in town and be his little wife. That ain't gonna happen, Jeffie.

Whoops! He just snarled at me to "turn off the fucking light." Good night.

▶ January 25

Not much excitement today. I caught Theresa and George the janitor together in the janitor's office. Mag and me were after some sponges when we walked in and saw them standing there all red-faced. Theresa said George was helping her look for cleaning supplies, then they both looked down at the floor. Mag told me later not to believe Theresa. She said she saw George kissing Theresa behind the bleachers last week. I know Theresa only likes seniors, but this is ridiculous.

Mrs. King gave us new assignments to do over the weekend. We've gotta write down one thing in the world that we'd like to do away with and why. The change doesn't have to be good for everybody, just our own opinion. God— where do I begin? I could make a list of stuff a mile long. Mag told me that she'd do away with physical fitness testing. It's cruel, she says. I said that didn't sound too practical.

Came home and Mom was sitting at the table with a pad in front of her, writing something. Asked her what it was and she said, "A letter to Dad." Looked over her shoulder when she didn't know it and saw what she wrote. "Dear Jonathon: I miss you awful bad." That was it.

January 26

Aaron called this morning and asked if I wanted to go with him and his Mom to Lipton to look for a car. His Mom felt an "urge" to buy one at midnight last night. I said, "Sure," and went with them. Mrs. Silver is a serious woman. She started talking about what a criminal Reagan is and how the poor should revolt. I looked around the BMW we were riding in and tried to figure out what she wanted to revolt against. Reagan seems to be doing okay by her. I like her, though. While she and Aaron were looking at cars, I watched Aaron. He looked kind of good in his sunglasses.

His Mom asked to try out three different cars and found something wrong with each one. The interior was "all wrong" on the first one. The horn sounded "the wrong key" on the second one. And the digital clock in the third one was "too bright." The dealer looked like he wanted to poke her one after she said "Goodbye" to him. She was kind of bugging me too.

When we left, both Aaron and her started laughing like crazy. I asked Mrs. Silver what was so funny and she said that was her way of irritating "another capitalist pig." I wanted to know who the "pig" was but I would have felt stupid asking. I didn't care. I got looking at how Aaron's hair curled.

We stopped at McDonald's on our way back. I almost died. Mom was standing behind the counter making french fries.

Her hat was on crooked and she looked sort of tired. I told Aaron I didn't want anything and ran to the bathroom before she could see me. I washed my hands quick and ducked out the back door. Met Aaron and Mrs. Silver in the parking lot.

I felt real bad when we were driving home. A lot worse than I would have felt if Aaron had found out. His Mom dropped me off at the store and I walked home. Aaron hasn't asked to come to my house. I'm not about to ask him over. Yet . . .

Came home and worked on my paper. It's hard. I was so happy after spending the day with Aaron, I couldn't think of anything I wanted to do away with. Decided to put it off until tomorrow.

9:04 P.M.

Just got done watching Timmy Will's nightly special. Tonight's deadly sin was "deviant sexual practices." Listened to Timmy condemn all gays, lesbians, and bisexuals straight to hell. AIDS is their punishment for "unnatural behavior," he says. It's their cross they have been given by God to bear.

Gonna work on my paper now. Just thought of something in the world that I wanna do away with.

11:55 P.M.

It just hit me. I haven't thought about Miles once today. I can write his name without feeling a jab.

Miles. MILES. MiLeS. mIlEs. Sort of rhymes with bile, vile, and pile. Of shit.

 ## January 27

Grandma had a cold today, so I got out of going to church again. Thank you twice, God. I asked her if Patsy would mind if she didn't check up on her. Grandma sneezed and said, "Patsy doesn't care. She's probably playing a kangaroo today."

Marsha came over this afternoon acting real sorry. She told Jeff she should have told him about Harvard when she first found out. Jeff acted mad at her and started dribbling his ball while she was trying to talk. Marsha got mad after a while and screamed at him to grow up. She punched him in the shoulder. Hard. So he dropped his ball.

Jeff got this dangerous look on his face and for a second I thought he was gonna slug her. It's the first time I've ever seen Marsha afraid. Jeff didn't hit her. He picked up his ball and dribbled out of the room. Marsha turned and slammed out the door. Grandma was in the living room watching *Timmy Will's Sunday Sing*. She heard doors slamming and came in. She wanted to know what was going on. I told her, "Jeff just blew it."

▶ January 28

Saw Marsha today at Student Council meeting. She acted very businesslike. Kimby told everybody her idea for a Valentine's Dance theme. She wants it to be "Love Is in the Air." She started going on about hanging heart-shaped balloons from the ceiling and piping scents of flowers and spices into the gym from a huge potpourri pot.

This had to be one of the stupidest ideas I ever heard. What if people are allergic to the smells? Marsha didn't seem to give a damn. She looked like she just wanted to get out of there. Nobody else had a better idea, so we took a vote on it. It was seven-to-one in favor of "Love Is in the Air." Kimby walked out of the meeting looking like the cat who ate the canary. God, I hate her.

Told Aaron I had a good time Saturday. He said we'd have to do it again. On the bus home Mag was all huffy because I wasn't around on Saturday when she called. She says it's like I don't want to be her friend anymore. Apologized to her and asked her over this Friday night. She said she'd think about it and then got off without saying goodbye.

▶ January 29

Had a great time today in French class with Aaron. We had to write a dialogue and perform it in front of the class. Aaron had the idea of doing it between two five-year-olds who are trying to eat Chinese food. He's trying to explain to me how to eat it. It got real funny after a while and the whole class was laughing, except for Mag. Old Lady Song gave us an A and said, *"Tres bien!"*

Aaron surprised me when we were doing it. He held my hand to show me how to eat with chopsticks. He grabbed it so quick and so gentle that I wasn't sure what to do. I started to pull my hand away from him, but that would've looked dumb, so I let him hold it. I felt my dick do a little jump when he let go. I hope nobody noticed.

Mr. Taylor cornered me today about Student Council and asked me how I like it. I told him it was "OK" and turned to leave. If I told him how I really felt he'd give me a detention.

Big B-ball game tonight. There's gonna be a big fanfare at each game from now on as Jeff gets closer to his thousand points. Mom and Grandma are both going. I wonder if Marsha's gonna be there.

► January 30

Mrs. King was all upset about my essay today. I wrote that I wanted to do away with televangelists, Timmy Will especially, because they use God to finance their lifestyles and the Bible to support their narrow ideas.

It turns out, Mrs. King is one of Timmy Will's followers. She got teary-eyed as she told me about everything Timmy does for the starving kids in Ethiopia. She said he went into one of their huts, rolled up his sleeves, and spoon fed a set of Negro twins. She got real mad all of a sudden and asked me if I was an atheist. I told her no and went back to my seat. Mrs. King scowled at me all through class. Got back my paper and she gave me a C– on it. Mag got a B+ for her paper on doing away with physical fitness testing. NOT FAIR. Went in the bathroom and wrote, "Mrs. King is a Nazi," on the stall wall.

In lunch, Aaron made everybody but Mag laugh. Aaron says Timmy Will's a clown "who feeds off the ignorant prejudices of the right wing." Then he started singing "How Great Thou Art" in a high-pitched voice like Timmy. Mag acted real irritated with him and left lunch early. Never got a chance to ask her to the game tonight. Asked Aaron and he said he'd like to go.

9:55 P.M.

Jeff had a great game tonight. Thirteen points. Two fouls. Aaron was real impressed that Jeff was my brother. He made me feel proud to admit it. Mag came up and sat with us for a few minutes. She got real moody after a while and left. She was gone before I even realized it. Aaron and me were too busy firing spit balls at the back of Kimby Quinn's head. I turned to look at Mag and she was gone. Seems like she's mad all the time now. Mr. Duff came over and reamed us out. We got kicked out of the game.

We walked around town for a while. Aaron asked me if I was happy in Tranten Township. I stayed quiet. I mean, what can you say about a town where the people get more excited about the opening day of hunting season than they do about their own kids' birthdays? I asked him if he likes it here and he said, "It's like living in a bad episode of *The Waltons* where Mary Ellen's shacking up with John-Boy."

That struck me so funny I couldn't stop laughing.

▶ January 31

Mag acted weird today. On the bus ride to school, she sat in a seat by herself instead of sitting with me. Asked her why and she said she was surprised I even noticed. She was wicked pissed with me. She said I've been treating her like dirt lately and she deserved better. I didn't have a clue. I guess I have been spending a lot of time with Aaron lately, but I don't think Mag should be upset about it. Aaron and me are going to the movies tonight. Asked her to come with us but she said she had other plans.

11:08 P.M.

What an awful night. Aaron and me went to see *Mad Max* at Lipton. Didn't watch it. Mag was there with Scott Pushard, a scuzzy dropout with greasy hair and grubby fingernails. She sat down right in front of us and looked at me with this smart-ass grin and said, "Hi, Ben," real sarcastic like. I said,

"Hi," back and tried not to look surprised, but I was IN SHOCK. Mag's pulled surprises in the past, but this one was a doozy. I didn't even know she spoke to Scott. He dropped out of school last year after he shoved Old Lady Song in detention. He works with his father in the woods. He's missing a finger on his right hand—chain-saw accident.

All through the movie he kept stroking Mag's shoulder with his grubby four-fingered hand. I just sat there and watched them both. I felt real angry—like Mag was doing it just to be mean to me. When the movie was over, Mag left without even saying goodbye. I'm pissed with her. If she wants to go out with sleazebuckets, fine, but she doesn't have to be so mean about it. If I didn't love her I'd hate her right now.

Aaron's leaving for Boston tomorrow night and coming back Sunday night. Gonna miss him.

▶ February 1

Grandma cornered Jeff today and asked him what was going on with Marsha. She wanted to know why Marsha hasn't been over all week. I could tell that Jeff wanted to tell her to butt out, but he doesn't dare. He just said they had a fight and broke up for a little while. I hope they make up. I can't stand having Jeff at home all day. He's so obnoxious. At least when he was with Marsha he had somebody he had to behave for. Act decent to. He left me alone. Now he spends all his time finding new ways to define *asshole*. This morning he told me to clear out of the bathroom because he had to shave. I told him to wait a goddamn minute. He just picked me up and carried me out of the bathroom. He dumped me on my bed and then ran back into the bathroom, locking the door. He started laughing real loud and calling me names through the door. I wanted to slug him.

11:35 P.M.

Jeff just climbed out of bed and ran out of the room. Asked him where he was going and he told me to go back to sleep.

2:35 A.M.

Jeff just came in plastered out of his mind. He said to me real sad like, "Tell me what to do." I told him, "Apologize to her." He's so wasted he doesn't have a clue.

▶ February 2

Went to church today with Grandma. I was dreading it the whole ride over, but it turned out to be kind of nice. The singing was nice and everybody was friendly. It seems like all these people who act like jerks during the week put on their happy faces when they walk into the church. It's like they forget all the mean stuff they did to each other and are ready to just be happy for an hour on Sunday. Les Numer was there acting holy with his mother and father. Kimby was there with a big toothy grin on her face. The big difference was, this grin was sincere—didn't have any horny plans behind it. It's nice (and kind of spooky) to see they've got that side to them.

The sermon was interesting, about the joy of being a Christian. Reverend Silk said just because you're a follower of God doesn't mean you have to live your life with a frown on your face. This is the day the Lord made. Have a ball. Sing. Dance. Love. Be loved. God gets a kick out of all of that stuff. He loves us no matter what. That was the first time I ever heard that before.

During the free prayer, I prayed that Mag would come to her senses, Jeff and Marsha would get back together, and Dad would get better. When the collection plate came around, I was surprised that I actually felt like giving. Think I'll go back next week.

Aaron's coming home tonight. HA-LAY-LOO-YAH!!!

▶ February 3

Saw Mag today first thing on the bus. She was looking real smug. When I asked her how her weekend was she said, "Great. How was yours?" I said, "Fine, considering." She sort of smiled at me and looked out the window. For some reason, I wanted to punch her. She started whistling some song I couldn't recognize. We rode all the way to school without saying a word. When the bus stopped in front of the school I asked her what was going on with her and Scott. She said, "We're dating . . . Possibly more."

I let her get out and followed her into the school. "He's bad news," I told her. I asked her if she forgot what Scott did to Old Lady Song. She said, "That was six months ago. He's matured since then."

"I bet," I said.

She made a face at me and said, "At least he notices me. That's more than I can say for you lately." Then she turns around and walks away from me. She didn't speak to me the rest of the day. Not even in lunch. She must have skipped it because I didn't see her anywhere in the cafeteria. Ralph asked, "Where's Mag?"

"God knows," I said.

In English, Mrs. King passed out copies of *Romeo and Juliet* and called it the greatest love story ever written. It's what we're gonna be reading for the next two weeks in honor of Valentine's Day, which is coming right up. Lesly groaned when she got her copy. Mrs. King raised her eyebrows at her but moved along. I looked at the guy and girl making moon eyes at each other on the book jacket and felt like groaning too. But I didn't dare.

Aaron wasn't in school today. That made the day even worse. In study hall Mag sat in a desk on the other side of the room from me. Without Aaron there, and Mag acting like a bitch, I didn't have anybody to talk to, so I read the first scene in *Romeo and Juliet*. Didn't understand a word of it.

5:58 P.M.

Just tried calling Mag. Scott answered. Hung up real fast.

6:32 P.M.

Aaron just called! He was late getting back from Boston last night so his parents let him spend the day in bed. He asked about homework. I told him we're reading *Romeo and Juliet*. He said, "Shit. I read it last year." Asked him if he was coming to school tomorrow. He said, "Yah, unfortunately." It felt good to hear his voice.

▶ ## February 4

Aaron was in school today. He had an earring in his left ear. That caused a stir. I've never seen an earring on a guy before, and neither had a lot of other kids in school. Asked him about it and he said that he and a couple of his friends had it done when he was in Boston. He asked me how I liked it. I said it looked cool, but I really didn't mean it. It looked strange to me.

In Phys. Ed. we were running laps around the track while some of the other guys were shooting baskets. Les Numer whistled at Aaron when he ran by. Aaron said, "No-brains shithead," under his breath and kept on running. I fell a couple of paces back from him because I didn't want Les whistling at me next. When Aaron and me were shooting baskets, Les walked over and asked Aaron where he got the earring, real sarcastic like. Aaron told him from his father, and Les said, "It's so pretty, I figured that your little sister gave it to you." Aaron told Les that he didn't have a little sister and Les laughed at him. Aaron gave Les a hostile look and went back to shooting baskets. He acted like Les wasn't even there. Les backed off after that.

Later on, when we were at our lockers, I warned Aaron about Les. Les has been looking for someone new to pick on ever since Kuprekski beat the shit out of him. Lately he's been tormenting grade school kids on the bus, but I know that's not gonna keep him content very long. Aaron and his new earring might be just what he's looking for. Aaron said, "The day I worry about Les Numer is the day Timmy Will whistles 'Dixie' through his ass."

Case closed. Aaron didn't seem afraid at all. I watched him shove his books into his locker and then turn and walk to study hall. Halfway down the hall he noticed I wasn't walking with him. He turned around and looked back at me. He said to me, "What are you waiting for?"

I thought for a split second that I wouldn't walk with him.

If I did, it could ruin my life in Tranten Township. But then I thought, It could just as easily save it.

I was beside him and walking in two seconds.

▶ *February 5*

"Why isn't Mag sitting with us?" Ralph asked me today during lunch. I said I didn't have any idea. Today Mag came to lunch, but she sat on the far end of the junior table with a bunch of Scott's cronies, the "Scuzzy Rejects." She seemed happy. Too happy. It was like she was putting on a show for us. I turned away from her and tried eating my shepherd's pie. Tasted like manure to me.

Student Council meeting this afternoon. Marsha and me got there early. She was pretty somber. While we were waiting for the others to show up, she asked me how Jeff is doing. I told her the truth: "Crappy." She sighed and started doodling on her notebook. "I know the feeling," she said.

She looked so miserable. I came close to groveling at her feet and screaming, "He's so sorry. He wants to get back together. Please take him back!" but Kimby, Dorian, and the other space cadets breezed in before I had a chance to. Dorian started talking about "Love Is in the Air" while Kimby grinned her trademark know-it-all stupid grin. Dorian said she's got a DJ all lined up, and that being Student Council members, we'd all better plan on coming early to help decorate the gym. Great ... I don't even want to go to the damn thing. Marsha didn't seem that excited about it, either. Kimby snagged me after the meeting and asked me if I had a date. The first person I thought of was Mag, but then I remembered Scott. So I said, "No."

Kimby said, "I didn't think you did. Now that Mag's seeing Scott and all."

How did Kimby know about Mag and Scott? How could she not know, is the question. News travels fast at Chappaqua High School.

I just looked at Kimby and said, "Do you wanna go with me?"

She said, "Sure."

Holy shit. What have I done to deserve this?

February 6

Woke up today and there was ten inches of snow on the ground. School got called off because of the snow, so I stayed home. I went into the kitchen and Mom was sitting at the table, looking at an old scrapbook she keeps locked in her hope chest. Asked her what she was doing and she said, "Thinking about your Dad."

She flipped the pages to the beginning and pointed at a family picture taken of all of us. I was just a baby and Mom's holding me on her lap. Jeff was about four and Dad's holding him. Mom and Dad and Jeff were all smiling away. I was screaming about something. Across the top of the picture "Sears Department Store" was written in tiny gold letters. Mom told me that was the first picture ever taken of me. Nanny Smith paid to have it done.

Next were a bunch of pictures of Jeff and Dad and me doing stuff together. Fishing, chopping wood, painting a wall. I was so young when they were taken that I didn't remember much about them. Different parts of them came to me in flashes. The smell of the paint, the way Dad laughed when I tried to bait my own hook, Jeff getting a splinter in his thumb. While I was looking at the pictures I could feel Mom's eyes watching me. I looked at her and she was trying to smile.

Next was a picture of the four of us sitting around a pup tent. I was seven and Jeff was ten when we went camping up in the Black Mountains. Mom talked about how she tripped over a tree stump and sprained her ankle when we went hiking on a mountain trail. Dad carried her back three miles down the trail to where the campground was. It all came back to me in bits and pieces. It was so long ago. Mom started getting serious again. She said, "Now it's my turn to carry your father. He didn't drop me, so I'm not gonna drop him. That's what love is."

I was gonna tell her that she didn't sprain her ankle every

day. How long was she gonna carry Dad? I didn't, though, because Mom seemed different to me all of a sudden. I understood what she was shooting for. She wants the life we had back in those old pictures. She wants it so bad she's willing to put up with any amount of shit to get it back. I can't decide if I want it bad enough. It's gonna take an awful lot of forgiving, and I'm not sure Dad or me are up to it. I know Jeff isn't. But Mom seemed up for anything today. For the first time in her life, she seemed sure of herself.

February 7

Almost died laughing today in English class. Mrs. King got reading *Romeo and Juliet* out loud in front of the class. When she got to the balcony scene, she started acting out all the parts, looking down when she was reading Juliet's parts, looking up when she was reading for Romeo. She started making lovey-dovey faces and smacking her lips together. It was so funny. When the dialogue got hot, she clutched her heart and closed her eyes. Then she made a kissy face. At first I thought she was having a heart attack, but when she stayed on her feet, I knew that she was just acting. I could tell Mag was getting ready to explode into laughs from the quiet little wheezing noises she was making behind me. I didn't dare look at her, because I knew if I did, that would set us both off laughing.

Mrs. King got done with the scene and smiled at us. She said next Monday she's gonna assign parts and we're gonna read the play out loud for the next few classes. Lesly groaned real loud when she heard that. After class, when we were out in the hall, I looked at Mag and we both started laughing like crazy. We didn't have to say a word to each other. It felt like the old days for a second.

I should've quit while I was ahead.

In study hall I sat down beside her and asked her if she wanted to come over tonight and she said she "had plans." She told me with a straight face that she's going to the Monster Truck and Tractor Pull Show in Augusta. At first I thought it was a joke. I tried picturing Mag at a tractor pull.

It struck me so funny that I started laughing. Mag got this defensive look on her face. "What's wrong with that?" she asked. "Scott's dad got us the tickets."

Mag looked hurt, so I stopped laughing. I was trying to think of something to say that wouldn't set her off when she out of the blue says, "Don't be afraid to fight for me."

That caught me way off guard. I was speechless for about a minute, and then I asked her what the hell she meant by "fight for me." She looked at me with this cold stare and said, "I can't wait forever for you."

"What are you waiting for?" I wanted to scream at her. "We're friends, for crying out loud. What the fuck are you talking about?" I didn't say a word, though. I was too confused.

Mag didn't even try to read my mind. She started reading *Romeo and Juliet*. I started reading my copy but it was tough. I could hear her turning pages in back of me. It sounded like she was coming close to ripping them out of the book, she was turning them so hard. She was pissed. I was too.

Aaron came in late to study hall all breathless. I asked him where he'd been and he said, "Duff's office," and he handed me a piece of paper. It turned out to be a note from Duff to Aaron's parents, telling them about the dress code. Aaron's earring is in violation of it. Duff expects Mr. and Mrs. Silver to "take action on the matter." I asked Aaron what he was going to do. He said, "Show it to my parents. They can use a good laugh."

He smiled at me and folded up the note like it was some precious piece of paper. He pulled out *Romeo and Juliet* and started reading. He was turning the pages pretty hard too. Harder than Mag. He was pissed too. I watched him whip those pages over and hoped his book wouldn't rip down the middle. Between Aaron and Mag, Mrs. King's gonna get back two mutilated books when we have to pass them back to her.

The bell rang and we all walked out of study hall. Mag and Aaron were both looking straight ahead, stone-faced. I looked from one to the other and didn't know what to say. When we got to the end of the hall, Aaron turned left to go to his locker. Mag turned right to go to hers. I stood there for a second, almost got knocked over by the traffic. Before I knew it, I was going left. Following Aaron.

 ## February 8

10:17 A.M.

Went to Aaron's house last night. He called at seven o'clock and said he was "bored." Grandma drove me over. When we got to Aaron's house she took one look at the mailbox and said, "Silver? Your friend's Jewish?" I said, "I guess so," and she got in an uproar. She said, "Watch out he doesn't try to brainwash you."

I asked her what she meant and she said Jews are tricky and "they have scales over their eyes when it comes to religion." I started getting out of the car when I heard Grandma say, "You believe in Jesus Christ, and I don't want to hear anything different."

At first I thought she was joking, but then I could see from her face that she was serious. She was scaring me, so I just said goodbye and shut the car door fast. In the house Mrs. Silver was sketching Aaron's dad in the living room. He was sitting in a big chair, looking at a peach like he was about to bite it. Mrs. Silver stood behind this big sketch pad and was drawing these long strokes. Mr. Silver kept laughing and Mrs. Silver would tell him to shut up. Aaron came in and said hi to me. Mrs. Silver hissed, "Quiet!" at him. She drew a few more strokes and said, *"Voilà!"*

We all looked at the sketch pad. It didn't look anything like Mr. Silver. It was just a bunch of black lines crisscrossing in different places. Mr. Silver sort of laughed and said it was like looking in a mirror. Mrs. Silver waved a piece of charcoal at me and said I was next. Aaron told her to leave me alone but I said I didn't mind.

I sat in the chair and Mrs. Silver started tearing into the picture. She kept saying, "Your eyes are letting me look into your soul," over and over. I tried to smile but I started feeling uncomfortable all of a sudden. Mrs. Silver was looking at me so intensely that I felt like I was naked almost. She got done with the picture and motioned me over to her to see it. When I saw it at first, I was confused. It didn't look anything like me. It's just two big eyes with tears streaming out of them. I held the picture in front of me and said it was like looking in a mirror. Mr. Silver laughed. Aaron hummed the *Twilight Zone* theme, and Mrs. Silver cleared her throat and started doing a sketch of Aaron. I just looked at the picture and didn't know what else to say.

Mr. Silver got out a Trivial Pursuit game and dared Aaron and me to try to beat him. Mrs. Silver got in the act and started making chicken sounds at Aaron. Aaron groaned and said, "An exciting way to spend a Friday night." I hate Trivial Pursuit, but it was fun playing with the Silvers. He'd pretend to think real hard and then come out with the right answer at the last second. She'd argue with him over the littlest thing, like the capital of India, and then storm out of the room when it turned out he was right. I had fun watching them. They really like each other. Aaron was looking pretty irritated by them. He kept telling me not to encourage them. They knew practically all the answers, so they wiped us out.

When we were done playing, Aaron pulled out the note from Duff and showed it to his father. Mr. Silver read it and crumpled it up. Aaron asked him what he should do about it. "We're going to fight it," Mr. Silver said, and tossed the note into the fireplace.

I watched the note burn and couldn't believe it. If I ever brought anything like that home, there'd be hell to pay. Grandma would fix my wagon. I was gonna ask Mr. Silver what he was gonna do to fight it, but I heard Grandma honking for me from outside. I thanked them and took off.

When I got in the car Grandma gave me the third degree. She wanted to know if the Silvers tried teaching me any yiddish chants. I don't know what the hell "yiddish" means, so I said no.

This morning I can't stop looking at the picture Mrs. Silver drew of me. I kind of like it. I tacked it up on my bulletin board. Jeff saw it and asked me what the fuck it was supposed to be. "My soul," I told him. He made a farting sound with his tongue and dribbled his way out of the room.

4:45 P.M.

Mom and Grandma just got back from Riverbrook. They said Dad looks skinny but healthy. They went to one of the group sessions with him and he started crying and apologizing to Mom for all the shit he pulled. Mom said he hugged her in front of everybody and asked her to forgive him over and over. Mom didn't tell us what she said back to him. Didn't have to.

She wants Jeff and me to go with her when she goes again in two weeks so we can talk to Dad and his counselor. I said "OK" but Jeff said he'd have to see what he's got planned. Grandma shot him a look that made me feel cold all over. Jeff ignored her and started dialing the phone. Whoever he was ringing wasn't home because he hung up and left the room in a flash. I wish Marsha was around. She'd whip him into shape.

6:57 P.M.

Grandma just sent me out to find Jeff and call him home for supper. I found him and a bunch of his friends at the store. They were playing the machines in the back room. Jeff had his arm around Cindy Jones and kept nuzzling her ear. She was acting all coy and pretending like he was bothering her, but she didn't fight him off too hard. I walked in and told him supper was on. He snickered at me and said, "Then go home and eat it."

Cindy laughed like that was the funniest thing she ever heard. I told him Grandma was upset with him and Cindy opens her mouth real wide and goes, "Ooooooooooooooh, Jeff. Grammy's upset." Jeff laughed at her and then says to me, "Tell Grandma to keep a plate warm for me. I'll be home when I'm good and ready."

He turned away from me and stuck a quarter in the Zaxxon machine. Cindy draped her arm around his shoulder and started playing footsie with him. I hightailed it out of there. When I came back, Grandma cornered me and asked me where Jeff was. I gave her Jeff's message, word for word. She got up and left in a huff. She's still not back yet.

7:35 P.M.

Grandma just got back with Jeff. He stomped in and shut himself up in our bedroom. There was a BAD SCENE at the General Store. I heard Grandma telling Mom all about it. She said she walked in and found Jeff with his hands all over "that Jones girl." Jeff was real surprised to see Grandma there and cut the "touchy-feely game" short. Grandma told him that it was time for dinner and if he had any sense he'd go home with her before she took him by his ear. Some of Jeff's friends started laughing at her but she didn't care. Jeff tried to ignore her and play a game, but she screamed at him to move his butt before she went home and got her strap. She pointed toward the door and Jeff walked out.

Mom said, "You shouldn't have done that, Ma," but Grandma didn't care. She is soooooooooo mad. I feel kind of bad for Jeff. Even though he was acting like a jerk, Grandma didn't have to go and embarrass him like that. Whoops! Mom just went into the bedroom and shut the door. I can hear them talking now.

9:10 P.M.

Just went into the bedroom. I waited for Mom to come out. She was in there for about a half an hour, talking to Jeff. I heard the two of them talking softly. She came out and whispered, "It's OK" to me. I went in and Jeff was on his bed spinning his basketball on his finger. Climbed up on the top bunk and didn't say a word. I didn't think Jeff noticed me, so I coughed a couple of times to let him know I was in the room. It was quiet for the longest time and then Jeff says, "You ever feel like saying to hell with everything?" I said, "Every day of my life."

It was quiet for a couple more minutes, and then Jeff asked me if I'd leave the room for a while. He wanted to be alone. I said, "No problem." I was so surprised that he was nice about it. He usually just tells me what to do and then tells me he's gonna beat me up if I don't do it. But this time he asked.

I got up and started to leave. When I got to the door, Jeff said, "I miss her so much."

I said I missed her too and left the room fast.

▶ February 9

Went to church with Grandma today. She was real happy when she saw me up and ready to go. During the ride up Grandma told me we had to be patient with Jeff. He's going through a tough time now. I was gonna tell her that she didn't help him much by embarrassing him in front of his friends, but I didn't. We got to the church and found a seat near the back. I was glancing through the program when I looked up and saw Kimby Quinn heading in my direction. The next thing I knew she was sitting next to me. She said hi and I said hi back. We didn't have a chance to say anything else because the organ player started pounding through a song. First we sang a couple of songs with the choir. Kimby and me had to share a hymnal because there weren't enough for everybody. While we were singing I kept losing my place and she'd have to point out where we were. Kimby was so close to me that I could tell she smelled like lilacs.

We all had to join hands for the open prayer. When Kimby took my hand, my dick did a little jump. That surprised me. While everybody was holding hands and praying, I was sitting there looking down at my dick, trying to figure it out. It acts like it has a mind of its own these days. As I was thinking about it, it started wandering out of the leg hole in my briefs. I started praying to God that it wouldn't go hard on me. I didn't have to worry. It stayed soft. After what seemed like an hour, the prayer was over and I had my hands back. I kind of squirmed in my seat and my dick worked its way back into my briefs. It could have been BAD. Grandma poked me with her program and whispered at me to sit still. I was so relieved to have my dick back in place that I didn't move a muscle for the rest of the show.

After the service, when we were outside, Kimby told me

she's looking forward to the dance this Friday. I lied and said I was too. She smiled at me and walked over to her house. I watched her go and tried to picture what she looked like naked. I couldn't because she was wearing a big bulky coat and a scarf around her head. Decided that I didn't care.

10:45 P.M.

Jeff just woke me up and shoved a ring box under my nose. "Look at this," he said, and opened it up while I was still blinking my eyes from the light. When I could see again I saw that Jeff was holding a ring. "It's half a carat," he told me. I was still half asleep, so I asked him who it was for. He says, "Marsha, you asshole. I'm gonna ask her to marry me."

That woke me up fast.

Jeff spent all the money he earned working at the feed store on the ring. I listened to him go on about picking it out in Portland and tried to understand. He's gonna propose on Valentine's Day. He told me not to tell anybody. He wants to take Marsha by surprise. She'll be surprised all right. I hope Jeff isn't surprised when he hears her answer. He's taking a shower now. I can hear him talking to himself. He keeps laughing.

Jeff wants to get married? It's like something out of the Twilight Zone. What about Marsha and Harvard? What about Jeff and college? His timing sucks.

▶ February 10

The class read *Romeo and Juliet* out loud today. I got stuck reading Capulet's part. Lesly read Lady Capulet and made me laugh every time I had a line. She'd whisper in my ear, "Careful, Cappy, our girl's a woman now," and I'd crack up. Mrs. King scowled at us but didn't say anything. Mag read the Nurse part and she was good. I forgot that I was mad at her and turned around and smiled at her. She just looked at her book. I didn't understand the story at all when I was reading it. It was like Greek to me. But then Aaron started reading.

When Mrs. King asked for volunteers to read Romeo, Aaron's hand shot up in the air. Nobody else raised his hand, so she had to pick him. He was GOOD. When he was reading it, I understood what was going on for the first time. After a while, I closed my eyes and pretended he was saying the lines to me. Aaron's voice sounded gentle and nice. Theresa, who read the Juliet part, kept saying the words wrong because she was so nervous. She stopped after every few words and took a deep breath. I thought she was gonna start hyperventilating. It was funny to see her like that.

After class I told Aaron he did good. He said, "Thanks," and smiled at me. I got shivers down my back when he smiled. When I looked at his earring I liked it—for the first time. It's starting to look good on him. Didn't have a chance to say anything else to him because he got called to the principal's office right when study hall started. Wonder what's up?

7:38 P.M.

Aaron just called. He's been suspended for not going along with the "dress code." Duff huffed and puffed at him about rules and how everyone has to follow them. And then he gave Aaron one more chance to take the earring off. When Aaron refused, Duff called his mother to come and get him. Mr. and Mrs. Silver are both pissed about it.

Aaron seemed pretty pleased on the phone. I asked him what he was gonna do and he said his father and mother are gonna go to the school board meeting on Wednesday night and "fight the suspension." He says his father's writing a speech now, and his mother is making a tape of sound effects and music to play while he's giving it. Aaron's real excited about it. He says it's gonna be "drama on a grand scale." It sounds like it's gonna be cool. Wish there was some way I could go and see it.

▶ **February 11**

Everybody talked about Aaron's earring today. It was sort of comical. Somebody passed out pieces of paper that said, "STUDENTS—FIGHT CONFORMITY!!! Come to the school board meeting February 12 and show your support in the battle!" It went on to tell about what happened to Aaron and how it violated his rights. I don't know who had them printed up, but Duff was pissed out of his mind. I saw him rip one down from the wall and crumple it up. During lunch, Lesly asked me if I'd spoken with Aaron at all. I told her yes and about what his father and mother have got planned. Her eyes went wide and she said she "can't wait to see that." She asked me if I'm going and I told her I don't think so. Grandma would pop a cork if I did.

Mag's still acting like a jerk. Ralph went over to her new lunch table today and asked her if she wanted to go to his house tonight and watch videos. She sort of looked off into space, like she didn't understand what Ralph said, and then laughed at some joke one of the "Scuzzy Rejects" cracked. She didn't even give Ralph an answer.

Read *Romeo and Juliet* again today. Without Aaron there, it was pretty bad. Ralph read the Romeo part and messed up every other line. Even Theresa sounded good compared to him.

February 12

Grandma read me the riot act this morning. She told me that I couldn't go to the board meeting tonight. She'd heard bad things about the Silvers. They like to break rules just for the sake of breaking them. She said if I did go to the meeting, she'd have my head on a platter. I said, "OK" because I was sick of the sound of her voice. I kind of want to go. I'm dying to see what Aaron's folks have got cooked up.

Nothing much happened today in school. Miles had my study hall. I could hear him talking softly to Les Numer all during the class. I think they were talking about baseball season, which is coming up. Whatever. I don't care. I don't feel anything when I look at him now. It's like I'm seeing a statue. He tries to get me to answer questions in History class, but I pretend like I don't know the answers, so he leaves me alone now. It's been a couple of weeks since I've even brought my History book home to do the homework. When Miles asks to see my homework now, I give some smart answer like "We ran out of toilet paper last night, so

I had to use my homework paper." He doesn't think I'm so funny anymore. It doesn't matter. I don't even try to think of ways to get close to him. I'm afraid if I can smell him it'll start the hurt all over again. I don't need that.

8:30 P.M.

Just got back from the board meeting. Mom took me. She didn't have class tonight because it got called off. She asked me if the Aaron Silver she'd heard about was the same one I know. I said it was and that I was dying to go to the meeting. She told me to get my coat on because she was interested in the issue too. When Grandma asked us where we were going, Mom told her, "The school board meeting." I thought Grandma was gonna throw a fit, but she just made a disgusted face and said, "Suit yourself."

Mom wasn't paying any attention to her. She had her coat on and was out the door before Grandma could say anything else. I didn't stop to see what kind of face Grandma was making at that.

When we got to the school, there were a bunch of people sitting on the bleachers in the gym. The board and Duff were on the gym floor, huffing and puffing. Mr. Silver was just getting ready to give his speech. I couldn't see Aaron anywhere. Mom and me found seats up in the bleachers and waited to see what was gonna happen next. Duff nodded to Mr. Silver and he tore into his speech. It was all about how nonconformists established America, and how we shouldn't be afraid of people who stray from the crowd. We should try to get to know these people so we can understand them better, and accept them for what they are. Persecution shouldn't even be an option if these people have done no harm. Partway through the speech, the Star-Spangled Banner started playing. I looked over to the far side of the gym and saw Mrs. Silver standing beside a huge boom box. She saw me and waved.

Mr. Silver got real emotional when he heard the music. He pounded the podium with his fist and started talking about conformity being the first step toward Nazism. I snuck a peek at Mom and she looked confused. Everybody else in the bleachers looked angry. Or scared. Mr. Silver's speech ended the same time the music did. The cymbals were crashing together for the finale just as he said, "Thank you all very much."

Mrs. Silver started clapping loud when the speech was over. I was gonna join her, but everybody else in the bleachers stayed real quiet, so I didn't. Duff walked to the podium and told the board not to let these dramatics cloud the issue. He said that earrings on male students were in strict violation of the dress code. He said it was important that students be given "moral absolutes" early on so they'll have a "good foundation" to work with. If we let one student get away with breaking the code, then soon we'd have anarchy. He looked up at the bleachers and said, "Is that what you want?"

Everybody screamed, "No!" Mom stayed quiet. Some old fart on the board said that he did some checking up on the Silvers. He said they took part in antiwar protests in the early seventies and they probably "smoke dope" for all he knew. Everybody started getting real nasty after that, making hissing sounds and catcalls. Mr. Silver walked to the podium again and told everybody he'd continue to support Aaron's individualism. Then him and Mrs. Silver walked out of the gym. They didn't even bother to take their boom box with them.

Everybody was real quiet after they left. I heard somebody whisper, "Uppity kikes," under his breath, but nobody said anything out loud. Duff said the meeting was over and people started filing out of the gym. Mom was with them so I got up to follow her.

When we were driving back I asked her what she thought of the Silvers. She said they seemed nice, "but they ought to choose their battles a little more carefully." I didn't ask her what she meant by that.

▶ ## February 13

Aaron wore his earring to school again today. I met him coming off the bus. When we walked into the building, Duff was waiting with a detention slip. He saw Aaron and the earring, said, "That's a detention for you," and started filling out the slip. Aaron whispered to me, "Ball-less moron," and kept on walking. Duff finished filling out the slip and went back into his office.

When we read *Romeo and Juliet* in class today, Mrs. King didn't even look at Aaron when he volunteered to read the Romeo part. She picked Ralph again. Old Lady Song was real happy to see Aaron. She smiled at him and said, "*Bonjour encore.*" Aaron smiled but didn't say a word to her. He was quiet all day, except for lunch period, when Lesly pointed to his earring and told him to keep it up. He said, "Thanks," to her.

The funny thing is, none of the students seems to care a flying fuck about the earring. Sure, the jocks have always got some brainless thing to say about it, but nobody with a triple-digit IQ listens to them half the time. It's Duff who made a national stink about it.

BIG basketball game in Longford tonight. Everybody says it's the night Jeff is gonna make his thousand points. There was an announcement about it this morning on the PA system. Mom and Grandma and me are all driving over to see it. I asked Aaron if he was going and he said no. He's not feeling very much school spirit right now.

10:17 P.M.

Jeff made his thousandth point! It was great! He needed to make nine points tonight to reach it and he made fifteen! He couldn't miss the basket if he tried. There were about twenty people there from Tranten Township, so when he made his thousand-point basket, the game stopped and we all cheered like crazy. Since the game was in Longford, nobody else knew what was going on. Jeff stood there while the coach ran out on the court with a microphone and announced what just happened. A photographer came out and shot Jeff's picture for the paper. The Longford team looked pretty irked that the game had to be stopped just to put on this little show. They stood around sweating and frowning at Jeff.

When the game started again, the center from the other team shoved Jeff out of bounds when he was going for a jump shot. Any other day, Jeff would've floored him, but he just grinned while the ref kicked the creep out of the game. After the game, Mom, Grandma, and me ran over to Jeff as he was coming out of the locker room and congratulated him. Jeff was real excited until he saw someone behind us. All of a sudden he made a face like he was seeing a ghost. We all turned around to see what he was looking at.

It was Marsha.

She was standing by the bleachers, just looking at him. Jeff was standing by the locker room door, just looking at her. Neither one of them was saying a word. Grandma started to say something but Mom shushed her. The next thing I know, Jeff's walking real slow over to where Marsha's standing. She said something quiet to him. I heard him say, "What?" and then he bent over so he could hear her better. He smiled a little and said something back to her. I wanted to stay there and see what was gonna happen, but Mom said, "Let's go," and almost pushed me and Grandma out the door.

During the ride back, Grandma talked about how Marsha was a good influence on Jeff, and maybe now he'll get his life in order. I didn't say anything, but I agreed with her.

I wonder if this means they're back together. God, I hope so.

11:56 P.M.

Jeff just came in and woke me up with his singing. I thought he'd been drinking but it turned out he was happy. I asked him if him and Marsha are back together. He nodded and said, "Tomorrow's the day."

 ## February 14

Valentine's Day. Turned out to be kind of nice. Woke up this morning and found my picture on the front page of the sports section. I'm sitting up in the bleachers screaming my head off along with Mom and Grandma. The caption says, "Family of Jeffrey Smith." Above it was a picture of Jeff after he made his thousand points. Later Grandma cut out the pictures and stuck them up on the refrigerator. She said we weren't a bad-looking bunch.

When I got to school, Marsha corralled me in the hallway and said I had to go to the office and help pass out roses to the teachers. Every year the Student Council buys a bunch of roses and gives each teacher one. Kimby and me were in charge of the freshman homeroom teachers. She said she wanted to give Miles his rose. I wasn't about to argue with her. I watched from outside the room while she skittered in and handed it to him with a wink. He's probably gonna go home and give it to his wife, Smurfette. Thinking about that made me dizzy, so I went into the French room and gave Old Lady Song her rose. She was so happy she gave me a kiss on the cheek. It caught me way off guard, she did it so fast. Les Numer and Kuprekski, who're both in Old Lady Song's homeroom, started whistling at me. I got out of the room fast.

Asked Aaron if he was gonna go to the dance tonight. He said he wasn't, because he's got detention. He wore his earring again today and Duff nailed him with another detention. During lunch Mag was toting around this box of chocolates I figured Scott gave her. They look cheap—like something he'd pick out. I think I saw them on special in the General Store for $5. She was acting real cocky about them, though. She'd smile at nothing in particular and pop one in her mouth. I don't know her lately.

After school I stayed and helped decorate the gym. While Kimby and me were filling balloons with helium, Marsha walked in with a huge bouquet of roses. I asked her who they were from and she said, "Guess." Jeffie-poo I bet. She was on cloud 9 and too happy to command, so she told Dorian to take charge. After Marsha left, Dorian cracked the whip and started bossing us all around. She got wicked mad when Kimby spilled a bucket of water we were gonna dump into the huge potpourri pot we're using to make scents for

"Love Is in the Air." Kimby left in a huff and I followed her. We made plans to meet tonight at 7:30.

11:57 P.M.

Just got back from the dance. What a great night. Mag was there with Scott Pushard. I knew she wasn't expecting me to show up with Kimby. When Kimby and me walked into the gym together, I saw Mag looking at us over Scott's shoulder. Her mouth dropped open and her eyes bugged out. She was IN SHOCK. HA-HA-HA!!! She HATES Kimby. HA-HA-HA again!!! Served her right. I couldn't help smiling. I didn't see her again the rest of the night.

Kimby and me walked over to the food table and got some 7-Up. She started talking about her family's Christmas trip to Bermuda and how she got drunk on Tornadoes. She said the bartender at the resort they stayed at didn't card her at all. I looked at Kimby real close and decided that she could pass for older if she wanted to. She looked kind of pretty to me. We danced a few times. During the slow dances, Kimby put her head on my shoulder and hummed along with the music. Her voice was off-key. But nice-sounding. It felt kind of good to hold her like that. Didn't turn me on, but it was sweet-feeling.

All of the sudden, this stink started filling the room. Dorian snagged us and told us to check the potpourri pot. When we looked in the pot, we found a rotten tomato and a dead bat some jerk(s) had dropped in it. I tried to laugh about it, but it stinked so bad that I felt like puking. Dorian charged in and threw a fit. She was pissed. Kimby and me took the pot outside and dumped it. When we got back, everybody was heading out the door to get away from the stink. Dorian asked us to stay and help clean up the decorations, but we snuck out when she wasn't looking.

Neither of us had a ride so we started walking home. It's almost five miles, but the night was pretty warm and the time went fast because we talked the whole way. Kimby started going on about how she knows that she comes on strong sometimes, but that's just the way she is. She likes to

137

touch people and get close to them. She asked me if there was anything wrong with that and I told her it depends on the people she touches. Kimby asked me if I minded it. I thought about it for a long time and finally said, "No. I don't." Kimby said, "Good," and took my hand.

We walked along for a second holding hands and then Kimby says she's gonna tell me a secret and I had to promise not to tell anybody. I did. She got all serious and told me she had a huge crush on Miles Mariner. She was real upset when he got married over vacation, and she still hasn't gotten over it. I listened to her talk about how it felt like he betrayed her. I didn't say anything, because I was trying to figure out why Kimby was telling me this stuff. We've never been that close before, because Mag hates Kimby and vice versa. Then I thought, I don't have anything to hate Kimby for. She's always been nice to me. It was Mag who got in the way.

She stopped walking for a second and said, "Normally I wouldn't tell a guy these things, but you're a friend." She smiled at me and started walking again. I felt real strange all of a sudden. Like I could count on Kimby or something. I wanted to be closer to her, to tell her a secret too. But we were quiet the rest of the walk. Kimby kept sneaking peeks at me, like she was waiting for me to say something. I almost told her that I had the same feelings for Miles, but we were just crossing into Tranten Township and it didn't seem right.

We got to Kimby's house and she told me she had a nice time. Then she kissed me on the cheek. When she stopped, she didn't pull her face away at first. I could smell her breath. It smelled like mint. The next thing I knew, I was kissing her on the lips and my dick did a little jump. Kimby pulled away from me fast and had a funny look on her face. I asked her if something was wrong and she said, "No, you just caught me by surprise." Then she smiled and disappeared inside the house. I came home and Mom was up, reading some book. She asked how the dance was. I told her, "Nice," and I wasn't lying. She told me I looked like I was real happy.

I am happy. But sooooooooo confused at the same time.

1:56 A.M.

Jeff's still not back yet. I didn't see him or Marsha at all at the dance. Hope everything's going all right for him. Can't fall asleep. Can't stop thinking about Kimby. Still very confused.

3:18 A.M.

Jeff just came in. He's furious. Marsha said no to his marriage proposal. He wouldn't tell me anything else when I asked him. He cursed and slammed the bathroom door.

What's life gonna be like tomorrow?

 ## February 15

Jeff's been pretty quiet all day today. He hasn't even gotten out of his pajamas. He told Grandma and Mom that his stomach was upset and he wanted to be left alone. When I walked into our bedroom, he was sitting on his bed, looking at the ring he bought for Marsha. He kept opening and closing the jewelry box so it made a *snap* sound. I asked him how he was doing and he said, "Get lost."

7:42 P.M.

Marsha's here and things are back to normal at last. I was up on the top bunk hiding under my blankets when she first walked in the room. I came in the bedroom to get away from *Hee Haw*, which Grandma's got cranked up to full volume in the living room. Jeff was sleeping when I climbed up on the bunk, so he didn't know I was in here. Marsha didn't notice me either when she stormed in and sat down on the bed beside Jeff. She was wicked mad. She reamed him out for running out on her after she told him no. She said, "Just because you don't like how things are, you can't run away from a situation. You didn't even give me a chance to explain."

"OK, explain," Jeff said.

Marsha started going on about how much she loved him, but she couldn't marry him yet. She has to go off on her own for a while and find out who she is. All her life people expected great things from her, now she needs to go out and see if she wants greatness for herself. "And I'm not going to find out if I stay here," she said.

Jeff acted irritated with her, and said, "Am I supposed to wait for you?"

Marsha told him no, she wants him to go away and find out what he can be too. "Far away," she said. The farther the better. She wants him to get away from everything that's holding him back. Jeff could do great things if he wanted to, but he's never had anybody to encourage him.

Jeff's voice got all quivery and he said, "I've got you."

They both stopped talking after that. I think they were making out because I could hear heavy breathing going on. After a while, I heard the jewelry box open and Jeff saying, "Take it." Marsha told him she couldn't accept it yet. "The time isn't right."

Jeff said he was gonna hang on to it until the time is right. Marsha said she was hoping he would. They both laughed and then got up to leave the room. I didn't dare make a sound while all this was going on. If Jeff found out I heard him get all goosey, he'd beat the shit out of me.

After they left, I started feeling really jealous of Jeff. He may be dumber than a fence post sometimes. He may be a mean son of a bitch sometimes. But he's got someone who he's crazy about, and who's crazy about him back. It must be so nice.

February 16

Mom went to church with Grandma and me today. It was kind of fun. We sat together in the pew and Kimby came over and sat with us. Me and Kimby shared a hymnal again and held hands during the group prayer. When the service was over, Kimby walked with us to the car. When we were going by Les Numer and his folks, Kimby whispered in my ear, "He's as dumb as a horse but I love his chest." I didn't say a word about his chest, even though I was thinking the same thing. I was trying to figure out why Kimby would say something like that to me when she said goodbye and turned up the walkway of her house.

6:26 P.M.

Jeff and Marsha are in the kitchen filling out a college application for Snyder College in Ellis. Marsha came over early this afternoon with the application and told him that March 1 was the deadline to apply. If he wants any hope of getting accepted he'd better get his ass in gear. Jeff shook his head and hemmed and hawed for a while about sports scholarships. Marsha listened to him and kept quiet the whole time, and then she punched him on the arm and said, "Snap out of it." She said if no college scouts had approached Jeff yet, it didn't seem realistic that they were gonna start crawling out of the woodwork now that basketball season is almost over. I'm so happy that somebody finally had the guts to say that to Jeff. I'm even happier that he listened.

Jeff took the application from her and started filling it out. He's gonna apply the old-fashioned way. I just went in and they were talking about majors and what Jeff wants to study. Jeff has to write an essay about his "career goals." He tried to get Marsha to write it for him but she refused. She says it's time for him to start thinking about it. He can't dribble a basketball all the time and expect to get anywhere.

▶ February 17

Got into homeroom today and Aaron was real moody. He wore his earring again and Duff nailed him with another detention. He told me he didn't know what he should do. I told him he could try not wearing the earring, and he got mad. He said that would be letting Duff win. I said, "Who cares?" and he said, "Of course, you wouldn't care, Ben. You're too busy passing out roses to the teachers."

It didn't take me long to figure out that he was mad at me. He thinks I'm letting him down. I asked him what he wants me to do and he said, "Take a stand on something.

Don't be like everybody else." I told him I would if there was something I cared about, but there's nothing really to take a stand on around here. What's there to get excited about? Improving the food in the cafeteria?

Kimby sat at our table during lunch today. Ralph seemed real happy to have her there, but Lesly looked bugged about it. Aaron wasn't very happy, either. He'd wince like he was in pain every time Kimby said something. I'd be laughing at him and Kimby wouldn't have a clue. She'd keep saying, "What's so funny?" and make a face at me while I laughed. Aaron wouldn't laugh, either.

Mag wasn't in school today. I wish she was. I'd give anything to see that look on her face again.

▶ February 18

Walked into school today and there was a big guy holding a huge video camera with "Channel 4 News" written across the side standing in the entranceway. A tall lady reporter was standing in front of the school seal, speaking into her microphone about civil rights and Chappaqua High School. Someone told me they came all the way from Portland. I watched the lady drone on and then saw Aaron wander over, wearing his earring. She asked him questions about what was happening to him because of the earring and he told about all the detentions he got. I looked over and saw that the guy holding the camera had an earring too.

Right then, Duff charged out of his office and barked at all of us to get to our homerooms. We were all frozen. Aaron ignored him and kept on talking to the reporter. After Aaron got done talking, the reporter turned her microphone on Duff and started giving him the third degree. Duff asked her to please step in his office, which she did, with Aaron and the cameraman following her. Before he closed the door, Duff scowled at the rest of us and screamed, "HOMEROOMS! NOW!" It was funny. I didn't see Aaron again for the rest of the day.

The whole school had a morning assembly today so Jeff could get his thousand-points plaque. The reporter must've scrapped the earring story, because she was nosing around the assembly, telling the camera guy where to set up. Jeff acted real noble as the coach handed him the plaque and everybody cheered him. Marsha ran up to him afterward and hugged him hard.

There was a short little blip about the assembly tonight on the TV news. The sportscaster said something about "rural pomp and circumstances" or something like that, and then they showed about five seconds of the assembly. Nothing about Aaron's earring. Tried calling Aaron to find out what happened but nobody was home at his house.

▶ February 19

Kimby acted so strange today. She sat at our table again at lunch and kept sneaking peeks at me. In History class, while Miles was droning on about the American Revolution, I looked over at Kimby and saw that her eyes were right on me. She jumped when I looked at her, and then turned back to Miles real fast. After class she came up to me and asked if I wanted to go to her house and study tonight. I said, "Sure," and she left me alone the rest of the day.

Mag was in school today, but she wasn't looking at me. In English, Mrs. King told us to break up into pairs with the people closest to us and write a limerick about winter. Aaron wasn't in school today, so I turned around and asked Mag if she wanted to work with me. She acted like I wasn't even there. She opened her notebook and started doodling pictures of Snoopy. Taking the clue, I worked on a limerick by myself.

A few times I'd turn around and read to Mag what I'd done, but she didn't seem to notice me. She'd keep drawing her Snoopy figures and not look up. I returned the favor and didn't bother turning around to speak to her. Mrs. King came over and asked us why we weren't working in a pair. I was wicked pissed so I said, "Mag doesn't want to." Mrs. King saw the page full of Snoopy doodles and hearts and started giving Mag hell, saying maybe Mag wanted to go to Duff's

143

office and work on her limerick there. Mag said, "Not especially." Mrs. King said, "Then get to work."

The bell rang then, so we got up to leave. Mag walked by Mrs. King and me with a glare on her face. She must've skipped study hall, because I didn't see her the rest of the day.

> There once was a kind girl named Mag
> Who showed off her dates like a flag
> Till her ex–best friend Ben
> Took out his swift pen
> And wrote, "Mag, you've turned into a hag."

Whoops! Kimby's here! Gotta run . . .

8:57 P.M.

"You're gay, aren't you, Ben?" That's what Kimby asked me out of the blue tonight when we were studying the Battle of Bunker Hill.

I was speechless for about a minute and then I said, "Hell no! Why do you ask?" She told me it was little signals I gave out. She's been watching me for the last couple of weeks. What tipped her off was something I did the day I found out Miles got married. She said my face looked like somebody told me my best friend was dead. She saw the same face that night when she looked at herself in the mirror. Plus, I guess Mag's been telling people that I never made a pass at her. That got Kimby thinking.

"If you are, don't worry. I'd never tell anybody."

Right . . .

I tried acting indignant about it. I kept saying over and over, "Kimby, you're crazy," while she kept her nose stuck in her book without saying a word. When I stopped talking, Kimby laughed and said, "You doth protest too much." I asked her what the fuck that meant and she said, "Figure it out." I was shaking by this time, and couldn't hold a pen. I told her I had to leave and she said, "Don't go. It's OK." But I took off like a bat out of hell. Didn't even say goodbye

144

to her. Ran all the way home. I'm trying to forget what she said.

2:23 A.M.

Holy Christ! Why did I have to run out like that? Why didn't I stay and deny it some more? Could Kimby tell I was lying? What if she was baiting me? She's famous for stabbing people in the back. I trust her as far as I can throw her. She wanted some gossip to spread around the school tomorrow. Why did I have to get so worked up in front of her? I feel real sick all of a sudden.

▶ **February 20**

Kimby acted like it was a normal day today. I avoided her like the plague. Didn't go anywhere near her. Snuck a few peeks at her, to see if she looked different to me at all. Every time I took a quick look at her she looked the same as always. I didn't dare speak to her and she didn't seem to care. Aaron wasn't in school today and I was relieved. I haven't seen him since he went into Duff's office with the news reporter. I'm not complaining. I don't wanna give Kimby any fuel for gossip.

I skipped the Student Council meeting today. Couldn't face Kimby. It didn't work, though. When Kimby got on the bus going home after school, she sat beside me and filled me in on what they talked about at the meeting. She started going on about the Spring Fling Dance in April and how Dorian wants to get her brother's band to play at it. Marsha tried to veto the idea but Dorian said they were the only band around that charges under a hundred bucks for a gig. Marsha changed her mind pretty fast. Kimby started laughing when she told me. I listened to her babble away and felt like screaming at her, "What the fuck are you up to?"

8:30 P.M.

Just called Kimby. I couldn't take it anymore. We talked about stupid stuff for about five minutes and then I said, "Kimby, you were right."

"About what?"

"I'm gay."

LONG QUIET SPELL. Kimby was so quiet I was getting scared, so I said, "I really don't know what I am."

"It doesn't matter."

"You're not gonna tell anybody, are you?"

"Of course not. It's nobody's business but yours."

Another LONG QUIET SPELL while I tried to figure out if she was being sincere. Then Kimby said, "I'm glad you told me."

I bet she is . . .

I said, "Goodbye," and hung up real fast.

For some reason, I trust her. Probably because I don't have a choice. I feel real sick.

February 21

11:12 A.M.

Staying home sick from school today. I told Mom I felt like throwing up and she let me stay. Had nightmares about Kimby all last night. Is she spreading the gossip around school now? I can't think about it or else I really will throw up. Grandma came in and crammed a thermometer in my mouth. She told me I looked "peaked." I told her I feel awful, which is the honest truth.

3:36 P.M.

Kimby was just here. At first, she was real talkative. She told me everything that happened in school today. She said Aaron came to school wearing his earring and Duff didn't do a thing about it. I stayed calm all through that long news flash. Just nodded my head and tried to smile. I was gonna ask her if she told everybody at school I'm gay when she started chattering away about Ralph having another seizure. She said this one was worse than the last one. Everybody thought he was gonna die. She started going on about the ambulance and the paramedics when I couldn't take it anymore. I interrupted her in mid-monologue and said, "What about my secret."

"What secret?"

146

"You know."

She had to think about it for a second, and then she finally said, "The gay thing?"

"Yah."

"I'm not going to tell anybody. What do I have to do to prove it to you?"

I said, "Swear," and she made a face and swore that she wouldn't tell. She spoke with a funny voice that sounded like Olive Oyl. I frowned at her and told her I was serious. She got mad at me and called me selfish. She expected me to be concerned about Ralph and his seizure and here I was all uptight about her giving away my secret. "It's really no big deal in the grand scheme of things," she said. Maybe not to you, Kimby . . .

I didn't want to make her mad. I couldn't *afford* to make her mad. After a minute, I told her I agreed with her and I was sorry about being selfish. Then I made her swear again, just to be sure. This time she was serious, and she seemed sincere. No funny voices. It's so hard to tell with Kimby.

She brought the books and homework I'll need over vacation. Her family's flying down to Cancun tomorrow. I've been so preoccupied by everything that I forgot February vacation starts today. A week off from school. It's just in time. Feel much better . . .

6:48 P.M.

Grandma just came in and asked me how I felt. "Better," I said. She was pleased, because tomorrow's the day Jeff and me are supposed to go with Mom to Riverbrook to see Dad and his counselor. When she reminded me I started feeling sick all over again. What a shitty way to start a vacation.

 ## February 22

Went to Riverbrook with Mom and Jeff today. It turned out to be a home for mental people. All the boozers have got their own wing on the far end. Jeff kept saying all the way up, "I don't need this shit." He made a real funny face when we walked in the entranceway and heard some woman scream. I just wanted to get out of there. I looked at Jeff and could tell he was thinking the same thing.

Met Dad and his counselor, a Captain Kangaroo look-alike, in a spare room in the boozers wing. Captain Kangaroo said, "Hi," to Mom and then to us. Jeff and me didn't say anything. Dad told us we looked great. He looked pretty good too, but I wasn't about to say that to him. Dad said he was voted leader of the ward and then looked shy at us. Mom told him, "Congratulations." Jeff and me didn't say a word.

Captain Kangaroo started in about how it was important for families to communicate. He'd heard Mom's side of the story and now he wanted us to tell Dad how we felt about him when he drank. Jeff and me still didn't say a word. It was quiet for a long time. I was feeling real uncomfortable. Dad looked real uncomfortable. Like he wanted to be anywhere else but where he was. He said, "Come on, Jeff."

Hearing Dad say his name must've set Jeff off, because he EXPLODED. The words poured out of him. He went on about how he made a thousand points in basketball and Dad was nowhere around. He asked Marsha to marry him and Dad was nowhere around. Dad embarrassed him practically every day when he drank, and he was damn sick of it. Jeff stood up and screamed at Dad, "To hell with you!" Then he walked out of the room. Dad said, "Wait!" to him, but he kept right on walking. Dad turned to the wall and said, "I love you"—to the wall. Captain Kangaroo looked at me and said, "How do you feel about your dad, Ben?"

That threw me for a loop. Nobody ever asked me how I felt about anything before. It was just a fact that everything was fine and dandy with me. Dad makes the scenes, Dad acts like a jerk. Jeff makes more scenes, then he acts like a jerk too. I go on, day after day, acting like everything's swell.

"I don't know," I heard myself saying. And that was the honest truth. Dad sat up in his chair and said, "Come on, Ben. How about the time I showed up plastered at your thirteenth birthday party?"

It all came back to me. I invited a bunch of kids over. Mom made this big cake. We were listening to records in the living room when Dad waltzed in, drunk out of his mind. He screamed at me and Mom about the racket, and then he knocked the record player over. I wanted to die. Never asked any of those kids over again. Couldn't. Except for Mag.

"I hated you," I said. That was the honest truth too. Dad nodded, like he was expecting to hear that. Then Captain Kangaroo got all tender and said, "You've gotta tell your folks when you feel that way. Your Dad told me you never talked to him about any of it."

I don't know why, but that pissed me off. Like it was my fault I never dumped on Dad all the time like Jeff did. Like he couldn't figure it out himself that he made me mad when he got drunk. Mom got into the act then and said in a real shaky voice, "You have to tell me when you're angry about something. I'm here to listen to you when you need me." Mom looked at Captain Kangaroo and he nodded at her. She took a deep breath and seemed relieved.

I just shook my head and said, "No." I can picture what would happen if I ever let it all hang out with Mom. She'd start crying and act goosey. She can barely handle her own problems. She'd slip over the edge if she ever heard what I was feeling half the time. I can't imagine what would happen if I started blaming Dad. All of my worst nightmares would come true, not that they haven't already. They've both got enough problems of their own to deal with. They don't need me adding to the pile. Jeff gives them enough for both of us, anyway.

"I can't," I said, and got up to leave. I'd only been in the room a half an hour but I couldn't wait to get out of it. When I was walking out, Dad said to me, "I love you." That was the last thing I wanted to hear. Got out to the car and Jeff was already there. When I got in the backseat, he said to me, "That was the biggest crock of bullshit I ever heard." Didn't say anything, but I agreed with him. Looked up at Riverbrook and saw how the trees in front of the building looked bare and dead.

Mom came out after a while. She seemed mad at both of us, but she didn't say anything. Just got in the car and drove.

149

We rode the whole three hours back in a dead quiet. The only time we talked was when Mom pulled into the drive-up window at McDonald's and asked Jeff and me what we wanted. We both said, "Nothing," at the same time.

 ## February 23

Woke up this morning and couldn't make myself get out of bed. Didn't have the energy to do anything but think. And even that wore me out before too long. I couldn't stop, though.

I got thinking about what a shitty year it's been so far. First Miles goes and breaks my heart. Then Mag flew off the deep end. Then Aaron got mad at me. Then the "Kimby scare." Whenever I think about that one my stomach drops a foot. Then the meeting with Dad.

I feel so old. Like I went from fourteen to eighty in the middle of the night. Just like those trees in front of Riverbrook that die every year because of the cold. I wish I'd never seen them, because I can't get them out of my head.

When is life gonna get easier?

I want it all to stop for a while.

I want it all to stop forever . . .

I feel real tired today. Tired and sad. I'm ready for another happy day. Some fun for a change.

February 24

Woke up this morning and felt lost. Thought about calling Mag, but didn't think that would be too smart, considering the last couple of weeks. Thought about calling Ralph, to find out how he's doing after his fit. But decided I didn't want to hear any more bad news. I found myself dialing Aaron's number. When he answered I felt real strange, but good at the same time. He asked me where I was on Friday and I told him: "Sick as a dog." He said I missed his triumphant return to school. He went wearing his earring and Duff didn't make a peep. I asked him how that came about and he said he thinks the television reporter did the trick. She had originally come to do a story about Jeff's award assembly. When Aaron told her what was going on with him, she agreed to help him out and interview him and Duff. Aaron says Duff was sweating bullets in his office when the reporter grilled him. He got scared at the possibility of bad publicity, so he promised to drop the earring rule from the dress code. The news report never went on the air after that. I tried to sound happy for him when I said, "Congratulations," but it came out in a squeak. Aaron asked if there was anything wrong. I told him I was bored and he asked me over.

When I got there, he was all alone. His parents drove to Portland today. He was acting kind of cold toward me. I figured he was still mad about me passing out roses when I should've been helping him, but I didn't feel like dealing with that. He asked me how my weekend was and I told him about it all. Dad and Riverbrook, the affair with Carol, Mom working at McDonald's, everything. I didn't plan on saying anything about it when I was riding over, but it just started pouring out of me and I couldn't stop. I told him things I've never told anybody before. Not even Mag. Stuff about how I was afraid to invite people over to my house because I never knew when Dad would show up plastered and embarrass me. How Mom just stands by and watches whatever shit happens to hit the fan. How Jeff acts like such a jerk sometimes and I can't do anything about it. Aaron's eyes kept getting wider and wider as I told him about the meeting we had at Riverbrook on Saturday. I started breathing real fast and my voice got all squeaky, but I didn't stop.

He didn't say a word until I was done. Then he said, "Holy shit, is there anything else?" Was gonna tell him about my heart breaking over Miles, but that seemed like too much to dump on his lap, so I kept quiet about it. Just shook my head and said, "No."

He sat there and looked at me. It was making me uncomfortable, so I looked out the window. After a while, I asked him what I should do, because I didn't have a single answer. He thought for a second and said, "Fight it all you can. Let your Mom know when you're pissed. Put your brother in his place when he deserves it, and talk to your Dad man to man. Just don't be quiet about it. That can make you crazy."

I told him that I couldn't complain. Everybody's got their own problems and they don't need me adding to them. He said, "You can come here and tell me when it gets bad."

I felt good all of a sudden. Told Aaron I felt like laughing. Aaron stuck *Police Academy* in the VCR and we laughed all through it. Grandma was outside honking for me just when the movie was ending. Before I left, I asked Aaron to come over tomorrow. He said, "Sure," without even stopping to think. I really like him.

▶ **February 25**

Aaron came over today. It felt strange leading him up the stairway behind the gas station to get to our apartment, but he was cool about it. He didn't even bat an eye when Mom waltzed in wearing her McDonald's uniform. She seemed real surprised to see him and didn't know quite what to do. She mumbled something about Mr. and Mrs. Silver being nice and then rushed out. Grandma creeped in next. She gave Aaron the once-over and then asked him where his earring was. Aaron told her he wasn't wearing one today, and she said, "Came to your senses, huh?" Aaron laughed and Grandma left the room. He thought she was joking. I didn't tell him that she was dead serious.

We didn't have anything to do but watch TV, so we sat around and watched *Oprah Winfrey*. She was talking to a bunch of people who claimed they were abducted by UFO's. After listening to them carry on for an hour, I was feeling mad that the Martians didn't keep them on the spaceships. They'd be doing everybody on earth a big favor. After the show ended, we went outside to walk around Tranten Township. As we passed different houses, Aaron talked about how he wants to "shake the area up a little." I told him he already did with his earring. He said that was just "small potatoes." He wants to do something that'll get people thinking. I told him when he finds out what it is, I'd help him. That's what people need to do more of around here—think.

▶ ## February 27

Got a postcard from Kimby today. It's got a picture of some beach on it. Kimby wrote, "Having a ball! Love ya, Kimby," on the back. Stuck it up on my bulletin board. Saw Mag and Scott in the General Store when I went with Grandma to pick up some hot dogs. They started fighting about what kind of soda to buy. Mag wanted Coke and he wanted Pepsi. Scott kept saying, "Coke tastes like piss," and picking up the bottle of Pepsi in his grubby hands. Mag would pick up the Coke and say, "Coke is the one." I know for a fact that Mag doesn't give a hoot if she drinks Pepsi or Coke. She just wanted to cause a scene because she saw me in there. I was embarrassed for her. I'm so sick of her.

Got home and called Aaron. He asked me over tomorrow. He says he's got a surprise for me. I told him I couldn't wait. Jeff came in after I hung up. He hasn't been around much since the Saturday meeting. He spends most of his time at Marsha's house now. Or the gym. I felt lonely and bored, so I asked him how he was doing, to try and start a conversation. He said, "I can't complain," and walked out the door to shoot hoops at school. He didn't ask me if I wanted to go with him. It might've been nice.

▶ ## February 28

Went to Aaron's house today and he showed me the big surprise. I walked into his room and he shoved a piece of paper in my hand. Across the top was a letterhead that said: "THE SCREAMER." Below that was a story with the headline "Are Civil Rights Dead at Chappaqua High School?" I read the story and it was real interesting. It told about the basic rights that are being denied us by the school regulations. Stuff like illegal locker searches and the dress code. Below that was a cartoon with the headline "Duff's World." It was a pencil drawing of Duff sitting on the hopper, writing something down on a piece of toilet paper. The caption below it said, "Important Administrative Decision-making."

I laughed at the cartoon and gave the paper back to Aaron. He told me it's gonna be his way of shaking things up around here. Every week he's gonna write a piece about something that's wrong in the area, and pass out copies to kids at the school. "Duff's World" is gonna be the "comic relief." He asked me if I wanted to help him work on it. I thought it over long and hard. I could get into deep shit if anyone ever found out I worked on Aaron's "radical" newspaper.

"Sure," I heard myself saying, without really believing it. There's something about Aaron. I knew he wouldn't take no for an answer. He gave me the paper and told me to start thinking of stories for next week's issue. When he gave me the paper, our hands touched for a second. I felt a shiver go down my back.

I'm home now and real confused.

6:15 P.M.

Jeff just came in from taking his SAT's at Lipton. Asked him how he thinks he did and he said, "Don't ask," and ran into his bedroom. From the sound of his voice, I don't think he did very well.

▶ March 2

Went to church with Grandma today. Saw Kimby. She was all tan and healthy looking. She sat with her family today but waved to me when she came in. Reverend Silk's sermon was called "To Know God Is to Love Him." He says that God is merciful and just. He's got a dandy plan for each of us, but we've gotta turn to Him and be open to His Word. I listened to Reverend Silk talk and tried to make sense out of it. I thought about the Ethiopian people and wondered if God had a special plan for them. If He does, when is the damn thing gonna start? They didn't do anything and they're dying left and right. Does He even know it's happening?

During the free prayer, when I was supposed to be praying for the world to turn to God, I prayed for God to turn to the world and to take a good look at all the crap that's happening to people.

After the service, when I was waiting for Grandma in the

parking lot, Kimby trotted over and asked me how my vacation was. Told her it was "fine" and asked her about Cancun. She whispered in my ear that the guys were all "babes" down there. Then she palmed a picture into my hand. I looked at it and almost passed out. It was Kimby on the beach standing beside this bronze god who's wearing nothing but a thong. Kimby's grinning in the picture like a Cheshire cat, while the guy looks like he's trying to pass a kidney stone. "That's Pedro," Kimby told me. "He gave me mouth-to-mouth one day."

"You lucky girl," I said, and we both laughed.

7:36 P.M.

Went to the National Honor Society lasagna supper tonight with Mom and Marsha and Jeff. It was in the cafeteria at school. Marsha had to help out on the chow line, but she came over and ate with us after she was done. The lasagna was the same shit they serve for hot lunch, except tonight they got three bucks for it instead of seventy-five cents. While we were eating, Mrs. Duff came over and asked Jeff what his plans for the future were. Jeff told her he was waiting to hear from Snyder College. Mrs. Duff started hounding him about his major and he kept saying, "I'm not sure yet," and she'd say, "The final buzzer's sneaking up on you, ya know." Jeff looked like he wanted to cram his plate of lasagna in her face.

After the dinner, there was an awards ceremony. The Honor Society gave Mr. Taylor (guidance counselor) a silver plate for helping them out this year. Marsha had her picture taken for the paper handing Mr. Taylor the plate. She was scratching her nose when the flash went off. The picture's probably gonna make it look like she's picking her nose. Wonder if anybody else noticed that.

When we were riding back, Jeff was all mad at Mrs. Duff, saying it was none of her damn business what he's gonna study next year. Marsha told him it was a "valid" question and he better start thinking about it. She's gonna make an appointment for him with Mr. Taylor this week.

▶ # March 3

Walked into school today and there was a big pile of different-colored papers on the heater by the front door. Picked one of them up and it turned out to be *The Screamer*. Looked around and practically everybody else in the hall had a copy in their hands. Some kids read a few words of it and then crumpled it up, while some others made paper airplanes out of them. I wondered if any of them were thinking, like Aaron wanted them to do.

I went into homeroom and Aaron was looking smug. He said he saw Duff pick up a pile of them and dump them in the garbage can. When Duff walked away, Aaron ran to his locker and got another pile and stuck it in a different place. "Every student is going to have a copy by the end of the day," he said.

Every student may have a copy, but I don't think very many of them will actually read it. I didn't tell Aaron that, though. He was too happy. I found myself looking at his dimple and wondering what it felt like to touch it.

I've been thinking about an idea for an article about Crazy Patsy. Was gonna tell Aaron about it but he got called into Duff's office before I had a chance.

7:12 P.M.

Aaron just called. Duff gave him HELL about the paper. He told Aaron that he didn't want to see another copy of *The Screamer* again as long as he's principal of the school. The "Duff's World" cartoon really pissed him off. He said it was disrespectful and in bad taste. He gave Aaron three detentions and told him to get out of his office. Aaron seemed real happy. I asked him if he was gonna keep on doing *The Screamer* and he said, "Of course." I told him my story idea about Patsy. He thinks it sounds good. He wants me to do a rough draft tonight and show him tomorrow.

11:25 P.M.

Just got done with my story about Patsy. I tell all about how she lives, what she eats and wears, and how her only connection to the outside world is one lone woman

(Grandma). The title of the piece is "God Help This Woman."
I'm real proud of it.

▶ March 4

Aaron read my piece today during study hall and liked it.
He says it's "powerful." He wants to make it the feature
story in next week's issue. I'm gonna go over to his house
on Friday and help him type it up. When the final bell rang
and Aaron was on his way to detention, I walked with him
to the detention-room door, where Duff was standing guard.
Aaron saluted Duff with his left hand and marched in. Duff
scowled at me and slammed the door shut. Something tells
me that Aaron's in deep shit again.

Jeff just came in all excited. He says he's found what he
wants to major in at Snyder College. "Business is the thing
to study," he said. I listened to him ramble on about the
salaries CEO's make, and the great offices they get to work
in, and then I said, "Don't you have to read books and study
to be a Business major?"

Jeff thought I said it to hurt his feelings, but I was being
serious. He asked, "What's your point?" and I said, "The
only time I've seen you crack a book this year was for that
research paper you did on African Pygmies." He photocop-
ied a picture from *National Geographic* of naked midget
women dancing around a campfire and stuck it on the cover
of his report. Mrs. King had a shit fit.

Jeff got all mad at me and said, "So what?" For a second
I thought he was gonna wallop me, so I said, "Nothing.
You'll be a great CAO." "That's CEO," he snapped at me
and stamped out of the room. When I went in the living
room he was thumbing through a catalogue for Snyder College's business program.

Maybe I should've kept my mouth shut.

8:34 P.M.

Aaron just called. He said, "It's me," and I started feeling
warm all over. I asked him what happened in detention and
he said that Duff tried the soft approach today, asking quietly

about why couldn't they reach some kind of compromise? Aaron told him, "There are no compromises," and Duff sighed and said, "I give up." "He's trying to make me crack, but it won't work," Aaron said. I could picture the way Aaron's face looked when he said that and it made me feel good.

4:59 A.M.

Just dreamed about Aaron. He was lying next to me, sound asleep. He looked like he was waiting for something. I started running my fingers over his face. Touched his dimple, his nose, his cheeks, his forehead and chin. They felt just the way I imagined they'd feel. The next thing I knew, I was kissing his face all over. Trying to swallow it up. Couldn't get enough of it. Thought about diving into that dimple and never coming out. I ran my fingers through his hair.

I wanted more but Aaron wouldn't wake up for the whole dream. I kept saying, "Wake up, Aaron, wake up," but his eyes stayed shut. After a while, I shook his shoulders a little, but he still wouldn't open his eyes. I tried slapping his face but nothing worked. I started feeling all these eyes on me and I couldn't figure out whose they were. Mom's? Grandma's? Jeff's? Mr. Silver's? Mrs. Silver's? Suddenly I felt so ashamed of myself. Finally, I gave up trying to wake Aaron and forced myself to wake up instead.

Was it a dream or a nightmare?

▶ March 5

Ralph was acting lovey-dovey toward Lesly today and vice versa. It's sort of been building up all week. After Ralph had his last fit, his mother made him stay in the house for the whole February vacation, and Lesly went over to his house practically every day to check up on him. She brought him books and magazines and talked to him for hours on end. Lesly told me all about it today during lunch. In the beginning she did it because she "felt sorry" for Ralph, but after a while she found out she was looking forward to the visits. "He needed me there," she said. "And it was great to be needed."

This morning on the bus, Ralph gave her a book of love poems and asked her to "go" with him. She said yes. She showed it to me. I looked through it and saw the different places where Ralph underlined. Lesly whispered in my ear, "I've known Ralph for a long time and he never looked so good to me." I gave the book back and looked across the table at Aaron, who was scarfing down a banana and reading *Time* magazine. I knew how Lesly felt.

I saw Ralph in study hall. He told me everything that Lesly did for him, and how great it made him feel to know that he was someone special to her. Ralph seemed so confident. He hardly blew his nose, and he didn't make a single funny face all day. It's nice to see him like that. This afternoon when we were leaving the building, Ralph carried Lesly's books to the bus for her. It's good to see that he's over Mag. Wish I could say the same thing about myself.

▶ March 6

Now that Ralph and Lesly are a couple, Ralph's a whole new person. He actually wore a pair of jeans to school today. Last night Lesly called him and busted his balls about the chinos he always wears, so he dug out the jeans and wore them. Kimby told him he looked like "a stud" and asked me if I agreed. I wanted to whack her, but instead I just said he looked cool.

This afternoon when Aaron and me were at our lockers, Aaron's arm sort of brushed up against my shoulder. Twice. I looked at him and he acted like he didn't know it happened. I knew it happened. Aaron just shoved his books in his locker and asked me if anything was wrong. I said no and turned away fast. While I was shoving books into my locker, he asked, "Do you want to work on *The Screamer* at my house tonight?" I said, "Sure." (I was thinking, Yes! Yes! Yes! So happy that it's Friday and I can stay out late.)

His mother's gonna pick me up on her way home from getting Aaron after detention. Whoops! She's outside honking now. Gotta run.

Todd D. Brown

9:34 P.M.

I wanna die. I kissed Aaron tonight. Ran all the way home after I did it. It snowed hard the whole way but I didn't feel wet.

Feel soooooooooooooooooo sick.

10:18 P.M.

Aaron kissed me back. I've been thinking about what happened: Did Aaron kiss me back? We were working together at the computer. I was reading my story and Aaron was typing it. I got talking about Mag and how much I hate her lately. Aaron was shocked that I said the word "hate." He told me I should try and concentrate on more "positive emotions" than hate. His face was SO CLOSE to mine. I could smell his hair. It smelled like Brut. He looked at me for a second. And I looked at him. The next thing I knew, I was kissing him. On the lips. It could've lasted an hour or five seconds. I don't remember. I had my eyes closed. Aaron didn't try to push me away. At least I don't think he did. I'm trying to remember if he kissed me back or if it was just coming from my side. I HOPE he kissed me back.

11:24 P.M.

Shit . . . How could I have been so fucking stupid? Aaron was probably so surprised that I kissed him that he didn't think to push me away. I keep thinking I should call him to apologize. Just can't make my fingers dial the numbers.

▶ **March 7**

12:05 A.M.

Turned out the light but I couldn't sleep. Can't call Aaron. I think I'd die if I talked to him right now. Thought about calling Mag. She'd still be awake now. I even dialed her number, but hung up before it went through. Thought about calling Kimby, but her parents throw a fit if the phone rings after nine o'clock. Jeff's not home yet, so I can't talk to him. I couldn't talk to him, anyway. Can't talk to anybody about it.

I feel so alone . . .

160

5:56 A.M.

Aaron was just here. He must've walked the whole way from Nome. I couldn't sleep. I was lying in my bed looking up at the ceiling when I heard him calling real soft outside my window, "Ben? Ben?" "Who the fuck is that?" Jeff asked, half asleep. I told him to go back to sleep and then I walked to my window. There was Aaron looking up at me. He motioned for me to go around to the door and I did. I opened it and there he was, shivering at the top of the stairs. He was looking at me with an expression I couldn't read. "Hi," I said to him. He didn't say anything back to me. I didn't know what to do. I watched him for a minute and then whispered, "Now you know everything about me."

He nodded but still didn't say anything. He looked at me with that strange expression on his face. All of a sudden he was coming at me. I started backing away from him but I ended up backing right into the wall. He walked right up to me and stood there, breathing hard. In the dim light it looked like he was glaring. I closed my eyes because I thought he was gonna slug me.

The next thing I felt were his lips on mine.

Then I felt his arms around my waist.

They ran up my back to my head and back down again.

I reached up and held his ears in my hands.

Then my fingers started going through his hair, down his back.

Aaron made a whining sound.

I made a whining sound.

Then I heard bells.

Whistles.

Drums pounding.

Or it could've been my heart.

Then everything went black.

I felt the floor rise up on me real slow. When I opened my eyes again, Aaron was gone. Grandma was crouched over me, calling my name. I looked up and I was lying on the front hallway floor. The front door was swinging open in the breeze. Grandma started giving me the third degree. "What are you doing out here? Why's the door open? Do you wanna catch your death of a cold?"

I couldn't say anything. I was trying to rehash in my mind what just happened. Grandma slammed the door shut and kept firing the questions at me left and right. Jeff staggered out of our bedroom like a zombie and wanted to know what was going on. Grandma told him she didn't have any idea and ordered him back to bed. She helped me to my feet and walked me into the bedroom, telling me there'd be no more sleepwalking this morning.

I waited for her to leave and then got up out of bed and walked to the window. I wanted to be sure that I didn't just imagine it. I looked down at the parking lot outside my window and tried to focus on the ground. I got real excited. The clouds cleared away and the full moon was shining bright, and I could see them as clear as day.

Aaron's fresh sneaker prints there in the snow.

4:45 P.M.

Haven't heard from Aaron all day. Thought about calling him this morning but couldn't take the sound of his voice right then. Dialed his number a couple of times this afternoon but hung up before it went through. Dying to talk to him. Dying to know what's going through his head. Wish I could make sense out of what's going through mine. One second I'm happy about what happened. The next second I start feeling sick and wishing it never happened. Grandma's been looking at me with this worried expression all day. She thinks I'm going senile. She asked me if I feel OK and I said, "Yes . . . fine . . ." She didn't believe me, because she put her hand on my forehead. She tried to get me to take some aspirin because she said I was "burning up."

I am burning up. But not with a fever.

Jeff came into the room and told me, "You look like crap today."

Thanks. I feel a lot better.

Mom came in and asked if there was anything I wanted to talk about. She was there to "listen" to me. There are a million things I want to talk about. But not with her. With Aaron.

"No," I told her.

She sighed (with relief?) and left the room.

6:38 P.M.

Aaron just called and asked me over for the night tonight. He wants to show me the latest issue of *The Screamer* and "talk about things." I told him I'd be right over. His mother's on her way here to pick me up.

What the hell is gonna happen?

▶ ## March 8

Life is beautiful . . .

Just got back from Aaron's house. It started out bizarre but ended up being fun. I walked into Aaron's room and he was sitting at his desk reading some book. He saw me and acted like everything was normal. He handed me the latest issue of *The Screamer* and asked me what I thought. I pretended to read my story about Patsy but I was really watching Aaron out of the corner of my eye. It felt like he was watching me, but I didn't dare look directly at him. The room was SO QUIET. I was getting ready to scream when I heard Aaron say my name. I put the paper down and looked at him. He said, "About last night . . . and this morning." I nodded and eyed the floor. Aaron walked over to me and put his hand under my chin. "Why do you always look down at the floor?" he asked me. He held my chin up so I was looking right at him. I wanted to touch that dimple more than anything.

He must have been reading my mind, because he took my hand and brought it up to his face. He left it there and said, "It's OK." I started running my fingers over his face, feeling his nose, his lips, his eyebrows, his dimple. After a while, Aaron started doing the same thing to me. His fingers smelled so nice and clean. The next thing I knew, we were hugging. Our arms got sort of tangled up. Neither one of us knew what we were doing. But we worked it out. Mine went on the inside and his went on the outside. My whole body felt right. Not confused at all. Just tingly and nice.

We walked over to Aaron's bed and sat on the edge of it. Aaron started talking up a blue streak. He said that he's known ever since he was five. He had a crush on his best friend in kindergarten. They used to play cops and robbers on the playground. After this kid moved away, he decided to "shut off" his feelings and not get close to anybody. He had girlfriends all through junior high. Each one he had he hoped would spark some feeling in him, but they all left him feeling empty.

Aaron told me that he started loving me the day we were doing some dialogue in French class. We were pretending to be little kids eating spaghetti or something. He held my hand and didn't want to let go. He said it was like a flash of light inside him. I guess my dick wasn't the only one dancing at the time. His old feelings snapped on again when he let go. He couldn't stop thinking about me ever since. He was surprised when I kissed him on Friday night. Happy and surprised. Happy and surprised and relieved.

His father knocked on the door and said supper was ready. I asked Aaron if his parents knew and he said, "No . . . they'd freak." I was surprised. I can't imagine the Silvers freaking over anything. But it's none of my business, so I kept my mouth shut all through dinner, except to say please and thanks. So did Aaron. The Silvers asked us to play Trivial Pursuit after dinner but Aaron and me went back to his room and closed the door.

I didn't know what Aaron had planned. It turned out we just sat across from each other on his bed and talked all night. Talked and kissed. Talked and kissed and felt right. My body never felt so right before. Aaron started laughing when he told me what happened when he came over to my house last night. I passed out right in the middle of our kiss. He heard someone moving around in the next room, so he knew he'd better get out of there. He checked me quick to make sure I was still breathing regularly and then took off. He smirked and said that was the first time he ever made anybody pass out with a kiss. All of a sudden I wanted to get closer to him. I needed to get closer to him. Before I knew it I was sitting next to him and wrapping my arms around his waist. I didn't even think about doing it. It just happened—like snow falling out of the sky. I put my head on his shoulder and we sat there real quiet for a minute. The only sound I heard was my heart beating.

I could feel his shoulder going down under my head. Suddenly my arms were around his neck and we were lying on the bed. He was breathing slow and steady. He started stroking my arm with his fingertips. I thought about kissing him, but then I figured that being that close to him was enough. We were both quiet for a long time, and then Aaron said, "Good night." I thought he said it as a cue for me to get off his bed and into my sleeping bag. But he didn't move a muscle. Just sat there, running his hand back and forth real slow along my arm. I didn't feel like moving, so I stayed put. I had a feeling it's what Aaron had in mind, anyway.

I felt so safe. Like I'd just walked through a wild storm and finally made it to a shelter. I always figured the first time in bed with a guy, I'd touch like crazy. Explore every inch of his body. But I didn't need to. Right then there wasn't anything else I could've wanted but to have that safe feeling.

We fell asleep like that. When I woke up, Aaron was snoring up a storm and my arm was numb from being under his head all night. I hated to move but I had to take a leak real bad, so I pulled my arm out slow from under Aaron's head and climbed over him to get across the bed to the floor. My hand got all wet from the sheets when I did. Smelled my hand and knew right away what the wet was. I didn't know whether it was mine or his. Didn't care.

Ran into Mrs. Silver in the hall. She was singing some Italian opera song. She stopped shrieking for a second and said breakfast was ready. All the time I was eating breakfast with them, it felt like they were looking at me funny, like they knew what Aaron and me did last night. I was feeling guilty for a while. But then Aaron walked in. I tried to keep cool but my heart was doing back flips. I wonder if his was doing the same thing? He said good morning to us all and acted sleepy. The only way I could keep from exploding out of my seat was if I didn't look at him. I talked to Mr. Silver about dumb stuff like the Contras. After a while, I started sneaking peeks at Aaron. He was eating away, not saying a word. It seemed like he was mad about something, but I couldn't tell what.

Aaron's mood didn't last long. After breakfast Mr. Silver offered to drive me home. Aaron came with us. He and Mr. Silver talked about the Celtics and how Bird's gonna take them all the way this year. Aaron looked at me when he said, "You've gotta love Larry," and smiled. He whipped his head around before I had a chance to smile back. He asked his father something about Danny Ainge.

I got home and Grandma was just getting back from church. She took one look at my face and said, "That's the first real smile I've seen from you in a long time." I told her I had a great night. She didn't ask me any more. And I didn't say any more.

I'm just sitting in my room now, replaying everything that happened in the last twenty-four hours. It was better than a great night. It was the best night of my life.

6:56 P.M.

Aaron called this afternoon. He said he had a nice time last night. Told him I did too. He went on about how he felt real lucky to have me as a friend. Nobody ever said that to me before. All of a sudden, I started feeling lucky too.

Marsha was here when he called. I got off the phone and she asked who I was talking to. "A friend," I told her. Marsha nodded her head and smiled. Jeff came in and asked us what we were talking about. Marsha said real quiet, "I think Ben's in love."

Jeff went, "Wooooooowee, Benny boy! Who's the unlucky girl?" I said it was none of their business and ran out of the room. They both laughed at me. I should be pissed at them but I'm not.

▶ ## March 9

Aaron brought a bunch of copies of the latest issue of *The Screamer* to school today. My name was on this issue alongside his. I was real proud when I saw that every kid in school had a copy. That means that everybody who reads the paper is gonna learn about Patsy. Duff popped a cork again. He hauled both Aaron and me to his office and gave us a long lecture. We were hoping since we dropped "Duff's World" that he wouldn't get angry. We were wrong. Duff was pissed.

He told me he was "shocked" that my name was on the paper. He said the paper isn't a school-related activity, so it's against the rules to distribute it on campus. Duff asked us why we didn't write about basketball games and bake sales. If we want to change it so it's a more traditional school paper, fine. We can go ahead. But *The Screamer* has to go. He wanted us to sign a paper that said we promised never to publish it again. He shoved the paper in front of us and waved a pen in the air, first in front of Aaron, then in front of me. I didn't know what to do. I looked at Aaron, who was just sitting there with his hands on his lap.

Aaron said, "No."

I said, "No."

Duff gave us both detentions.

The day got worse. I caught hell from Mrs. King today because I blew off a book report I was supposed to write over the weekend. Actually, I blew off reading the book too. Didn't tell that to Mrs. King. Said it would be on her desk tomorrow.

Wuthering Heights. UGH!!! Read the first couple of chapters in study hall and almost fell asleep. Couldn't care less about Cathy and Heathcliff. Finally I decided to read every twentieth page. It went pretty quick doing it that way. I think I know enough about the story to write my book report.

9:47 P.M.

Jeff just came in carrying a crumpled up copy of *The Screamer*. He pinned it up on our bulletin board in front of my nose and asked me what it was supposed to be. "A thought provoker," I said. Jeff made a disgusted sound and told me nobody cares about "some old broad who eats dog food for breakfast." Everybody at school thinks the paper is "a joke." And "If Mom or Grandma find out you're writing stuff like this, your ass is grass."

"They won't find out about it," I told him, and I ripped it off the bulletin board and dumped it into the trash can. Jeff was quiet for a long time, and then out of the blue he asked me what was going on with me and "that earring kid." "We're friends," I told him.

Jeff made another disgusted sound and said, "You don't need friends like him."

I wanted to scream at him. As if he has any right to judge a friend of mine. Most of his friends are illiterate and can't speak in complete sentences. I didn't say anything. Kept my mouth shut and let Jeff dribble his ball while I worked on my *Wuthering Heights* book report.

▶ ## March 10

Aaron came over today after school. We had a close call and we had to talk about it. It was too close. It could've been horrible for both of us. I was coming out of a Student Council meeting and he was standing by the water fountain, taking a drink. Dorian was walking in front of me. She met her boyfriend Clyde and gave him a kiss on the cheek. They both took off down the hallway. I saw Aaron standing there and the first thing I thought of doing was kissing him. I don't know what in hell I was thinking about, but I walked right up to Aaron and started to put my hand on his shoulder. Aaron's eyes went wide and the next thing I felt was his foot tangling my feet out from under me. I hit the floor face first. It must've looked like I tripped, because I heard a few kids laughing at me. Kimby came up behind me and asked, "What happened?"

Aaron bent over me and gave my shoelaces a quick yank. "He tripped on his shoelaces," he said. I cursed and stood up. I scowled at Aaron and took off down the hall. Almost tripped on my shoelaces for real when I did. I was pissed at him. Kimby was right on my heels, asking me if I was OK. Didn't say anything to her except, "Yah," which was a lie.

"You've got to be more careful," Aaron told me tonight when he came over. He wasn't mad. He was just stating a fact. I agreed with him. Was gonna tell him the story of Dion Hatch to show him I understood why I had to be careful. But then I thought, Aaron probably already knows a Dion Hatch story. He probably knows dozens of them. We both talked and decided we wouldn't touch each other at all where other people could see us. And we're not gonna be seen together so much for a few weeks. It's gonna be tough. But it's safer that way.

Aaron stayed for a little while tonight. Nobody was around, so the apartment was real quiet. We sat beside each other on the top bunk and just talked. About everything. School, parents, you name it. It's funny. I wanted to do more with him. I had a feeling he did too. But I didn't want him to think I'm pushy, so I kept my hands polite. I was also afraid Grandma would barge in waving a cross at us and damn us both to hell.

▶ March 12

Kimby, Aaron, and me worked on an experiment together today in Earth Science class. We had to dissect a perch and label different body organs. While Aaron picked around for the stomach, Kimby flirted with him and really ticked me off. She did the old pick-the-lint-off-the-sweater trick with him again and again. I wanted to pop her one. When it was her turn to find the perch heart, she made her "little-girl-lost" face and asked Aaron if he'd help her. He said, "Why? You're not helpless."

He made Kimby find her own heart. She pouted the whole time. I could tell she wasn't really bugged, though. She kept tossing coy grins in Aaron's direction. After a while, I got sick of her and helped her look. She kept her eyes on Aaron's ass. When we were walking out of class, Aaron said to Kimby, "You would make Phyllis Shlaffy so proud." Kimby asked me who Phyllis Shlaffy is. I told her I didn't know but that I didn't think Aaron meant it as a compliment. Kimby didn't care. She smiled at me and huffed in my ear, "I think I'm in love." I didn't dare get mad at her. She's kept my secret so far. I'm not gonna do anything to tick her off.

On the bus ride home, Kimby asked me if Aaron has a girlfriend. I thought fast and said, "Yes. Her name is Connie and she lives in Boston." Kimby said, "Uh-huh," and looked all hot and bothered out her window. I'm not too worried about her. She's been going with Bert Dane for about a month now. He'll keep her busy for at least another couple of months. Hopefully she'll forget about Aaron in the meantime.

▶ March 13

Mr. Mariner gave me hell today. I was supposed to make up a list of questions about Archduke Ferdinand and Sarajevo and ask them in front of the class but I forgot. Actually I remembered, but I got busy last night talking on the phone with Aaron. He called up all excited about next week's *Screamer*. He wants the feature story to be about the TV ministry craze. Aaron's already got the focus of the article figured out. A couple of weeks ago he met a man from Lipton who lost a leg to cancer. When the man first heard he had cancer, he sent Timmy Will fifty dollars a week to pray for his cancerous leg. The weeks went by, the leg got worse, and Timmy never mentioned the man's name during any of his TV shows. When the leg finally had to be amputated, the man wanted to sue Timmy Will for negligence. Aaron says it's "a real American tragedy." We ended up talking and talking, until I looked up at the clock and saw that it was almost ten. Grandma charged over and barked at me to get off the phone and go to bed.

Miles—Mr. Mariner—didn't want to hear anything about that. He had his heart set on Archduke Ferdinand. I told him in front of everybody that I "just forgot" about the assignment and he blew up at me, saying it was a lame excuse and that I was full of lame excuses lately. He wants a 500-word paper on Ferdinand next Monday.

What did I ever see in him?

When he was done yelling at me about the paper, I almost asked him, "Bad night with your wife last night?" But I didn't. I was too mad. Aaron walked with me out of the class and said, "Who put the bug up his ass?"

"Smurfette," I told him.

While I was sitting in detention I tried writing about Ferdinand, but every time I opened the book my eyes glued themselves shut so I couldn't read it. I couldn't take my eyes off Aaron, anyway. He was sitting across the room from me, writing his story for *The Screamer*. He was easier to study than Ferdinand any day.

10:57 P.M.

"Do you believe in God?" That's what Aaron asked me tonight when we were working on *The Screamer*.

I told him I did. I didn't even think about it. Aaron could've asked me if geese flew south for the winter. It's just something I never bothered to think about before. God is up there in heaven as sure as I breathe. Aaron didn't say anything. He just started typing on his computer. I was getting ants in my pants, so I asked him if he believed in God. He told me, "I used to . . . but not anymore."

That threw me for a loop. I was waiting for a lightning bolt to crash through the window and zap him. I never heard anybody say flat out that they don't believe in God. "Why not?" I asked him.

He got going on this jag about all the suffering in the world and how God must pick out his favorites early on, because it's always the same people who end up landing on their feet, and the same people who end up getting the shaft. I was gonna tell him I was wondering the same thing when he asked me, "Why do you believe?"

I didn't know what to say at first. Nobody ever asked me that before. Finally I told him, "Because I never wanted to believe anything else." That was the honest truth. Aaron said to me, "You know, you can't walk through your life accepting everything people tell you. Nine times out of ten, they're going to be wrong."

That made me a little mad, so I asked him if believing in God is wrong. Aaron said, "No. But believing in God just because it's convenient, or because it's been pounded into your head since the day you were born—that's wrong." Then he said I've gotta go out and find what I know is true. Make up my own mind for a change.

He looked like he was mad all of the sudden. He asked me why I didn't sign Duff's paper saying I wouldn't write for *The Screamer* anymore. I said, "Because you didn't."

That got Aaron really mad. He said that doing what other people do is no way to make decisions in life. I've gotta decide what's important to me and stick with it. I can't sit on the fence and jump from one side to the other whenever the spirit moves me.

"Show me how," I said.

He said it's something I've gotta learn on my own. He shut off his computer and looked at me a long time. I couldn't tell what he was thinking. I wanted to kiss him so bad. Didn't think he'd appreciate it, though. I heard Grandma honking the horn outside, so I got up to leave. As I was walking out the door Aaron said he'd call me tomorrow.

Was quiet all the way home. Thought about what Aaron said. Decided he's right.

 ## March 14

Went to Aaron's house today. Had a good time. When we were riding over, Mom asked me, "What are you gonna do at his house all day long?" Told her, "Homework mostly." That was a lie, but it was a lot easier than telling her the truth.

It's kind of strange with Aaron and me. Neither one of us knows what the rules are. We don't have anybody to copy, so we make it up as we go along. Whatever feels right, we do. Actually, what we do mostly is talk. Built a model airplane this morning and talked about when we were little kids. Aaron told me about growing up in a nudist colony.

When he was four, a social worker pulled him away from his parents because she figured he must be getting abused in such a place. I told him about growing up in Tranten Township and how Dad used to beat me with his bamboo cane. No social worker ever knocked on our door.

Read magazines this afternoon and talked about what they said. In an issue of *Time* there was a letter some guy named Bill T. Walsh wrote about gays causing the end of the human race because they don't reproduce. Bill was terrified that everybody on the planet would suddenly decide to "turn gay," and then where will we be? The human race will die out. Asked Aaron what he thought about that and he said, "It's bullshit. There are enough straight people in the world to guarantee at least ten more generations on the planet . . . if the earth lasts that long." Aaron says there are more important things to worry about than everybody on the planet suddenly turning gay. "Like the homeless . . . and what Nancy Reagan spends on White House china."

Watched TV tonight and talked about what was on. We got watching the spokesmodel competition on *Star Search*. The contestants were a blonde named Bambi Lynne and a brunette named Jasmine Findley. Asked Aaron which one was his favorite. He was quiet for a long time, just watching those two prance around in swimsuits. Finally he looked at me and said, "Ed McMahon."

I laughed and threw a pillow at him. It must've taken him by surprise because he fell off the bed. I laughed at him and asked if he was all right. He jumped up from the floor and landed on top of me and started kissing me up and down my face. I couldn't stop laughing until he got to my lips and stayed there. My whole body turned on like a 1,000-watt light bulb. Could feel my dick going hard. Could feel his too. Aaron stopped kissing and took a deep breath. I worked my face into his dimple and started kissing his neck. Felt him breathing real hard in my hair. It felt like dynamite was going off between us, but instead of blasting us apart, it was making us crash together. Again and again. We kissed and kissed and kissed. Each other's cheeks. Noses. Foreheads. All the stuff that built up over the week exploded in ten minutes. One mini-explosion after another. BANG! BANG! BANG! Mrs. Silver walked by Aaron's door singing. Aaron heard her voice and jumped a foot. I jumped too. Then I felt my dick shrivel up and play dead.

Aaron and me moved to different sides of the bed and pretended like it never happened. I felt sooooooo guilty. Guilty and mad at the same time.

We didn't talk much the rest of the time I was there. We watched TV. It was easier than looking at each other. Mom came and picked me up at eight.

"What did you do all day?" she asked me.

"Homework mostly," I told her.

7:15 P.M.

Just saw Scott and Mag in front of the gas station. They were filling up Scott's car with gas. Scott was holding the nozzle, and Mag was standing in back of him, with her arms around his waist, holding her hands over Scott's. When Scott got done, Mag moved her hands up to his chest and kissed the back of his neck. I almost puked when I saw it. I ducked from the window quick.

▶ ## March 15

9:54 A.M.

Aaron asked me over again today. Told him I couldn't come. Dad's coming home from Riverbrook tonight and Grandma wants Jeff and me to stick around the house today and get it ready. She shoved a feather duster in my hand and told Jeff to start scrubbing the kitchen floor. She keeps tearing through the living room with the vacuum cleaner going at full throttle. Asked her why we had to clean everything and she says we've gotta show Dad how well we got along without him.

4:56 P.M.

Mom just brought Dad back from Riverbrook. I expected Mom to be happy as a clam, but she seemed kind of bugged about something. Dad looks slim and healthy. He asked me if there was anything I wanted to get off my chest now that he's home. Was so happy about Aaron that I didn't care. "Welcome back," I heard myself saying. Dad's walking around the apartment now, looking at everything. He says it's the first time in a long time he's seen it with "sober eyes."

I think we're all scared, Mom most of all. The last couple of months she's thought about how her new-old "scrapbook life" is gonna be. I look at Dad and try to see the same man who's in the pictures in her scrapbook, but it doesn't work. Those pictures were a different time. Different people. I wonder if Mom found that out tonight during their ride back.

March 16

Met Aaron in the school parking lot this morning. He was passing out *Screamers* to kids getting off the bus. I grabbed a stack from him and handed them out to the kids from Tranten Township. Tried to give Jeff a copy but he shoved it back into my hands and said, "Keep that damn thing out of my sight." Duff hauled us into his office during homeroom and told us we both had detentions again. He said that if we openly defied him again, he was gonna take "drastic measures." When we were walking back to class, I asked Aaron what kind of drastic measures Duff was talking about. Aaron said, "He's probably going to make us take hot lunch for a month." I laughed, even though I didn't think it was funny.

Came home right after school and Dad was sanding down the coffee table. Refinishing furniture was one of the things he learned at Riverbrook. He's real quiet except when the sander goes on, and then he sings some song about "smiling Irish eyes" or something like that. He seems to be happy. Haven't really spoken to him since he got back. Haven't decided whether it's a good thing or not. Dad acts like he was never away. He made himself right at home again.

Don't care. Got Aaron now. Everything's good.

▶ ## March 17

Woke up this morning and Dad made a speech for us all. It was about broken promises and how he needed all of our help if he was gonna make it the next few weeks. We're a "team," he said, and he's gonna be the captain. Jeff and me looked at each other and made faces. The speech sounded like something that Dad's been rehearsing the last couple of weeks. He did a great acting job, though. Grandma even got up and kissed him. She said she'd be here for him when he needs her.

Mom was real quiet through the whole thing. She didn't even nod when Dad said he was gonna be the "captain." She looked sort of angry about it.

9:30 P.M.

Bad fight tonight. Mom and Dad. Mom got back from working the afternoon shift at McDonald's and Dad started giving her the third degree. He wanted to know how many nights a week Mom worked there, and what her take-home pay was. Mom told him "Five shifts a week, $3.45 an hour." Dad said, "$3.45 an hour? That's shit." Dad wasn't saying it to be mean. He was just stating a fact. $3.45 an hour *is* shit. For Mom. Or anybody.

But Mom didn't hear it like that. She got wicked pissed. I've never seen her so mad. She told Dad, "It may be shit, but it kept this family going when you were gone. And it's mine." She whipped her coat off and flung it on the table in front of him. Dad looked scared. I probably did too. He said, "Hey, cool down. I didn't mean it like that." Mom asked him, "Do you want me to quit?" But she wasn't asking. It was almost like a dare. Like she was saying, "I dare you to try and make me."

I just sat there and watched her. I was IN SHOCK. She started going on about night school, and did he want her to quit that too? Did he want her to stay home all day and cook his meals like "the old days." When she said "the old days," the words came out of her mouth like a glob of spit.

By this time, Dad got pissed. "HELL NO!" he screamed.

"Work your butt off for diddly-squat. I don't care. It's your life."

Mom said, "That's right," and stomped out of the room.

We were both quiet for a couple of seconds, then Dad looked at me and said, "What the hell was that?"

I told him I didn't have any idea.

10:26 P.M.

Can't sleep. Dad's in the kitchen making a racket sanding the supper table. Mom's in the bedroom. Not making a peep. Jeff just came in and doesn't have a clue what just happened. He's all excited because a couple of his friends heard from Snyder College and they're getting heavy-duty financial aid. Marsha told him that was a "good sign." I listened to him babble away about Pell Grants and GSL's, but wasn't really paying attention. Jeff didn't even seem to hear the sander going in the kitchen.

▶ March 18

Got home tonight and Dad had rearranged the furniture in the living room. He said the room needed "spiffing up." He asked me how I liked it and I said it was great. Mom just came home and seemed bugged about it. Dad asked her how she liked it and she said, "Have you ever heard the saying, 'If it ain't broke, don't fix it'?" Then she left the room. Dad shook his head and slumped down on the couch. I felt a little bad for him. At least he's trying to make it work. Mom seems hell-bent on fighting with him. What's she thinking of?

Dad just went to the store to pick up some chips. Right after he left, this dame named Edith called and left a message to remind him about the AA meeting on Friday night. What the hell is AA? Gonna ask him when he comes back.

▶ March 19

Aaron and me figured out next week's feature story for *The Screamer*. Aaron wanted it to be something controversial. We thought for a long time today during lunch and then

Aaron had a great idea. The article's gonna be about the lack of sex education at Chappaqua High School. We're gonna work on it tomorrow night when I go over to his house.

Grandma's all upset tonight. Crazy Patsy's gonna be moved into the "Sunny Meadows Home for the Aged" in Lipton this weekend. Reverend Silk pulled some strings with his brother-in-law, who knows the chief of admitting. Grandma's not sure how it's gonna work out. Patsy will have to share a room with another old lady. "Patsy doesn't like to share anything," Grandma says. I told her it couldn't be any worse than the way she's living now and Grandma said, "Sure it could. Patsy's happy now. Who knows how she'll be in that morgue."

▶ March 20

Came home tonight and Mom and Dad were having an argument about AA. (I found out that it means "Alcoholics Anonymous" today from Aaron.) Mom kept saying over and over that Dad had to go to the meeting. It's part of his treatment. Dad didn't want to go to the meeting. He said, "It would be letting everybody know I'm an alcoholic." I don't know what he's so worried about. Everybody in town knows about Riverbrook. He told Mom he'd go to AA next week, when stuff is "less crazy" in his head. Mom said, "OK," real quiet, like she knew she was making a mistake.

Dad said there's a bingo game in Lipton tonight. He told Mom to get her bag while he warmed up the car. Mom did. She asked me if I wanted to go with them and I told her no. I'm going to Aaron's house tonight to work on *The Screamer* and hopefully do some other things.

11:45 P.M.

Just got back from Aaron's house. Except for kissing a couple of times, we didn't do anything but work on the paper. It wasn't as much fun, but the time flew by like it always does when I'm with him. The mood didn't seem right tonight. Aaron was tired and I couldn't stop thinking about

Dad. Oh well ... There's plenty of time tomorrow to get close.

Our article about sex education is great. It starts out with a question: "Do your parents talk to you about sex? If they do, you're lucky." It goes on to tell about how few parents really do talk to their kids about it. Aaron asked me if mine ever did. I told him no. The only thing I remember about a sex talk is once last year before Dad took off with Carol. We were chopping wood and he got talking about a "man's responsibility" once he gets a woman pregnant. I didn't even know how a woman got pregnant until Jeff told me last summer. The school nurse did give a sex talk last January. She even told about condoms. But some parents got wicked mad about it and made the PTA put a stop to it.

Aaron says Sex Ed. should be a mandatory course. After thinking about it for a while, I agreed with him. It seems like there's always some girl in school who gets ready to drop a calf. This year it's a sophomore from Nome named Angie. Angie's single and already has one baby. The father of her first baby was this old guy named Rufus. Angie told everybody he raped her one night when she was coming home from a youth group meeting. Rufus denied it, and told everybody he was sterile. He said he'd prove it to anyone who didn't believe him. Everybody believed him. The rape charges were never filed, and Angie had a cross-eyed baby girl by immaculate conception. Her parents kicked her out of the house after the baby came, so she went to live with her grandmother.

These days Angie's big again and ready to have her second baby. The father of this one is Kent, one of Jeff's friends. I heard Kent tell Jeff all about it. Angie got drunk at a party last summer and Kent drove her home. When they got to her house, Angie took off her bikini top and refused to get out of the car until Kent showed her his thing. Kent asked her if she was on the pill and Angie said, "What's the pill?" After Kent explained the pill to her, Angie told him they wouldn't need it. It wasn't her "time to get PG."

Kent kept saying over and over, "The bitch wanted it. She

wanted it." I couldn't tell whether he was happy or upset. Until I heard Jeff and him cracking up. Now Angie's as big as a houseboat, and Kent's gonna be a daddy. He's not cracking up these days. He offered to pay for an abortion, but Angie's grandmother wouldn't allow it. She thinks if Angie has another kid, she can get more AFDC.

I feel kind of bad for Angie. I see her sometimes in the store. Every time I see her she looks older. And fatter. It's scary. She looks like she's about fifty years old and she's only fifteen.

I asked Aaron if he ever saw Angie around town, and he said, "Yah . . . What's her story?"

I told him all about Rufus and Kent and Angie's grandmother. Aaron shook his head when I got done and said, "It's tragic what straight people do to each other."

▶ March 21

11:30 A.M.

Came to the table for breakfast this morning and Mom and Grandma were having a deep discussion about Dad. Mom was saying things like, "I can't just let him take over again." And Grandma was saying, "He's the man of the house, you know."

Mom was all upset because last night Dad told her he'd be in charge of seeing that the bills got paid from now on. He wants her to deposit her paycheck into his checking account. Mom told him it was "her money" and he told her it was "their money."

Mom wanted to scream, "For how long?" at him. She wants to know how long he'll be on the wagon. How long he'll be living with us. How long he wants to be in charge. She doesn't dare ask him because she's afraid he'll get upset and start boozing and fooling around on her again. "It's like I'm living with a time bomb," Mom said.

Grandma kept her mouth shut while Mom carried on. When Mom finally stopped to take a breath, Grandma said, "When he left you for that cow, I told you, 'Divorce him.'

When he came back drunk as a skunk, I told you, 'Divorce him.' When he was hitting you, hitting the boys, and spending all your money on booze, I told you, 'Divorce him.' Now he's back and sober. He loves you and wants to take care of you. Your old problems are gone. I'm telling you to give him another chance."

Mom didn't say anything. She just sat puffing away on a cigarette. Grandma stood up and said, "You probably won't listen to me now, either," and then she left the room.

Mom said, "I don't know what I want anymore." Not to me, to the air. I was gonna ask her if she looked in the old scrapbook lately just as Dad walked in and told us we were going for a drive today. He wanted to spend some time together as a family. I got up and left the room. Nobody asked me what I thought, anyway. I don't care what they do. I'm going to Aaron's house today.

6:30 P.M.

Just got back from our "family outing." Dad made me go. I told him I already had plans but he said this was more important. When I called Aaron and told him I couldn't come over today, he said, "Shit!" I knew what he was thinking. No touching today. I wanted to swear too, but Grandma was sitting in the room reading *Guideposts*.

The family outing turned out to be soooooooo boring. We drove along dirt roads and looked at scenery like Dad wanted to do. During the whole ride, Jeff looked out his window and said, "This sucks," real quiet. Nobody heard him but me. He had to cancel a date with Marsha, so I knew he felt the same way I did.

Dad kept saying, "It's great to be free," over and over. Mom asked him if he'd called his AA sponsor back. He shook his head and said, "Later . . . later . . ." He kept grabbing her hand and holding it up to his cheek. She kept pulling her hand away from him.

Dad said, "How about McDonald's for lunch?" Mom said no, she wanted Burger King. Dad said, "Big Macs, Whoppers—what's the difference?" Mom said he'd know if he worked at McDonald's all the time. Dad stopped at McD's anyway. When he asked Mom what she wanted, she told him, "Nothing." He ordered her a Big Mac, but she wouldn't touch it.

▶ ## March 22

Grandma and me went to see Crazy Patsy today after church. It's not going well for her. She's sharing a room with an old lady named Ruby who stays in bed all day and sleeps. Ruby must be in real bad shape because she doesn't even get up to go to the bathroom. She's hooked up to a tube and she just pees whenever she feels like it. It was so gross. Ruby just lies there, out like a light, while her pee comes full-throttle through her tube and into a plastic container at the bottom of the bed.

Patsy hates Ruby. She says Ruby's mean and steals her food. I looked at Ruby and couldn't imagine her having the strength to stand up, much less steal anything of Patsy's. Patsy's convinced that Ruby's got it in for her, though.

A nurse brought in Patsy's lunch while we were there. I hated her the second I saw her. She called Patsy "Honey" and told her to eat all her food "like a good girl." It was like she thought Patsy was three years old or something.

Patsy seemed real quiet today. Quiet for her, anyway. Grandma told me after we left that they give her drugs to calm her down. When Patsy arrived on Friday night, she tried to run away twice during the night. They'll take her off the drugs as soon as she "settles in."

6:35 P.M.

Dad just came in holding two bowling-team shirts. He entered him and Mom in the Lipton Bowler's League as a pairs team. Mom asked him, "Why bowling?" and he said so they could start working together as a team again. Give and take. Support each other. Every Saturday night all the pairs in the league get together at the bowling alley and compete against each other. They hand out trophies and "have a blast," Dad said.

Mom didn't say anything at first. She just stood there, looking at the ugly pink shirt Dad gave her. It had "Lucher's Hardware" written on the back. Suddenly, she tossed the shirt in his face and said, "Why didn't you ask me before you went and entered me?" Then she left the room.

Dad went after her. They're screaming at each other now. Mom keeps saying, "You never ask me nothing!" and Dad keeps saying, "I don't have to! You're my wife!"

Whoops! One of them just cranked the radio up. Can't hear anything but Waylon Jennings. Something tells me they won't be bowling anytime soon.

▶ March 23

Aaron and me caught hell again today for *The Screamer*. When we were passing them out in the parking lot, Duff hauled both of us into his office and gave us detentions. He skimmed the article about Sex Ed. and said this time we'd gone too far. His next step was gonna be to notify our parents about it. I got scared but Aaron was cool as a cucumber. He called Duff a fascist. Duff told us to get out.

When we were walking back to class, Aaron told me the only way Duff can nail us is if he can prove our grades are suffering. Aaron gets all A's, so he's not worried. He asked me if my grades were good and I nodded.

During lunch, I tried to figure out if *The Screamer* was worth all the trouble. None of the kids looked any different to me. None of them seemed to be thinking about anything except getting in line and playing with their hot lunch. I don't think most of them even read the Sex Ed. story.

Came home tonight and got scared to death every time the phone rang. I thought it was Duff calling Mom and Dad, telling on me. But it never was. The first couple of times it was Marsha for Jeff. The third time it was Dad's AA sponsor. Dad told me to tell her he wasn't home.

▶ March 24

The shit hit the fan today. During homeroom, I got called to Duff's office. I almost died when I walked in. Mom and Dad were sitting in there. Mom looked nervous. Dad looked pissed. Duff had copies of *The Screamer* on his desk, and he had his constipated face on. I didn't have to ask what was going on. I knew.

Duff told me to sit down and then he went on this jag about how I was failing in my schoolwork because of my participation in "non-school-related" activities. He had a note from Mr. Mariner/Bastard, saying that lately my grades were unsatisfactory. I wanted to scream at him about the real reason I was flunking History, but he was talking so steady I couldn't get a word in if I tried.

Duff gave Mom and Dad copies of *The Screamer* and asked them if they were aware of the paper. Dad pretended to read it but I knew he couldn't read that quick. Mom didn't even pretend. She had her eyes glued on me. She had a strange look on. It was like her face was asking me, "You too?"

Duff sent me home with them. When we pulled into the driveway, Dad turned around and said, "You're grounded for a month. You come straight home after school. No more of this shit." He crumpled up *The Screamer* and tossed it at my face quick so it bounced off my forehead. I felt like throwing it back at him, but I knew there'd be hell to pay if I did. Instead, I looked at Mom, waiting for her to say something. She turned out to be just as bad as Dad. No. Worse . . .

She fixed her eyes on the dashboard. She said, "I don't want you going to that Silver boy's house anymore." She was out of the car before I could say anything. Dad told me to go to my room and not come out until suppertime. Then I figured it out. The two of them found something better than bowling that they could team up on: punishing me.

I keep pinching myself to try and wake myself up, but it's no use. Dad's been home for less than two weeks and already my worst nightmare has come true.

8:38 P.M.

Jeff just came in looking happy as a pig in shit. "Benny boy, you really did it this time," he said. Mom and Dad are in their bedroom talking softly. They keep laughing about something.

▶ ## March 25

Saw Aaron first thing during homeroom today. He came right over and asked, "What happened?" real quiet. Told him I'm in deep shit. Told him I couldn't come over to his house anymore. And I couldn't work on *The Screamer*. He looked like somebody just told him he had a day to live. He said, "We'll think of a way."

I thought he was talking about *The Screamer*, so I told him there was no way I could work on it anymore. My parents mean business. He shook his head. It turned out he wasn't talking about *The Screamer*. He said he's giving up on it. It's pointless to keep printing it up. He found that out when he went into the men's room yesterday and found a stack of them where the toilet paper should've been. "We're offering real ideas to apathetic clones," he said. He was quiet for a long time, and then he whispered, "We'll think of a way to see each other." Then he said he could live without *The Screamer* but he couldn't live without me.

I didn't know what to say to that. I felt like I was floating and falling at the same time. I got scared and couldn't look at him. Then kids started pouring into homeroom and we couldn't say any more. I was relieved. Aaron went back to his seat and didn't talk much the rest of the day. He was too busy thinking.

Walked into history class and I wanted to slug Mr. Mariner. But he acted like everything was A-OK so I would've felt dumb. He came up to me after class and said he was sorry he wrote the note to Duff but I hadn't given him any other choice. He put his hand on my shoulder and told me he'd help make up a study program for me so I could get my grade back up.

A few months ago my heart would've jumped out of my chest if he made an offer like that to me. But not today. Not anymore.

"No thanks," I told him, and walked out.

▶ ## March 26

Aaron, Kimby, and me worked together today in French class. We had to write a conversation between three people

185

and perform it for the class. Kimby was all upset because she suffered her fifth broken heart of the year last night. Bert Dane told her to take a hike when she asked him to go steady. Kimby kept saying, "I really liked the guy." I pretended to listen to her whine, but I was too busy watching Aaron out of the corner of my eye. He was doing the same thing. I know because he put his hand on my knee a couple of times and gave it a squeeze. I squeezed his thigh back, and I could feel his dick jump.

Kimby talked away while Aaron and me felt each other up under the table. She was so wrapped up in her own problems with Bert that she never figured out what we were doing. All we had to do was say, "Uh-huh," to her and she'd talk away. Aaron and me were saying more to each other under the table than we were to Kimby. But we weren't talking to each other. We weren't even looking at each other half the time.

Old Lady Song came around and told us to get cracking on our conversation. Kimby had the idea of setting it in a restaurant. She and Aaron would be eating dinner and I'd be the waiter. When we got up to perform it, Kimby hammed it up, acting snobby and sending her food back. I made everybody in the class laugh when I made a disgusted face and mimed shooting Kimby in the back of the head. She didn't have a clue.

8:16 P.M.

Grandma just came in and gave me a long talk this evening. She thinks Aaron "was" a bad influence on me. She doesn't know why I don't hang around with the old Tranten Township gang anymore. They're "such nice boys." I listened to her babble away about how Les Numer goes to church every Sunday and always sits right in between his parents. Sometimes he even helps pass the collection plate. I was gonna tell her about some of the things that Les does when he's not in church but I didn't.

Grandma doesn't know about *The Screamer*. Mom told Dad and Jeff not to breathe a word about it to her. As far as

Grandma's concerned, I'm flunking history because I goofed off "with that Silver boy too much." Mom knows that Grandma would pee in her pants if she ever read *The Screamer*. I keep thinking I should've saved a few copies of it to show to Grandma. A good pee in the pants once in a while never hurt anybody.

March 27

Something real strange happened between Les Numer and Kuprekski this afternoon on the bus. I guess Les figured since he couldn't beat Kuprekski up anymore he might as well ask him to join him. He grabbed a junior high kid's notebook on the bus and screamed, "Hey, Kuprekski!"

Kuprekski turned around and Les threw the notebook at him. At first I thought Les was aiming it at his head, but the notebook came in for a landing on Kuprekski's lap. Kuprekski sat there holding the notebook in his lap. He was in shock. Then he smiled. He must've been real happy to get some attention from Les that didn't involve physical pain and embarrassment. He tossed the notebook back to Les and the junior high shrimp squawked again.

Pretty soon the notebook was sailing across the aisle, back and forth between Les and Kuprekski. They were both laughing like crazy. The junior high shrimp was blubbering. The bus got to Les's stop and he got up to leave. He handed the notebook to Kuprekski and they high-fived each other. It was so strange. When the bus got to Kuprekski's shack, he tossed the notebook at the back of the junior high shrimp's head and got off the bus, laughing like an idiot. I've never seen Kuprekski so happy before. It was scary.

Les and Kuprekski are bad enough when they're alone. I can't imagine the hell they're gonna raise together. The next time Grandma asks me why I don't hang around with them anymore I'm gonna tell her the truth: I can do better than that.

9:17 P.M.

Friday night and I'm stuck at home. Mom and Dad are at bingo. Dad passed on AA again. Mom made him promise he'd go next week. Jeff went with Marsha to her parents' silver wedding anniversary party. Married for twenty-five years. Shit. How can they still stand each other? I can't imagine living with anybody for twenty-five years. Not Aaron. Nobody. Grandma went with a church group to hear Timmy Will preach in Augusta. He's doing a special nationwide fund-raising campaign to bring a bunch of starving people from Ethiopia over to America. Grandma says usually she wouldn't feel right about helping "colored people," but if Reverend Timmy says it's OK, then it must be blessed in the eyes of God.

I wonder what Aaron's doing tonight.

I can't stop thinking about him. The way his dimple feels when I touch it with my lips. The smell of his hair. His arms. The way his eyes go all squinty when he's thinking hard. Or when he's just angry. It's funny. Everything about him turns me on now. Even the things I used to think were weird. An hour goes by and all I've done is think about him. It's a nice way to pass the time.

▶ March 28

Bad fight today. Jeff and me. I don't know what brought it on. All this anger has been building up in me all week and I guess I had to let it out. It didn't start out like anything special. Jeff came into the bathroom and told me to get out. He needed to use it to get ready for a date. I said no and kept brushing my teeth. He said, "Why are you being such an ass about it? You're not going anywhere tonight." I told him he was the one who was being the ass, and then I picked up a can of shaving cream and shot some in his face.

This made Jeff MAD. He bent over to pick me up and I shoved him into the wall. He shot to his feet and started punching me, saying, "You think you're so goddamn smart." Every time Jeff punched me, I punched him back. My punch seemed to take away the hurt of his punch. Sometimes I'd punch him back twice and then I'd be ahead of him on the pain. It was like I was on cruise control.

Jeff didn't look surprised that I was hitting him back. He

looked like murder. His eyes were flaring and his breathing was heavy. The next thing I knew, I was on the floor and I didn't have any idea how I got there. He was on top of my back and trying to get me in a headlock. I drove my elbow into his stomach and listened to him gasp. I think Grandma came in then because I heard someone shriek, "Boys!!! Stop it!!!" I couldn't see anything but the rug my face was buried in.

The next thing I felt was Jeff flying up off from me, like he was a rocket taking off. I rolled over and saw Jeff, Grandma, Mom, and Dad looking down at me. One of Jeff's eyes was swollen shut and his cheeks were all red. Dad was pissed. "What the hell is going on?" he screamed at us.

"I just asked him if I could use the bathroom," Jeff said.

"Bullshit," I said back.

"I want this crap to stop here and now," Dad said.

Jeff said, "Fine," and ran out of the apartment. Dad told me to stay in my room and not come out for supper. Grandma and Mom both looked at me with hate in their eyes. Went into the bathroom to look at my face. It doesn't look as bad as Jeff's. That made me feel good.

▶ March 29

Went to church with Grandma today. Dad wasn't gonna let me go, but Grandma told him it would do me good to get some God in my system. I didn't really want to go. But it was either go to church or sit around the apartment all day. It's getting tougher and tougher to sit through the services now. I keep thinking about what Aaron asked me: Why do I believe in God? I still don't know the answer.

It seems like God means different things to different people. For some people, He's like a teacher you've got in detention. They don't dare make Him mad. They walk around on tiptoes all day, afraid to say anything bad. So they end up *thinking* the bad. To other people, God's like a fuel. You can see them filling up on their God every Sunday, singing the hymns, praying like crazy, hoping that they've got enough God in their system to last them a week. To other people,

God's like doing jail time. They sit in church from 9:00 to 10:15. If the sermon runs over, they get up and leave. They've given their hour and fifteen minutes to God for the week. Now they just wanna be left alone. To other people, God's a miracle worker, tossing down good things on the earth like they're Tootsie Rolls. Someone's cancer gets cured, it's "God's work," they say. A baby gets born healthy, it's "God's work," they say. Three thousand people get killed in an earthquake, it's "God's wish," they say.

I don't know what God is to me. All of the above? None of the above?

We went to see Patsy after the service. She didn't say a word to us. She was in her bed, out like a light the whole time. The nurse told us she tried to escape again on Friday night so they had to sedate her. I looked from Patsy over to Ruby, who was making whining noises but wouldn't open her eyes. Ruby's pee bag was full. I noticed today Patsy had a pee bag too.

9:18 P.M.

Jeff just came in. He's still pissed about the fight. He said if I ever crossed him again I'd know what it feels like to eat the floor. I told him, "No problem." He expected me to be scared of him, but I wasn't. I was sick of him instead.

 ## March 30

I felt like strangling Kimby today. Ever since she broke up with Bert, she's set her sights on Aaron. She came up to him today in lunch and asked him if he'd like to pose for a yearbook picture (Kimby's a yearbook photographer). Aaron said, "Sure." Then Kimby handed me her camera and asked me if I'd take the picture, and she sat her pointy little ass down beside Aaron, grinning like a fool. It was all a trick to have her picture taken with him.

Later on, Kimby and me had to go to the supply closet for Mrs. King to pick up a few reams of paper. I was gonna tell her to keep her mitts away from Aaron, but I was afraid I might make her mad, and suspicious. She doesn't have any idea what's going on between Aaron and me. Nobody does. Kimby was too busy talking about Bert for me to say anything. She's still upset about the breakup. When we got to the supply closet, Kimby walked in and sighed like she was in agony. Asked her what was wrong and she said, "Bert and I used to come in here and make out during lunch."

I looked around the supply closet and decided it was the perfect size for making out. Think I'll tell Aaron about it tomorrow.

▶ ## April 1

Terrific time today. Aaron and me went to the supply closet during lunch. It was easy enough. I asked the teacher on duty in the cafeteria for a pass to go to the bathroom. On my way to the bathroom I cut through the boys' locker room, went through the gym and then into the supply closet. A few minutes later, Aaron did the same thing and I met him in there. Kimby told me how it worked. As far as she knows, nobody else knows about it. She said she had to be careful not to be gone for more than ten minutes, and she and Bert never came back to the cafeteria together. Nobody caught us. Nobody was suspicious. We acted like we were there to pick up art supplies until we were sure nobody was there.

We turned the light out and kissed and felt each other the whole five minutes. Aaron's body felt different in the dark. It was like I was feeling it for the first time. The way his back curves and the muscles in his shoulders turned me on today. I never noticed them before. We didn't say much to each other. Didn't have to.

The whole time we were doing it, I had a feeling that somebody would come in at any second. That should've scared me to death, but it only made it funner.

▶ ## April 2

"People are starting to talk about you and that earring kid," Jeff told me today after school. I asked him, "Who? And what were they saying?" Jeff wouldn't tell me. He just said that if Dad finds out I'm hanging around with Aaron

I'll get the crap beat out of me. "Remember the bamboo?" he asked me.

I told him Dad wouldn't find out, and Jeff said, "That's what you said about that half-assed newspaper you were writing for." Then he smiled at me. Now I can't stop thinking about the bamboo cane and the bruises it left. Got scared.

▶ April 3

Ate lunch at the table with Aaron, Ralph, and Lesly today. It was the same as it usually is, except I could feel Jeff's eyes on me. I looked over at him and saw that he was watching me with a poker face. I nodded to him and tried to look cool. He turned away quick. I got up and moved to the other side of the table from Aaron. He asked me why I moved and I whispered at him, "My brother's watching me," real quiet so Ralph and Lesly couldn't hear. I shouldn't have worried. Ralph and Lesly were going at it hot and heavy, anyway. Ralph bought Lesly lunch today. She thanked him by spoon-feeding him pudding. She smeared some on his nose as a joke, so he smeared some on her cheek. They both laughed.

They're so happy lately it makes me sick to see them.

For some reason, seeing Ralph happy makes me mad. Today I found myself hoping he'd have another fit. I felt real guilty after I thought it, though, and I tried to laugh along with them, like I thought they were funny. Aaron didn't even try. He said to them, "Don't you two have anything better to do with your time?" and then he left to dump his tray.

"What's with him?" Lesly asked me. I told her I didn't know, even though I did. Aaron came back and didn't say anything the rest of the time. The bell rang and Ralph and Lesly grabbed each other's hands and walked out together. Aaron and me grabbed the air and walked out five feet apart.

▶ April 4

It's Friday night and I'm stuck at home with nothing to do. Today was hell. Didn't talk to Aaron all day. Didn't dare. It seemed like Jeff was everywhere I looked. He was slinking around the halls this morning when Aaron came up to me in homeroom and asked me how I was doing. I gave him a look that said, "Leave me alone." Aaron started to ask me something. I turned away from him and acted like I couldn't hear him. When I turned back around he was sitting in his seat. Couldn't tell whether he was mad, upset, or *anything*. His face just went blank, like he wasn't thinking about anything at all.

Can't think about that. I've got ten chapters of History to read this weekend. Mr. Mariner made me a list of things to do to raise my grade. I've decided to do them. Repeating History with him would be the end of me.

10:26 P.M.

Just found a note from Aaron stuck in my History book. He must've stuck it in during study hall when I went to the bathroom. It says, "What's going on with you? Do you want to break up? Write me and tell me what's going on. I can't accept not knowing." It isn't signed or anything. I can tell it's from Aaron, even if he did try to disguise his writing. Also the way it smells—like soap—makes me think of him.

Miss him. Miss him bad . . .

11:48 P.M.

Just got done writing my letter back to Aaron. Told him everything that's going on. How my brother's getting suspicious, and how I don't know if he's gonna tell Dad on me or not. How I didn't know what Dad would do if he found out. Told him no, I don't want to break up with him. We're just gonna have to lay low for a while—lower than we have been, if that's possible. I ended the letter by telling him he was the most important person in my life right now. It hit me while I was writing it that Aaron's the reason why I get up in the morning. It made me feel happy and blue at the same time.

Gotta figure out a way to get the letter to Aaron. He's gotta know how I feel, now that I do myself.

▶ ## April 5

Another "Smith Family Day" for the history books. Mom and Dad fought again. Dad told Mom he went to AA last night, but Mom found out that he spent the evening at bingo again. She got wicked mad at him and told him AA was for his own good. Dad tried to change the subject by telling a joke about state road crews. Mom and Grandma both made sour faces. Jeff just sat munching his corn flakes. He wasn't listening at all. I laughed, not because I thought the joke was funny, but because it might've made them stop being mad at each other. Didn't work. They all looked at me like I didn't have the right to crack a smile. I've been quiet ever since.

Tonight the three of them went to a baked bean supper at the church. Didn't ask me if I wanted to come. That was fine with me. It's awful being cooped up in a room with gassy old people.

Before they left, they told Jeff that I wasn't supposed to leave the apartment for any reason. Jeff didn't care. The second they were gone, he was telling me, "Have a ball" and zipping out the door. I was seriously thinking about walking to Nome and talking to Aaron in person. Then I thought if they ever caught me, I wouldn't be able to sit for a year. Decided to mail the letter. Stole a stamp from Grandma's desk and trucked over to the mailbox down the street. As I was dropping the letter in, I thought I might just keep going down the street. Leave everything behind, think about myself for a change. Then I thought about Aaron. It would kill me to leave and never see him again. Before I knew it, my feet were walking back to the Texaco station.

▶ April 6

Bad fight today. Grandma and me. We were riding to church and Grandma started giving me a lecture about obeying my elders. I guess one of her "church friends" showed her a copy of *The Screamer* (she called it "that *Streamer* paper"). She said it was the most disgusting thing she'd ever read in her life. I didn't ask her which issue she read. Then she said, "Aren't you ashamed for all the grief you put your parents through?"

It was all I could do to keep from screaming at her.

She started going on about the "Ten Commandments" and

how they say it's a sin not to honor your mother and father. I was mad by this time, so I said, "How can you believe the Ten Commandments? For all you know, they were chiseled out by some guy who thought he was playing a joke on mankind."

I heard Aaron say that a couple of months ago in French class. I hadn't planned on repeating it. Especially not in front of Grandma. But I was mad. Grandma was madder. She stopped the car and told me she'd never heard such blasphemy and I'd better pray to God for forgiveness when I got to church. I couldn't let that slide.

"What God?" I asked. It was the first time I ever said I had doubts. I wanted Grandma to prove to me that there was a God. I asked her, "Why do you believe in God?"

Grandma looked at me like I'd slapped her. Her lower lip started quivering. She said to me, real cold and direct, "Because I want to go to heaven." Then she started driving again. She didn't say a word the rest of the way. There was a lot I wanted to ask her. And there was tons of stuff I wanted to say about Timmy Will. But I had a feeling talking to Grandma then would've been like talking to a wall. When we got to church, Grandma told me not to bother to go in. I sat out in the car and watched people go by. Saw Kimby, but didn't feel like talking to her.

When the church service was over and Grandma got back, she said, "Your mother and father are right to keep you away from that Silver boy." She wouldn't say anything else. She wouldn't even let me go in to see Crazy Patsy with her when we stopped at the nursing home on the way back. She wanted me to sit in the car and think about what I'd said. When she came out and I asked her how Patsy was, she told me, "Comfortable."

 ## April 7

Didn't talk to Aaron all day. He wouldn't look my way, so I couldn't give him the "A-OK" look I practiced last night. The look that would've told him "We're still on." He avoided me all day long like he was mad at me. Maybe he is. It hurts to think that, but there wasn't a damn thing I could do about it. Aaron and me acted like we didn't even know each other were in the room. It was safer. Hopefully he'll get my letter in the mail tonight. Then he'll know what's going on. Then the bad feelings will go away. I hope . . .

Nobody seemed to notice that we weren't talking to each other. Life went on as usual. Kimby and me worked together in History today. We had to draw a map of Europe. She's all excited about the Spring Fling Dance this Friday. I skipped the last few Student Council meetings, so I don't know what they've got planned. Kimby asked me if I had a date yet. I told her that I'm grounded. "Too bad," she said. She doesn't have a date yet, either. I'm kind of relieved that I have an excuse not to go. Dancing with Kimby is the last thing I wanna do right now.

She was scaring me. She kept finding all these excuses to walk by Aaron's desk. First she had to sharpen her pencil, then she had to get a piece of paper, then she had to sharpen her pencil again. I had to act like I didn't know what she was up to. Once she stopped in front of his desk and said something to him. He said something back. I couldn't hear what it was, but Kimby was smiling when she got back. Asked her why she was so happy and she said, "Aaron has got some mouth on him."

You can say that again, Kimby.

Mr. Mariner came poking around, asking how we were doing with the map. Kimby and me both acted nonchalant toward him. He asked me if I'm ready for the test tomorrow and I told him, "As ready as I'll ever be." He smiled and said, "That's what I like to hear."

What a creep . . .

April 8

"Why doesn't Aaron eat with us anymore?" That's what Ralph asked me today during lunch. "It's tough to explain," I told him. That wasn't a lie. How could I tell Ralph the truth? That "people are talking." It's too ridiculous to even say. Ralph was happy with my answer. He and Lesly started doodling on each other's notebooks and I scanned the room for Aaron. He wasn't anywhere in the cafeteria.

I found him waiting in the supply closet. We hadn't said a word to each other for almost five days and my body was craving him. I saw him standing there and I started needing him like a drug. He said he got my letter last night. He was relieved. He didn't know what was going on all weekend. He thought I was mad at him. Told him I was sorry for how I acted on Friday. Told him it was because I was scared. He put his arms around my waist. I put my arms around his neck and held him tight. His face was there, ready and waiting. We didn't bother to turn out the light. We just went at it. I don't know if we made noises or not. We must've made noises. All I could hear was the heater buzzing above our heads. I started kissing his cheeks and nose, because that's what I saw some woman named Trina do on a soap opera once. The five minutes flew right by. Then the next ten minutes seemed to go even quicker. Then the bell rang and lunch was over. Felt like crying when I had to leave. Aaron whispered in my ear, "See you here tomorrow." Then he was gone.

When I got out into the hallway a couple minutes later, I saw Les Numer and Kuprekski firing rubber bands at all the kids coming out of the Special Ed. room. They do everything together now. Eat lunch, ride the bus, pair off in Phys. Ed., you name it. Kuprekski's the star of the outdoor track team. Les is the star of the JV baseball team. When these two "stars" get together, they think they really light up the galaxy, but they're just making everybody miserable. I wonder why people don't care that *they* hang around together so much?

▶ April 9

Student Council meeting today. It was so stupid. They had to make last-minute preparations for the Spring Fling Dance. Dorian was all huffy because Marsha doesn't like her brother's band. Marsha says they sound like "pigs in heat." That struck me funny, so I laughed. Dorian pouted for the rest of the meeting. Kimby was upset because she still doesn't have a date for the dance. I listened to her whine about going to the dance alone and tried hard to keep from smacking her. She doesn't have a clue about what real problems are.

I spoke with Marsha for a while afterwards. It'd been a long time. She's usually busy with Jeff or schoolwork or something. I didn't realize how much I missed her. She said Jeff told her I was having a tough time. I said, "Yah." Didn't feel like telling her any more. I think she already knew.

She told me about how once in the fifth grade she was friends with a sixth-grader named Ginger. Marsha thought Ginger was the coolest kid she ever knew, until one afternoon when she went over to Ginger's house. Ginger turned out to be a boozer and a chain-smoker. She offered Marsha a beer. That was when Marsha knew Ginger was bad news. She said, "You never can tell about people until you really get to know them. All you can do is decide for yourself if you want to take the chance."

I guess it was pretty cut and dry for Marsha. I thought about what she said and it made sense to me. Especially the part about deciding for myself. I made my decision and met Aaron in the supply closet. Learned things about him today that I was happy to know. Thanks, Marsha. Thanks a lot.

I got a 92 on my History test. Mr. Mariner wrote on it: "See what you can do when you apply yourself?" Looked across the room at Aaron and he was crumpling up his test. I did the same to mine and threw it away when I got home.

April 10

Aaron's taking Kimby to the Spring Fling Dance. That's what Kimby told me this afternoon on the bus. I tried not to look surprised, but I was IN SHOCK. He didn't say a thing about it when we met in the supply closet during lunch. It turns out Kimby asked him during study hall this afternoon. She said that when she asked him, he said, "Sure." He didn't even stop to think about it.

The more I think about it, the sicker I feel. Kimby was acting pretty proud of herself. She didn't realize that she just stuck a knife in my heart. I couldn't say anything. Couldn't pretend to be happy for her. I just looked out the window and watched the trees fly by. Kimby leaned over and whispered in my ear, "Don't worry, Ben. You'll find somebody."

10:35 P.M.

I'm dying to call Aaron and find out what the hell is going on. But I'm afraid what the answer's gonna be. Can't use the telephone, anyway. Grandma's in the living room watching TV. Mom and Dad are in the kitchen playing rummy.

I keep trying to tell myself Kimby was lying and that it's not really gonna happen. It doesn't work.

 ## April 11

Met Aaron in the supply closet today. We didn't kiss. We fought. I asked him how he could say yes to Kimby like that, didn't he care about me? He said his parents were bugging him to get out more and meet people. He's just going to the dance so they'll get off his back. "Besides," he said, "you went to the Valentine's Dance with her and it didn't mean anything."

I told him that was "before."

He leaned forward to kiss me but I was too mad about the shit I went through last night. "What are you afraid of?" he asked me. I couldn't answer him. He should've known.

He got mad. He said if I didn't trust him enough to let him go out on one date with a girl, then that doesn't say very much for our relationship. Then he walked out of the closet. I almost went after him. But I was afraid if I did I'd make a fool of myself in the gym. I kept trying to shoot "sorry" looks at him all afternoon, but he never looked my way.

The whole thing is driving me crazy. I don't know what bugs me the most, the fact that Aaron's going out with a girl or that it's Kimby. I feel mad at both of them, and I'm not sure why.

They're both at the dance now. Dancing together. Touching each other. If Aaron likes it, I'll die.

 ## April 12

8:25 A.M.

Didn't sleep at all last night. Every time I dozed off I had a nightmare that Aaron fell in love with Kimby and wanted to break up with me. It would make things a lot easier for him, and God knows it would make my life simpler. It would also ruin it.

1:39 P.M.

Kimby just called. Tried to keep cool. Asked her how the dance was. She said, "OK." Like she didn't want to talk about it. Asked her what kind of a kisser Aaron was and she said, "How would I know? I don't kiss on the first date."

Suuuuuuuuure you don't, Kimby.

I tried to get more information out of her, but it was like pulling teeth. She said the band sucked eggs, the decorations almost caught fire, and a bunch of seniors got kicked out for smoking in the cafeteria.

I kept trying to find out how Aaron was, but Kimby kept dodging the questions. All she'd say about him was that he's "going to be a challenge." I didn't dare ask her what she meant by that. I'm taking it as a good sign. I'm praying nothing happened.

7:48 P.M.

Just called Aaron. Jeff was out with Marsha, Dad and Mom ran out to the store, and Grandma was in the living room with *Star Search* at full blast. I was alone in the kitchen, saw the phone, and grabbed the chance. Aaron seemed real surprised to hear my voice. Asked him how the dance was and he said it was one of the strangest nights of his life. Kimby kept disappearing into the ladies' room. She'd stay in there for ten-minute stretches. Every time she came out, her hair was different. Once it was in braids, then it was down

200

straight, then it was in a ponytail, then it was piled up on top of her head like a haystack. Aaron said it must be a woman's thing to change her hair every five seconds, just like they change their minds.

We both laughed, and then he asked me if I was still mad at him. I told him no, that I've been thinking about it a long time and I decided I didn't have any right to keep him from dating other people. It's probably better for both of us if he does. That way people won't get suspicious. I asked him, "Did you like dancing with Kimby?" He was quiet for a second. I almost passed out. Finally he said, "It wasn't bad. But I'd rather dance with you any day."

Hung up the phone quick and now I'm walking on air.

▶ April 13

Grandma wouldn't let me go to church with her today. I got up this morning and she was dyeing Easter eggs in the kitchen. All the kids at church were going on an egg hunt after the service. I kind of wanted to go. Not for the egg hunt but to see how Patsy's doing. I asked Grandma if I could go and she said, "Why? So you can insult God in His own house?"

After she got back, she told me she'd spoken with Reverend Silk about me. She set up an appointment for me to speak with him next Sunday. I told her, "OK, I'll go." She said I didn't have a choice in the matter. I was going whether I wanted to or not. She said Reverend Silk is a very kind man and he'll help me get my act together.

Great . . . I can hardly wait . . .

▶ April 14

Bad news. They found rats in the supply closet over the weekend. They're fumigating it this week. They moved all the supplies to the janitor's office. All the homeroom teachers announced it to their homerooms this morning. Now if we want supplies, we have to go to the janitor's office. The supply closet is off limits for a week. I heard the news and felt my stomach do a swan dive. Looked over at Aaron and he was staring off into space. That's what he does when he's covering up that he's upset. He slips the "I don't care" mask on his face and acts like everything's normal. Come to think of it, that's what I do too. The mask goes on real easy with a little practice.

Kimby didn't give a damn about the supply closet being closed off. She was too busy all day flirting with Aaron. I've never seen her so lovesick. Today she sat with him in the cafeteria. It's not like Kimby to sit at a table one-on-one with anybody. She likes a crowd around her all the time. I tried not to look over at them, but I couldn't help it. Every time I did, Kimby was laughing at something and Aaron was smiling his exasperated smile. When we were walking out, Kimby walked up behind me and said, "I think I'm in love."

April 15

Dad's decided that he's gonna get a job. Somebody told him that we weren't eligible for Aid if he was living with us, so he's decided that it's time to go back to work. He said, "No more living off the government for me." I wonder how long he's gonna feel that way. I have a feeling if something doesn't come through in a couple of weeks he's gonna be hitting the welfare office again. Or hitting the bars. We'll see.

Mom's happy because she's got her own checking account now. She flat-out refused to hand her money over to Dad, so he made a deal with her: she could have her checking account if she didn't bug him about AA. He still hasn't been to AA yet, but Mom says as long as he stays off the bottle, she's not gonna worry about that. They both go to bingo instead. Mom says it keeps Dad's mind off drinking, so it's good for both of them.

I try to be happy for them, but I can't because of how they feel about Aaron. Like today Mom asked me about "that Silver boy." What trouble did he stir up at school today? I pretended like I didn't have any idea. Like I didn't even care. Dad frowned and said, "I want you to keep ten feet away from people like him." They both think Aaron's a part of my past. Let them think that.

Actually, I really didn't have any idea what Aaron did today. The only thing that went on between us was looks. He'd look at me quick and I'd look at him quick.

8:30 P.M.

Jeff came home real concerned tonight. All of his friends have heard from Snyder College. They've all been accepted. He's the only one who hasn't heard anything. Marsha told him not to worry. He applied real late, so of course he'll be one of the last ones to be accepted. Jeff wasn't convinced. After Marsha left, he looked at me and asked, "What am I gonna do if I'm not accepted?"

"I don't know," I told him. And that wasn't a lie. What will Jeff do? Stay in Tranten Township and work at Plumbco? It's the strangest thing. Once people start working at Plumbco, they stay there for a long time, sometimes their whole lives. It can't be because they like the work. They just get comfortable and wake up one morning and figure that Plumbco's as good as it's ever gonna get. They keep working there and lose things as the years go by. It starts out small, like fingers getting hacked off. And then it gets bigger, and then they lose their hopes. I think that's the last thing Jeff wants to do. But it's not like he's gonna have much of a choice.

He looked real scared. I told him not to worry about it yet. Marsha was probably right. His acceptance letter was probably in the mail. He said he hoped so. Before he walked out of our room, he looked out the window at the factory across the street. I could tell he was thinking the same thing I was.

▶ April 16

Talked with Aaron today. Not really, but it felt like a talk. Mrs. King was reading these poems by Yeats and Donne, two old-fart poets. She asked for a volunteer to read one of the poems, and Aaron's hand went up. He started reading this poem about loving somebody with red hair. His voice sounded strange to me, so I looked over at him. I almost passed out when I did. He wasn't looking at his book at all. He was looking at me, saying the poem from out of his head. Everybody had their faces buried in their books so they didn't notice. Mrs. King was squirting nasal spray up her nose, so she didn't notice.

Aaron got done with the poem just in time for Mrs. King to clear out her nose with a loud honk into her tissue. I cracked up because she sounded like a foghorn. I guess I laughed pretty loud because everybody looked at me. Everybody except for Aaron. He had his nose stuck in his book. Mrs. King asked me what was so funny and I didn't know what to say, so I laughed again.

Right then, Ralph sneezed a juicy one. It hit him so fast he didn't have time to cover his mouth. He ended up giving the back of Theresa's head a shower. Theresa shrieked, "Gross!" and everybody looked at her and laughed. The bell rang so we all got up to leave. Mrs. King glared at me and said she didn't want any more laughing in her class. I nodded and shot a look at Aaron. He was smiling at me.

That smile made my day. The poem was nice, but the smile was the kicker. Everything else may be all wrong in my life, but Aaron's smiles make it seem better. These days, they're all I have.

▶ *April 17*

Walked into the boys' room today and felt an arm go around my shoulder and pull me into a stall. Almost screamed, but then I saw that it was Aaron's body connected to the arm. He looked like he'd been crying. Asked him what was wrong and he showed me a picture of a swastika and said somebody stuck it up on his locker door. He was real upset about it. I didn't know what to do. He looked like he wanted to punch somebody. I put my arms around him and blew "Shhhhhhh" in his ear because that's what Mom used to do to me when I was upset. He seemed to calm down, but I was freaking out. Every time I heard somebody walk by in the hallway I'd look up fast.

Aaron started whispering in my ear. He said he's gonna

wait across the street from my house tomorrow night from six to nine o'clock. If there's ever a chance that he can come over, for five minutes even, I'm supposed to flash the light in my bedroom on and off three times. He'll be up the stairs as quick as he can make it.

I tried to tell him the chances of everybody in my family being gone for any amount of time tomorrow night are slim, but he was out of the stall before I had a chance. I sat on the hopper for a minute and tried to calm down. Couldn't get my hands to stop shaking.

Kimby got on the bus all excited this afternoon. She's going to the movies tonight with Aaron. They set up the date during study hall. Asked her what they were gonna go see and she said, "Something with a lot of sex in it."

I felt a pang when she said that. I don't think I have to worry, though. Kimby's parents are probably taking them. If that's the case, it'll be a "Disney date" for sure.

April 18

There is a God. And He does love me. Well, He loves Dad, anyway. Dad won big at bingo last night. Thank you, God! He's taking Mom and Grandma out to dinner tonight at the Rusty Nail to celebrate. Thank you, God!! Jeff's driving to Portland with Marsha to go to a rock concert. Thank you, God!!!

All systems are go. Hope Aaron can make it.

9:15 P.M.

Aaron was just here. It was so easy it scared me. Dad, Mom, and Grandma left for Lipton at 6:00. Jeff left at 6:30. I flashed my light three times, and a minute later Aaron was at the door. The first thing we did when we saw each other was kiss. Long. I felt his hands reaching around to touch my ass and didn't stop him. I wanted it. Let him feel my ass. Felt his too. It felt like two soft/hard pillow balls in my hands. He said, "Let's go lie down."

We got in the bedroom and made M+M's (Masturbation Memories). They're something that Aaron thought up. We didn't know when we'd be together like that again, so we'd better do things that turned each other on, things that we could think about when we jerk off. M+M's. It turned out to be pretty fun.

I put my head on Aaron's lap and let him play with my hair. It felt nice. After a while, Aaron unbuttoned his shirt so I was looking at his belly button. I stuck my finger in it and he laughed. I started running my fingers over his nipples and Aaron got goose bumps all over his chest and stomach. I looked at my arms and I had goose bumps too. Aaron whispered at me to "Sit up," so I did. He put his face near mine and started kissing. Put my hand on his chest and his heart was doing a drum roll.

Aaron unbuttoned his jeans and took my hand and brought it down to his dick. The next thing I knew, I was holding his dick in the palm of my hand. It was so hot and slimy-feeling that I let go of it and put my hand behind my back. Aaron asked me what was wrong and I didn't say anything. I couldn't tell him I was scared. Aaron reached for my hand again and said we'd take it slow. I felt better about that, so I gave him my hand.

All of the sudden, there was this loud KNOCK on the front door. We jumped about three feet in the air. Aaron must've bitten his tongue because he screamed "Ow!" and grabbed on to his cheek. The knock turned out to be Kent, one of Jeff's jock friends. He was supposed to go to the concert with Jeff tonight, but Jeff forgot to pick him up. I could tell Kent wanted to come in and wait up for Jeff so he could give him hell, but I shut the door in his face.

Got back to the bedroom and Aaron had buttoned his shirt back up. He looked scared. I told him it was "OK" and then I sat back down beside him. I wanted to take up where we left off, but Aaron was shaking. He said, "Sometimes life is such a bitch." I didn't say anything, even though I agreed with him. I looked at my own hands and they were shaking too.

I thought he might be mad at me for pulling my hand

206

away, so I said, "Sorry ... about what I did." I told him he just caught me off guard. I'll be ready next time.

He was quiet and that made me crazy. I wanted to make it up to him. I told him he could stick his dick anywhere he wants and I wouldn't care. That made him mad. He said, "Jesus Christ," under his breath and said I couldn't just go make offers like that to people. It's stupid. I've gotta think about my own life first.

He asked me what I knew about "safe sex." Told him, "Nothing." Sex (safe, unsafe, or whatever) isn't a topic of conversation at our dinner table. The only thing I know about AIDS is that everybody's afraid of catching it from a toilet seat, because it hides on the rim and waits for people to sit down so it can crawl up their behinds. The school nurse came and told us how you can catch it, but the PTA told us to disregard everything she said. I don't know who to believe. Decided tonight that Aaron is a reliable person. Asked him to show me what it is. I wanted to know all about it. But he shook his head. ("Later, later ...")

We were quiet for a second, while I tried to figure out if he was still mad at me. He had this serious look on his face that scared me. Was gonna ask him straight-out, but then he said, real gentle, "Don't ever let them tell you it's wrong."

I knew right away what "it" was. I put my head on his shoulder and thought, How can "it" be wrong? "It" is the only right thing in my life.

We sat like that, just thinking. Before we knew it, it was 7:30 and Aaron had to take off. I felt sick. Aaron said, "See you in the supply closet," kissed me, and was out the door. I watched him go down the stairs and felt like I was watching a piece of myself walk away. Wanted to run after him, but ...

Whoops! Grandma, Mom, and Dad just got back. They all sound happy as pigs in shit. Gonna pretend to be asleep so they'll leave me alone.

▶ ## April 19

This morning I had my meeting with Reverend Silk. Grandma was right about one thing: he's a kind man. He also turned out to be real smart. I thought he was gonna ream me out for what I said about God, but he didn't. He didn't even mention God at first. He asked me stuff like, How is school? What are my grades? and What's my favorite subject? I gave him all the stock answers. Then he got serious and said, "Your grandmother is very concerned about you. She doesn't think you have any guidance in your life."

I thought about it a second and decided that Grandma's right, though she shouldn't be worried about it. I've always gotten by pretty good. Reverend Silk started talking about how important it is to develop a moral code early on and stick to it. I told Reverend Silk I know what's right and wrong. I ran down the list of things that I know for sure: giving of yourself is right, and stealing is wrong, loving is right, and hating is wrong (Reverend Silk nodded real fast when I said that), and acceptance is right and prejudice is wrong. Reverend Silk raised his eyebrows when I said that. I think he was surprised that I used two three-syllable words in a single sentence. He looked at me for a second and then he asked, "What does your moral code mean to you?" I told him I didn't think having good morals had anything to do with God or religion. Some of the most "religious" people I know wouldn't know right from wrong if it hit them over the head.

I thought he'd get mad but he didn't. He laughed a little and said "Amen" real quiet. He told me not to condemn all Christians just because a few might be a little too enthusiastic or hide their sins behind the Bible. Then he told me he'd heard I had doubts about God. I thought he'd be real mad about that, but he wasn't. He said at my age it's natural to question what I believe. He said, "Go on questioning until you find an answer that satisfies your spirit."

We talked about other things like heaven and hell, and the importance of making the most of our time on earth. He didn't say "Believe in God or you'll go straight to hell" or anything like that. I walked in expecting a lecture and came out feeling great. Grandma met me outside and asked me how it went. Told her, "Good." She smiled at me and said she loved me.

We stopped and saw Patsy on the way back. She seems to be settling in finally. She likes Ruby now. What's not to like about Ruby? Sharing a room with her is like sharing it with a cucumber. Patsy gave Grandma an ashtray she made out of a bunch of sea shells. Grandma acted real happy about the gift. She kissed Patsy and said, "Thank you, sweetheart." Patsy just giggled away.

April 20

The supply closet reopened today. Aaron and me celebrated by spending all lunch period in there. We didn't even bother to go to the cafeteria for a pass, we just went straight to the closet. Had a nice time kissing and talking. There were two big chemical drums in there left by the exterminator, so it was a little cramped. We made room. Told Aaron about my meeting with Reverend Silk and he said it's good that I'm asking questions. He didn't make fun of it or make me feel weird like I was afraid he would. The bell rang and we became strangers again. Acting like we didn't know each other existed.

8:42 P.M.

Just saw Mag and Scott in the General Store. They were fighting. Mag was all mad at Scott about something he said to her before they walked in. She told him, "You take that back." Scott just laughed at her and slapped her rear end. Gary Gould was standing behind the cash register, trying to look away from them. He was wishing he was somewhere else. Mag called Scott a pig and went over to the soda cooler. I could tell she was embarrassed. I almost went over and spoke to her, but Mag wasn't hearing anything then. She was just glaring at Scott like she wanted to kill him.

Scott started talking to Gary, asking him about his plaque. Mag walked back to him, shaking a can of Pepsi like crazy and calling Scott's name. When Scott turned to face her, she sprayed him with the Pepsi. She got him good. Some of it went in his eyes so he couldn't see anything. Scott screamed and lunged at her but he ended up ramming into the potato chip rack and knocking it over. He landed face first on a bag of Fritos. He got up quick to go after Mag again. I was gonna step between them, but Gary had already jumped from behind the counter and grabbed Scott. Gary told Mag she'd better get out of there. Mag looked cool at Scott and said, "Don't you ever call me a cunt again."

Mag looked like she hated Scott right then. I know I did. When she was stomping out, our eyes connected. I wish they hadn't. Because she looked like she hated me. She walked out and slammed the door. I almost went after her. But then I figured I was the last person she'd want to talk to. Scott was MAD. He had corn chips hanging from his beard and Pepsi coming out his nose. He shook Gary off and ran out. The last I saw him, he was running down the street, screaming Mag's name.

Wonder how Mag feels tonight. Dying to talk to her. Something like this would've kept us on the phone until midnight in the old days. But it's not the old days.

▶ *April 21*

Dad got a job. I tried to act unexcited but he was so happy it was rough. Grandma found it for him. He's gonna be cutting wood with a crew in Nome. Dad kept saying over and over again, "It just goes to show you what willpower can do for you." He looked at me and Jeff and asked, "What do you think of your old man now?"

Where do I begin?

I didn't know whether to tell him the truth and piss him off, or make up a lie and let him keep on being happy. I was gonna plead the Fifth when Jeff saved the day and said, "We're both real happy for you, Dad."

Even though I heard him plain as day, I couldn't believe it. Dad didn't have any trouble believing it. He swallowed it like it was a Bud Lite. I looked at Jeff and Mom looked at Dad. We all had smiles on our faces, though some were false and some were sincere. Right then I couldn't tell which was which.

I cornered Jeff in our room and asked him why he said we're both happy for Dad. He said, "Because we don't have any choice." Jeff says he's been thinking about it long and hard. Dad's a loser with a capital L (it took Jeff seventeen years to realize that). There's nothing we can do about that. Everybody knows it and nothing's gonna change their minds at this stage. Jeff says he thinks even Dad knows it. But as long as nobody tells him straight out, he can pretend it's not true. So we've gotta applaud his victories and keep on letting him pretend so he won't fall off the wagon again. After Jeff explained it to me, he took off for a keg party down by the river.

Jeff's lucky because he's leaving home in a few months, but I'm stuck here for at least three more years. What's it gonna be like when I'm here alone? Don't want to think about that. I feel sick when I do. It won't be too bad if Aaron's around. As long as he's a part of my life, nothing could be that bad.

▶ *April 23*

Awful day today. Aaron called me "insecure" in the supply closet. He asked me if I minded if he took Kimby to the prom in a couple of weeks. I minded. A lot. I think I was hoping he'd ask me to go with him, even though I know that's impossible. And crazy. And dangerous. I told him, "No, I don't mind." But I tried to look hurt. It must've worked, because Aaron asked me what was bugging me. I told him I hate the idea of him doing stuff with Kimby. Expected him to be sympathetic, but he wasn't. He got all mad and said he couldn't exactly take me, could he? He said, "I don't want you to think that you need me so much that I can't make plans that don't include you."

And then he called me insecure.

He said there was no reason why I should be that way. He said that's why he broke up with Connie. She was the kind of girl who couldn't make up her own mind, always had her arms around him, and got jealous every time he made other plans. He was suffocating with her. That's why he likes me. I go my own way and let him go his. He can breathe with me ... Except when I start complaining about Kimby, and then I sound just like Connie. He told me, "You're too strong a person to worry about Kimby Quinn."

I felt a little better, but not so strong. At that moment I felt sooooooooooooo weak.

Aaron started talking about my finding a date for the prom. He says we can double date. I didn't say yes or no. I was still getting used to the idea of him going with Kimby.

▶ ## April 24

Saw Aaron first thing this morning in homeroom. Kimby was planted at his desk, jabbering away. I pretended not to notice. Decided to make *him* feel insecure for a change. I flirted with Theresa. I talked to her about Algebra and gave her the "eye." I saw some hunk give this bimbo the "eye" on a commercial for *Dynasty*. I've seen Jeff give Marsha the "eye" right before he kisses her. I've seen Dad give Mom the "eye" right before they disappear into the bedroom. The "eye" is a look that tells somebody, Hey! Let's do something. Now.

I gave Theresa the "eye" for five solid minutes while we talked about $X = Y \times Z$. Theresa looked up at me and asked if my eyesight was getting bad. I dropped the "eye" real quick.

I was probably wrong for wanting to make Aaron jealous, but for the first time, I was mad at him and not Kimby. He was talking to her like they were best friends and it bugged the hell out of me. I wanted to let him know how it felt to see his boyfriend making "eyes" at a girl. I think it might've worked. After Theresa asked about my eyesight, I laughed. LOUD. I could see Aaron's head jerk around and look at me. I couldn't tell his expression. I hope it was shock. I edged closer to Theresa and pretended to study the pattern on her sweater. Didn't look at Aaron again the rest of the day. Not even in the cafeteria. I kept thinking of excuses to talk to Theresa so that everybody saw us. Aaron especially.

Theresa loves to put people down. She kept making fun of the flannel shirt Old Lady Song wore today. She said it must've been made from an old Salvation Army blanket. I laughed like I thought she was funny and smiled at her. She didn't have a clue what was going on. She didn't seem to care.

April 25

I got up this morning and Dad told me I wasn't grounded anymore. Because I followed the rules so well I was a free man. (What Dad doesn't know won't hurt him.) When I was walking out the door, Dad told me he didn't want me going to "that Silver boy's house."

Went to Aaron's house anyway.

When I got there, Mrs. Silver was real surprised to see me. She said, "It's been a long time," and let me in. Aaron looked even more surprised to see me. I told him that my grounding was over and I was a free man. He didn't act happy or sad about it. I asked him what he did last night. It turns out, Kimby called him and kept him on the phone for an hour. I lied and told him that Theresa called me. I looked for a reaction from him but his face was blank. He said, "You *know* Kimby doesn't mean a thing to me." Then he lay down on his bed and asked me why I was such a jerk with Theresa yesterday. I wasn't so sure, so I turned the tables on him and asked him what he and Kimby talked about for an hour last night. He said, "Absolutely nothing." He says discussing current events with Kimby is like trying to explain sunbathing to an Eskimo. The concept's too foreign.

He started to say more but he couldn't talk through my hair. I'd jumped on top of him and buried my face in his neck. I don't know why I did it. It was just automatic. Maybe it was because he put Kimby down and all my fears went flying out the window. Aaron nudged me off him and pulled off his shirt. It seemed like he knew what I wanted. It hit me later that he wanted the same thing. I pulled off mine. He laid down flat and I started stroking his chest. He unbuttoned my pants and then pulled his own pants down. His dick was jumping all over the place. "Milk it," he said.

I knew what to do. I'd had plenty of practice with my own. I took it in my hand and played with it like it was mine. I rolled it between my hands and it throbbed. I squeezed it gently and it throbbed. Aaron kept rubbing my dick with his thighs, so it was growing right along with his. It seemed like both our pulses were going two hundred beats a minute. All of the sudden, Aaron sat up straight and grabbed my head in his hands. He swished my hair around and started to kiss the air. He fell back flat and pulled me down on top of him. His dick throbbed against my stomach. My dick was still between his thighs, feeling like it was in heaven. He rolled me over so we were lying side by side, face to face. I pulled him to me and ran my arms down his back. He groaned. Then he came. All over my stomach so it got covered with milky white. I came too. All over Aaron's thighs, and I thought I could see love for the first time in my life. Real Love. It felt so different from the times I do it on my own. It was like the stuff had a place to go. It belonged there on Aaron's thighs, making white rivers on his leg hair.

We lay there for a minute, just breathing hard. I felt different afterwards too. It wasn't an empty feeling at all. It definitely wasn't an angry feeling. Instead, I felt like I was flooding over with good feelings. The good feelings lasted longer with Aaron there. Like five minutes at least.

Later on, when we were washing up, we talked a little bit about dumb stuff. No matter how hard we tried, we couldn't get a conversation started. Everything seemed so unimportant compared to what we just did. I came home.

The second I walked in, Grandma took one look at me and asked, "What happened to your hair?" I looked in the mirror and saw that it was going in a million different directions. I combed it down quick and told Grandma the wind messed it up. She believed me, even though the air today is as dead as a doornail.

▶ April 26

Went to church with Grandma today. I think Reverend Silk told her to let me make my own decisions about God, because she didn't lecture me once during the drive up. I was so happy today that I felt the Spirit going through my veins full throttle. If Grandma had asked me, "Do you believe in God?" today, I would've said, "Yes!" with a smile. Then again, if Grandma had asked me, "Do you believe in Santa Claus?" I would've said, "Yes!" with a smile. Hell, I would've believed in the Tooth Fairy today.

The service was nice. Reverend Silk talked about how God holds love above all other human emotions. To love is to know God. I couldn't have agreed with him more.

After the service we stopped and saw Patsy. She seemed happier than usual today. She grinned the whole time and talked about her husband. Not to us, but to Ruby. Patsy pretended like we weren't even in the room today. She said hi and then turned to Ruby and yammered away. I guess her husband was some lover. Patsy told Ruby that she and him made love every night the first year they were married. Ruby snored. Grandma blushed. I edged closer to Patsy to hear some more. Patsy talked about how her husband loved to try "new things." She didn't say what the new things were, but she said they felt awful good. It hit me then that Patsy must have hundreds of M+M's stored away in her mind. All she has to do is pick one and do whatever it is old ladies do to turn themselves on, and then she'll be happy. I stopped feeling so sorry for her then.

When we got out to the car, Grandma told me not to believe a word Patsy says. "The drugs cloud her mind so she doesn't remember things right."

▶ April 27

Kimby charged onto the bus first thing this morning and told me that Aaron asked her to go to the prom last night. Didn't have to ask her if she accepted. I knew. Kimby was real excited. I listened to her carry on about the dress her mother's buying for her. It's peach-colored and it has ruffles and shit around the shoulders.

When I got to school I asked a couple of girls if they'd like to go with me. They both had dates already. EVERY-

BODY has a date already. Except for Theresa. I figured she's
holding out for a senior to ask her. I watched her make the
rounds of the senior tables during lunch this afternoon. I
don't think she had much luck. She'd stop at a senior table
and try to strike up a conversation with one. The second she
left, they'd be looking at each other and laughing. I felt a
little bad for her, but she was asking for it, setting herself
up like that. They think she's the biggest joke since disco.
How can she be so blind?

Ralph and Lesly talked about the prom. They're both
going. Lesly thinks it's gonna be a drag, but Ralph seems to
be looking forward to it. They asked me if I had a date yet.
Told them I didn't. Ralph told me I'd better hurry up, the
prom's only a week from Friday. I acted like I couldn't care
less and they looked at each other with these superior faces.
I pretended not to notice.

► April 29

Jeff wasn't accepted at Snyder College. The letter came this
afternoon in the mail. He was upset, and I can't blame him.
Everybody else from Chappaqua High who applied to Snyder got accepted except for Troy Wilcox, and he's got mental
problems. The rejection isn't gonna do a hell of a lot for Jeff's
ego. The letter said his SAT scores were "unsatisfactory" and
"We welcome you to apply again in the spring."

"Fat chance," Jeff said and went over to Marsha's place.

Dad came home from his first day of work all sweaty
and grumpy. Mom showed him the letter and he acted
irritated when he read it. He's been real quiet all night.
He's sitting in the kitchen now. Mom's sitting beside him,
waiting for him to say something.

► April 30

Came home from school tonight and Dad and Jeff were
having a deep discussion in the kitchen. It struck me as odd
to see them sitting together like that. It turned out they were
talking about the future.

They went back and forth, talking as if Mom and me weren't

even in the room. Dad asked Jeff what he was gonna do, as if Jeff had his life all mapped out. Jeff told him, "I don't know. I was thinking about hitchhiking across the country." Dad got mad and told Jeff not to expect any financial help from him. He had his own ass to worry about. And Mom's and Grandma's and mine. He couldn't send money out the window so Jeff could leave home and party in "Californeeya."

That got Jeff mad. He told Dad he didn't expect anything from him and headed out the door. Dad watched him go and then said to Mom, "What's that kid gonna do with his life?"

Mom said, "You should have thought of that before you filled his head with garbage about basketball scholarships." Then she left the room.

7:45 P.M.

Jeff just came into the room. Thought he'd tell me to get lost, but he didn't. He sat at the window looking across the street at Plumbco. His body started shaking. Couldn't tell if he was laughing or crying or what. Left the room because I didn't want to know.

► ## May 1

Bad day. I finally worked up the balls to ask Theresa to the prom and she turned me down. She said that she already has a date. I was gonna ask her "Who?" just to see who she'd come up with for a lie, but I figured she wasn't worth the trouble.

She seemed shocked that I asked her. Like I broke a rule or something. She sort of smiled and said, "I've already got a date." Nothing else. I really did my best when I asked her. I was sincere. Well, I pretended I was sincere. That's more than a lot of people do. I deserved more. I know I'm just a freshman. I know I'm from Tranten Township and she's from Lipton. I know my parents don't make much money. But she could've at least said, "Thank you for asking."

The horse-faced bitch . . .

I met Aaron in the supply closet and told him I don't have a date yet. He said, "So go stag." Right. Like I'm really gonna go alone. He told me he hopes I go. He wants me there for moral support. I wouldn't say one way or the other. I was too busy feeling up his ass. Aaron started sucking on my neck. All the worries disappeared.

10:15 P.M.

Just dialed Mag's number. Was gonna ask her if she wanted to go to the prom with me. I hung up when I heard her voice on the other end. I feel so dumb now. She probably would've told me to go to hell. Every time I go near her these days she looks away or walks away or makes me feel like a leper. She and Scott officially broke up. I heard Scott talking about it a few days after the big soda incident. He was telling this guy in the gas station that Mag wasn't the kind of woman he wanted. He started going on about how she's hairy in all the wrong places. I wanted to slug him, but then I asked myself, What do I care? Mag brought this on herself.

That's the truth. Still, I see Mag these days and I hurt all over on the inside. She looks so unhappy. Angry. Alone. Love sucks . . .

► ## May 2

Went to Aaron's house again today. Mom and Dad and Grandma all drove to Wheeler to visit Dad's cousins. They left directions with Jeff to keep an eye on me. Jeff moped around the apartment all morning—it felt like a tomb. Told him I was going out and he said, "Why should I care?" I left in a flash.

Got to Aaron's house and Mr. and Mrs. Silver were out planting flowers around the house. Met Aaron inside and we went straight to his bedroom. We explored each other's bodies today. I ran my hands all over his body and found out something pretty amazing. I used to think it was the hardness of a guy's body that I liked, but today I found out I like the soft parts just as much. The way his ass feels on my fingertips, the sponginess of his stomach, his nipples, his

218

neck, the small of his back. Aaron said the human body is "a miracle of engineering." Amen to that.

Aaron got dressed and looked out the window at his parents. He asked me, "Do you think we'll ever have that?" I walked to the window and saw Mr. and Mrs. Silver were sitting on the grass sharing a 7-Up. They were laughing about something. I knew what Aaron meant when he said "that."

I didn't know what to say. I try not to think about the future. Just getting through tomorrow is all I can think about most days.

"I hope so," I said.

Aaron didn't say anything. He closed the shade and put his clothes back on.

▶ May 3

"Jeff's going into the army." That's what Dad announced to Grandma and me today when we got back from church. Mom was sitting in the kitchen beside him. Nobody asked him, "What are you talking about?" Grandma looked shocked when he told her. I knew the question was on her mind. Dad had the answers all worked out in his head. He said that since Jeff really isn't sure what he wants to study, why should he worry about college? The army will pay him to learn skills. It'll make a man out of him. Give him discipline. Dad said Jeff and him talked about it a long time this morning and they both agree. Jeff wasn't here to say whether he agreed or not. "Where's Jeff?" I asked. Dad said, "Out for a drive."

Dad was excited enough about it for the both of them. I listened to Dad yammer away and tried to understand. It made sense for a second. The army is a way Jeff can get out of Tranten Township, and away from Plumbco. He'll see new things and learn a lot. But the army changes people. I've seen some of the wildest guys who ever came out of Chappaqua High School come back from the army looking like they had a lobotomy. They looked stunned, like all the spirit was beat out of them. I just can't picture Jeff taking orders from a stranger. And marching in a line with a bunch of other people. It scares me to think about it. But maybe the change'll be good for him.

After Dad got done with his ten-minute commercial for the army, he went out for a walk. Grandma and Mom stayed in the kitchen. Grandma shot Mom a look and asked, "Are you crazy? Do you want Jeff going to the Philippines and fighting for that Aquino woman? That's what's gonna happen."

Mom said, "Jeff's made his own bed and now he has to lie in it." The outcome isn't what she wants, "but try and think of a better idea for Jeff." Grandma and me were both quiet. I was trying like hell to think of something, but it wasn't coming today any better than it did last week. My mind went blank.

6:30 P.M.

Just was in Mom's room. She was looking at her scrapbook, running her fingers over pictures I couldn't see. She saw me and jumped, like I scared her. She asked me what I wanted.

"Things to be okay," I said.

She sighed and said, "I know how you feel."

She held out her arms and I hugged her. I looked down at the scrapbook. It was turned to pictures taken of Dad the day he shipped out to Vietnam. It was scary, the similarity between Dad then and Jeff now.

9:58 P.M.

Jeff just got back from wherever he's been all night. He's in a BAD mood. Asked him about the army and he said, real sarcastic like, "It's pretty fucking exciting, isn't it?" Asked him how Marsha feels about it. He said, "She doesn't know yet."

He said something else about how he hated being railroaded into doing something. I couldn't hear him because he was slamming drawers so loud. He went into the bathroom before I could ask him to repeat what he said. I'd offer to talk to him about it, but I don't know how that'd go over. I'll keep quiet.

▶ ## May 4

Marsha snagged me in the halls and asked me what was bugging Jeff today. He wouldn't talk to her all day. And he skipped his meeting with Mr. Taylor. I was late for the supply closet, so I told her quick what's going on. She just said, "Damn," and took off down the hall. When I got to the supply closet, Aaron said I looked blue. I told him about Jeff and the army. I had nightmares all last night that Jeff was on a battlefield and bombs were going off all around him. I looked up in the sky and Dad was the person dropping the bombs. My voice got squeaky when I told Aaron about the nightmare. I said, "I don't know why I'm so upset about this. It's not like it's happening to me."

Aaron said, "You're upset because you love your brother. What's wrong with that?" I started to deny it but I couldn't. I do love Jeff, even though he can be such a creep sometimes. I don't know how I would've got through the last year without him around. Not that he was a help to me. He was just *around*. I felt better knowing that. Safer.

I love Jeff. But it's a different feeling from the one(s) I have for Aaron. It's a lot less confusing.

Aaron kept telling me things would be okay, but it was tough trying to believe him. He doesn't know how logic works in my family. I put my hand over his mouth and said, "Shhh." We spent the rest of the time just leaning on each other. I felt better doing that. It was enough.

Got home from school tonight and Grandma told me that Jeff and Dad and Mom drove to Portland to talk to an army recruiter. They're still not back yet.

9:20 P.M.

Jeff and them just got back. Marsha was here waiting with us when they walked in. Jeff saw her and said, "Hi, Marsh. Got a surprise for you," like he was real happy. Maybe he was. *Is.* He took her into the bedroom while Dad told us how the meeting went. The recruiter was this nice guy named Barry. He made the army sound so good that Dad

221

almost re-enlisted. Dad was smirking when he said it, so you could tell he was kind of joking. Dad says the more he thinks about it, the more he's convinced that it's the right thing for Jeff. The army made a man out of him and it'll do the same for Jeff.

Marsha came out of our bedroom and said goodbye to us. It might've been my imagination, but I think I saw her make a disgusted face at Dad when his back was to her.

Went into the bedroom and asked Jeff how it went. He said, "Terrific," but what he meant was "Shitty." He kept bouncing his basketball off his bed headboard and catching it. He cursed under his breath every time he caught the ball. I thought he was gonna break the bed. I told him if he wanted to talk I was there. He looked at me like I was crazy, and then he shut himself up in the bathroom. Now he's bouncing the ball in there. Cursing louder.

May 5

Ralph had an asthma attack today. George the janitor was sweeping the parking lot in front of the school and kicking up a lot of dust. Plus the pollen in the air was so bad Ralph had to leave during homeroom. I never had a chance to see him. Lesly told me about it during French class. She said Ralph started gasping for air after the bell rang. She helped him down to the nurse's office and called Ralph's mother. She held Ralph's hand while he sucked on an inhaler.

She said Ralph's mom came cruising in and told everybody she'd take care of things from now on. She didn't even say thank you to Lesly. I told Lesly that Ralph was real lucky to have her around and she said, "You're right about that."

May 6

Got a date for the prom. Lesly asked me if I'd go with her today. Ralph's mother told him he couldn't go, but he wants Lesly to go anyway. Lesly said he looked so pitiful sucking on his inhaler with his mother looming over him that she didn't have the heart to tell him she didn't want to go. He already bought the tickets and everything. Lesly just wants to stay home and watch TV, but Ralph insisted that she go. I was surprised when she asked me. She said it's just gonna be a friendship date. Fine with me . . .

Got in the supply closet and told Aaron I've got a date. He looked relieved. Kimby's driving him crazy lately. She's upset with him because he won't rent a tux. Aaron says tuxedos are "pretentious and dumb." She gave him directions on what color corsage she wants. I guess it has to be made from "salmon-colored roses" so it won't clash with her peach dress. Aaron asked me what the hell color salmon is. Told him I didn't have any idea. Aaron's bugged because Kimby wants him to come by her house early so her parents can take plenty of pictures of them together in their prom clothes. He looked so miserable I didn't feel right about laughing at that.

▶ May 7

Close call today. Came walking out of the supply closet after lunch and Kimby saw me. She had on her sly-looking face. I could see the light bulb clicking on over her head. Could see her brain start working double time.

She asked me, "Who?" I didn't answer her right away because she took me by surprise. She jerked open the closet door and peeked inside. It was empty. Thank God Aaron had to leave early. If Kimby'd seen us walking out together that would've been awful. She faced me again and asked, "Who?" "Nobody," I said. I told her I was just in there picking up art supplies and she said, "Suuuuuure." Kimby whispered in my ear, "Boy or girl?" I acted like I didn't know what she was talking about and walked away from her. I avoided her all afternoon. Every time I snuck a peek at her, she was looking at me. She looked so happy she was ready to bust.

▶ May 8

Got to school today and Lesly met me in homeroom. She told me she'd come pick me up at seven tonight. I'm kind of looking forward to it. The theme of it is "Blast Off into Paradise." The gym is decorated to look like a jungle with crepe paper palm trees and a lagoon. I looked close at the lagoon and saw that it's somebody's wading pool. There are all of these different-colored lights at the top of the bleachers and there's a papier-mâché volcano set up in the middle of the gym. It's supposed to erupt a bunch of confetti and streamers at midnight. That should be kind of exciting. Lesly said if the band sucks, they're gonna get tossed into the volcano as a human sacrifice. Ha-ha . . .

Kimby came up to me all excited because her mother bought her a feather boa to wear with her dress. She says it'll be her way of making a "fashion statement." I laughed at her and told her I couldn't wait to see it. Actually, I'm more excited about seeing Aaron in a suit.

Kimby kept bugging me all day today. She found out I'm going to the prom with Lesly, so she asked me if Lesly was the one I was in the supply closet with. I told her no and she grinned her stupid grin. I must've blushed because she said, "Don't be embarrassed." Then she pretended to ream me out for not thanking her. I asked her, "For what?" and she said, "For telling you about the supply closet. It's great, isn't it." I didn't say anything, even though I agreed with her.

11:59 P.M.

Just got back from the prom. It was sort of neat. And a little exciting. Lesly looked almost pretty. She had on contact lenses instead of her glasses. I never noticed how green her eyes were before tonight. She wasn't interested in dancing. Mostly what we did was talk and eat. Old Lady Song was standing by the food table, making sure nobody spiked the punch. Lesly kept going back for seconds and thirds on the cake. The band was pretty good. They were called the Missing Link. I think they only knew five songs, because they all started sounding the same after a while. I wasn't really paying attention to them. I was too busy watching Aaron and

Kimby out of the corner of my eye. Aaron had on this blue suit with a paisley bow tie. He was looking good.

The prom was a disaster for Kimby. She had on her peach dress with the ruffles around the shoulders. She also had on this six-foot-long boa that was sewed onto her dress at the waist. All night she'd flip it over her shoulders and swing it in the air when she and Aaron danced. She was snooping around taking pictures of everybody for the yearbook. Things were going fine for her until she tried to get a shot from on top of the bleachers. She wanted a sweeping shot of the whole gym, so she climbed up on top of the bleachers and stood right in front of the lights. Her boa must've been super-flammable, because it started smoking. Kimby didn't know what was going on until somebody screamed at her. She looked down and saw that her boa was on fire. She started screaming and trying to rip it off from her dress. When it wouldn't rip off, she ran like a wild woman down the bleachers and across the gym floor, shrieking at the top of her lungs, her flaming boa trailing behind her. Everybody cleared a path for her as she ran. Duff came charging in with a fire extinguisher and aimed it right at her. Kimby must've been worried about ruining her dress, because she saw him coming and took off in the other direction. I hate to say it, but it was almost comical watching Kimby run from Duff and his fire extinguisher. By this time, her boa was pretty well burned and the fire started spreading to the ruffles around her shoulders. Kimby screamed louder and ran toward the exit. Mr. Mariner headed her off at the pass. He picked her up and tossed her into the wading pool. She rolled around in the water and that put the fire out. But then she became hysterical. She let out these screams that sounded like laughs. I wasn't sure if she was upset because she almost got char-broiled or because her dress was ruined.

Aaron seemed to appear from out of nowhere. He looked concerned. He walked over to Kimby and put his hand on her shoulder. Kimby started crying. She didn't seem to be hurt at all. She was just soaked. And she smelled like burnt rubber. I felt bad for her because nobody seemed in any hurry to help her. Everybody stood around, waiting for somebody else to make the first move. It dawned on me that nobody likes Kimby all that much. It must've dawned on Duff too, because he walked over to her and asked if she wanted to lie down. He actually asked her nicely. Marsha offered to take her to the hospital to get checked out. She sent Jeff out to get his car started, and she wrapped her arm around Kimby and walked her across the gym floor. Aaron followed them. They left together, and that was the end of the fire show.

The band didn't seem to know what to do. They asked us for requests. Somebody suggested "Up in Smoke" and everybody laughed. Duff got mad and told us to knock it off. Lesly and me left early, because she wanted to see Ralph tonight. When we were riding back, Lesly told her father all about "Kimby the Human Torch." I couldn't help laughing. Lesly laughed too.

2:14 A.M.

Jeff just came in. He said Kimby's fine. She had a minor burn on her back, but aside from that, she was in great shape. I'm relieved. Kimby may be an obnoxious pain sometimes, but I wouldn't want to see her get hurt. Now I feel bad about laughing at her. The more I think about it, the worse I feel. Think I'll go visit Kimby tomorrow.

▶ May 9

Snuck over to Aaron's house today. He was pretty shaken up from the "Flaming Kimby Show." He said she cried all the way to the hospital. She kept screaming at him, "Where were you when my boa was on fire?" She was pissed with him. He told her he was in the bathroom. He was really hiding in the supply closet. He saw the boa catch on fire and took off. He got scared. He knew if he put out the fire, he and Kimby would be linked from now on. He didn't want that responsibility. He made sure somebody else put the fire out and then he showed up. After the fact.

Kimby told him the bathroom was a stupid place for him

to be. She wanted to know why he didn't run out when he heard her screaming. Aaron didn't have an answer for her. I guess Kimby hates him now. Last night when he walked her to her door, she told him she never wants to see him again. If he can't be there for her when she needs him, then he can go to hell.

(I felt sooooooooooo relieved when I heard that.)

Aaron said he'd been feeling guilty all day. Guilty about running away from a person in trouble. He kept asking me if I understood why he didn't help Kimby. I said I did.

I wanted to make him feel better, so I started unbuttoning his pants. I thought that would do the trick. But he wasn't in the mood. He buttoned his pants back up and said, "Not today." I had a feeling he just wanted to be alone, so I left.

▶ May 10

Crazy Patsy's dead. When Grandma and me went in to see her, her bed was empty. Ruby was there, still breathing away. A nurse came in and told us that Patsy died in her sleep last night. Grandma kneeled down at Patsy's empty bed and started praying. It was eerie. It was almost like she thought God was in the room with us. Her voice was steady and clear. Every time I heard her say the name "Patsy," I felt this pang in my stomach. It was almost like indigestion, only without the pukey feeling. I didn't know why I felt that way, until it hit me: Patsy wasn't there anymore. I felt real cheated all of a sudden. Kind of like I do when I'm watching the *Late Movie* on TV and I fall asleep before the ending so I don't know how it turns out. I wished I'd been there at the end for Patsy. I started feeling sad. And then empty. And then dizzy, like I was gonna pass out.

I knelt down beside Grandma and put my hands together. I was a little embarrassed at first. Then I remembered that the only other person in the room was Ruby, and she was so out of it she wouldn't've cared if I mooned her. I told God everything I wanted Him to do for Patsy. Things like "Make sure she can watch the *$25,000 Pyramid* every day" and "Be sure she's got plenty of jelly beans." Patsy had a lot of likes, so I wanted to cover all the bases.

I felt so happy. Like I do when Aaron smiles at me and tells me I look good. Real happy. Like someone was really paying attention to ME and was worried about what I'm thinking and what I have to say. I figured out why people like praying so much. It's a way they can stop feeling alone when they're having a rough day. Somebody's always there for them to listen to their problems. I'm still not sure who that Somebody is. It could be a God, or a statue, or even a puff of smoke.

I felt real good when we were driving home from the nursing home. Grandma was too. I looked over at her and she was smiling. I was smiling too.

May 11

Felt so bad for Kimby today. Some jerk took a picture of her running around with her flaming boa. Whoever it was ran off copies on the xerox and wrote at the bottom of the picture "Peach Flambé." The pictures were EVERYWHERE today. Wherever I looked, somebody was holding one and giggling about "Peach Flambé."

It seemed like Kimby was pissed at everybody. She came up to me during homeroom and asked me why I didn't go to her house to see her over the weekend. Didn't I want to make sure she was OK? I told her that Jeff told me she was OK, and I didn't think she'd feel like having any visitors. She said, "Bullshit," and walked away. I felt guilty all of a sudden. Lesly didn't even pretend to be concerned when Kimby confronted her. She told Kimby, "I didn't come visit you because I didn't care if you were OK or not."

That made Kimby real mad. She stamped off and I didn't see her until study hall this afternoon. She wouldn't even look at me.

When I met Aaron in the supply closet today, he just felt like talking, so we left the light on. He still felt bad about Kimby. I kissed him a couple of times. Long. To let him know I'm there for him. He hugged me back. Kimby rode by herself this afternoon on the bus. I cleared the seat beside me for her but she kept on walking down the aisle to an empty seat at the back. I heard somebody whisper "Peach Flambé" when she sat down. She must feel awful tonight. I'll apologize to her tomorrow.

▶ ## May 12

Horrible day. My life is definitely over now. I walked into school today and there was a mob of kids passing xeroxes around. They were all laughing and gasping. They saw me and quieted down. Somebody handed me one of the papers. At first I thought it was just another copy of Kimby's "Peach Flambé" picture, but when I looked at it, I saw it was of two people kissing. I didn't recognize who the people were because the pictures were fuzzy and dark. Then I took a closer look.

They were Aaron and me.

Kissing in the supply closet.

Somebody wrote below the picture: "Another day in the supply closet."

Suddenly my breakfast shot up to my mouth and I almost gagged trying to keep it down. It felt like everyone around me was laughing and oohing and aahing. The faces all blurred together so I couldn't recognize anybody. I heard "faggot" over and over again in high-pitched whispers. I pinched myself to wake up but the nightmare was real. I felt somebody grab my arm and looked and saw it was Duff. He screamed at everybody to get to their homerooms and then he hauled me into his office. Aaron was already in there. He looked white as a sheet. Embarrassed. Ashamed. Sick. Duff was upset. Angry.

I was numb.

Duff looked back and forth between us for about a minute. I didn't know if he was gonna smile or scream. It turned out he didn't do either. He started going on about "appropriate behavior" and "when and where" stuff like what we did was appropriate. He said we were suspended from school for three days, to give us time to think about what we did.

He said he'd called our parents (Aaron sucked in a breath when he heard that). I didn't dare look at him.

Mom and Dad walked in and I wanted to die. They were both holding copies of the picture. They must've picked them up out in the hall. Dad looked mad. He looked at me and Aaron like he wanted to kill us both. Duff told them I was suspended for three days. Mom looked like she was in shock. The picture shook like crazy in her hands. Duff said he was "sorry this unfortunate incident happened."

Not half as sorry as I was.

Rode home with Mom and Dad. Before he started the car, Dad shoved the picture in my hands and asked me how long it's been going on. I told him the truth. I thought he was gonna explode at first, but he didn't. He started the car and drove. Neither one of them said a word the whole ride back. Got in the apartment and Dad had the bamboo cane ready. Didn't even try to get away from him when he came at me. He let me have it. I lost count at twenty. My ass felt like it was on fire. And then it went numb like the rest of my body. Now I'm in my room and it's way past dark outside. I've been in here since right after the beating. Trying to rehash what happened, and trying to forget it at the same time.

▶ May 13

Jeff didn't come home last night. And he's been gone all day today. I wonder what's going on with him.

My life is hell. Went to the table this morning because I was starved. Dad saw me and told me to get out of his face. I went to pick up a roll to take to my room and he nailed my hand and told me to get lost. I went to my room and sat around all morning.

Mom came in at noontime with a sandwich. She was upset. She asked me, "Why?" I tried to tell her I was sorry, but she wouldn't let me. She told me not to say a word. She and Dad have just gotta work this out in their heads and try to find some answers. She said they're gonna tell Grandma about the picture tomorrow. They were gonna try to keep it from her, but that's impossible.

Grandma knows I've been suspended but she doesn't know what for. Mom and Dad told her I got caught smoking in the boys' room. I haven't seen her at all. Haven't left my room.

Mom started crying and asked me, "How could you?" like she was furious with me. Then she ran out of the room. She cried and cried and cried. The loudest I ever heard her do it. Louder than she ever did for Dad. It killed me.

10:57 P.M.

Been lying awake, trying to figure out all night who took the picture. Whoever it was, was hiding behind the chemical drums when they took it. Waiting for us to come in. Who could have it in for me so bad that they'd do something like that?

Kimby keeps popping into my head. I keep pushing her out again. She was/is mad at me. And Aaron. She knew about the supply closet. And that I'm gay.

I hate to think she did it. I hate to think anybody did it.

▶ May 14

Grandma found out before Mom told her. She was in the store when one of her friends asked her how I'm doing. Grandma said, "Fine. Why?" And then her "friend" told her all about it. Could hear Grandma slam into the apartment after she found out. Then talking on the phone. She sounded hysterical. She slammed the receiver down and I could hear her charging down the hall. I wanted to hide under my bed. She came in and looked at me for the longest time, like she was trying to find something she never saw before. She said, "I don't care what Oprah says. It's a sin!"

Didn't have to ask her what "it" was.

She said it's in the Bible in black and white. Ask any Christian. I was led astray by the wrong kind. The worst kind. She knew that Silver boy was trouble the second she met him. Reverend Silk told her there was still hope for me. I can change my ways. Make a different choice. Get back on track. She made an appointment for me with Reverend Silk for next Sunday. She said, "You can beat this thing."

Jeff didn't come home again today. Dying to know where he is. I'd ask Mom or Dad, but talking to me is the last thing they wanna do.

2:00 P.M.

Dad came into the room first thing this afternoon. He wanted to know everything I did with Aaron. I couldn't tell him the truth. I said we just kissed. He said, "Just kissed? Holy Jesus," and looked out the window. He didn't look at me again the whole time he was in here. He kept his eyes glued to the Texaco sign.

He asked me if I knew the hell that him and Mom have been through the past few days. They can't leave the apartment without hearing some remark from somebody. He says everybody in town knows about it now. I listened to him carry on about how much I embarrassed them and thought about tossing the words back at him. He was the last person I wanted to hear a lecture on shame from.

He said he's been thinking about it a long time, trying to let it sink in. But it won't. Every time he tries to think it through he gets sick to his stomach. He had no idea. He doesn't know whether to be angry or embarrassed.

He wants to know who to blame. He knows he hasn't been the best father in the world. Did I do it to get back at him? He started going on about all the times I'd looked at him like I was ashamed of him. At parent-teacher conferences, at Jeff's sports things, at the store. At Riverbrook. He said he could see the shame in my eyes whenever I looked his way. He asked, "How do you think that made me feel, to want your respect and to just get that ashamed look, even when I was sober?"

He said I picked a hell of a way to get back at him. Now he has to look at me in public with that same ashamed look. He hates himself now for driving me to it.

I listened to him go on and tried to understand. It all seems so crazy to me. Dad blames himself for "it." Grandma blames Aaron. Mom blames me. The funny thing about it is, nobody's to blame.

232

9:30 P.M.

Jeff's home again. I guess he was staying with Marsha and she made him come home. He has a shiner on his eye. Asked him how he got it and he told me to "go to hell." He said he's not gonna stick up for me anymore. If somebody calls me a faggot, he's gonna agree with them because it's "the truth." He looked like he wanted to punch me.

He asked me, "How did you *get* that way?" I told him I didn't know. He cursed me worse than I've ever heard him curse anybody and then he told me to get lost. Told him I wasn't supposed to leave the room and he snorted in my direction. He started changing into his pajamas in front of me, but then he hightailed it into the bathroom and slammed the door in my face. I think he's sleeping on the couch tonight. I haven't seen him since he left our room.

11:09 P.M.

I just remembered. I'm gonna have to face Aaron tomorrow. What the hell is gonna happen? How is he gonna act? How am I gonna act? Does he hate me now? I'm not sure how I feel about him. I've been trying hard not to think about him the past three days. Every time I do, I see that awful look he had on his face in Duff's office. Like he wished he was dead. It scares me when I see it.

▶ ## May 15

"Aaron went to live with his uncle." That's what Mrs. Silver said to me today. I couldn't believe it. I stood there like a dummy and watched her while she cleaned out Aaron's locker. When I found my voice again I asked her how Aaron is. When is he coming back? She wouldn't say any more to me. Wouldn't even tell me where Aaron's uncle lives. She kept looking at her watch and cramming stuff in the bag. When she was done and Aaron's locker was empty, she looked at me and said, "I'm shocked at both of you. There's a time and a place for everything. You picked the wrong time and the wrong place."

I watched her pick up the bag of Aaron's stuff and thought

about crying. Screaming. Dying. She was the last person I expected to act like that. I guess some people are liberal only as long as the issue doesn't hurt *them*, then they turn into Timmy Will.

I walked through school today in a daze. Didn't notice if anybody was staring at me or not. I heard "faggot" a few times, but didn't know if it was somebody talking to me, or a pet name between two friends. Didn't care. My teachers were all talking to themselves today for all I cared. I felt Old Lady Song's hand on my shoulder once, but all the rest of them were strangers to me. Didn't dare go to lunch. Went to the supply closet. It was locked. Went to the bathroom and sat in a stall for the whole time. A couple of people spoke to me this afternoon. Ralph or Lesly, I think. I wasn't hearing what they said. Pretended to be deaf so they'd leave me alone. Came home and sat by the telephone all afternoon and all night. I was hoping Aaron would call and tell me what's going on. The phone stayed quiet all night.

▶ May 16

The apartment's like a tomb. Couldn't make myself go outside and face people. Hell, it was hard enough just getting out of bed. Mom, Dad, and Grandma all look at me like they hate me, like they can't believe I have the nerve to breathe the same air as everybody else. Jeff doesn't look at me at all.

Don't care. Miss Aaron. Miss him real bad.

▶ May 17

I had my meeting with Reverend Silk today. It was so strange. He treated me nice, like he always does. I was hoping he'd be mad and scream at me. Then I'd have an excuse to get mad and scream back. I need to scream at somebody. But he didn't, so I couldn't.

He talked about confusions of puberty, and how my hormones are doing funny things now. He says it's no wonder I'm mixed up. It's normal for teenage boys to be attracted to the same sex. The secret is, not to give in to the feelings. Make the "right choices." I'll outgrow it, he says.

I listened to him babble away and wished it was that easy. But it isn't. It's not like walking into a McDonald's and deciding you want a Quarter Pounder instead of a Big Mac. ("Let's see ... I had a man yesterday, so today I think I'll try a woman.") It's more like deciding if you'd rather eat than starve.

He kept calling it my "problem." "I can help you with your problem," he said. At first I was confused. Did he mean my family? Or the fact that I feel so empty that I'll never smile again? But Reverend Silk doesn't know the first thing about my family. And he didn't give a hoot about my face. But he thinks he knows all about "it." To hear him talk, you'd think he was around when they thought the idea up. He said I could be "cured" of "it." Right. As if.

I thanked Reverend Silk. I was polite. He deserved it. He's so nice. He told me he's gonna pray for me tonight. That made me sick. I said goodbye and got out of there. Knew there was no way I'd ever be going back. Couldn't imagine what his "cure" could be. Decided that I couldn't care less.

▶ May 18

Walked into the locker room today before Phys. Ed. and felt my face ram into a locker. And then I kissed the floor. Got up tasting blood in my mouth. Heard Les Numer and Kuprekski laughing. Looked in their direction and got a fist in my face. Then I hit the floor again. Waited for somebody to help me. Nobody did. I was in there alone with them. I tried to get to my feet but I got kicked every time. Kept hearing "Faggot! Faggot! Faggot!" over and over. And then it got quiet.

Mr. Nolier came in and asked what the hell was going on? He saw me spitting blood and walked me over to the showers. He told me to clean up and that I should skip Phys. Ed. today. He asked me who did it to me. I told him I didn't know. Mr. Nolier must've told the class what happened, because while I was in the shower Ralph poked his face in. He asked me if there was anything he could get me. I told him, "A new body."

He pulled his face out quick so I couldn't see his reaction.

Got home tonight with my eyes swollen shut and my face puffy. I came straight to my room. Didn't feel like facing Mom or Grandma or anybody.

May 19

Hellish breakfast this morning. Walked to the table with my face all purple and Grandma and Mom freaked out. Jeff just sat there like a statue. Mom asked me what happened. I was gonna lie to them, but the truth made more sense somehow. A lie would have been stupid, considering how bad my face looks. The truth was the only way I could've explained it to them.

Mom got all mad. Not at me, like I was expecting, but at Les and Kuprekski. She was gonna call Duff, but I told her not to. Grandma was quiet for once in her life. I was hoping she'd say something about God condemning Les and Kuprekski to hell, but she didn't. She just stared down at her coffee and moved her lips with no sound coming out. Jeff ate his cornflakes and wouldn't look at me.

Meanwhile, Mom kept picking up the receiver and putting it down again. She took a deep breath, dialed some numbers, and said, "Hello, Mr. Numer." It took me a second to realize she was talking to Les's father. I wanted to die. Mom told Mr. Numer what happened, and then asked him what he was gonna do about it. Mr. Numer said something like "Boys will be boys" and Mom said, "Not when one of them is my son."

Mr. Numer laughed long and hard at that. As his voice boomed out of the phone, I saw the years add up in Mom's eyes. She must've aged a decade every time Mr. Numer took in a breath. I wanted to kill myself. And Mom. For putting both of us through it.

When Mr. Numer finished his laughing fit, Mom told him, real cold like, "You tell your son to leave Ben alone."

I thought Mr. Numer would start laughing again, but he got mad instead. He wanted to know who Mom thought she was talking to. Mom told him, "I know full well who I'm

236

talking to." Mr. Numer started calling her all kinds of names, like stupid broad. Mom hung up on him. Then she stuck some ice in a plastic bag and told me to place it on my eye. I threw the bag down on the floor and went to my room. I'm sooooooo mad at her. If my life sucked before, then she just made it ten times worse.

Been sitting in my room since breakfast. She hasn't bugged me about going to school today. I'm gonna blow it off. Wish I could skip the rest of the year.

Les and his father are probably wetting their pants from laughing so hard. Damn.

No. Damn her.

▶ May 20

I got beat up again today. This time I was walking out to the bus after school and I felt an arm go around my shoulder. Then my feet went out from under me. I looked up at the sky and saw two shadows laughing down at me. One of the shadows picked up my books and drilled them down at me. I thought about getting up and fighting back. But then I figured it was pointless. There were two of them, maybe more. It would've been a losing battle. I kept asking myself, Where's Duff? Where's Duff? It seemed like he was too far away to stop it. To help me. I had a scary thought. One of the shadows could've been Duff.

Got home and saw Mom studying in the kitchen. She asked me how my day was. I didn't answer her. I slammed into my bedroom. Mom came in without even knocking. Told her to get out. She didn't move. Wanted to tell her to go to hell, but I didn't dare. She said, "The people who love you won't let you suffer alone, no matter how bad you want to."

I didn't say a word. It was the stupidest thing I ever heard.

▶ May 21

I felt an arm go around my shoulder today when I was walking out of school. Turned and saw it was Marsha. She kept her arm around me all the way from the school to the bus. Some kids stopped and looked at us. They were trying to figure it out. I knew right away what was going on. Nobody would dare lay a finger on me if Marsha was walking with me. She's got clout around Chappaqua High, and she was using it to help me.

At first I was gonna ask her to leave me alone, but then I thought, I want her with me. I put my arm around her shoulder and we walked to the bus like that. Marsha didn't say anything until we were on the bus, then she sat beside me and whispered in my ear, "How are you doing?"

I looked out the window because I was afraid I'd start crying. Marsha understood. Suddenly what Mom said last night made a lot of sense to me.

▶ May 22

I saw Kimby walking up Main Street after school tonight. I went after her, screaming, "Kimby! Kimby!" She took off up the street, like she was pretending I wasn't there. Like she's been doing all week in school. Only tonight she wasn't pretending. She was wishing. I headed her off at the front of her house. She looked real irritated with me, like I was putting her out. She asked me what I wanted.

"Did you do it?" I asked her.

"Do what?" she wanted to know. Before I could say anything, she ran up her walkway and disappeared into her house. I knew then that she was the one. I didn't need her to admit it. Her running away was all the information I needed.

It's a good thing she ran away. I'm not sure what I would've done if she'd been within reach.

▶ May 23

I missed Aaron bad today. I sat around the apartment and didn't do a damn thing. It's always worse when I'm bored, or just waking up in the morning. Those are the times when my head is the most clear. I keep hoping he'll come back, keep telling myself that he hasn't left for good. I can't stop looking at the picture his mother drew of me, the two eyes with tears coming out of them. I know what she meant when she said it was my soul. I've cried so much on the inside that I don't think I have anything left to cry with.

▶ ## May 24

Marsha and Jeff had a fight tonight. About me. They both came in and Marsha said, "Hi," to me. I said, "Hi," back and looked at Jeff. He looked the other way and walked into the kitchen. Marsha followed him and punched him. I know she punched him because I heard Jeff say, "Ow!" Then she started talking a blue streak. I couldn't hear most of it, but what I did hear made me feel better. Marsha told Jeff that I was his brother. Whatever he or I did doesn't change that. I'm still the same person, but now he's got the chance to understand me a little better. Jeff said he didn't want to understand "*that*." Marsha said something real quiet. I couldn't make it out. I think it was "You'll try if you love him."

Jeff was quiet after that. Marsha did all the talking. I could hear bits and pieces of what she was saying. Things like "He needs you now" and "He's always been there for you when you needed him."

I don't think Marsha's talk did much good. Jeff came out and walked right by me again without even looking my way. Marsha came out and shrugged her shoulders at me. Something tells me she wasn't through with Jeff yet. She was out the door right after him. They're still not back.

▶ ## May 25

Something strange happened today. The bell rang for the end of History class. I must not have heard it, because I was doodling in my notebook. Everybody got up and left. I looked up and I was all alone in the room with Mr. Mariner.

He was just looking at me funny, like everyone looks at me these days. He walked over to me and said, "Your grade is really improving, Smithie." I didn't know what to say to that. My History grade was the last thing on my mind right then. I think he knew that, because he looked uncomfortable. I started getting my stuff together to leave. I dropped my pen and he picked it up. When he handed it to me, our hands touched a little. I pulled mine back quick. I was terrified of touching him. He pretended not to notice what I did. He started talking about the test we're gonna have tomorrow on the Great Depression. I watched his lips move and tried to flash back to the time when all I had to do was look at him and I was happy.

He walked with me to my locker. When we got there, I wanted to die. Somebody had taped up a piece of paper that said "FAGGOT" on it. Below the word was a picture of a guy sticking his dick in another guy's mouth. Somebody wrote below that: "This is what turns Ben on." I wanted to sink into the earth. It was so embarrassing. I crumpled up the paper and crammed it in my locker. I waited a few seconds before I looked at Mr. Mariner again, because I didn't want to see his reaction. Shouldn't have worried. When I turned around, Mr. Mariner was gone. I was grateful. And sad.

May 26

Ate lunch today with Lesly and Ralph. In the cafeteria. It was the first time in a long time. Ralph and Lesly were cool about it. Ralph asked me over to his house to watch videos tomorrow night. It was so funny. A couple of sophomores at the other end of the table wouldn't stop staring at us (me). Lesly walked over and told them to "Take a snapshot. It lasts longer." Me and Ralph both cracked up. For a few seconds, I forgot about all the shit that's happened the last couple of weeks. I felt good.

May 27

Awful night tonight. I went over to Ralph's house to watch videos. Things were going fine until Ralph's mother came in. She saw me sitting there and I thought her eyes were gonna pop out of her head. She called Ralph into the other room and reamed him out for asking me over. She didn't even try to keep her voice quiet. I have a feeling she wanted me to hear her. She asked Ralph how he could invite me over? Does he want me to make him even sicker? She said I've probably got AIDS for all anybody knows. She doesn't want me sitting in their chair, using their toilet, drinking from their cups, nothing. She screamed at Ralph that she wanted me out of there. Ralph said he couldn't just ask me to leave, and she said, "If you don't, I will."

I didn't hear the rest. I was walking out the door fast. I think Ralph told me to wait, but I kept on going. Ran the whole way home. Got home and I feel dizzy.

▶ May 29

I went to the nursing home today and had a long talk with Ruby. I told her everything that's going on and she snored away, out like a light bulb. It felt good to get everything off my chest, even though Ruby is lost to the world. After a while, I found myself crouching down by the bed in the praying position. It seemed easier to pray to Ruby. She gave me someone to look at. Grandma told me once that Ruby's soul is "with the angels." In that case, I figured that Ruby was God's ears. It was the best talk I've had in a long time.

A nurse came in and asked me if I was related to Ruby. Told her I was, but she didn't believe me. She told me to get out. I did, after I patted Ruby's hand. I was surprised at how warm it felt. I guess there's some life left in her after all.

▶ May 31

Jeff and me went to get our hair cut today. Mr. McPheran called Jeff over to the chair first. He started cutting away and talking to Jeff. I got reading a magazine, so I wasn't really paying attention. Their voices were just a buzz to me. All of the sudden, it got real quiet and McPheran said, "Customers are scared of diseases." I looked up from my magazine and McPheran was looking right at me. I was gonna ask him what diseases when McPheran told Jeff, "I can't cut your brother's hair." Jeff asked, "Why not?" and McPheran said he didn't want his customers thinking they'd get a disease from the scissors. I didn't know what to say. Jeff had his back to me, so I couldn't see his face. I didn't know what he was thinking. I just left.

I was walking home alone, kicking a can, pretending it

was McPheran's head, when I heard somebody walking behind me. Turned around and saw it was Jeff, with his hair
half cut. He said McPheran was a constipated old bastard.
He didn't say any more. And I didn't ask. We came home
and Marsha cut our hair.

June 2

I keep trying to figure out what I did wrong. I had a
relationship with Aaron. We kissed. We talked. We made
each other happy. What was so wrong about that? It's crazy
the way people's minds work. We got caught. Suddenly it
became this horrible, wrong thing. I don't understand.
What's the crime? Tell me, please.

June 5

Dad's drinking again. It's a nightmare for everybody. He
came home late last night drunk out of his mind. He wasn't
violent as usual. He was just sad. Crying. He kept asking,
"How much do I have to take?" Mom held him in her arms
and shot me a helpless look. She came into my room first
thing this morning and told me that the guys Dad works
with in the woods have been razzing him about his "queer
son."

I don't know what to do. I feel so guilty. Should I apologize for it? What would I say? Something tells me if I apologize now, then I'll be apologizing the rest of my life
whenever Dad falls off the wagon. If he ever gets back on
again.

What do I do?

June 6

10:15 A.M.

I sat by my bedroom window last night, just looking out
it. Jeff came in and asked me what I was doing. Told him,
"Just thinking." When Aaron didn't come, I dug around in
Jeff's bureau and found a bottle of booze. Don't even know
what it was, but I drank and drank. It went down hard at

first, but then my mouth seemed to go numb and the stuff wasn't so strong. The room started spinning and all my problems went flying out the window.

It was great.

I didn't feel anything. It was like a vacation. Now I know why Dad likes it so much. It's a picnic. No worries. No pain. Just give me more. Give me more. I forgot everybody.

It made me so happy. The booze made it easier to pretend I was back in the supply closet with Aaron. I kissed my pillow. Jerked off with the lights out. Laughed. Sang. And woke up this morning, puking buckets.

5:10 P.M.

Jeff was real mad at me for drinking all his gin. He reamed me out and made me pay for it. I cracked open my bank and dug out twenty dollars in quarters and nickels and dimes to pay him back. Told him to pick me up another bottle with the difference. He did. It's in my sock drawer now.

I'm gonna wait by the window again for Aaron tonight. If he doesn't come, I'm gonna dip into the sock drawer. It beats every other way I know of to cope. It's impossible to pretend on my own that things are fine. I need help.

▶ June 8

Dad lost his job. He missed work too many times and his boss didn't have any choice but to fire him. He came home, opened a bottle of Jack Daniel's, and said his boss was a "worthless piece of crap." Nobody else was around. I didn't argue with him. I let him drink and then I took the bottle from him and poured it down my throat. We talked about everything. He told me he was afraid to go to work, because he didn't know what they'd say to him. He wasn't mad at me or anything. I told him to "screw them all. They're all stupid."

He said, "Amen," and took another swig.

We passed the bottle back and forth between us. Drinking away, getting happier. I felt real close to him all of a sudden. The closest I've ever felt to him. Like I was seeing him clearly

243

for the first time. He told me, "Careful, Ben. They're all out to get you. The only friend you've got is this."

And he took another swig.

I reached over to get my share of my only friend. Dad gave it to me with a smile on his face. I took it and pretty soon I was smiling too. Forgetting. Loving Dad.

▶ June 10

Got up this morning and took a swig of whiskey to help get me going. Went to school with a little buzz. The people on the bus sounding like they were making music with their voices. I started singing along. Mag kept looking over at me like I was crazy, so I sang even louder. Ray the bus driver shook his head when I got off. I shook my head back at him and laughed.

Took another swig before History. Mr. Mariner cracked a joke. I think it was a joke. It was funny, whatever it was. I laughed, so Mr. Mariner cracked another joke. I couldn't stop laughing. Mr. Mariner looked at me funny and shook his head.

Took another swig before lunch. Ralph and Lesly were both real funny. They kept cracking jokes. I think they were jokes. I couldn't stop laughing. They both shook their heads and told me to "Quiet down . . . Duff's coming by." I did, and Duff walked right by. Then I started laughing again.

After lunch, Jeff grabbed me in the hallway and asked me what the fuck I was doing? Told him, "Surviving." He shook his head and looked at me funny.

Took another swig before study hall. I must've fallen asleep because I don't remember anything from the beginning to the last bell.

Took another swig before I got on the bus. Kuprekski tripped me when I walked by him. I went flying down the aisle and landed flat on my face. He laughed. I laughed. It was sooooooooooooo funny.

Got home and emptied the bottle down my throat. I'm still flying. Everything's great. Everything's funny. HA-HA-HA!

▶ **June 12**

Mag was just here. I was shocked to see her. We hadn't talked to each other in over three months. We were both too busy being mad at each other. I forgot what we were mad about. She looked good. I was hung way over, so I looked like shit. She got me a glass of ice water and told me it works great for hangovers. She didn't ask me why I was drinking. She was real quiet while I drank the ice water, then she told me, "I never knew about you."

I didn't know what to say to that. Nobody knew. Nobody needed to know. She said, "You know, Kimby's telling everybody that you told her you're gay a long time ago." Mag was upset that I hadn't told her. She wanted to know how I could have trusted Kimby with a secret like that. I said I didn't want to talk about it. It was a very complicated story.

Mag was quiet for a long time. She seemed to be itching to start a conversation, like she had to get something off her chest. She started going on about how happy she is that Scott's out of her life. He turned out to be a pig (I could've told her that). He wanted her to drop out of school and "have a litter of brats and cook for him all day." I didn't say anything because my head was pounding. Mag was quiet for a second, then she asked, "Do you miss him?"

It took me a second to figure out that Mag meant Aaron. Nobody thought to ask me that before. Nobody cared. Or nobody wanted to know. It hit me all of a sudden that I do miss him. Still. This aching feeling in me isn't embarrassment. It's a broken heart. I had a feeling Mag understood that, so I told her, "I miss him bad."

Then suddenly I started crying. On the outside. Like crazy. All of these feelings like hurt and guilt exploded out of me. I felt so bad about what's been going on in my life. About what I did to Mag. And myself. She put her arms around me and told me she's never been as lonely as she was when me and her stopped being friends. When she broke up with Scott, the lonely feelings got even worse.

It hit me then how much I missed Mag. I felt real bad for wanting to make her jealous. For ignoring her when I was with Aaron. She deserved better than that from me. Sure, she ran off with Scott, but who cares? She just did what anybody would've done in that situation. Sure, she was obnoxious about it, but so was I.

The next thing I knew we were hugging. Then saying "I'm sorry" to each other over and over again. I started telling her all about Aaron and me. The supply closet, the secret meetings, everything. Her eyes got wider and wider. But she didn't say anything bad. Didn't put me down. Just listened like a friend. I'll do the same for her sometime down the road.

It got late and Mag had to leave. After she left, I dug around in my sock drawer for my new bottle of gin. Opened it and dumped it down the toilet. The buzz is nice for a while, but when you come back to reality, you've still gotta face this scary world. It's better to face it with your head clear. With a friend like Mag.

▶ *June 13*

Grandma came home from a Bible Meeting all upset today. She said they read something called "Romans" where the Bible puts down homosexuals. All the ladies at the meeting looked at Grandma when they read that verse. Nobody said a word, but Grandma said it was like she could read all their minds. She didn't know what to say. How could she stick up for me when it was right there in black and white for everybody to see?

We talked for a long time. This talk was different from any other ones we've had in the past. Grandma was quiet for once. She didn't shoot Bible verses back at me and give me her black-and-white viewpoints on everything. She listened.

I told her that it's not as simple as two men idolizing each other's bodies. Love plays a part in it too. (Grandma made a face when I said that, but she didn't say anything.) Reverend Silk told me once that God views love between two people as the most sacred thing on earth. Reverend Silk didn't say love between a man and a woman, he said "two people." A lot of people think God made Eve for Adam so

246

they could have kids, but that was just a part of it. He made Eve so Adam would have somebody to pass the time with. To share his life. That's what he wanted. That's all any of us want.

I told Grandma what Aaron told me once about how the original Bible was written during a completely different time than today. There wasn't even a word back then that meant a "gay man." It was the people who translated the Bible through the ages who stuck their own gripes in where they thought they belonged. These gripes caught on, and they got to be habits after a while. There are only about five verses in the Bible that supposedly condemn gays, but people have taken them and spread them around like wildfire so it seems like there's a lot more.

Grandma asked me, "How can you be a Christian and still be that way?" I told her I didn't see what one thing had to do with the other. Who I love doesn't automatically make me a sinner. It's not gonna stop me from helping people who need it, or being nice to somebody who's having a rotten day.

When we were done talking, Grandma didn't seem totally convinced. She asked me if I'd try to change for her. Try and let girls turn me on. Shut off the feelings for good. Her eyes were so hopeful that there was no way I couldn't say, "Yes, I'll try to change."

Grandma nodded. She was a little happy, and I was a little disappointed. In other words, things are a little better between us.

▶ June 14

Duff called me into his office today. He wanted to know how things were going. I told him I couldn't complain, which wasn't exactly a lie. There are still bad times. I get called "faggot" an average of three times a day now, which is basically the average for everybody. I still find dirty pictures on my locker every once in a while. (I give them to Mag and she takes them home to show her mother. Mag's mother gets a kick out of stuff like that.)

Phys. Ed.'s getting a little better now. Better than it was, anyway. For a while there, the locker room was hazardous to my health. The guys couldn't stand the thought of being naked in the same room with me. They figured since the incident that I was gonna start gawking at them. As if. I mean, most of them are so ugly, they're not worth gawking at. But I couldn't convince them of that. After the third time I got beat up, I got permission from Mr. Nolier to go in early and make sure my business is done before the other guys come in. I can usually time it so I'm done getting dressed, but sometimes I don't make it. When that happens, I don't look left or right, I pretend to be blind, deaf, and dumb. I can't hear them when they call me faggot. It's all so stupid and unnecessary. But it's safer.

I eat lunch with Mag and Ralph and Lesly. We're in all the same classes, so it works out pretty good. Ralph came to school with some new wire-rimmed glasses the other day. Mag and Lesly both teased him. They said he looked like Mr. Hooper from *Sesame Street*. I didn't join in. I've had enough teasing for a while.

Mrs. King still gives me cold looks whenever I walk up to her desk now. Old Lady Song is great. The other day we talked about me going over to France for a year and studying as an exchange student. She thinks I have a knack for learning languages. I know I've got about as much chance of going to France as winning the lottery, but it was nice to know Old Lady Song thought I could do it. That I'm smart enough. I told her I'd think about it, and I really will.

(Mr. Mariner is still Mr. Mariner. Nice to look at, but off limits. It's a relief.)

Duff and me talked for about a half an hour today. Could've told him that life at Chappaqua High School is a bowl of cherries. But that would've been a lie. Could've told him life at Chappaqua was hell. But that would've been a lie too. I told him life is going on, some of it better, and some of it worse. He accepted that.

▶ June 15

Jeff turned eighteen today. And Mom got her night school diploma in the mail. Grandma made a cake and Marsha and

Mag came over. It was almost fun, but then Dad came in. He had a six-pack in one hand and a bottle of vodka in the other. From the looks of his hair, he'd just had a haircut. This time when I looked at him, I didn't see somebody who was mad. I saw somebody who was scared. To death.

Mom told him we were having a party for Jeff and he said, "Sorry, Son, but I'm getting good and plastered. You can thank your little brother for it." And then he pointed at me.

I didn't know what to say to that. I felt Mag take my hand under the table and give it a squeeze. Then something amazing happened. Mom stood up and said, "Don't pass off your drinking on Ben."

It looked sort of funny—Mom's five feet and four inches standing up to Dad's six feet three. She took the vodka from his hand and said, "Ben screwed up big time, but you can't blame him for this." Mom said Dad should be able to take crap without boozing. People do it every day and they get by just fine. It's time to grow up and face facts. Things are just the way they are. Some of them can change and some can't. Mom didn't say what the facts were that we had to face, but I think we all knew. I guess we all have different facts to face.

Mom told Jeff to start cutting the cake. He asked Mag and Marsha if they wanted any. They both said, "Yes." Dad just stood there, watching us all, but paying most of his attention to Mom. It was like he was testing her, seeing how much more she dared to say. Mom was real quiet while she ate her cake. Just when it looked like she was getting ready to say something, she looked down at her plate. Dad picked his bottle of vodka up, and told Jeff, "Happy Birthday." Then he looked at me like everything was hopeless and disappeared into his bedroom with the booze. I guess he's more ready to face some facts than others.

▶ June 16

Reverend Silk told Grandma about a place down east called Camp Sunlight that young men can go to free of charge. A bunch of churches pool together and sponsor poor kids so they can go to it. Reverend Silk didn't say "poor kids," but I figure that's who it must be for, since everybody can go for free. It's something called a youth fellowship. They meet from the end of June to the middle of August, seven weeks. Grandma asked me if I'd like to go. Reverend Silk has to know so he can get the paperwork ready. Grandma told me it's a great chance and I should be thrilled. At first I was gonna say no. It sounded like a pain, but then I thought, It's a chance to get out of Tranten Township for a while and be with some different people. People who don't know. I told Grandma I'd go.

She looked real happy about it. She called Reverend Silk and told him I was willing. When she got off the phone, she hugged me and said, "This camp will change you. I know it."

Didn't say anything. She was so happy.

▶ June 17

Ran into Mrs. Silver today in the General Store. I thought she'd try to avoid me, but after a minute she walked right over and asked me how I was doing. I was so surprised to see her up so close that I didn't know what to say. I mumbled something like "Pretty good." Asked her how Aaron's doing. She made a face and said, "Fine."

She asked me how school was going. I gave her my stock answer: I can't complain. She nodded like she understood. I asked her where Aaron's living now. She said, "Boston," and looked at the candy bar display. I asked her when he's coming back. She looked at me real funny and said, "Aaron's not coming back."

I pretended like I didn't hear what she said. I was gonna turn around and run out of there so I wouldn't hear the rest of it, but my feet wouldn't move. And she kept talking. She told me she tried to talk him into coming back to face the music. She said they never should've given him a choice in the matter, but they don't believe in forcing him into doing something he doesn't feel right about.

I couldn't believe it. I always figured Aaron's parents

forced him to leave. But he had a choice whether he could stay or leave. His parents gave him a choice. Holy Christ . . .

Mrs. Silver started going on about how she always let her conscience guide her. What about Aaron's conscience? I wanted to ask her, but I didn't. I ran out of there. I wasn't in the mood for any more of her phony liberal bullshit. Nothing she could've said would've made things any better. When I got out to the parking lot, I picked up a rock and thought about smashing the windshield of her BMW with it. But then I thought, The Silvers are screwed up enough as it is. They don't need any help from me. What would a broken windshield prove? I tossed the rock down and ran the hell away from there.

11:55 P.M.

Sat by the window today, not looking for anybody special. Just looking down at the street. And thinking.

I keep wishing that Aaron had given me something breakable. Something that I could toss out the window and smash into a thousand pieces. That would make me feel better. But how do I smash confidence and self-respect? Why would I want to?

The only thing I've got to remember him by is the picture. It's all crumpled up and faded now. It's been through a lot, just like me. It's so out of focus, you can barely make out that it's Aaron and me doing the kissing. The two people in the picture could be ANYBODY.

Some days when I'm feeling really low, I take it out and look at it. It reminds me of what we had. I try to imagine that Aaron's looking at it too, at the same time, remembering. Maybe he is. Maybe he isn't. Maybe he just wants to forget all about it.

Maybe that's what I ought to do.

 ## June 19

It's taken me a couple of days to let it sink in. He's not coming back. I won't wait by the window for him anymore. The telephone can ring off the hook and I won't pick it up.

I won't drink myself crazy feeling sad about him. It isn't worth it. Nothing's worth it.

I burned the picture. I had more reasons to destroy it than to keep it. It's time to move on. Time to start living again.

June 20

I've been like a ghost ever since I talked to Aaron's mother. I couldn't deal with anybody around here. I just moped around like a slug and tried to think of excuses to leave. I overheard Mom and Grandma talking. They thought I was moody because I'm going through puberty. Grandma said, "The taller they get, the moodier they get." I couldn't exactly argue with her. I've grown a couple inches in the last few months. Now I'm almost as tall as Jeff.

Thank God for Mag and her mother. They were the only people who knew what was going on. I went over to Mag's house yesterday and spent the night. Her mother had lots of good advice for getting over a broken heart. She told me to run out and find somebody new. I would if it was that easy, but it isn't. Mag's mother wasn't afraid to talk about my being gay. She has two cousins on different sides of her family who are. I was real surprised when I heard that. Sometimes it feels like I'm the only one in the whole world. Mag's mother told me that wasn't true. She said I'd be surprised at how many gay people there are in the world. Even in Tranten Township she knows of a couple. I asked her, "Who?"

"None of your business," she said. And she was right.

I asked her how she found out about them. She said when she worked as a bartender people used to come in and tell her stuff when they were drunk. She said, "Of course, that's different from what happened to you. I wouldn't wish what happened to you on anybody."

Neither would I.

June 21

Jeff graduates tomorrow. Two days after tomorrow he's leaving for Biloxi, Mississippi, for basic training. I've seen him maybe five minutes all week. We've both been breezing in and out of the apartment so much. This morning when we were eating breakfast together for the first time in a couple of weeks, Jeff looked at me quick and asked, "Is it live or is it Memorex?"

Graduation's supposed to be this big deal, and I guess it is. Don't know if I'm going or not. Things are getting back to normal again and I don't want to take any attention away from Jeff.

Whoops! Mom just came in and asked me if my Sunday suit was clean. I asked her why? and she said, "So you can wear it to Jeff's graduation."

Guess this means I'm going.

June 22

Just got back from graduation. Everybody was there. We sat near the back. Dad was sober (thank God!). Mom was grinning from ear to ear. She looked so happy and content. You never would've guessed the shit she's been through. I saw everybody I know in the gym. Saw Mr. Mariner and Smurfette, or whatever her name is. Kelsey! That's it. They both looked real happy. Old Lady Song was there with George the janitor. That was a surprise. I wonder if they're an item now. That could be interesting. They both had smiles on their faces. Saw Duff handing out diplomas. He had a smile on, like he was having a good crap session. Saw Mag and her mother. They looked happy. Mag's mother had a new boyfriend with her. I think his name is Barry or something. I met him a couple of days ago. Saw Kimby. She looked happy. Don't know how I felt about that. I should hate her right now for what she did to me. Sometimes when I see her these days I think about getting revenge on her. But how could I? Nothing I could do to her could cause half the harm she did to me. So I leave her alone, and hope that somewhere in her brain she feels bad about what she did. She was looking so happy and proud of herself I almost walked over and sat beside her. I was dying to see what she would've done. She probably would've pretended like the picture was never taken. She would've grinned and acted like we were still friends. Or she might've gotten up and switched seats to get away from me. Who knows? Who cares?

Everybody looked happy.

Don't know what the reason for all the happiness was. Maybe it was sincere. Maybe it was just an act. Didn't care. I was just wishing things like graduation could happen every day, to give people a break from the sadness of the day. Some people find their breaks in stupid things like violence and booze and hate. What kind of a break is that?

When Marsha walked up to get her diploma, the whole place went bananas. She's the hope of Chappaqua High School. When Jeff went up to get his diploma, everybody cheered again. I heard myself clapping along. Feeling happy. Wondering about the future. Just like everybody else in the gym.

When graduation was over and everybody was leaving, I looked down at the ground and walked out with the crowd, trying to blend in. Nobody seemed to notice me. I was glad.

▶ June 23

Jeff just went to bed. Me and him had a long talk tonight. He came in and he was real serious. He tried to pretend like he wasn't nervous, but I could tell by the way he kept sitting and standing that he was. I tried to think of something to say that would make him feel better. I ended up telling him he'd be fine. It sounded dumb when I said it, and I wish I could've taken it back. Jeff just looked at the ceiling. I asked him if he was scared. He shook his head no and said, "I'm excited." He thinks the army will be good for him. When Dad first suggested it, he was dead set against it because it was Dad's idea, but the more he thought about it, the more it makes sense to him. I felt better when Jeff told me that. It's gonna make it easier to watch him leave.

He told me to look after Mom and Dad and keep him posted about anything new that happens. He kept trying to tell himself not to care what happens to them, but that's tough. He said, "Like it or not, we're a family. We've gotta look out for each other." Sure, we all screwed up at one time or another, but that doesn't take away the fact that we've got the same blood running through our veins. It's okay if we hate each other for a while, but then let it go.

I couldn't believe Jeff was saying this kind of stuff. I don't think he's so dumb after all.

June 24

Jeff's gone. We drove him to the bus station today. He was real quiet and sober the whole ride up. He tried to smile and crack jokes, but I could tell he was scared. He kept looking at Marsha and kissing her. When we got to the bus station, Jeff asked us if we'd stay until the bus left. Mom said, "Of course." It was odd. There was so much that was on our minds, but nobody said anything. It made me feel bad that we didn't have ESP, since none of our tongues were working. Dad said something dumb about not taking any wooden nickels, but aside from that, we were all real quiet. Jeff and Marsha whispered things back and forth from time to time, but I couldn't make out any of what they said.

Jeff's bus came and I didn't think Mom was ever gonna let him go. She hugged him longer than Marsha did. Of course, Marsha had the longer kiss. Jeff gave Grandma her hug and kiss. After she kissed him, Grandma stuck her gold cross necklace in his hand. She was trying to do it like it was a secret, but we all saw it. Jeff looked a little confused at first, but he stuck the cross in his pocket, then he shook Dad's and my hands. Dad looked real uncomfortable, like he didn't know if he should hug Jeff or not. I was wondering the same thing. Jeff didn't make any move to get close to either of us, so it wasn't a problem.

Jeff got on the bus quick. He looked so old to me when he sat down and looked out the bus window at us. Like he was twenty-five or something. When the bus was pulling away, we all waved like crazy. I looked up at Marsha's hand because I saw some gold flashing in the sun. When she brought it down, I saw that it was the engagement ring Jeff bought for her. "Next June," she said.

Marsha didn't say another word about the ring the whole way home. She and me kept looking at each other and smiling. There was a lot of stuff I was dying to ask her, like why'd she change her mind? Nobody else seemed to notice the ring. Grandma and Dad talked about the new bridge that's going up in Tranten. Mom was just quiet, looking out the window. When we dropped Marsha off at her house, she whispered in my ear, "Jeff and I want to keep it a secret, OK?"

I figured that was the best way to handle it. There's no point in getting everybody excited about it. Who knows what's gonna happen in the next year? Who knows what's gonna happen tomorrow? Life is just one big question mark these days. Maybe that's why Marsha finally said yes.

11:09 P.M.

Just had a terrible nightmare. Jeff was lost in this sea of men wearing army uniforms. I was up in the sky looking down at him. He wanted to know how to get out of the group. I screamed down at him, "Turn left! Turn right!" but Jeff couldn't hear me and he did the opposite of what I said every time. Suddenly, he fell down this hole and I couldn't see him anymore. I screamed, "Jeff! Jeff!" but he was gone. I woke up and looked down in the bottom bunk for him. But he's gone.

It's so strange. I miss him already and he's only been gone a few hours. I never expected I'd feel this way. I figured I'd celebrate and try to forget about Jeff when I finally got the room to myself. Instead, I feel like remembering.

▶ June 25

Mom came into my room this morning looking like she wanted to talk. She said she was missing Jeff bad. I told her I was too.

She started going on about how she's tried to come to grips with "it." But she can't. It seems so unnatural to her. She told me she wasn't gonna try to understand it anymore. She'd given up. But she still loved me. Seeing Jeff leave reminded her that I was gonna be leaving soon. She wanted me to know that before I left.

For some reason, "I still love you" was all I needed to hear. Maybe it was because after all the crap Mom's taken, that's all she had the strength to say. It hit me all of a sudden how much guts it took for Mom to say it. She could just as easily hate me. Hell, she could just as easily kick me out of the house and say she never wants to see me again. But she decided not to.

Then it hit me how much guts it took for Mom to do everything she's done: go back to school, get her driver's license, date Chuck, deal with Dad. And Carol. And Jeff. And me. There were times when she must've been so scared, looking in any direction for a helping hand, only to find out she was alone. I thought she was so weak all the time. But she was the strongest of us all.

▶ June 26

Dad had an accident tonight. He was smoking and reading the newspaper in the living room when he fell asleep and dropped his lit cigarette on the newspaper on the floor. Grandma and me were in the kitchen when we smelled smoke. We ran in with the fire extinguisher. It was so odd. Dad was so passed out from booze that he didn't have any idea there was a fire two feet away from him burning a hole in the carpet. Odd and scary.

After Grandma put out the fire, she and me helped Dad get into bed. He woke up a little bit and moaned a couple of times, but he didn't say anything. Mom got home and smelled the smoke and panicked. I heard her in the kitchen shrieking at Grandma, "Is Ben OK? Is Jonathon OK?" I walked into the kitchen and she ran up and hugged me. I was so surprised to be hugged by her that I didn't know what to do, so I hugged her back.

Grandma and me told her everything that happened while she kept shaking her head. After we got done, she told us, "It's time to do something about this."

Then she called somebody named Edith. I think it was

257

something about AA. She wanted to know about meeting times and if you could just walk in without calling first. While she was on the phone, I went into the bedroom and wrote Jeff a quick letter. Told him what happened with Dad. Started out the letter, "Dear Jeff, Dad almost burned the apartment down today."

Well, Jeff did say he wanted me to keep him posted.

▶ ## June 28

Mag was just here. She came to help me pack for Camp Sunlight. She's worried because she's afraid I'll come back religious and talk about God all the time. I told her I'm coming back with a tan and that's it. She still didn't seem convinced. She said if I start quoting Bible verses at her she's gonna slap me silly. I said, "If I start quoting Bible verses, I'll slap myself silly."

We packed all the summer clothes I own—three pairs of shorts and five T-shirts—and sat and talked. Mag's got her summer all worked out. She's gonna go live with her grandparents and work at a Dairy Queen near where they live. Her grandfather arranged the job for her. The first few days Mag's gonna be a trainee and learn how to dip cones and make slushes and stuff. She's real excited about it. She says it'll be the first money she ever earned on her own.

Mag's been on the lookout for a guy ever since she broke up with Scott. Her grandmother told her that the guy who's gonna be her boss is "really cute." We'll see about that. I've talked with Mag's grandmother before. She thinks Lawrence Welk is "really cute." I can just imagine what Mag's boss looks like. I reminded Mag about that and she said, "Granny means well."

Mag asked me if I was gonna look for romance this summer. I told her, "No way!" Life is just getting simple again. I'm gonna play it safe and keep my feelings locked up for the summer. No. For the year. Mag didn't argue with me. She handed me something wrapped in tissue paper and told me to open it later. Then she got up to leave. We both hugged and kissed each other on the cheeks. Mag said, "Give 'em hell, Ben." I told her, "You too." Then she left.

I watched from my window as Mag walked up the street. She got smaller and smaller. Suddenly she stopped and turned around. She looked right up at my window and waved. I don't think she could see me, but I waved back anyway.

6:28 P.M.

Just opened the present from Mag. It's a green bathing suit. She stuck a note on it that says: "Don't break too many hearts this summer. Love, Mag." The suit's got tiny hearts in the material. They're so small you've gotta look close to make them out.

I miss Mag already . . .

▶ ## June 29

Mom starts work at Plumbco tomorrow. She's all excited about it. She won't be able to drive me to Camp Sunlight. Grandma says she isn't up to driving that far. Dad says he's gotta look for work. Grandma called Reverend Silk and asked him if he'd drive me. He said he'd be happy to.

Tonight Grandma made my favorite fish sticks for supper. She told me to behave myself and make her proud while I'm at camp. Dad said the same thing to me that he did to Jeff about not taking any wooden nickels.

I feel strange tonight. Excited and nervous and scared all at the same time. I could only eat three fish sticks. I usually eat six or seven. Grandma asked me where my appetite was and I said I didn't know. Grandma tried spooning some potatoes onto my plate and Mom stopped her and said I ate enough.

9:36 P.M.

Dad was just in my room. He wished me luck for tomorrow. I wished him good luck too. And that I hope he gets cured of alcoholism. He made a face and said he'd never be cured. It's taken him six months to realize that. He used to think he could just stop drinking and that'd be it. But the want for booze will always be with him. It's just like a disease.

I got kind of sad when I heard that. Didn't have time to think about it, though, because then Dad said to me, "I hope you get cured."

I knew right away what he meant. I should've been mad, but I wasn't. Dad looked so sincere. He honestly wants me to "get better." I didn't know what to say. I couldn't exactly tell him there's no cure. That I don't want to "get better." The want will always be there. I stayed quiet and let him believe.

▶ June 30

Got to Camp Sunlight today. Reverend Silk drove me. Leaving home was so awful. When I said goodbye to Mom and Grandma and Dad my voice kept cracking. I couldn't get out to Reverend Silk's car fast enough. But when he pulled away from my place, I started feeling sick. When I crossed the Tranten Township line I felt my stomach drop. It hit me that this was the first time I'd ever gone anywhere by myself. Reverend Silk looked over at me and asked me if I was OK. I wanted to jump out of the car and run back home as fast as I could. I think Reverend Silk could tell I was scared. He turned on the radio. That made me feel a little better.

We drove for a long time and finally got to the camp. It's a bunch of tiny cabins by a lake. There's a big cabin off to the side where we eat and everybody gets together. It was real bizarre driving up. I figured the people here would all be in dress-up clothes, like they were getting ready to go to church, but they were in shorts and T-shirts just like me. These two girls who looked a little older than Marsha—Pia and Denise I think their names are—were passing out name tags and saying hi to everybody coming in.

We all got together in the meeting hall and this guy named Uncle Lloyd gave a "welcome" speech. He said we were "lucky kids" because some "very good people" care about us and sent us here. I didn't feel lucky. I felt sick. He said the purpose of Camp Sunlight was to bring kids from different backgrounds together to see how we can get along. He said stuff about morning activities and "fellowship exercises" in the afternoon. I wasn't really paying attention.

Uncle Lloyd read off our names and what our cabins were. I'm in a cabin named "Oak" with three other guys and a counselor named Simon. One of the guys I'm bunking with is named Vinnie. He's here to get out of Boston. He's got a police record, so a church sponsored him to get him out of the city and out of trouble. I know this because he told us all about it when we were unpacking. He served time in juvenile hall for stealing car radios. Vinnie has a tattoo on his arm that says: "DON'T FUCK WITH ME."

One of the guys is named Trip and he wears hearing aids in both ears. He doesn't say much. The only way you'd know he's in the room is because his hearing aids start ringing every ten minutes. The third guy is named Peter, and he's weird. The second I saw him I thought about Dion Hatch. Peter's got this femmy voice and a face that looks made for makeup. When I saw him first, I thought he was more pretty than handsome. I wondered if Peter ever got strung up on football goalposts at his high school. He's got these clothes that're real strange, like a T-shirt that's got "Bee Gees" written on it and plaid shorts and bell bottoms. When Peter was unpacking his clothes, Vinnie picked up his "Bee Gees" shirt and said, "Jesus, is this pitiful."

I laughed, because it was kind of funny. Simon reamed out Vinnie and told him to leave Peter's clothes alone. Simon's kind of a geek. He reminds me of the guy from the commercials who gets upset every time somebody squeezes the Charmin.

Whoops! Simon just said "Lights out." Gotta go to bed.

 ## July 1

Awful night last night. Trip and Vinnie both snore loud. Vinnie sleeps above me and Trip sleeps to my right, so when they go at it, it's coming at me in stereo. Peter talks in his sleep, so I've gotta put up with two snorers and a talker. I didn't get any sleep at all. Got up this morning with bags under my eyes and nearly puked up my breakfast. I got excused from morning activities and ran to the office.

Called up Mom this morning and told her I wanted to go home. This morning was BAD. I missed EVERYBODY. Even Dad. I figured when I got away from him I'd be so happy I wouldn't care about anything else. Now whenever I think about him I feel bad about all the mean things I've done to him. I wish I could take back every bad thing I ever said to him. It's such a weird feeling.

Mom told me there was no way she could make it down. She's gotta work all week. I told her to ask Reverend Silk if he'd come and get me. She said she wouldn't do that. He was nice enough to drive me down here, I couldn't expect him to drive back. I started freaking out. I HAD to get home again. My voice started getting all shaky and I felt like bawling. Mom said goodbye real quick and hung up.

I got off the phone and felt lost, then I saw Pia walk in. She was real nice. She asked me if anything was wrong and I just said, "No." I felt real dumb and babyish all of a sudden.

I think she heard me talking on the phone, because she sat down beside me and talked up a blue streak about her family in Connecticut and how she misses them sometimes. It was like she could read my mind. I told her I was missing my family bad. Told her about Mom and Grandma and Dad and Jeff. Didn't give her any gory details. Just told her the good stuff because that's all I wanted to think about right then. She's got an older brother in the army too. He's stationed in Germany. We talked for about a half an hour. It was so strange. When I walked into the office, I didn't know Pia at all, but when I left, I knew all about her. She walked with me to Oak Cabin and I was ready to go back in.

▶ July 2

Things are a little better today. Spent the morning activities with Peter and Trip and Vinnie. We swam in the lake and played tether ball. It was fun. Trip isn't supposed to get his ears wet, so he has to wear a life jacket. He's tall and skinny, so he looks kind of comical with it on, but nobody laughed at him, not even Vinnie. Vinnie was too busy making fun of Peter's bathing suit. It's got a picture of Kermit the Frog on it. Vinnie said the last time he saw something like that was at a losers' convention.

Vinnie wore this French-cut bathing suit that I couldn't figure out if I liked or not. I tried to keep away from him while we were swimming. I didn't want him making out the tiny hearts on my bathing suit and teasing me next.

This afternoon Pia and Denise led us on a nature hike. They both got real excited about finding some mushrooms that we could eat. The mushrooms looked so gross I wouldn't have stuck them in my mouth if my life depended on it. Didn't tell them that, though. Vinnie kept whispering in my ear, "Don't you love her tits?" about Pia. I'd smile back at him and pretend like they turned me on. Peter didn't even try to pretend. He'd just roll his eyes and make faces at me like he thought Vinnie was the stupidest person he ever knew. I don't think Vinnie noticed what Peter was doing. He was too busy checking out Pia's behind.

 ## July 3

The "fellowship exercise" this afternoon was to get together with a partner, blindfold him, and lead him around the camp. It's supposed to teach you how to trust somebody else. I paired off with Vinnie. He must work out, because he's got big biceps and triceps. I never noticed them before today when I had to hold his arm. I took him on a real off-the-beaten-path trail. We walked around the dock. When we got to the edge of it, Vinnie asked me where we were. I almost pushed him into the lake, as a joke. But then I figured it wouldn't be a good idea to get him mad. Decided to follow his tattoo's advice. I led him back off the dock and let him lead me around for a while.

July 4

Big Fourth of July party tonight. When we were getting dressed for it, Vinnie kept saying to Peter, "Stop staring at me, faggot." Actually, I was the one who was looking at his body, just for a second. I couldn't help myself. It wasn't turning me on or anything. It was just nice to look at. But not touch.

Peter might've glanced at Vinnie, but anybody with a pulse would've. Vinnie wouldn't let Peter off, though. He kept telling him to stop staring at him. He must've had Peter pegged as a fem from the first day. Peter put his clothes on and tried to ignore him. I felt kind of bad for him. He's a nice guy, but Vinnie hates him for some reason. It's strange. Vinnie's so mean to Peter but he's nice to Trip and me. He helps Trip out a lot. Like this morning when we were making birdhouses, Trip was having trouble sawing a board straight. Vinnie showed him how and even helped him sand it down.

I felt a pang when Vinnie called Peter "faggot" over and over again. I didn't do anything, except promise to myself to be nice to Peter, to sort of make up for Vinnie's being so mean. Simon walked in then and Vinnie shut up quick.

The party turned out to be pretty boring. Some counselor from a different cabin played records and tried to be a DJ, but the records kept skipping and he'd have to take them off and try again. All the guys stuck with people from their own cabins, so there wasn't much talking. Nobody seemed interested in getting to know anybody else. I didn't notice if any of the others were cute. Didn't care. Simon had these rinky-dink fireworks he lit and threw up in the sky. They'd make a few colored sparks and then die out.

All during the party, Vinnie kept walking over to Pia and asking her what her plans were for tonight. She'd look at Denise and they'd both crack up like they thought he was funny. That didn't make Vinnie too happy. When we were walking back to Oak Cabin he told me, "Pia must be a lesbo," and then he sort of laughed. I laughed too.

 ## July 6

Our fellowship activity today was to go off in the woods and find a list of different stuff and bring them back. It was kind of a contest between cabins. Pia and Denise called it a "scavenger hunt." It was kind of fun. When we were in the woods, Vinnie tore the list in half and told me and Peter to find half, and him and Trip would find the other half. Before he took off in the woods, Vinnie said to me (loud so Peter could hear), "Be careful the faggot doesn't try to make a pass at you." I looked at Peter and he was just looking at a tree. I felt bad, so I didn't laugh at Vinnie.

When we were alone and looking for some beechnut leaves, I asked Peter if he minded that Vinnie picked on him all the time. He said, "Yah." I told him he should try fighting it. He asked me how. I didn't answer him right away because I wasn't sure myself. It's a no-win situation no matter what Peter does. I copped out and told Peter, "I don't know how, but you've gotta take a stand on this. Don't let Vinnie walk all over you."

Peter asked me why he should have to take a stand. Why should he have to prove to Vinnie that he's not a faggot? When Peter said "faggot" he made a face. I think I made a face too.

Peter got mad at me then. He said I wasn't any better than Vinnie. I just stood by and watched it happen. Why didn't I help him out? I didn't answer him but walked back to camp quick.

► July 7

Vinnie made Peter cry today. We were getting changed into our bathing suits when Vinnie accused Peter of looking at his body again. Peter was just sitting at the table writing a letter. Vinnie started flicking Peter with his towel and hissing "Faggot" at him. Peter tried to write his letter, but Vinnie wouldn't stop. I kept feeling like I should've done something, but Trip was ignoring them. I pretended to be deaf too.

Peter started crying when Vinnie flicked his face. He told Vinnie to cut it out, and then he called him a "dumb motherfucker" real loud. Then he ran out of the cabin. All three of us pretended like nothing happened for a minute. I asked Vinnie why he treats Peter so bad. He said, "Because he's a fucking homo. I can tell them a mile away. You've gotta give them the score before they jump your bones and rape you."

I didn't know what to say to that. Vinnie was as ugly to me as a piece of horse shit.

Simon came charging in and wanted to know what was going on. I guess Peter told him what Vinnie'd been doing to him the past week. Simon looked at Trip and me. We both looked up at the ceiling. Simon got wicked mad and dragged Vinnie over to a corner and reamed him out. He told him to go to Uncle Lloyd's office and wait for him.

Simon stalked over to Trip and me. He was mad at us. He told us the purpose of a fellowship is to help out friends when they're in trouble. He told us, when one of us gets harmed, we all get harmed. I didn't need the lecture. I felt guilty enough already.

Vinnie's been moved to a different cabin. He's in Maple, which is the bad-news cabin. Simon says he'll be moved back when he can prove he can handle it.

I hope he never comes back.

▶ July 9

Vinnie came over and sat with me during breakfast this morning. I tried to ignore him, but he wouldn't stop whispering in my ear. He told me he was gonna get Peter's head on the wall. Nobody finks on him and gets away with it. He's gonna bide his time, and when Peter least expects it, BANG!

I started feeling cold all over when Vinnie told me that. He sounded so nonchalant when he said, "I'm gonna get Peter." It was like he was talking about getting a gallon of milk at the store. I tried to pay attention to my scrambled eggs, but Vinnie kept asking me to think of ways that "we" could get Peter. I wouldn't look at him, and that made him kind of mad. He asked me if I was gonna help him get Peter. Didn't I hate Peter for finking on him? I didn't know what to say. I got up to dump my tray. Vinnie couldn't take the hint. When we were outside, he told me to "think about it."

I'll think about it, all right.

Peter didn't say a word to Trip and me all day today. He's

still mad at us. I don't blame him. I keep thinking I ought to apologize to him but he won't look at me long enough to let me.

6:45 P.M.

Got a letter from Mag this afternoon. She's as happy as a pig in shit. She says her grandmother was right for a change, her boss is "MAJOR CUTE." She sent me a picture of him she took while she was in training. She says she thinks he looks like a very young Tom Selleck. I looked at the picture and decided that Mag must've drunk one too many slushies, the ice is affecting her judgment. The guy is no Tom Selleck, young, old, or otherwise. Still, he isn't bad, even if he's wearing a dorky Dairy Queen uniform. Mag says he's studying computers at college and he's wicked smart. She says if he doesn't ask her out soon, she's gonna throw herself at him and ask him out herself. She says it's great being a liberated woman. I thought for a second how lucky Mag is sometimes.

▶ *July 11*

There was kind of a bad scene this morning at breakfast. When Trip and me sat down at our table, Peter got up and left the hall. Simon got mad at us all over again and told us to stop bugging Peter. He thought we said something to Peter that hurt his feelings. He sent us back to our cabin to make up with Peter once and for all. We tried to talk to Peter when we got back, but he ignored us. That made me mad. I was just gonna tell him to "go to hell" when Uncle Lloyd came in and gave us all a lecture. He told us that we're on this planet for a short time. We owe it to ourselves and each other to get along. Tolerate. I think what he said must've sunk into Peter, because he said he was willing if we were. Trip and me said we were too. We all had to shake hands and pretend like we automatically liked each other.

Something tells me it's not gonna be that easy. After Uncle Lloyd left, Peter climbed up on his bunk and started writing a letter. We asked him if he wanted to play cards and he said, "No."

8:15 P.M.

Today during lunch, Uncle Lloyd and Simon watched us like hawks, waiting for us to start talking and acting friendly. I tried to get a conversation going a couple of times, but Peter wouldn't bite. Trip wasn't any help either. He hummed a song to himself and spaced out. We were all uncomfortable.

This afternoon's fellowship exercise was something Simon called "The Peanut Butter River." He had a wading pool full of water placed between two trees. A rope was tied from one tree to the other so it went over the wading pool. Simon gave us a bucket of sand and said it was nitroglycerine. We had to get it and us across the Peanut Butter River without spilling the nitro or else it would explode. Simon said nitro always explodes when it comes in contact with peanut butter. Duh . . .

It was one of the dopiest things I ever heard, but Trip got right into the game. He volunteered to be the one to carry the bucket. That was fine with me. I crossed the river first. It was pretty easy. We did sort of the same thing in circuit training in Phys. Ed. I got over to the other side and waited for Peter. He was just standing there, looking up at the rope. I asked him what he was waiting for and he said the rope was too coarse for his hands. He was afraid he'd get blisters if he had to cross it. No matter what I said, Peter wouldn't put his hands on the rope. He started whining and saying his allergies were acting up. I pulled out a handkerchief and started to walk around to give it to him and Simon told me I was cheating. So I crossed back on the rope, gave Peter my handkerchief, and then crossed back over again and waited.

Peter blew his nose and then figured out a way to use the handkerchief to protect his hands from the rope. He made it across and asked me if I wanted the handkerchief back. I told him, "No thanks." We both watched Trip, who spilled the nitro the second he got over the river. Simon screamed, "BOOM!" and we had to start over again.

We went on like that all afternoon. I must have crossed the damn river twenty times. Simon got a real kick out of screaming "BOOM!" every time Trip spilled the nitroglycerine. My hands were getting wicked sore, and I was thinking about asking for my handkerchief back, when Peter dropped it in the stupid "Peanut Butter River" and Simon wouldn't let him get it out. He said peanut butter eats handkerchiefs. I wanted to cream Peter. He asked me if I had another handkerchief. "Suffer," I told him.

Peter started crossing the rope without the handkerchief. He whined and carried on. I just laughed at him. He started laughing after a while. Every time Trip spilled the nitro, we'd both scream "BOOM!" along with Simon. It got to be funny.

It was suppertime when we finally made it across. When we were walking to the main cabin, Peter showed off this tiny blister he had on his thumb. I showed him my own hands and told him to stop complaining. He just laughed at me and said, "Poor baby." Trip called us wimps and said next time Peter'd carry the damn bucket.

We were all quiet when we were eating, but it was a comfortable quiet. After a while, we couldn't look at each other without laughing.

▶ ## July 12

Things got a little better with Peter today. He's starting to see that Trip and me aren't like Vinnie. I'm starting to like him too. Once you look past the clothes he wears and his fluttery hands, he's not a bad person. This afternoon during fellowship activity, we had to tell about the best present we ever got from somebody and why it was so special. I went first and told them about a sweater I got from Mag last Christmas. I said it's special because Mag made it just for me. She told me I looked good in that shade of green.

When it was Peter's turn, he pulled out a ratty old wallet and said it belonged to his brother. His parents gave it to him after his brother fell from a tree and died. He said it was special because it made him think of his brother. After Peter told us that, he looked at Trip and me like he was daring us to laugh. I didn't feel like laughing. All of the sudden, I started wishing that I had something that made me think of Jeff. I don't even have a picture of him. When he left, we were both too afraid of making asses of ourselves to give each other anything.

I asked Peter what his brother was like. He said they used to fight all the time, but once in a while, he'd do something nice for Peter and everything would be OK again. Peter didn't sound sad when he talked about it. He sounded almost happy. I couldn't figure out why.

▶ July 14

6:15 A.M.

Just had an awful dream. I was in bed with Aaron, doing the stuff we did. We were laughing and having a ball. It was just like the old days, except in the dream, I was happier than I ever was in real life. Aaron kept smiling at me and caressing my dick. It felt like this big party was going on in there. I came all over the place. When I stopped coming, I closed my eyes and fell back on the bed. When I opened them again, Aaron was gone. I screamed his name, "Aaron! Aaron!" but he wouldn't come out from his hiding place. I got mad and buried my head in my pillow. I woke up screaming, "Aaron!" and my hand was wrapped around my dick in a puddle of wet. I was terrified. I looked all around me for Aaron because for a second I forgot. I thought for sure he was hiding somewhere in the cabin.

When I remembered, I looked all around me to make sure nobody heard me. Simon wasn't in the cabin for some reason. Trip was snoring loud. His hearing aids were out so I didn't have to worry about him. I heard Peter talking gibberish. I was so relieved I thanked God then and there.

I've just been lying here watching the sun come up. It feels strange thinking about the dream. It makes me miss Aaron all over again. I still love the guy after what he did. When's this feeling gonna go away?

Love sucks.

The more I feel it, the more I understand why Mom couldn't break up with Dad. If Aaron came to me now, I'd take him back in a second. I never wanted to understand that feeling. Now that it's been pushed on me, I'm kind of glad I do.

8:15 P.M.

Vinnie was nice to Peter today. It surprised all of us. We were in the main cabin making bookends because it was raining out. The bookends are square blocks with designs on them. Simon showed us how to burn the designs on with a wood-burning kit. He told us the designs could be of anything, then he took off. I was good and burned a sailboat on mine. Peter put a horse on his. Trip put a marijuana leaf on his. I thought he'd get in trouble for that but Uncle Lloyd came by and said, "Why did you put a poison ivy plant on your bookends, Trip?" We almost died laughing.

Peter was painting his bookends when Vinnie walked over to our table and offered to shellac them for him. Vinnie winked at me and I got scared. Peter sort of backed away from him. I think he was afraid of getting a face full of shellac. But Vinnie was good. He sprayed the shellac on nice and offered to do Trip's bookends for him. Peter was so shocked he didn't even say thanks.

When Vinnie was done shellacking Trip's bookends, he smiled at me and did mine. For a second, I forgot what a monster he is.

▶ July 15

Peter and me paddled a canoe all the way around the lake today. It was kind of fun. We got talking about Uncle Lloyd's lecture during breakfast this morning. I guess he was feeling holy, because while we were eating our pancakes, he stood up and told us about how God told Moses to lead the people out of Egypt. Peter said that was one of his favorite stories from the Bible. I wanted to be funny, so I said that Moses must've peed in his pants when God spoke to him. Peter said if God ever spoke to him, he'd know right away what to do. There wouldn't be any second thoughts.

I asked Peter if he believed in God. He said, "Of course," and looked at me like he couldn't believe I asked such a stupid question. He told me to look out across the lake at the sunset. It was really beautiful. All different shades of red, pink, and purple. He asked me who else but God could make something like that?

I was gonna say the sunset probably would be there whether God was around or not, but Peter started going on about how God's always been there for him when he needs it. It makes him feel better knowing that his brother's up in heaven with God. It helps him deal with it and even makes him happy sometimes. I asked him how he knows there's really a heaven. He said, "I don't know, but if there is, I wanna live a good life so I know I'll make it in. If there isn't, then it won't matter."

To Peter, God's like this voice that tells him things are gonna be all right. If he has a problem, he just stops and thinks about it. God gives him the answer. He told me if I wanted to hear God, to walk out in the woods by myself sometime and just listen. I didn't tell him I thought that sounded crazy.

When we paddled by the beach, I saw a couple of girls sitting on the sand. They waved at us. Peter waved back. One of the girls was built. I was waiting for Peter to say something. He didn't, so I whistled and said, "Not bad," because it felt like the right thing to do. It seemed like one of us should say something. It's what Jeff would've done. And also about four-fifths of the rest of the guys I know. The other fifth would've done something more graphic.

Peter didn't say anything to that, and I started feeling like a jerk. When we got back to camp, Pia met us and asked us if we saw anything worthwhile. Peter told her, "Ben saw some pretty sights." Pia showed me a book she wanted me to read. It's something called *Lord of the Flies*. It's about a group of rich boys who crash on an island. She lent it to me and told me to enjoy it.

▶ July 17

Got a letter from Grandma this morning. She told me that Reverend Silk said I was doing fine and that she's proud of me. She's got a new old person that she checks up on now. Her name is Jane and she's paralyzed from the waist down. Grandma likes Jane because she's "got all her marbles." She doesn't drive Grandma crazy all the time like Patsy used to. Grandma didn't say much about Mom and Dad. She just said they're both "going to their meetings."

Meetings?

9:25 P.M.

Just got back from the cookout. It was kind of fun. And something neat happened at the end of it.

Uncle Lloyd put on this apron and chef's hat and cooked hamburgers. Vinnie came over and talked to us. He asked Peter how he was doing, real loud, and made sure everybody saw him shake his hand. Peter acted uncomfortable the whole time, like he was afraid of what Vinnie might do next.

We found out quick enough what Vinnie had planned. For Simon, not Peter. During dinner, Vinnie stuck a lit firecracker in Simon's back pocket. When it went off, Simon jumped a foot into the air and started patting his butt hard like it was on fire. We looked, and there was a hole in his pants. Vinnie was laughing loud, and that's how we all knew who did it. Simon dragged Vinnie over to the main cabin, where he stayed for the rest of the night. With Vinnie gone, Peter seemed to start having fun.

After we ate, Pia played her guitar and we sat around the campfire. She started playing "Allentown." She told us we could sing if we wanted to. Peter was sitting beside me singing real loud, so I felt like singing too. Trip joined in, and we sang like we were crazy. I looked around and found out we were the only ones singing. Our voices seemed to go together good. The guys from Maple Cabin looked at us like they couldn't believe it. I didn't care. I WANTED to sing. For once in my life, I didn't care how stupid I looked. It was the first time I sang since my voice stopped cracking. It felt good singing with those guys. And I think I hit all the right notes. Everybody must've liked it, because they all clapped when we were done.

When we were walking back to our cabins, Uncle Lloyd told us we oughtta work up an act for the Family Day Talent Show. Simon told him, "You bet we will." What a loser . . .

Simon asked me how come I never told him I could sing. I told him I didn't know I could before tonight. I remember singing in music class in grammar school. My voice used to be real flat and I couldn't carry a tune to save my life. I'd sing quiet because I didn't want the guys making fun of me. Simon said I have a great voice—sort of a cross between Neil Diamond and Billy Joel. I took it as a compliment, even though where I'm from anything that reminds you of Neil Diamond is supposed to make you puke.

Now I'm trying to fall asleep, but I wanna sing. Use my voice. It's strange. It took me so long to find something that I'm good at. Who would've guessed I'd find it sitting by a campfire?

Feel good. Feel real good.

▶ July 18

"Who's Aaron?" That's what Peter asked me this morning when we were swimming. I didn't know what to say. I almost swallowed a gallon of water when I went under. I came up coughing and spitting. I asked him, "Why?" and tried not to sound defensive. He said, "Because you kept saying 'Aaron' last night."

That threw me for a loop. I didn't even dream about him last night, not that I remember, anyway. I said, "A friend."

Peter sort of smiled and said, "She must be some friend."

I didn't argue with him. I was trying to remember if I dreamed about Aaron. My mind went blank. I must've. Why else would I say his name like that? I don't think it was a wet dream, because my sleeping bag was all dry this morning. At least I think it was. God, I've gotta be careful about what I dream now.

Peter started asking me questions. He asked me if he was ever gonna meet Aaron/Erin? Is she nice? Is she pretty? Do I have a picture of her? I went underwater and swam away so I wouldn't have to answer his questions. When I came up for air, Peter was grinning like crazy.

▶ July 19

Peter's writing another letter. Trip's got his headset on and he's in a trance. He keeps peeking at a new copy of *Playboy* he's got hidden under his mattress. He had an old copy, but Simon found it and took it away from him. Trip bribed some guys from Maple Cabin to buy him a new copy. They did for twenty bucks. Trip showed it to me because he thought I was interested. The name of the "Playmate of the Month" is Candy Roberts. She's this brunette with big squishy boobs and enough hair in her crotch to make a wig out of. Trip keeps saying, "Candy's dandy," over and over again.

Whatever . . .

I'm writing in this. It's been kind of a quiet day. We practiced a song for the talent show this morning. We're gonna sing "Get a Job." We got the idea from one of Pia's records. Trip sings the "ba-booms" and Peter sings the "da-da-da-das." I sing the words. It's fun. Pia plays the guitar for us. After we practiced for a while, Denise came in and said we sound just like the guys on the record. I don't think we're that good, but we don't sound half bad.

▶ July 20

This afternoon we had "free time" so I took *Lord of the Flies* down by the lake and read most of it. I really like it. While I was down there, Vinnie came up to me and asked me how Peter's doing. He said he felt real bad for all the stuff he did to him. He sounded sincere. He says every time he tries to apologize to Peter, Peter walks in the other direction. I told him he should try just leaving Peter alone. He said, "That's boring." Then he laughed in my face.

He looked at me a long time and said he noticed I've been getting real chummy with Peter lately. I asked him, "So what?" He said, "If I didn't know you better, I'd swear you two were sweethearts." Then he grinned this scary smile. I'd seen that same smile before, right before I got the shit beat out of me.

I was gonna tell him he didn't know me at all, but I didn't dare. Instead, I said, "When hell freezes over. I like bitches."

I felt so dumb saying that, but it seemed to make Vinnie happy. His smile stopped being scary and got more friendly. He told me, "I'm glad you're still with me."

That made me feel sick to my stomach.

He told me to say hi to Peter for him, and then he ran up the hill. He's up to no good, I can tell. I'd tell Simon about it, but I don't want Vinnie getting mad at me. He seems to like me and I wanna keep it that way. I'm trying to just forget I ever spoke to him.

▶ ## July 21

10:49 P.M.

Just returned Pia's book to her. And had a shock. It was after "lights out" and I was walking through the woods quiet, trying to hear God, like Peter told me. All I heard was wind, so I gave up and walked quick to Pia's cabin. It was dark and quiet when I walked up to it. Was gonna leave the book on the front porch, but I heard laughing coming from inside. Denise was in there with her. The shades were all pulled down and the lights were off. The only sound I heard was laughing and music playing soft. I don't know why I did it, but I sort of peeked under the shade and saw them dancing together.

Slow dancing.

I ran all the way home. It was one of the strangest things I've ever seen. Two women dancing together. I still can't get over it. Vinnie told me once that Pia's a lesbian, but I thought he was just kidding. I wouldn't have believed it even if he'd been serious. I asked Jeff one time what lesbians look like. He told me they were big ugly women who look and sound like men. I always used to think Mag's mother was a lesbian, until Mag and me spied on her one day. She was skinny-dipping in the river with a guy. After a while they stopped swimming and went all the way underwater for whole minutes at a time. Mag told me what they were doing. I found out then and there that Mag's mother is definitely not a lesbian.

Pia and Denise are both real pretty, and kind of small. I'm so confused. Now I know how Mom and Dad must've felt. To them, a homosexual was anybody but who they know.

▶ July 22

Walked around today dying to tell somebody what I saw. But I decided that I'm just gonna shut up about it. I thought about it all last night. Who knows what would happen if somebody found out. Pia and Denise would probably be fired, and that would be wrong. They're two of the best counselors at this camp.

This afternoon during fellowship activity, we had to paint a poster to hang up outside our cabin for Family Day this weekend. Pia helped us out with ours. She asked me if anything was wrong. She said I was looking at her funny. I tried to shrug it off and say no, but I couldn't stop looking at her. She seemed different to me, and I hated myself for feeling that way.

Denise came in with some more paints and I saw Pia's face light up. I knew exactly what she was feeling. It seemed kind of strange to me at first, but then I decided it didn't matter what I thought about it. It's their lives. I started feeling bad about how I saw them. Sneaking around and peeking under the shades. It reminded me of what Kimby did to Aaron and me. It made me feel like a creep, like I was intruding on them. It must be hard enough keeping it under wraps like that. They were dancing in a dark room with the shades down. That can't be easy.

No . . . It isn't easy . . .

6:15 P.M.

We just hung up our poster. It's three stick figures surrounded by musical notes. The stick figures' arms are connected so they make sort of a circle. Pia and Denise came by and told us it looks great.

 ## July 23

Got a letter from Mom today. She says everybody's doing great. Dad's been to AA five times since I've been gone. Mom was going with him for a while, but then somebody told her about something called Al-Anon. Now she drives twenty miles both ways to go to this "Al-Anon" thing. She says it's a big help to her.

Her job at Plumbco is going well. She works on one of the packaging lines, sealing packages ready to be mailed out. She says the work gets boring after a few hours, but she just shuts off her brain and thinks about the paycheck. At the end of the letter, she told me that they wouldn't be able to come to Family Day this weekend. Grandma's car's in the shop and Dad's car died last week. It needs a new transmission.

I was kind of relieved when I read that they're not coming. Uncle Lloyd told us about Family Day a couple weeks ago. We were all supposed to write our parents and ask them to come. Uncle Lloyd must've sent them the invitation, because I didn't say a thing about it. I never really thought they'd come. We're supposed to sing our song for the parents for the talent show. I think I'd die if I had to sing in front of Mom and Dad. I'm sooooooooo glad they're not coming.

6:32 P.M.

I've been feeling guilty all afternoon. I kept rereading the letter from Mom. Peter asked me who the letter was from. I said, "My mother." He wanted to know how she was doing. He talked about his mother and father and everything they'd done for him. I wasn't paying attention to him and he knew it. He said, "Think about all the things your parents have given to you." I thought: a black eye, a loose tooth, grief, grief, grief!!! But I didn't say it out loud.

Peter didn't care. He started going on about all the sacrifices his parents made to send him to Camp Sunlight. His father doesn't believe in charity, so he worked two jobs and his mother collected returnable cans so they could raise the money for him to go. That's why he stuck it out when Vinnie was being such an ass to him. He couldn't go home early after everything his parents had done to send him here. He owes it to them to have a good time.

Hearing that reminded me of something from a couple years ago. I wanted a digital watch for my twelfth birthday. Mom told me they couldn't afford it and that was that. My birthday rolled around and I got the digital watch. I never stopped to think about what Mom and Dad did to buy it. I don't think I even told them, "Thanks." I slapped it on my wrist like I knew all the time I was gonna get it.

The more I think about it, the guiltier I feel. It makes me wonder how many other times they sacrificed for me and I didn't have a clue. Why didn't they tell me?

It's easier if I don't think about it. But it keeps creeping into my head. It's been such a sucky afternoon.

▶ July 25

It was Family Day today. Peter's family came. They all talked like they'd been away from each other for a year. I know that his family lives less than thirty miles away from Camp Sunlight, but they all acted like it was at least a hundred. When Peter's father asked him how things were going, he said, "Great." He didn't bother to mention the problems with Vinnie.

Peter's parents are both nice. They remind me of the mother and father from *The Brady Bunch.* They even wear the same kind of clothes. His mother had on a weird pants suit with real baggy pants. His father had on this flowered shirt that looks like somebody puked on it. Peter told me tonight that his father doesn't believe in buying new clothes, so they have to wear whatever the Salvation Army has in stock. He sounded proud when he said that, so I didn't laugh.

We sang our song for the show tonight. It was a big hit. We got a standing ovation. Peter's parents led the applause. Maple Cabin did the grossest thing for the talent show. They sang a song about how important it is to brush your teeth twice a day. While they were singing it, they passed a toothbrush back and forth between the five of them and took turns brushing their teeth with it. It made me want to puke. Vinnie looks real happy with those guys. Good for him.

 ## July 26

This afternoon during "free time," Peter, Trip, and me went for a walk in the woods. We got singing "Get a Job" and laughing. We were still feeling good about the show last night. It seems like the more we practice, the better our voices sound together.

When we got to a clearing, Trip stuck in his headset and vegged out. Peter and I talked. Peter laid down flat on the moss and looked up at the sky. It looked comfortable, so I did too. Peter says that he likes to go off by himself sometimes and just think. It was so quiet. I tried to hear God, but all I heard was the birds singing. Then Peter said something that hit my ears like thunder.

"Tell me about Aaron."

I didn't know what to say at first. I thought that Peter forgot all about Aaron. I tried to think of some lies when Peter asked me something that really sent me flying.

"Have you ever done it with her?"

I said, "Yah," and tried not to sound too cocky about it. What Peter doesn't know won't hurt him.

Peter was quiet for the longest time. I was afraid he knew I was lying, but it turned out he was thinking something else. He told me lately he's been having "feelings" for somebody. Was gonna ask him who, but he told me before I had the chance.

Simon.

I almost choked when I heard that. I always thought Peter was gay, but not in love with Simon. Simon's the last person I'd figure anybody'd have a crush on. He's such a Dudley Do-Right sometimes. I never really looked at his body before, either. Peter told me that he loves to look at Simon when he sleeps. He says it makes him want to rest his head on Simon's chest. When I look at Simon when he sleeps, I think about suffocating him with my pillow. It's a case of different strokes for different folks, I guess.

Peter told me if I told anybody what he said he'd never talk to me again. I promised that I wouldn't. He said he had to tell somebody how he felt about Simon before he went crazy. He knew I wasn't the kind who'd blab it all over town, so he took a chance and told me. I was gonna tell him I admired his guts, but the words started pouring out of him. I just let him talk.

Peter's sooooooo confused right now. He doesn't know if girls turn him on or boys turn him on or what. Some nights he dreams about Kim Basinger. Some nights he dreams about Richard Gere. I felt kind of bad for him. It must be hell being confused like that.

It *is* hell . . .

I told him to take his time. I said, "But whatever you are, don't ever let them tell you it's wrong."

I was surprised at how sure of myself I sounded and felt. Then I remembered who told it to me first, and I understood why I felt that way. Peter wasn't so sure. He said, "It's tough."

I didn't say anything even though I agreed with him. It is tough. Everything about it. But it can also be great.

We heard Simon calling for us, so we got to our feet quick and woke Trip up. Simon came by and told us it was time for dinner. When Simon went tromping back through the trees away from us, I heard Peter take a deep breath, and I knew how he felt.

▶ July 27

Uncle Lloyd found Trip's *Playboy* this morning and we all caught hell for it. He ripped up the magazine and gave us a lecture about the sins of lust. He told us that to look at someone with lust in your heart is the same as committing adultery.

I asked Uncle Lloyd why God gave us hormones if he doesn't want us to lust. Trip laughed at that, but I was serious. Uncle Lloyd said that God gave us hormones so we'd grow mustaches and beards and our voices would change right. When he said that, I was the one who was laughing. Uncle Lloyd looked at me angry and told us to go to breakfast. I don't think he likes my questions that much.

Don't think anybody paid much attention to the speech. From the sounds of the heavy breathing going on all around me, it sounds like everybody's jerking off to beat the band. Lust is flying through the air like fireworks tonight.

Trip's probably thinking about Candy Dandy. Peter's probably thinking about Simon. Or Richard Gere. Or Kim Basinger. Who knows? I'm gonna think about Miles in the weight room. For old times' sake.

▶ July 28

Big controversy today in the newspaper. Timmy Will got caught in a whorehouse in Mexico. He claimed he went to the place to "save souls." He was gonna convert all the prostitutes to Christianity. I guess he got a little carried away when he was converting, because somebody snapped a picture of him dancing a Mexican hat dance with this señorita who's a high-priced hooker. It's kind of a comical picture. Timmy's got on this sombrero and he's holding a bottle of tequila in one hand and the hooker in the other. Pia had a copy of the paper on her porch and I read the article. I cracked up when I saw the picture.

I wonder how Grandma's taking it. I wonder how all of Timmy's followers are taking it. How's God reacting to it? Is He laughing, crying, or screaming? Uncle Lloyd acted like he didn't know anything about it. Maybe he really doesn't. Maybe he thinks Timmy Will's a clown just like I do. During lunch I was gonna ask him what he thinks about it but decided I better not. He didn't look like he was in the mood to answer any questions today. Especially any questions from me.

▶ July 29

Got a letter from Jeff today. It's short and quick. He said that basic training "sucked" but he made it through. His captain was an asshole and hated his guts. The second day of boot camp, Captain Strang made Jeff scrub the latrine floor for talking back to him. Jeff says he learned to keep his mouth shut after that.

He misses everybody. Marsha most of all. Tomorrow, he's gonna find out where he'll be stationed next. I was happy, because he sent me a picture of himself. He's standing in front of this army barracks beside two other guys. His head's all shaved so he looks sort of like a chimpanzee. I wonder how Marsha likes that.

Peter asked me what I was reading. I told him, "A letter from my brother." I showed him the picture. Peter told me I was lucky to have a brother. He'd give anything to talk to his brother one more time. I looked at the picture and started feeling lucky. And proud.

July 31

Vinnie's gonna be moved back to Oak Cabin. We found out this afternoon when we played baseball with the other cabins. Vinnie came over and told us, grinning his "I'm a perfect little angel" grin the whole time. I tried to act happy about it but my stomach was churning. I ran over and asked Simon if it was true. He said yes. Vinnie's been behaving himself, so he's gonna be moved back in with us as a reward.

Great . . .

I almost told Simon what Vinnie's up to, but I didn't. Last night I had a nightmare where Vinnie snuck up behind Peter and hit him over the head with a baseball bat. I forced myself to wake up before he came at me with it too. I couldn't tell Simon about my nightmare. I ran back to the cabin and grabbed our poster. I was afraid when Vinnie saw the stick figures forming a circle he'd rip it to pieces. I folded it up and stuck it in my locker for safekeeping.

August 1

Vinnie moved back in today. He acted nice to everybody. He high-fived Trip and winked at me. He looked over at Peter and asked, "How're you doing, buddy?"

Peter didn't say anything.

Simon came in and gave us all a lecture about tolerance and learning to get along with each other. Vinnie did a great acting job, nodding his head and looking all serious, like he really gave a damn about what Simon was saying. For the first time I was happy that Simon follows the rules all the time. I just hope he's around when Vinnie goofs.

I feel so strange tonight. Like I'm gonna see something that I don't want to see. I used to feel this way when Dad got home from drinking.

▶ August 2

Pia told us about a show they put on at the end of camp. It's called the "Sunlight Spectacle." Different cabins get up and perform. She wants us to work up a song for it. I said, "Maybe." Peter didn't look like he was up for anything. He moped around the cabin all day and acted afraid to say anything. It's like he's waiting for some bomb to go off in his face. If Mrs. Silver drew a picture of his soul today, it would've looked like a big black hole.

Vinnie pretended like he didn't think anything was wrong. He and Trip went out for a hike in the woods with Pia. I almost went with them, but I thought about some of the stuff that Vinnie did to Peter and decided not to. I spent all afternoon in the cabin with Peter. He was so depressed. I tried to make him feel better by telling him that Vinnie seems to have changed. He said, "People like Vinnie don't change. They just get good at pretending."

When Vinnie got back, he asked Peter and me how we two "lovebirds" were doing. I laughed like I thought it was funny. I was relieved when Vinnie started laughing with me, not at me. Peter got up and left. He said he was going for a walk.

▶ August 3

Vinnie asked me to go canoeing with him this afternoon. I went, because I didn't want him thinking I spend all my time with Peter. I also figured if I kept him busy canoeing, he wouldn't have a chance to hang around the cabin and bug Peter.

When we were out in the middle of the lake, Vinnie started talking about his father. He got out of jail a few months ago. He did time for assault and battery. It turns out, he assaulted Vinnie's mother. He used to toss lit cigarettes at Vinnie. Vinnie showed me the burns on his shoulders. They look almost like freckles. Big freckles. Vinnie's father is a recovering boozer and his mother collects welfare. They got a divorce after his father went to jail. Vinnie hasn't seen his mother in over a year. He's living in a foster home now. When he gets back to Boston, he's gonna move back in with her.

It hit me all of a sudden how much alike our families are. Except there used to be love in my family, and there still is every once in a while. There was never any love in Vinnie's family. Just crying and burning cigarettes. And I've got a feeling there'll never be love.

Vinnie doesn't seem to care about it. It's like he just wants to concentrate on surviving. He hates people because that's all he's ever been taught to do. Listening to him talk about his parents made him seem like a human being to me today. A scared, mixed-up human being.

Came back and wrote Mom and Dad a short letter. I told them that I'm doing fine and I hope they're both good. Peter'll be happy that I did that. I know I'm happy.

▶ *August 4*

Pia came over this afternoon and we thought of an act for the "Sunlight Spectacle." We're gonna sing "Runaway." Vinnie's gonna get all these different props and act out the song while we're singing it. Peter got a little more cheerful when we were talking about it. He even spoke to Vinnie a couple of times and acted like maybe they can be friends. Everybody got along good. I hope it lasts.

After we were done working on the act, I felt safe enough to bring out our poster and hang it up again. Trip and Peter both looked surprised to see it, like they hadn't even noticed it was gone. Don't think Vinnie cared one way or the other.

▶ ## August 5

We practiced our song today. I think it's gonna be pretty funny. While Peter and Trip and me sing the words to the chorus, Vinnie jumps out and acts out the song. As soon as the chorus is over, he ducks behind us and hides while we sing the verses, and then he comes out again when the chorus starts up. It'll be a big hit.

While we were practicing the song, this girl came in and gave Simon a long kiss. He looked shocked to see her. Vinnie let out this high whistle so we all stopped to look at her. She was pretty, I guess. Simon introduced us to her, saying she was his fiancée. I was surprised to hear that. I can't imagine anybody wanting to marry Simon. Her name is Dina or Daphne or something like that. We sang the song for her and she seemed to get a kick out of it. After we sang, Simon told us to go back to Oak Cabin and wait for him. When we were walking back, Vinnie and Trip couldn't stop talking about Dina/Daphne. I tried to act excited about her. It was pretty easy. I just followed Vinnie and Trip's lead.

Peter was quiet when we got back to the cabin. He just lay on his bunk and looked up at the ceiling. Vinnie asked him if it was "that time of the month." The way he said it was so funny I couldn't stop laughing. Peter didn't laugh. He slammed out of the cabin.

▶ ## August 6

I got a letter from Mag this morning. She had some gossip. Les Numer and Kuprekski were arrested for raping a twelve-year-old girl. Mag says her mother told her about it. Mag was pretty sketchy about the details. The girl was a retarded cousin of Kuprekski's. She was visiting him and his father when Les got the bright idea. They figured since she was retarded she wouldn't know enough to scream, but they were wrong. She screamed and Kuprekski's father came running in and saw Les on top of her and Kuprekski holding her arms down. He called the police and watched as they took away his son and his son's best friend. Les's father hired a big-time lawyer to get Les out on bail. Kuprekski's on his own. His father hasn't even been to visit him in the center. He tells everybody he "ain't got no son."

Mag wrote at the end of the letter: "It's about time somebody caught Les with his hands on his prick. He plays around with that thing so much you'd think it'd fall off after a while."

Leave it to Mag to say something like that. I wish I could handle it as easily as she is, but I'm in shock right now. I don't know if I feel happy or mad or what. I've known both of those guys for practically all my life. I never really thought they'd amount to anything, but did they have to blow it so soon?

5:18 P.M.

Went fishing with Trip and Vinnie this afternoon. I had to get out for a while. I spent all morning thinking about Les and Kuprekski and it was driving me crazy. I asked Peter to come with us, but he said he had better things to do than that. I tried to talk to him but he acted like I wasn't even there. I wasn't in the mood for his moody junk, so I left.

When we got out on the lake in a rowboat, Vinnie talked about his girlfriend Monique and the different positions they did together. He started showing off about it after a while, telling mostly lies. I was gonna ask him if he remembers to use condoms, but I didn't think he'd appreciate that. Instead, I heard myself telling them about my girlfriend, Aaron/Erin. I said "she" was a great lay. They both acted kind of silly when I told them that. Not half as silly as I felt, though.

Vinnie caught this rinky-dink little sunfish and was happy about it. He said he was gonna take it home and mount it for his mother. I threw it back in the lake when he wasn't looking. A couple minutes later he asked me what happened to his fish. I told him the fish must've escaped. He pretended like he was mad about that and whipped off his shirt and dove in the water. Asked him what he was doing and he said, "I'm chasing the fucking fish." Then he started rocking the boat from underwater. The next thing Trip and me knew, the boat was tipping over and we were in the water. We came up for air and Vinnie was sitting in the boat laughing like crazy at us. So we tipped the boat over and sent him in the water again.

Trip started whining that he didn't have his earplugs in and his hearing aids were probably ruined. I dunked him to shut him up and he came up spitting out water. He looked so funny I started laughing at him, but then I felt Vinnie's hands on my shoulders and I went under. When I came up for air, Trip snuck up behind Vinnie and dunked him. We didn't know whether to be mad at each other or not. After a second, Vinnie laughed, so we did too.

We docked the boat and decided to go for a walk in the woods. We kept on hiking until we got to the beach. I almost died. There were two girls sitting on the sand, sunbathing. The same two girls Peter and I saw a couple weeks ago. Vinnie said, "Jackpot," and hid behind a bush. Trip and me ducked behind him. He was breathing hard and saying, "One for you two, and one for me." Trip said, "We want the one with the tits."

I didn't say anything.

Vinnie told Trip he was crazy if he thought the big-boobed one would go for him. "She's the kind who needs a man." I asked Vinnie where the man was, and he gave me the evil eye. Vinnie and Trip went back and forth, putting each other down. Finally, Vinnie yanked out one of Trip's hearing aids and tossed it in the woods. Trip dove after it and Vinnie made his move. I followed him.

When we walked out on the beach, I started wishing I was anywhere but there. The girls looked a lot older close up. They saw Vinnie and me coming and started to laugh. Big Boobs asked us what Cub Scout troop we were from. I hated her right away. Vinnie told her we were seniors in high school. She said, "If you guys are seniors, then I'm turning 40 next week."

Little Boobs laughed like that was the funniest thing she ever heard. I was just gonna tell Vinnie we should forget it when Trip came running out of the woods, sticking his hearing aid back in. He tripped on something and fell flat on his face. Big and Little Boobs both almost died laughing when they saw that. Vinnie was pissed by this time and told them, "If we're ever in the mood for sloppy seconds, we'll come looking for you two." And then he walked back into the woods. We followed him. He told us it was all part of his plan. Make them think we don't care about them, and then they'll come crawling to us when we see them again. Trip asked when we were gonna see them again and Vinnie said, "In a few days we'll come back." From the look on his face, I have a feeling Vinnie doesn't plan on coming back to the beach, ever.

The funny thing is, I had a good time. It was fun being with them like that. It felt good being one of the guys for a while. I've been on the outside looking in for soooo long, it seems.

Peter hasn't talked to me since we got back. He just mopes around the cabin and acts like he wants to be somewhere else. I don't know what's wrong with him.

▶ August 8

2:37 P.M.

I feel embarrassed for Peter today. He talked in his sleep last night. Some of the things he said were pretty bad. He asked Simon to take off his shirt. Simon was half asleep and didn't really know what was going on. When Peter asked him, he said, "What?"

Peter said, "Will you take off your shirt for me?"

Simon was quiet. Trip was quiet. I was quiet.

Vinnie laughed. A long, cold laugh.

Then Peter said, "You don't love her. You can't love her."

Vinnie laughed again. I was thinking about waking Peter up, but he wouldn't stop talking. He got going about taking off pants. Vinnie wouldn't stop laughing. Simon hissed at him to go to sleep. This morning when we were getting dressed, Vinnie asked Peter how he slept last night. Peter said, "Fine." And Vinnie said, "You sure had some sweet dreams."

Peter turned white. Simon told Vinnie to cool it. Peter looked at me and wanted to know what Vinnie was talking about. I told him, "Nothing important. You just did some talking in your sleep last night, that's all."

Vinnie laughed again. Peter turned whiter. I couldn't look at him. I turned away and started feeling lucky that Peter was the one who did the talking and not me.

All morning, Simon avoided Peter. He wouldn't sit next to him during breakfast or anything else. I think Peter knows what's going on. He doesn't need me to tell him any more.

▶ August 9

Vinnie told some people about Peter today. It had to be Vinnie. Simon and Trip wouldn't have said anything about it. And I know I didn't. When we were eating lunch, a couple of guys from Maple Cabin came over to our table and asked Peter if he'd like to screw one of them for fifty bucks. Peter got up and left without eating anything. I looked all over the place for Simon, but he'd disappeared. I haven't seen him all afternoon.

When we were sitting around the cabin for free time this afternoon, Peter found a makeup kit in his locker. He got mad and slammed it into the trash can. Then he ran out of the cabin. I feel a little bad for him. Who knows what else happened to him today? I tried telling myself that Vinnie wasn't the one who leaked the news about Peter. I almost got myself to believe it too, until out of the blue Vinnie said, "That sorry queer has been asking for it all the time."

I was gonna ask Vinnie to leave Peter alone. He doesn't need to take any more shit than what he's already taken. But I got scared of how it might make me look to Vinnie, me sticking up for Peter. Yeeeesh. So I kept quiet.

▶ August 10

Peter and I went to the clearing in the woods today. This morning I told him if he wanted to talk, I'd be there for him. He said, real cool like, "Yah, I do want to talk." I was hoping he wouldn't say that, but I went with him anyway. I made sure nobody was watching us when we left together because I didn't want people getting the wrong idea about us. When we got to the clearing, Peter reamed me out. He was mad at me for not helping him with Vinnie. He said, "You see what he does to me. Why don't you help me?"

I tried to tell him that we don't have any proof that Vinnie's behind any of this. Anybody could have told the guys in Maple Cabin. Anybody could've planted the makeup kit. Peter said, "Bullshit." He was so mad his whole body was shaking. I wanted to just get away from him. Pretend like I didn't know what he was going through. That was the easiest thing to do. If Peter found out my secret, there's no telling what he'd do. I said, "Camp's almost over. Pretty soon you won't have to put up with it."

I wanted to walk away then, but Peter wasn't about to let me get off that easy. He screamed at me that I'm a coward and afraid of Vinnie. I'd shave off my head if Vinnie told me to. That made me so mad. What makes him think he knows what I'm thinking? I told him he was way out of line and he'd better learn to fight his own battles. He got mad and told me to go find Vinnie so I could kiss his butt. I wanted to punch him. He didn't have any right to say those things to me.

▶ August 11

Peter almost drowned this afternoon. It was the freakiest thing. We were having free time in the water. I saw Peter go under, but not come back up. I dove down but couldn't find him anywhere. I screamed for Simon to help and he dove in. Simon came up gasping for air and had his arms around Peter's neck. Trip and me helped Simon get him on the dock and we all watched Simon give him mouth-to-mouth. Peter started puking up water and then he breathed. Everybody was looking shook up by this time except for Peter. He looked sick. Simon let him lie there for a while, and then he helped him walk to the infirmary.

Uncle Lloyd came poking around and wanted to know what happened. Simon said it was nothing to worry about.

He said Peter must've bumped his head under the dock and then passed out. I was relieved when he said that. And a little mad at myself for being relieved. I had a sick feeling that Peter's almost drowning wasn't an accident, but I didn't dare say anything about it. What if I'm wrong?

When I got back to Oak Cabin, Vinnie was reading a magazine. He asked me, "What's up?"

Wanted to tell him about all the stinking problems his big mouth caused. Wanted to ask him how he'd like it if somebody spread rumors about him. Didn't though. Instead, I told him, "Nothing much." And got into my bunk.

I can't wait for camp to be over.

▶ *August 12*

Peter stayed in the infirmary all day today. The nurse kept telling him he was "in perfect health" but he wouldn't come outside for anything. I went in to see him this afternoon. He looked depressed. I asked him how he was feeling. He said, "I feel so stupid."

Didn't ask him what he meant by that. Because I didn't want to know.

4:48 P.M.

Simon just left to try to talk Peter into coming back. I'd love to be a fly on the wall for that conversation. Before he left, he told us he doesn't want us mentioning Peter's talking in his sleep or anything about it. He was looking right at Vinnie when he said it. Trip and I both promised we wouldn't. Vinnie put on his serious face and said, "I promise."

After Simon left, Vinnie cracked a joke about him and Peter. He called them "Mr. and Mrs. Joe Blow." He looked at Trip and me and waited for us to laugh. Trip giggled a little, but I stayed quiet. I want to tell Vinnie that I'm getting sick of it all, but he keeps looking out the window and humming "Here Comes the Bride."

6:27 P.M.

Peter just came back. Vinnie ran right up to him and said, "Welcome back, buddy." I heard Peter whisper loud to him,

292

"Don't bother me anymore or I'll get a rake and beat the shit out of you."

Vinnie looked like he got hit by lightning. His mouth dropped open and he was speechless. I was speechless too, but cheering like crazy on the inside. I guess Peter's been thinking about it all day. It's either kill or be killed.

Vinnie backed away from Peter and let him pass without a word. Simon came in then and looked at each of us. Then he smiled and said, "It's nice to see everything's back to normal in here."

God ... If he only knew ...

▶ August 13

Tonight was a nightmare. We had practice for the "Sunlight Spectacle." Things were going fine until we got to our song. Vinnie got the props mixed up. He pulled out the umbrella at the wrong time and accidentally on purpose goosed Peter with it. I saw him do it. Peter turned around and started screaming at him. I guess all the crap just got to be too much for him. Simon ran up on the stage and wanted to know what was wrong. Peter told him that Vinnie was poking him with the umbrella. Vinnie said it was an accident and tried to act innocent. They both looked at Trip and me to back them up. We didn't say anything.

Simon took Vinnie aside and talked soft to him. I heard Vinnie say over and over, "I didn't do it on purpose." Simon shook his head and told him to listen. Vinnie came back scowling and said he was sorry to Peter. Peter didn't even look at him. I got scared all of a sudden. I've never seen Vinnie or Peter so angry before.

▶ August 14

Vinnie got a letter from his mother today. His father's in jail again for beating up a guy in a bar. Simon came in and told us what was going on. Trip wanted to know all about jail, but Simon told him that wasn't the point. He said we had to support Vinnie and be here for him if he needs us. He said we should offer to talk to him if he wants to. Peter didn't say anything to that, and I guess Simon understood why.

Vinnie came into the cabin looking pissed. Simon asked him if he wanted to talk about it. Vinnie told him no, he wanted to be left alone. But then he asked me to stay in the room. Simon looked at me like he couldn't believe Vinnie would rather talk to me than him.

When we were alone, Vinnie told me what happened. His father went in the bar because he felt like drinking. A "faggot" started making eyes at him and his father beat him up. It turns out the "faggot" was a cop. Vinnie's father had cops on him and throwing him in jail before he knew what hit him. I listened to Vinnie go on and tried to figure out what the truth was. I don't think anybody but his father and the "faggot" will ever know. Vinnie's mother wrote, "The world's gone out of control when a man can't protect himself from queers in a bar."

The news about Vinnie's father wasn't the worst news in the letter. At the end of the letter his mother said she couldn't take him back yet. She's got a new boyfriend and he hates kids. She told Vinnie, "You know how it is, baby." Vinnie tore up the letter after he read me that part.

Now Vinnie has to go back to social services when he gets back to Boston. A social worker will be waiting for him at the bus station. Vinnie says hell will freeze over before he goes anywhere with any social worker. Now he's in the bunk above me, not making a sound. The quiet's both scary and nice at the same time.

August 15

6:35 P.M.

It's almost time for the "Sunlight Spectacle" tonight. We're supposed to be resting for it, but I'm too nervous. I hope I don't screw up the song and mess everybody up. Vinnie's been cheerful all day. I can't figure that out. Peter's had a bug up his ass all day long. He won't talk to anybody. It's like he's just counting the seconds until he can get home again.

Whoops! Peter just walked out the door. I heard Vinnie tell him, "Goodbye, Tinkerbell." He didn't bother to turn around and look at him. I thought Vinnie said it to be funny, but he's not laughing.

Whoops! Vinnie just walked out the door too. Wonder where he's going.

9:56 P.M.

It's been a hell of a night. I still can't believe everything that happened.

The "Sunlight Spectacle" was in full swing, and still no sign of Peter and Vinnie. I told Trip I was going to go look for them. I'd be right back. Was walking through the woods, when I heard a Voice say, "Go to the clearing." It was real deep. Don't know if I really heard it or it was in my imagination. Don't care. I ran to the edge of the clearing and saw them there. Vinnie was standing over Peter with a broomstick in his hands. Peter was lying on his stomach. His underwear was down around his ankles and he was crying. His face was all black and blue and shaking. Vinnie was saying, "So you thought you could beat the shit out of me, Tinkerbell?" I was so scared I ran away from there as fast as I could. I was running through the woods when I heard this Voice telling me, "Go back. Go back."

I tried to ignore the Voice but it kept ringing in my ears. The only way I could make the Voice stop was to turn around and go back, so I did. I ran back to the clearing and saw Vinnie start to stick the broomstick up Peter's butt. He saw me standing there and didn't even look surprised. He grinned at me and motioned for me to come closer. I did. He said, "You go first."

He handed me the broomstick. I didn't know what to do with it. I stood there like a dummy. Vinnie said, "C'mon. He won't move. If he moves or makes a sound I'll slug him again."

Peter made a sound. It was a little sound. A sentence. He

said, "I screwed a girl last week." I didn't think Vinnie heard him. Peter looked up at me and said, "Tell him, Ben."

Vinnie told him to shut up or he'd kill him. My voice was gone. But the Voice kept ringing in my ears, "Stop this! Stop this! STOP THIS!!!" I felt so awful. I didn't know what made me sicker, what Vinnie wanted me to do to Peter, or Peter feeling he had to prove he screwed a girl. I just wanted to get out of there.

I dropped the broomstick and started to back away from Vinnie. He looked so scary to me. He said to me, "Take the damn thing and cram it in. He likes that stuff. C'mon."

He was so mad/happy, there was snot running out of his nose. I felt the broomstick in my hands again. I saw Vinnie grin at me, and I knew I'd seen that look before. On Les Numer's face. On Kuprekski's face. On Kimby's face. On Timmy Will's face.

The Voice took over my brain and told me what to do. I drove the broomstick into that face. I hit that face again and again with the broomstick. The look went blank. Vinnie fell over. I closed my eyes and swung again. Over and over. Hitting Vinnie with the broomstick. Every swing was for somebody. One was for Peter. One was for Pia. One was for Denise. One was for Aaron.

The rest were for me.

When I opened my eyes again, Vinnie was gone and I was hitting a rock. Peter was sitting up, pulling his pants up and wiping his face off. He looked at the ground and said, "Thanks." Then he started to cry. He snuck a peek at me and asked, "Why?"

I didn't know what he meant. It could have been a dozen different things. I told him, "I don't know." And then I started crying too. I was mad at everything, but mostly mad at myself. For letting the situation get this far. For being such a coward. For telling myself what was happening to Peter didn't have a thing to do with me.

Peter needed help walking back to camp. He kept falling over when he'd try to stand. "Dizzy," he said.

I carried him back. I was surprised at how light he felt to

me, like I was carrying a pillow. When we walked into camp, people were just pouring out of the "Sunlight Spectacle." The whole group of fifty guys were staring at the two of us, trying to figure it out. I told them that I had to get Peter to the infirmary quick. They all just stood there. Uncle Lloyd or Simon or Pia didn't seem to be anywhere around. It was so quiet, I could hear the guys from Maple Cabin whispering and laughing, but trying to keep themselves quiet.

Peter started getting heavy by this time. I was afraid I might drop him. I think people could tell that I was straining, because a guy from Birch Cabin came over to help me. Then a guy from Elm. As we were walking to the infirmary, a guy from Pine joined us. We made a real group, the four of us. I don't know any of their names (I didn't bother to learn them over the summer), but it felt like we'd known each other all our lives.

The other guys parted a path for us as we walked, didn't offer to help us or anything, but didn't get in our way, either. I don't think it would've mattered if anybody had tried to stop us. We could've carried Peter through the Patriots' defensive line if we wanted to. When we got in the infirmary, we set Peter down on the bed and looked at each other. That's when I knew we *had* known each other all our lives. We couldn't have looked any more different. One of them was black. One of them looked Chinese or something. The other one was short and chubby. But they were me. And I was them.

Uncle Lloyd and the nurse came barging in, asking questions left and right. The nurse screamed at us to clear out. Uncle Lloyd tried to corral me and find out what happened, but I got away from him and—

Whoops! Simon just came in and said Peter's got a concussion. They're taking him to the hospital for observation. I'll go with them. I'm still waiting for Vinnie to make an appearance. Still waiting for the shit to hit the fan.

▶ August 16

Just got back to the cabin. Tired as hell. Stayed with Peter in the hospital all night. He came around at exactly 2:30 this morning. He kept saying he felt fine, but every time he'd sit up, he'd get a head rush. He fell asleep and I sat by his bed, saying I was sorry over and over again. Peter's parents walked in and I got out of there quick. I couldn't take any more tears or anger. Maybe stuff like this has happened to Peter before and it's old hat to them. Or maybe this is the first time it's ever happened. I didn't want to know, either way. I got thinking how lucky the *Brady Bunch* parents were. They never had to deal with anything like that.

I told Simon what happened. Had to. He cornered me and told me he wanted to know. I didn't give all the details. I didn't tell about Peter's underwear being down or about the broomstick. I figured Peter could tell that part later if he wants to, though I have a feeling he won't. I just said that Vinnie beat him up. Simon asked me what my part in it was. I told him that I helped Peter fight off Vinnie. I didn't tell about all the times I hit him. Simon asked me and I said, "A few."

It could've been more or it could've been less. I don't know just when Vinnie ran out and I started hitting the rock. Simon told Uncle Lloyd what happened. Uncle Lloyd gave me a lecture about turning the other cheek and then told me to say a prayer for "that poor lost soul of a young man." Then he went to call the police.

I'll say a prayer for Vinnie tonight. I'll pray that he gets hit by a train.

6:30 P.M.

Peter just came back. I was surprised to see him. I figured since camp was almost over, he'd go home with his parents and call it a summer. But he's back. He looks awful. His face is all puffy and he's got a bandage around his head. Asked him how he was feeling and he said, "Like I've been to hell."

Told him that I was surprised to see him and he said, "Why? Camp's not over yet."

He climbed on his bunk and started reading. I just looked at him for a minute. I couldn't believe the courage it took for him to walk through that door. Was gonna say so to him, but the next thing I knew, he was thanking me for helping him. That made me feel terrible.

▶ *August 17*

They found Vinnie this morning. Simon told us about it, shaking his head the whole time. He was trying to steal cash from a cash register in a 7-Eleven in Monroe when the owner caught him and called the police. There was a chase on foot. When the police finally caught him, his face was all black and blue like he'd been beat up. When the police asked him who did it he said, "Uncle Lloyd."

They thought it was a case of child abuse. When Uncle Lloyd was questioned, he explained what he thought happened. He said a couple of "his boys" got in a little disagreement and Vinnie ran off when he realized the error of his ways. The police came and questioned Peter and me. We told them what I told Simon: that Vinnie attacked Peter and I helped Peter fight him off when I saw it. It didn't seem like Vinnie was interested in telling the whole truth, and neither were we. The cop looked at Peter's face and said, "Holy Christ!" It does look pretty bad. He asked Peter if he'd be willing to testify in court and Peter said no really quick. The cop didn't push it.

Simon told us that Vinnie's been taken to the youth detention center, where he belongs (I hope he's sharing a room with Kuprekski). I thought Peter would be happy when he heard what happened to Vinnie, but he looked upset. He asked me, "Why did Vinnie hate me so much?"

I didn't answer him, because I honestly don't know. You can't chalk it up to a lousy childhood. Lots of people who had good childhoods hate gays too. Who can explain why? Who'd even wanna try? I know I don't. It's like trying to explain why some people hate all blacks or Jews or people with red hair. There's no logical reason, except the ones they make up for themselves.

Peter looked out the window and said, "He's still out there."

I went to the window with him and agreed. We looked out together at a world full of Vinnies and were quiet.

▶ **August 18**

Peter and I paddled around the lake again today. He started going on about Aaron, and how excited I must be to see "her" again. That made me feel worse than ever. I couldn't take it anymore.

"Him," I said.

DEAD SILENCE from in back of me.

I said, "Aaron was a guy."

Before Peter could say anything else, I told him all about what happened with Aaron. Everything that we did together. How it all just blew up in my face. How I still miss him after all this time. How I've known I was "it" for almost two years now.

I don't know what I expected Peter to do when I was done. I thought maybe he'd tell me "Thanks" for telling him. I turned around to sneak a peek at him and saw he wasn't in any mood to thank me. He was pissed with me. It seemed like the more he let it sink in, the angrier he got. Told me I was no better than Vinnie. He called me every bad name I ever heard. Started screaming about what a creep I was. "Quiet down," I told him. "Go to hell," he told me.

I got scared then. I thought maybe he'd stand up in the canoe and start screaming, "Ben told me he's gay!" to everybody standing on shore. I couldn't imagine anything worse than that. I wanted to just get away from him. Was gonna tip the canoe over and swim for shore, ready to deny everything that Peter said about me.

But then it hit me, nothing could be worse than living with the secret cooped up inside me. It's been such a pain in the ass pretending. Passing myself off as something different from what I am. Laughing at jokes that I don't think are funny. Telling all these insane lies to myself. And then forcing myself to believe them. I worked so hard all summer to shut off the feelings. I ended up shutting off myself at the same time.

Decided that I didn't care who knew. It was time to stop being scared. It's the Truth, for God's sake. Ben Smith *is* gay. If I act ashamed of it, then everybody will keep treating me like shit when they find out.

I told Peter I didn't care if he told anybody.

He couldn't believe it. He asked me if I was crazy.

Told him no.

He didn't say anything to that. I thought maybe he was getting his lungs revved up to scream it across the lake. He had every right to do it. But he wasn't saying anything. He was being so quiet. All I heard was the sound of him paddling again, so I did too. When we got back near the beach, Peter said, real quiet, "I won't tell anybody."

I turned around and looked at his face, which still had big purple bruises on it. It looked like hell, but not angry anymore. Just too tired and hurting to do any talking. I knew then that Peter wasn't going to tell anybody. That was my job.

I started screaming "I'm gay!" as loud as I could. My voice didn't crack once. It echoed across the lake so strong that the trees seemed to shake every time I let loose with the words. Guys started popping out of the cabins until a small crowd formed on the beach and watched me. Uncle Lloyd was with them. That should have scared me but it didn't. I screamed the words ten more times and never felt better in my life. Hell, if it was a song, I would've sung it. I could tell from Uncle Lloyd's disgusted face that he was thinking, Great, another one. But I didn't care. The only thing that matters is what I think, and I think I'm pretty damn okay.

After my screaming jag, we paddled and talked for a long time. Peter's known ever since he was a baby. He says he thinks he came out of the womb that way. I didn't tell him that I thought we *all* came out of the womb that way, because I knew what he meant. He called me a "late bloomer" for not knowing until a couple years ago. He laughed like crazy when I told him about my crush on Mr. Mariner. After a little while, I started laughing too. It's funny now when I think about all the lame stuff I did to get close to him.

Peter got quiet all of a sudden. "Look at that," he said.

I turned to where he pointed and saw the sun was just setting over the lake. It looked ten times better than I'd ever seen it look before. All different shades of pink, from pastel to hot, glowing out from that one sun. No Voice spoke to me right then, but I knew from the colors shining down on the water that I was making Somebody happy.

We docked the canoe and walked to dinner together. A couple guys whistled our way when we got to the main cabin, but it didn't faze us. Trip and the guys from Pine and Birch who helped me carry Peter were sitting at our table. We joined them. It was the first time all summer that people from different cabins ate together. The guys from Maple Cabin gawked at us, but we didn't care. Not being alone felt too good.

► August 19

10:14 A.M.

The last day of camp. We're all packing and getting ready to leave. I think Peter's still a little mad at me, but I'm not about to ask him. Things are sort of nice again. The poster's still in one piece, and there's no doubt in my mind about who the stick figures are. I asked Trip and Peter if they wanted the poster. They both said no, so I'm going to keep it. It doesn't mean as much to them as it does to me. Whenever I look at it from now on, I'll think about what we had. And what could be.

Whoops! Simon just called in to us to get our stuff out on the porch and ready to go. Yeeeeeeeeha!

6:55 P.M.

I'm home again. Mom and Dad and Grandma all came to pick me up at camp today. I was really happy to see everybody. I was surprised at how happy I was. They were even happier. Mom ran up and hugged me hard. Then Grandma did the same thing. It was a little embarrassing, but I didn't push either of them away. I hugged them back hard. Dad didn't say much at the camp. He acted shy and unsure.

All three of them looked different to me. They looked like people separate from me. Like they were a part of me but not a part of me. For the first time, I felt like their lives weren't wrapped up around mine. I was standing next to them and I could breathe on my own. They got along fine without me. And I got along fine without them. It felt good to know that.

Before I left, I asked Peter for his address and told him I'd write to him. He said he'd write back. Something tells me we'll be keeping in touch. We've been through too much not to.

When I got in the car, Mom told me that Jeff was coming home for a few days next week. And Marsha's coming home before her classes begin at Harvard. They both told Mom they have a big announcement to make. Mom asked me if I knew what it is. I played dumb and said, "No."

Mom drove and we were all quiet for a while. Grandma kept sneaking peeks at me. She told me I got taller while I was away. Mom asked me how camp was. What was my favorite thing to do? How was the food? All kinds of stuff like that. I answered every question and watched Dad's face. He looked so great, like he hadn't touched a drop all summer.

We stopped to get gas and they got out to stretch. I watched them standing as Dad pumped the gas. They weren't a bad-looking group of people. Not perfect by a long shot, but they don't give up. They roll with the punches that come at them and try to do good. I saw my reflection in the rearview mirror and realized I was one of them. I could see their features in every part of my face. I went out to stand with them, happy.

When we were rolling again, Grandma asked me, "What did you learn this summer?"

I know she was expecting me to repeat a Bible verse back to her. Or some Bible story. But that wouldn't have scratched the surface of what I learned.

All of the sudden, I started singing. Loud and strong. On key. Nobody looked at me like they couldn't believe it. They all just took my singing in stride. Like they knew I could do it all the time. Mom and Grandma joined me. Dad was quiet in the beginning. After a while, though, he started humming too. I can't remember the name of the song, or how we all happened to know the tune, but we were doing it together. We sounded good.

When we were driving over the Tranten Township line, it hit me how easy it'd be for me to leave next time. It's just a matter of deciding to do it. Wanting more than what I've got. When the want gets bad enough, I'll leave and be on my own. I'll figure out a way. It's as easy as driving over a line in the road.

When we drove through town, it seemed weird to me how nothing had changed. It seemed like I'd been gone forever, but everything still looked the same. Then it hit me that the only changes were the ones inside of me. And it wasn't just my voice. I started singing even louder.

When we were eating dinner tonight, Mom couldn't stop looking at me. She kept reaching over and squeezing my shoulder, like she was making sure I was really there. Dad kept laughing at her and saying, "For crying out loud, he's only been gone two months." I laughed too. Later, while Dad and Grandma were clearing the dishes, Mom sat at the table and kept looking at me. She told me I looked "so different." I told her, "I sure feel different."

She smiled and said, "That's a relief." She kissed me and said, "I knew you could beat this thing if you wanted to. We can all do anything if we try hard enough."

Case closed. I didn't bother to explain my answer, because she wouldn't have wanted to hear it, and I wasn't in the mood for a fight so soon after coming home. There's plenty of time to explain later.

▶ August 20

This morning, Grandma gave me the embroidery she's been working on for me. It says, "THOSE WHO FORGIVE ARE THE TRULY BLESSED." I asked her what book of the Bible that verse is from. She told me it's not from the Bible.

It's something she thought up on her own. She said she wants me to hang it up over my bed and think about it every morning when I wake up.

After she gave me the embroidery, she showed me how she'd reorganized my closet. I got a little mad when I found out she threw away some old magazines I had. I was just getting ready to start a fight with her when she asked me if I wanted to go to church with her next Sunday. I said, "Sure."

I was gonna ask her about Timmy Will. How did she feel when she found out about him? But I figured that would've been like rubbing salt in the wounds. She's worked it out for herself and found some peace of mind. That's all any of us wants to do.

After she was gone, I took the hanging into the hallway and hung it up out there so everybody could see it and think about it. There's so much that we've all got to forgive each other for. Maybe the hanging will get us going in the right direction.

6:37 P.M.

I just went to the General Store to pick up some chips. When I passed the front window of the barbershop, I saw Les Numer getting a haircut from Mr. McPheran. They were both talking and laughing about something. Les was acting just as cocky as ever. It doesn't look like a short visit to the youth detention center changed him much. He's worked his way back into the town's good graces. I was gonna go in and ask him how Kuprekski's doing but decided I'd better not.

Some people always land on their feet.

▶ August 21

Mag just called! She's back from her grandparents' house!!! Asked her how her summer was. She said, "I never wanna dip another goddamn ice cream cone in my life." Asked her if she found romance. She said the only romance she found was a date with her boss where nothing happened. I didn't ask her any more about it. She sounded grumpy. She asked me how my summer was. Told her, "It's a long story." She said, "Come on over, we'll have all night." I said, "OK." Her mother's coming to pick me up.

I can't wait to see her.

That reminds me. School starts in a week. Chappaqua High School. I sort of dread it, and I sort of want to see how it's going to be. Better? Worse? No. It couldn't be any worse. After last year, anything will be better. I'll make it better. I know I can.

I'll be a sophomore—a "wise fool." Perfect. That's exactly what I feel like now. Wise, because of everything I've learned. A fool, because of—where do I begin?

I won't. I'll concentrate on the wise part. The things I've learned. They could fill a book.

They *have* filled a book.

I'd better pick up a new notebook the next time I'm at the General Store. I think I'll get a green one. Or maybe a blue one. Red, maybe? Orange? Black? Yellow?

No . . . hot pink is good.

Whoops! Mag's mother is outside honking for me. Gotta run.